The stirring stor  hard
Bolitho is told in vels,
all available in A

Colours Aloft!

ALEXANDER KENT

ARROW BOOKS

Arrow Books Limited
62-65 Chandos Place, London WC2N 4NW

An imprint of Century Hutchinson Limited

London Melbourne Sydney Auckland
Johannesburg and agencies throughout
the world

First published by Hutchinson 1986
Arrow edition 1987

Printed and bound in Great Britain by
Anchor Brendon Limited, Tiptree, Essex

ISBN 0 09 950190 2

Contents

Kim, my love

'And the sailor lost his heart to her,
but she had given him hers long before.'

I

Ebb Tide

It was unusually cold for mid-September and the cobbled streets of Portsmouth Point shone like metal from the overnight rain.

Vice-Admiral Sir Richard Bolitho paused at a corner and stared back at the George Inn where he had stayed for two days since his arrival from Falmouth. There was the old Blue Posts Inn too, a plume of smoke pouring from a chimney, a reminder of long-lost times when he had begun a voyage as a lowly midshipman.

He sighed and turned to his companion who was waiting for him and as they rounded the corner Bolitho felt the Solent's chill wind like a challenge.

It was morning and yet the narrow streets were all but deserted. For this was 1803 and the fragile peace had been swept away in the first broadside of May. No young man or casual idler loitered here for fear of the dreaded press gangs. Like a lesson repeating itself with little learned from before, he thought. He saw his nephew watching him, his eyes troubled, and was reminded of a remark made at the George Inn just that morning while he and Adam had played out a last cup of coffee. The man had been a traveller and had been watching the two sea officers in conversation, and later had said that he had originally taken them for brothers.

Bolitho faced his nephew, hating the moment of parting but knowing it was selfishness to detain him further. Adam Bolitho was twenty-three and in his uncle's eyes was little changed from the day he had first joined his ship as a midshipman.

But there was a difference, a marked one. Adam had

gone through danger and pain, sometimes at his side, other
times not. The line of his mouth and the firmness of his
chin showed he had learned well, and the solitary gold
epaulette on his left shoulder said all the rest. A
commander at twenty-three and now with a ship of his
own. The little fourteen-gun brig *Firefly* lay out there
beyond the wall, lost amongst the sprawling anchorage
with its big men-of-war, transports and all the life of a
naval port at war.

Bolitho looked at him fondly without really seeing him,
but catching glimpses of small, swift pictures of what they
shared.

He said almost without realizing it, 'Your father would
have been proud of you today.'

Adam stared at him, his eyes anxious but pleased. 'That
was good of you.'

Bolitho tugged down his gold-laced hat to compose
himself. Then he said, 'If I had to discover a reward for
myself in all this, it is here and now, seeing you about to
sail with your own command.' Impetuously he gripped
his arm. 'I shall *miss* you, Adam.'

Adam smiled but his eyes remained sad. 'You were
looking back just now, Uncle?'

'Aye.' They fell in step again and Bolitho tried to contain
the feeling of depression which had been his shadow since
leaving Falmouth. Was this then the last time? Was that
the cause of his apprehension? Would he end up like so
many others on some torn and bloodied deck never to
return home?

Adam said, 'He thought we were brothers. A compli-
ment to me I thought.'

He laughed and Bolitho saw the midshipman again.

Bolitho adjusted the boat cloak about his shoulders. His
flagship was waiting for him too. Perhaps the weight of
responsibility which lay in his sealed orders would drive
away his doubts and lose them far astern like the land.

They would all be out there waiting for him. Thank
God he had managed to keep Valentine Keen as his flag-
captain. There would not be too many other familiar faces
this time, he thought.

The Peace of Amiens, as it was called, had lasted less than a year but in that time their lordships and a complacent government had seen fit to run down the fleet in numbers and men to a maniac proportion. Sixty out of a hundred sail-of-the-line laid up, and forty thousand sailors and Royal Marines thrown on the beach. Bolitho had been lucky to stay employed when so many had lost everything. It was ironic that his last flagship, *Achates*, had fought and won the first real battle after the Peace against the odds at a time when the fleet needed to hear of a victory of any kind. It was a further twist of fate that the French admiral's ship *Argonaute*, which they had taken as a prize after one of the fiercest close actions Bolitho could recall, was now about to break his flag at the foremast. *Achates* had been an old ship and would remain in the dockyard for many more months. She had never really recovered from her earlier battles in the Caribbean. *Argonaute* was new by comparison and had been on her first commission when they had beaten her into surrender.

He wondered briefly if prize ships ever resented their new masters and onetime enemies. Bolitho had once been flag-captain in a prize ship but could not recall any strange behaviour in his command.

Anyway there was no choice. They needed every ship and experienced seaman they could get. For whereas England had allowed her strength to sap away, the old enemy across the Channel had done the reverse. New ships, young, eager captains, and a vast army bent on final victory painted a gloomy picture for the future.

Some Royal Marines were sheltering by the sally port wall and sprang to life as the two officers drew near.

It felt strange not to have Allday with him at this moment, Bolitho thought. Hogg, Keen's coxswain, would be at the stairs with the barge this time. Allday had asked to go and visit someone. That in itself was strange. Allday never asked favours or discussed personal matters, and for a moment Bolitho had wondered if he had intended to accept his earlier offers to stay ashore. He had been at sea all his life apart from a brief spell when he had learned to be a shepherd. He had earned his freedom from the navy

a thousand times over. And in *Achates* his life had nearly
ended. Bolitho often thought of that day when his
coxswain had taken a sword thrust in the chest which
should have killed him instantly. He was usually his old
cheerful, irrepressible self, but the wound showed itself
none the less. He found it hard to straighten his back
when he walked, and Bolitho knew just how much it hurt
his pride. He had often compared Allday with an oak, or
a faithful dog. He was neither. He was a true friend, one
whom he could trust, who saw more of Bolitho the man
than any other.

They reached the stairs and Bolitho saw the barge
swaying below him, Hogg, the coxswain, and a young
lieutenant standing by the boat, faces upturned, heads
bared. The tossed oars were in perfect white lines, the
tarred hats and checkered shirts of the bargemen saying
much for what Keen had already achieved with a new
company.

Keen would be watching him right now with his telescope, and probably his new flag-lieutenant, Hector Stayt,
whom he had also sent on ahead of him. Stayt was a fellow
Cornishman whose father had served with Bolitho's father.
He was highly recommended but looked more like an
adventurer than someone who was supposed to show
diplomacy when so required.

A thousand worries and regrets rushed through his mind
but his face was composed as he turned to his nephew
once again. From one corner of his eye he had seen Adam's
little gig standing well clear while they waited for their
youthful commander.

The tide was on the ebb and he saw an old man gathering
driftwood where the shingle showed itself. The man
glanced up and looked directly at the two officers. They
could be brothers. Each with black hair and the same
steady grey eyes. Adam's hair was cut short in the new
fashion for sea officers; Bolitho retained the queue at the
nape of his neck.

The man on the shingle threw up a mock salute and
Bolitho nodded. A last farewell.

He said, 'Take each step with care, Adam. You'll get your frigate after this if you stay out of trouble.'

Adam smiled. 'I am sailing for Gibraltar with your dispatches, Uncle. After that I fear the fleet's apron strings will tether me.'

Bolitho returned his smile. It was like seeing himself being reborn. 'Apron strings can stretch.' He clasped him against his boat cloak, oblivious of the rigid marines and the watching bargemen. Almost to himself he said, 'God be with you.'

Then, as Adam doffed his new gold-laced hat and allowed his raven hair to ruffle in the wind, Bolitho hurried down the stairs. He nodded to the lieutenant. A face from the recent past, except he had been one of *Achates'* midshipmen then.

'Good day, Mr Valancey. It will be a hard pull in this wind.'

He saw the flush of pleasure on the youngster's face because he had remembered his name. Any link would help.

He seated himself in the sternsheets and then waved to Adam as, with oars dipping and rising like wings, the smart, green-painted barge thrust clear of the piles.

With unseemly haste the little gig pulled towards the stairs, and as they swept around the stern of an anchored transport the sally port was hidden from view.

There were many vessels at anchor, their black and buff hulls shining dully in the rain and spray. Beyond them the Isle of Wight was little more than a misty hump, but the wind was steady. Was he glad to go this time?

The lieutenant coughed nervously. 'The frigate yonder is *Barracouta,* sir.' He flinched as Bolitho glanced at him. The frigate must have dropped anchor this morning otherwise he would have been informed. She was to be one of his new squadron under Jeremy Lapish who had commanded a brig like Adam's when he had last served under him. In war the chance of promotion, like death, was ever present. But it was sensible of the lieutenant to tell him and also showed that he took an interest in the comings and goings within the fleet.

Bolitho said, 'What is your appointment?'

'Sixth lieutenant, sir.' One step up from the gunroom.

Hogg swore under his breath and snarled, '*Oars!* Easy there!'

The oar blades hovered, dripping and motionless, as Hogg put his weight on the tiller bar. A longboat was cutting directly across their path, so full of people it looked almost awash.

Hogg glared at the youthful lieutenant and when he remained silent cupped his hands and bellowed, 'Stand away there! Make way for a King's officer!'

Somebody waved and the longboat veered towards some nearby transports.

Bolitho saw that one of the passengers was a young girl, her head and shoulders unprotected against the spray and wet breeze. She twisted round between two companions to see who was shouting and Bolitho's eyes met hers across fifty feet of tossing whitecaps. He stared at one of her hands as she gripped the gunwale. She wore manacles on her wrists, but she turned away before he could see more.

He asked quietly, 'Who are those people?'

Hogg eased the tiller carefully, still outraged that such a thing could happen under the eyes of *his* admiral.

He said gruffly, 'Convicts, sir.'

Bolitho looked away. Going to Botany Bay probably. What had she done, he wondered? Who was she?

'Ready, bowman!' Hogg was gauging the last cable or so with great care.

Bolitho saw the tapered masts of *Argonaute* as the barge swept around another two-decker. She was a fine-looking ship, he conceded, shining in her new livery with a huge Red Ensign streaming out from her poop to welcome him aboard. She had fine graceful lines and Bolitho knew from hard experience she was an excellent sailer. Her poop deck was rather longer than her English counterparts but otherwise she was little different from any seventy-four, the backbone of the fleet.

But as she drew closer Bolitho saw there were slight differences which any Frenchman would notice. The stronger bow and stiffly raked jib boom and the gilded

stern gallery which seemed almost flamboyant after earlier
French ships. It was hard to see her with her decks puddled
in blood, as embattled men hacked and thrust at each other
to hold their ground. Many good hands died that day and
on their way home to Plymouth. The dockyard had done
magic with their battered charge, Bolitho thought. He had
been tempted to visit his new flagship several times during
her refit and repairs but had stayed away. Keen would
hardly have been pleased to have his admiral come aboard
in the midst of such confusion.

Bolitho had wanted to go, needed to see and speak
with people he understood. He tossed the cloak from his
shoulders to reveal the gleaming epaulettes, each with its
two silver stars. Vice-Admiral-of-the-Red, apart from
Nelson the youngest on the Navy list. Even that he could
not get used to. Like the title which had made everyone so
pleased but which left him feeling awkward, embarrassed.

More pictures flashed through his mind as he watched
the ship and gripped the old family sword between his
knees.

London, the bright liveries and bowing footmen. The
hush as he knelt before His Britannic Majesty, the lightest
tap of the sword on his shoulder. Sir Richard Bolitho of
Falmouth. It had been a proud moment surely? Belinda
had looked so radiantly happy. Adam and Allday beaming
like schoolchildren. And yet –

He saw a cluster of figures around the entry port, the
blues and whites of the officers, the scarlet of the marines.
His world. They would be watching his every move.
Usually Allday would have been on hand to make sure he
did not lose his balance or trip over his sword.

The thought of ever being without Allday was beyond
belief after what they had seen and endured together. He
would be aboard before the ship weighed. He must. *I
need him more than ever.*

He saw the lieutenant staring at him and for a terrible
moment imagined he had spoken aloud.

But Valancey was merely anxious and stood aside as
Bolitho waited for the barge to sway heavily against
Argonaute's fat flank.

Then he was swarming up the side and through the entry port, his ears cringing to the slap and click of bayoneted muskets presenting arms, and the fifes and drums breaking into 'Heart of Oak'.

There was Keen, his fair hair visible as he doffed his hat and strode to meet him, even as Bolitho's flag broke smartly from the foremast truck.

'Welcome, Sir Richard.'

Keen smiled, not realizing that the greeting had caught Bolitho unawares. It sounded like somebody else.

'I am glad to be here.' Bolitho nodded to the assembled officers and the watch on deck. If he had still expected to see some sign of the battle he was disappointed. Newly paid deck seams and blacked-down rigging. Neatly furled sails and every upper-deck eighteen-pounder with all its tackles and gear perfectly in line as if on parade.

He looked along the deck and through the criss-cross of standing and running rigging. He could see the white shoulder of the figurehead, depicting the handsome youth who had been one of Jason's crew in the mythical *Argo*. Less than three years old from the day she had slid into the water at Brest. A new ship by any standard, with a full complement of six hundred and twenty souls, officers, seamen and Royal Marines, although he doubted if even the resourceful Keen had gathered anywhere near that total.

They walked aft beneath the poop deck. By making it longer than in English third-rates, the builders had given better and more spacious accommodation to the officers. In battle, however, as in any man-of-war, the deck would be completely cleared from bow to stern so that every gun, large or small, could be worked without obstruction.

They ducked beneath the deckhead beams and Bolitho saw a marine sentry marking the screen doors of his quarters right aft.

'When Allday comes aboard, Val, I want – '

Keen glanced at him curiously. 'He preceded you, Sir Richard.'

Bolitho felt a great sense of relief, as he had of fear when Allday had been hacked down on that terrible day.

It was quite dark between decks and Bolitho allowed his feet to guide him by instinct. The smells were like old friends. Tar, oakum, paint, damp canvas. Like the ship's fabric itself.

He nodded to the marine sentry and entered the stern cabin. A spacious dining table brought from Falmouth, the wine cabinet which followed him from ship to ship, and aft in the broad day cabin a fine carpet laid upon the black and white check canvas covering of the deck.

Keen watched his reactions as little mole-like Ozzard, who had been aboard for several days, hurried from the sleeping space. He too watched as Bolitho walked slowly to The Chair.

Bolitho had had it made in Falmouth. Belinda had disagreed about it and thought he should have something more elegant, as suited his position.

Bolitho touched the high back, which, like the rest of the chair, was covered with dark green leather. It was soft as a woman's skin under his hand.

He handed his sword to Ozzard and sat down in the chair which would become so important when he could share none of his doubts and worries with his subordinates. Strong arms to rest on, a high back to shut out things or people when needed.

Keen grinned. 'Came aboard an hour before we quit Plymouth Sound.' Feet pattered overhead and Keen moved towards the door.

Bolitho smiled, 'Be off with you, Val. You've much to do. We shall speak later.'

The door closed and he watched his cabin servant padding about with a tray and some glasses. Was Ozzard sorry to be leaving the security and safety of Falmouth? If so, he did not show it. Bolitho waited for Ozzard to place a glass of claret by his side and then withdraw to his pantry. A fine servant, dedicated even beyond his unfailing terror whenever a ship cleared for action. He was well read and full of surprises for one so small and mild. He had once been a lawyer's clerk. It was said he had gone to sea to escape jail or worse. Like Allday, he was totally dependable.

He glanced around the great cabin. Contre-Amiral Jobert must have sat here often enough in those other days. Must have cocked his head when he heard the lookouts cry out that they had sighted *Achates*.

The other door opened and Yovell entered with the usual pack of letters under one arm.

'Good day, Mr Yovell.'

'Good morning, Sir Richard.'

They smiled at one another like conspirators. For if Bolitho had gained a title, Yovell's status had been raised from mere clerk to secretary. With his sloping, fat shoulders and small gold-rimmed spectacles he looked like a prosperous merchant.

Yovell had found a new clerk to assist him, a fresh-faced youth named John Pinkney, whose family had lived in Falmouth for many generations. Ozzard too had gained an assistant; his name was Twigg, but Bolitho had only seen him once when he had called at the house in Falmouth.

He found he was on his feet and was pacing the cabin as if he was trapped.

There was so much he had wanted to say to Belinda. There had been a strangeness between them since their visit to London. She loved him, but because of the difficult time she had had during Elizabeth's birth there had been a barrier. A coolness. He could not be certain if –

He looked up, angry without knowing why, as the sentry tapped his musket on the deck and called, 'Admiral's cox'n, *sir!*'

That marine would soon get to know that Allday came and went as he pleased.

Allday came in and stood in the middle of the carpet, his head just beneath the skylight.

He looked little changed, Bolitho thought, in his blue jacket with the special gilt buttons, and his nankeen trousers to mark him out as the admiral's coxswain.

'All done, Allday?' Perhaps he would shake him out of his gloom.

Allday stared around the cabin and then back to Bolitho and the new chair.

'Fact is, sir.' He fidgeted with his coat. 'I had a bit o' news.'

Bolitho sat down. 'Well, what is it, man?'

'I've got a son, sir.'

Bolitho exclaimed, 'You *what?*'

Allday grinned sheepishly. 'Somebody wrote a letter, sir. Ferguson read it to me, me not bein' able – '

Bolitho nodded. Ferguson, his steward in Falmouth, could always keep a secret. He and Allday were as thick as thieves.

Allday continued, 'There was a girl I used to know. On the farm, it was. Pretty little thing, smart as paint. Seems she died, just a few weeks back.' He looked at Bolitho with sudden desperation. 'Well, I mean, sir, I couldn't just do nothin', could I?'

Bolitho sat back in the chair and watched the emotions hurrying across Allday's homely face.

'Are you certain about this?'

'Aye, sir. I – I'd like you to speak with him, if it's not too much to ask?'

Feet moved overhead and somewhere a boatswain's call trilled to summon more hands to hoist some stores inboard. In the cabin it seemed apart, remote from that other shipboard life.

'You brought him aboard then?'

'He volunteered, sir. He's worn the King's coat afore.' There was pride in his voice now. 'I just need – ' He broke off and looked at his shoes. 'I shouldn't have asked – '

Bolitho walked over to him and touched his arm. 'Bring him aft when you're ready. Blast your eyes man, you have the *right* to ask what you will!'

They stared at each other, then Allday said simply, 'I'll do that, sir.'

The door opened and Keen looked in at them. He said, 'I thought you should know, Sir Richard, *Firefly* has just weighed and is setting her tops'ls.'

Bolitho smiled. 'Thank you.' He looked at Allday. 'Come, we'll watch him leave, eh?'

Allday took the old sword down from its rack and waited to clip it to Bolitho's belt.

He said quietly, 'He'll need a good cox'n of his own afore long, an' that's no error.'

They looked at each other and understood.

Keen watched them and forgot all the demands, the signals which awaited attention and which he must discuss with his admiral. Bolitho and Allday were the rock which would stand when all else fell. He was surprised to discover that this realization still moved him deeply.

Several of the hands working about the quarterdeck withdrew as Bolitho and their captain walked to the nettings. Bolitho could feel their eyes even though his back was turned. They would be pondering on his reputation both as their leader and as a man.

The little brig was heeling over to the wind, showing her copper as she tacked between two anchored seventy-fours.

Bolitho took a glass from the signals midshipman. The youth seemed vaguely familiar. He trained the glass across the nettings and for a few moments saw *Firefly*'s commander staring across at him, near enough to touch. He was waving his hat slowly from side to side, then one of the ships shut him from view. Bolitho lowered the glass and the scene fell away into the distance.

He handed the telescope to the midshipman. 'Thank you, Mr –'

'Sheaffe, Sir Richard.'

Bolitho eyed him curiously. Of course. He should have remembered that Admiral Sir Hayward Sheaffe had made a point of putting one of his sons in *Argonaute*. It was unlike him to forget such things. Even Keen's comment, 'Lose the brat overboard and I'll lose my command to boot!'

He had visited Sheaffe at the Admiralty several times since his return to England. One rank only separated them. It could have been an ocean.

Keen was watching him and as they walked to the opposite side said, 'There was no real urgency to come aboard just yet, sir. It may be another week before the full squadron is assembled here.'

He thinks I need to leave the land, Bolitho thought.

He said, 'A small enough squadron it will be too, Val. Four sail-of-the-line, *Barracouta* and the little brig *Rapid*.'

Keen grinned. 'There is also *Supreme,* sir.'

Bolitho smiled ruefully. 'Tops'l cutter. She hardly ranks with her name, eh?'

He considered the three other seventy-fours. One familiar face amongst them. Captain Francis Inch was in command. Bolitho swung round, his voice almost pleading as he asked, 'What has become of us, Val? *We happy few,* remember?'

Keen said, 'I think of it often.' Bolitho's mood disturbed him. He had heard the reason, or some of it, the rest he could guess. Bolitho's beautiful wife was concerned about his career, although to most sailors a vice-admiral, with or without a knighthood, was about level with the Almighty.

She wanted him to leave Falmouth, to purchase a fine residence in London where his name would be noted and acted upon.

Leave Falmouth? Keen had been at their wedding there, and knew the Bolitho house below Pendennis Castle better than most. Bolithos had always lived there; it was as much a part of them as the sea itself.

Bolitho was looking across at his one frigate *Barracouta.* Lapish, her young captain, had less than three years' seniority, not even posted. The sight of the anchored frigate, her yards and decks alive with working seamen, jabbed at another memory. The first time he had spoken sharply to Belinda. She had been talking about Nelson. Practically everyone did in London, but not of his courage and his victories, but about his outrageous and unacceptable behaviour with *that woman*.

Belinda had said, 'You rank the same as Nelson, but he has a fleet whereas you are being given a squadron!'

Bolitho had said, 'A fleet is not built on favours!'

Curiously enough, despite his fame and his position, Nelson had only two frigates for his whole command, but Bolitho had been too upset to mention the point at the time.

The little admiral had hoisted his flag in *Victory,* that old and respected first-rate, and had sailed for the Mediterranean to seek out the French at Toulon or make sure they stayed bottled up like those in the Channel Ports.

He had seen Belinda recoil at his tone and they had stared at each other like strangers.

She had said quietly, 'I say and do things because I care.'

Bolitho had retorted, 'Because you think you know best! *This* is our home, not London!'

Now, watching the ships, remembering lost faces, he wondered what had really provoked him. Enough to bring him here, no matter what it was.

He said softly, 'All those men, little more than boys some of them. Farquhar, Keverne, Veitch,' he looked away, 'young John Neale, remember? And the rest, where are they? Dead, maimed, ekeing out their lives in one poxy hospital or another, and for what?'

Keen had never seen him like this before. 'We'll beat the Frogs, sir.'

Bolitho gripped his arm. 'I daresay. But a lot of good men will have to pay for others' complacency and stupidity.'

He controlled his voice and said calmly, 'I will go aft and read my dispatches. Dine with me tonight, eh, Val?'

Keen touched his hat and watched him leave the quarter-deck. He saw Stayt, the new flag-lieutenant, strolling towards the poop and wondered if he could replace Bolitho's nephew or the previous aide Browne. He smiled sadly. *With an 'e'*.

Keen walked to the quarterdeck rail and rested his hand on it. Soon the ship would be alive again, a working creature, driven by her pyramids of canvas, expected to deal with anything, anywhere. He glanced up to Bolitho's flag at the fore. There was no man he would rather serve, none he respected more. Loved. From the moment he had joined Bolitho's ship as a midshipman he had found his affection growing. Amidst death and danger in the Great South Sea, when Bolitho had almost died of fever, he had still found the strength to support him in his own loss. Keen still thought of the lovely Malua, who had died of the same terrible fever. Unlike most sea officers, he had never married, had never really recovered from losing her.

He looked along his command and felt vaguely pleased with all they had achieved in so short a time. He recalled the never-ending broadsides, the carnage above and below decks in that last battle. He touched his left shoulder where a splinter had smashed him down. It still ached on occasions. But he was alive. He looked at the men high above the decks working at their endless splicing and other ropework.

It had been his good fortune to retain some of the older, seasoned men from *Achates*. Big Harry Rooke, the boatswain; Grace, the carpenter, who had been worth his weight in gold during the refit at Plymouth. Even Black Joe Langtry, the fearsome looking master-at-arms, had come aboard *Argonaute*. But they were still well short of seamen. He rubbed his chin as he had seen Bolitho do when he was considering a problem. The port admiral and a local magistrate were doing their best, but Keen wanted prime seamen, not felons. The thought made him glance across at the two big transports, one an ex-Indiaman by the look of her. They were to carry convicts to the new colony. Was it the right way to expand a place, he wondered? A felon was a felon and the gallows a fitter end for his kind.

Paget, the first lieutenant, crossed the deck and touched his hat. 'Permission to exercise the lower battery during the afternoon watch, sir?'

Keen saw him glance aft to the poop and smiled. 'Have no fear, Mr Paget, our admiral greatly approves of efficient gunnery! So do I!'

Paget walked away. A good lieutenant, slightly older than the others, he had been in the merchant service for a time during the Peace of Amiens. He should have a command, albeit a small one. The little *Supreme*'s new commander, Hallowes, had been Keen's fourth lieutenant until the battle. Keen could see it now. Adam Bolitho and Hallowes in a madcap attack on *Argonaute*'s stern. With a handful of men they had placed charges around the mainmast and brought it down like a gigantic tree. The enemy had struck almost immediately. So why not Paget? His report was good and he seemed competent enough.

Keen began to pace up and down, his chin in his neckcloth, momentarily oblivious to the rattle of blocks and
the hoarse cries of his petty officers as more stores were
hauled aboard. Time would tell. One thing was certain, it
would be a harder war this time. The feeling of being
cheated, even betrayed, after so short-lived a peace would
put an edge on every temper.

It would be good to see Inch again, to watch his long
horse-face light up when he met Bolitho. It was a sobering
thought to realize that Inch and himself were the only
post-captains in the squadron. Inch's two-decker *Helicon*
would arrive from the Nore at any time. Then, under
orders once more, they would put out to sea where every
sighting would likely be hostile. To Gibraltar, and then?

While Keen paced the deck immersed in his thoughts,
Bolitho wandered about his unfamiliar quarters as Ozzard
and some extra hands moved his possessions into their
new places.

The old sword was on its rack above the fine presentation one from Falmouth's public subscription. He could
remember quite clearly his father giving him the old blade
in the grey house where he had been born.

He said gravely, 'England needs all her sons now.' He
had been grieving for Hugh's disgrace, his desertion from
the Navy. Hugh should have been given the sword. It
would be Adam's one day.

Bolitho walked into the sleeping compartment and
stared at himself in his mirror. Where had the years gone?
He would be forty-seven next month. He looked ten years
younger but the thought, like the others, disturbed him.

He thought of Belinda, back in Falmouth. Would there
be more changes when he returned? He grimaced at his
reflection then turned away. 'If, more like.'

Ozzard started. 'Sir?'

Bolitho smiled. 'Nothing. I have been ashore for too
many weeks. The next horizon will cure that directly.'

Ozzard was packing things into drawers and a fine
hanging wardrobe. He liked to be busy. He hesitated over
one drawer and made to tidy some new shirts. His fingers

touched a miniature portrait of a girl with long chestnut hair and green eyes. She was so beautiful, he thought.

Twigg, his new assistant, peered over his shoulder. 'Shall we 'ang it, Tom? I would if I 'ad a wife like 'er!'

'Get about your work!' Ozzard closed the drawer carefully. It was not Twigg's fault, the miniature looked very like Lady Belinda. But Ozzard knew differently: he had heard Bolitho call out her name when he had been badly wounded. *Cheney.*

Why did she have to die? He picked up a pair of shoes and regarded them unseeingly.

The deck rolled slightly and Ozzard sighed.

This was a life he had come to understand. Better than those poor devils in the convict ships. He gave a gentle smile. If fate had been less kind he might have taken the same one-way passage.

Three days later the small squadron with *Argonaute* in the van stood down-Channel in a brisk northerly wind.

They had sailed on the ebb, but there was no letter. Bolitho locked his own in the strongbox and watched the land slipping away into the dusk. *My England, when shall I see you again?*

It was like a cry from the heart, but only the sea replied.

2

In Distress

Bolitho walked across the poop and idly watched the other three ships-of-the-line following astern. It was two long days since they had weighed anchor at Spithead and, apart from sail and gun drill, there had been little to break the monotony.

Inch's *Helicon* was directly astern, with *Dispatch* and *Icarus* in direct line although not without a few forthright signals from the flagship.

They had to learn good station-keeping and to respond to every signal without delay. There would be no time later on.

Far away on the starboard quarter, with only her pale topsails showing above the sea and spray, the solitary frigate *Barracouta* held carefully to windward, ready to dash down and investigate any sighting or support her heavy consorts if so ordered. Bolitho could picture them all, and their captains whom he had seen just briefly prior to sailing. The brig *Rapid* and the small, rakish cutter *Supreme* were sweeping far ahead of their flagship, Bolitho's eyes and intelligence.

Bolitho had decided to leave the briefing to Keen when the captains had assembled in *Argonaute*'s wardroom. He had always hated speeches just for the want of making them. When they reached the Rock he would know better what was expected and would then lay his intentions before the others.

Inch's face had been creased with delight when Bolitho had greeted him aboard. He had not changed. Still eager and completely trusting, Bolitho knew he could never share his doubts with one so loyal. Inch would agree with everything he said and did, even to the mouth of Hell.

He turned to watch the hands at work on the gundeck. He had noticed several faces he knew from the *Achates*. He had remarked to Keen that it did him credit they had volunteered to serve under him again. He had not seen Keen smile to himself, just as it had never occurred to him that they might have volunteered because of their admiral.

He had seen the loping, misshapen Crocker, the gun-captain who had blown down this ship's mainmast and so finished the battle, looking no different despite his new uniform. He had gained promotion to gunner's mate and was rarely far away when the drills were carried out.

He saw Allday on the larboard gangway with a fresh-faced youth he guessed was his newly discovered son. It did not seem possible, and he wondered when Allday would decide the time was right and proper to bring him aft to the great cabin. Allday would know better than anyone Bolitho's dislike of showing favours in a crowded man-of-war. He would doubtless judge the moment perfectly.

Two bells chimed out from the forecastle and Bolitho stirred restlessly. He felt so apart from the ship and those who followed his flag. Keen and his officers dealt with everything, and day by day *Argonaute*'s company were led, encouraged and driven into a working team. Minutes were knocked off the time for clearing for action, for reefing and making sail, but Bolitho could only share it at a distance.

The hours dragged heavily and he found himself envying Keen as well as the other captains who had their ships to fill their days.

He walked to the opposite side and stared at the dull, grey sea with its serried ranks of wave crests. One hundred miles abeam was Lorient. He glanced forward to the figurehead's pale shoulder. They had passed Brest in the night, where this ship had been built. Did *Argonaute* feel it, he wondered?

Curiously enough Inch's *Helicon* was also a French prize, but had had her name changed as was the custom when the battle where she had been taken had been badly fought.

Bolitho touched the nettings. Nobody could say that about this ship. She had fought well from start to finish. Nelson would be hard put to control the Mediterranean if the enemy had more admirals of Jobert's breed.

'Deck there! *Rapid*'s signallin', sir!'

Bolitho glanced up at the masthead lookout on his precarious, swooping perch. The wind had backed slightly and was almost directly astern. It would be lively up there.

He opened his mouth to speak but Keen was already present.

'Get aloft, Mr Sheaffe, with haste now!'

Bolitho watched the slim midshipman swarming up the shrouds. He was sixteen but looked older, and rarely skylarked with the other 'young gentlemen' off duty, or during the dog watches.

He wondered momentarily if Adam would have been so serious had he been his son.

Eventually Sheaffe was able to level his big signals telescope and shouted down to the deck.

'From *Supreme*, repeated *Rapid*, sir!' All eyes were raised to his foreshortened silhouette. The clouds seemed to be racing directly above the masthead.

'Sail in sight to the south'rd!'

Keen exclaimed, 'I wonder?' He looked at Bolitho. 'Frenchies, sir?'

Bolitho said, 'Doubt it. We saw some of the blockading squadron yesterday. The enemy would have to slip past them first.' He smiled at Keen's expression. He was disappointed. It was as clear as if he had said it aloud.

Bolitho said, 'Signal *Supreme* to investigate. She carries only pop-guns, but can outpace anything that floats.'

The signal dashed up to the yards and broke stiffly to the wind. *Rapid* would be waiting to repeat it to the cutter which was out of sight from the flagship. He knew Lieutenant Hallowes' reputation for recklessness and hoped he would take care. Otherwise his new command would be shortlived.

Bolitho heard a step beside him and saw his flag-lieutenant watching the signal party critically as Sheaffe slid down to the deck again.

Stayt said, 'Slow. You must do better, Mr Sheaffe, or I shall know why.'

Bolitho said nothing. At least Stayt did not care about reprimanding an admiral's son.

Stayt said, 'Whoever it is will probably turn and run, sir.'

Bolitho nodded. If it was a merchantman, no matter what flag she wore, her master would not wish to lose any of his prime seamen to a King's ship.

He wondered about Stayt. His father had quit the sea a sick man and owned some land around the little village of Zennor. Stayt's brothers were both clergymen but it was hard to picture the lieutenant wearing the cloth.

Stayt had a swarthy complexion and dark restless eyes. Like a gypsy. He was not handsome like Keen, but had the rugged good looks which would appeal to women.

Bolitho knew that Stayt always carried a small pistol under his coat and wanted to ask him why. A curious habit, as if he was expecting trouble.

Sheaffe spoke urgently to his assistant midshipman and then climbed swiftly up the mizzen shrouds with his telescope. He was smarting, whereas most midshipmen would have taken Stayt's comment as part of their lot. A midshipman was neither fish nor fowl, who stood between the lieutenants and the people, and was respected by neither for the most part. It was strange they never remembered that fact when they became lieutenants, Bolitho thought.

'From *Supreme*, sir!' Sheaffe's voice was sharp. 'She's the *Orontes*!'

Keen said, 'One of the convict ships. But they sailed two days before us.' He eyed Bolitho questioningly. 'Strange?'

'From *Supreme*, sir. Ship requires assistance.'

'Make to *Supreme*.' Keen had seen Bolitho nod. '*Heave-to and await the flag.*' He waited for the signal to break out. Now a general signal. '*Make more sail.*'

Stayt closed his glass with a snap. 'The squadron has all acknowledged, sir.'

Bolitho watched the hands dashing up the shrouds and out along the yards to set more sail. The other ships were doing likewise. There was no obvious danger but the squadron would keep in formation. Bolitho had known traps in the past, his own and the enemy's. He was taking no chances.

The deck staggered and spray lifted above the taffrail as *Argonaute* responded to the extra pressure of canvas.

'We'll be up to them by noon, sir.' Keen watched the set of each sail and then shouted, 'Another pull on the weather forebrace, Mr Chaytor! Your division is in confusion today!' He lowered his speaking trumpet and turned aside. There was little wrong with the lieutenant's division, but it did no harm to drive them a bit more. He saw Bolitho smile and knew that he had seen through his guard.

Luke Fallowfield, the sailing master, watched the hardening sails and put another man on the big double-wheel. He had been master in flagships before but had never known one like Bolitho's. Most admirals stayed away in their great cabins, but not this one. Fallowfield was short, but massively built like a huge cask. He had no neck and his head sat directly on his shoulders like a great red pumpkin. He was a shabby, shambling mass of a man, who usually cast the smell of rum in his wake, but his knowledge of navigation and ship-handling was unsurpassed.

Bolitho was getting to know their faces, the way they responded to their superiors and subordinates. It kept him in touch. Without this small contact he knew he would be forced into his shielded quarters. In his heart he admitted he did not want to be left alone with his thoughts.

The *Orontes* grew and lifted from the grey water with each turn of the glass. Lying-to nearby, the *Supreme* remained an onlooker, her hull rolling and pitching in the troughs.

As soon as *Argonaute* was within signalling distance Keen observed, 'Lost their rudder, damn them!'

Stayt said, 'The other ship was an ex-Indiaman and in

good condition.' His lip curled. 'This one is a hulk. I'm glad for their sakes the Bay is being kind.'

Bolitho took a glass and watched the slow exchange of signals. Stayt was right about the ship's appearance. More like a slaver than a government transport.

He said, 'If we take her in tow, Val,' he saw Keen's dismay, 'and assist her back to port, we will reduce our strength and slow our passage. We cannot abandon her.'

Old Fallowfield mumbled, 'Squall gettin' near, zur.' He stared blankly at the officers. 'No doubt in my mind.'

'That settles it.' Bolitho folded his arms. 'Send a boat across and discover what has happened to her consort, the *Philomela*.' He watched Big Harry Rooke, the boatswain, beckoning a boat's crew towards the tier. It was bad luck, but they had no choice.

'We will escort her to Gibraltar.'

Keen protested, 'But we shall take days longer with her in tow, sir.'

He was eager to get there. More so to become involved against the enemy. He did not alter.

The first lieutenant clambered down into the waiting boat and was soon speeding across the water towards the drifting vessel.

What a way for the convicts to begin what was already a terrible voyage, Bolitho thought. He tried to shut it from his mind and concentrate on what he must do. If he left the squadron and went on ahead in *Barracouta* or *Rapid* to discover what was required of him, there might be an unexpected attack during his absence. A barely trained squadron without its admiral would certainly attract the French if they learned of it.

He made up his mind. 'Signal *Barracouta* to close on the flag. Captain to repair on board.' He could already see Lapish's youthful face, grateful to be released from his ponderous companions, to be free of authority.

'Then signal *Helicon* to prepare to tow.' Inch was by far the most experienced captain, but he would not thank him for it. Not even loyal Inch.

It took the remainder of the day to pass the massive hawser to the rudderless transport, and some hundred

sailors from Inch's command to do it. By the time they
had formed up once more in some sort of order *Barracouta*
was already hull down on the horizon and soon out of
sight altogether. Lapish would carry dispatches from
Bolitho to the Governor and commander-in-chief. At least
everyone would know they would eventually arrive under
the Rock.

Darkness closed in and when Bolitho went aft to the
great cabin he saw that the table was carefully laid, the
sides and deckhead glittering to the swinging lanterns and
new candles.

The exercise with the *Orontes* and the passing of the
tow had given Bolitho an appetite. It had helped to pass
the time, to see his squadron doing something other than
running out guns or shortening sail.

Ozzard watched him and was satisfied. It was good to
see Bolitho in a warmer mood. He would dine with the
captain and the new flag-lieutenant. Ozzard was reserving
his opinion on the latter. There was something false about
Lieutenant Stayt, he decided. Like the lawyer he had once
worked for.

Ozzard said, 'The cox'n's waiting, Sir Richard.'

Bolitho smiled. 'Good.'

Allday was right aft by the big sloping windows. He
faced Bolitho and touched his forehead. Even that he did
with massive dignity, Bolitho thought. There was neither
subservience nor indifference there.

'How is it coming along?' Bolitho sat on the new chair
and stretched his legs. 'When do I meet, er, your son?'

Allday replied, 'Tomorrow forenoon if it suits, Sir
Richard.'

Even the title rested easily with Allday. He seemed
prouder of it than its recipient.

Allday continued, 'He's a fine lad, sir.' He sounded
anxious. 'I was wonderin' – '

Now to the truth of the matter. Bolitho said encouragingly, 'Come on, old friend. There are no admirals or
coxswains down here.'

Allday watched him worriedly. 'I knows that, sir. I've

always known it. You treated me like one of the family
in Falmouth. I don't reckon anyone would forget *that*.'

He tried again. 'I get a bit o' pain from time to time,
sir.'

'Yes.' Bolitho poured two glasses of claret. 'I fear there
is no rum within reach.'

The memory brought a slow grin to Allday's bronzed
features. *Remembering*. The rum which had brought him
back to life, if only because his reeling mind had recorded
that Bolitho was drinking some out of despair. Bolitho
never drank rum. In some strange way it had dragged
Allday across the margin of survival and death.

'I wants to do my duty for you, sir. Like always. But
somehow – '

Bolitho said gently, 'You think I might need a second
cox'n, is that it?'

Allday stared at him. Awe, astonishment, gratitude, it
was all there.

'God bless you, sir.' Allday nodded. 'It would help the
lad, an' I could keep an eye on him like.'

Keen entered and stopped by the screen door. 'I beg
your pardon, sir.' It seemed quite natural to find the big
coxswain having a quiet drink with his admiral. Keen had
cause to know and respect Allday. When he had been a
midshipman under Bolitho's command he had been cut
down by a great splinter which had driven into his groin
like a bloody lance. The frigate's surgeon had been a
drunkard and Allday had carried the barely conscious
midshipman below and cut the splinter away himself. It
had saved his life. No, he would never forget, especially
as the respect had become mutual.

Bolitho smiled. 'All done. With your permission, I'd
like to take, er – ' He glanced at Allday. 'What name does
he use?'

Allday looked at his feet. 'John, like me, sir.' He became
serious, 'Bankart. That was 'er name.'

Keen nodded, his handsome features expressionless. His
own coxswain, Hogg, had told him about it.

Bolitho said, 'A second cox'n. Good idea, eh?'

Keen replied gravely, 'None better.'

They watched him leave and Keen said, 'God, he even looks like a father now!'

Bolitho asked, 'Do you know this Bankart?'

Keen took a glass from Ozzard and held it up to a lantern.

'I saw him sworn in, sir. About twenty or so. Served in the *Superb* before the Peace. A clean bill.'

Bolitho looked away. Keen had checked up already. To protect him or Allday, it did not matter which.

Keen said, 'I am in despair over the *Orontes*, sir. Her master ignores Captain Inch's instructions and I am fast becoming impatient with the fellow.' He eyed Bolitho thoughtfully. 'I've a mind to go aboard tomorrow.'

Bolitho smiled. 'Yes. I think my flag-captain will get more done than Inch's lieutenants.'

Stayt entered the cabin and handed Ozzard his hat. He too had apparently been considering the *Orontes*.

'I think I have discovered why the other transport sailed on without *Orontes*, sir.' He leaned over to move a chair and for a second or so revealed the bright pistol beneath his coat. '*Philomela* carries gold as well as human beings. The paymaster for New South Wales is with it.'

Bolitho rubbed his chin. That was strange. Nobody had mentioned it before.

Keen said bitterly, 'Afraid to put his money in a man-of-war, is he? In case we have to fight for him, damn his eyes!'

Ozzard hovered by the other screen door. He had heard everything but would keep it to himself. He had known all about the gold, as did most of the squadron. It was funny that the officers were always the last to hear such matters, he thought.

'Dinner is served, Sir Richard,' he said meekly.

When Bolitho went on deck the following morning he saw the disarray in his ships after a mounting overnight gale. Now, as each captain endeavoured to place his ship on the required station, the wind just as mischievously dropped to a wet breeze, to leave the heavier vessels rolling uncomfortably in the troughs, their sails flapping and banging in confusion.

Keen glared across at the *Orontes*. Quite rightly Inch had cast off the tow during the night to avoid a collision and now it would have to begin all over again.

Keen sounded exasperated. 'Call away the gig. I shall go over to her.' He took a glass from the midshipman-of-the-watch and trained it on the drifting transport. Half to himself he said, 'I have already had words with my carpenter, Sir Richard. With his aid I intend to coax *Orontes*' master into rigging a jury rudder.'

Bolitho raised his own telescope and studied the other vessel. Her decks seemed to be full of people, crew or convicts it was impossible to tell. No one appeared to be working and he said quietly, 'Take some marines with you, Val.'

Keen lowered his glass and looked at him. 'Aye, sir.' He sounded uneasy. 'Some of their people are drinking. At this time of the day!'

The gig and then a cutter were lowered alongside while the flagship came into the wind and lay hove-to, her reefed canvas flapping wetly in the spray.

Keen hurried to the entry port and Bolitho said, 'Go with him, Mr Stayt. You may learn something less basic then seamanship today.'

Keen waited impatiently as a squad of Royal Marines clattered down into the cutter with their junior officer Lieutenant Orde. He was a haughty young man who obviously resented the idea of soaking his immaculate scarlet coat on the crossing.

Keen touched his hat to the quarterdeck and then hurried down the side where Hogg waited with his gig.

Keen had no doubts in his mind that the next months would be crucial as England and her old enemy circled one another to seek out and exploit a first weakness. He wanted to begin, to use his ship where she was most needed. For Keen it was like a driving force. He had nothing else.

Once he glanced astern and saw his ship riding easily in the swell and Bolitho's straight figure by the quarterdeck rail. *Argonaute* would serve him well, Keen thought. *I owe him that and so much more.*

The coxswain swore silently as the gig shuddered alongside and hooked onto the main chains. The cutter, caught on a sudden crest, was carried past, the marines watching with amusement as the oarsmen fought to regain control.

Stayt stood aside to allow Keen to climb the ladder. After the lively motion and stinging spray the *Orontes'* broad deck seemed almost sluggish and without wind.

There were figures everywhere, on the deck and gangways, even in the tops overhead. A few carried weapons, guards probably, the rest looked like the sweepings of a jail.

But Keen saw only the drama being enacted below the poop. The rigged grating, a great brute of a boatswain's mate with what looked like a long whip in his hand as he stared at the figure seized up for flogging.

Keen hated the savage ritual of a flogging, more so the occasional need for it. Ever since he had seen his first punishment as a young midshipman, like most sea officers he had fought to conceal his revulsion for the sake of discipline. Others, it seemed, could watch it without turning a hair.

But this was different. He felt his spine go cold as he stared at the spreadeagled form on the grating.

A seaman exclaimed behind him, 'Christ A'mighty, sir, it's a girl!'

She was stripped almost to her buttocks, her face and shoulders hidden by her hair, her arms stretched out as if she had been crucified.

Keen stepped forward but before he could speak the boatswain's mate drew back his arm and curled the whip across the girl's back with the sound of a pistol shot.

Keen saw her arch her body, her torn clothing falling still further. But she did not scream for the force of the blow had smashed the breath from her body. Then, after what seemed like several seconds, a bright scarlet line showed itself from one bare shoulder to the opposite hip and then the blood ran down her back, and as the man drew back his arm she began to struggle.

Keen said sharply, '*Belay that!*' He felt Stayt beside him
but did not take his eyes from the scene. Around and
above him he could hear a baying chorus of voices. Anger,
disappointment – they had *wanted* to watch her flogged.

In the sudden silence Keen said, 'Mr Stayt! If that man
so much as lifts his whip I order you to shoot him dead!'

Stayt stepped forward, the pistol already cocked in his
hand. He raised his arm, not like a man going into battle,
but as a duellist would balance his weapon for that one,
vital shot.

A portly figure in a blue coat pushed towards Keen, his
jowls jogging with fury.

Keen regarded him calmly although he was feeling cold
anger sweeping through him, blinding him to everything
but the desire to smash this man, the master, in the face.

'What the hell do you think you're about, blast you!'
The man was almost incoherent with rage and drink.

Keen met his angry glare. 'I am Sir Richard Bolitho's
flag-captain. You abuse your authority, sir.' He felt his
relief as he heard the marines scrambling up the side. At
last. Inch had obviously withdrawn his own men before
the squall. In another moment, he, Stayt and the others
might have been overwhelmed. Most of the crew looked
too drunk to be able to think, let alone take orders.

Lieutenant Orde seemed unable to respond to what he
saw, but Blackburn, his big sergeant, rasped, 'Fix
bayonets, Marines! If they moves, cut 'em down!' Blackburn did not trust anyone who did not wear the scarlet
coat of the Corps.

The rasp of steel seemed to shock the vessel's ungainly
master.

He said in a conciliatory tone, 'She's a damned thief,
that's what. No better than a common whore! I must have
order and discipline in my ship! If I had my way – '

He broke off as Keen said gently, 'Cut her down. Cover
her with something.'

A seaman called, 'She'm fainted, sir!'

Keen made himself cross to the grating. He saw the way
her slight figure was dragging on her bound wrists, the
blood running down her spine. Her breasts were pressed

into the grating, and he could see where her heart pumped against the scrubbed wood.

She had fainted, but the pain would be waiting for her.

Hogg had appeared on deck and Keen heard him sheathe his cutlass. He must have thought the worst to quit his gig and come aboard without an order. A riot, a mutiny, Hogg was ready to save his captain. Like Allday had done for Bolitho.

Hogg strode over and cut the bonds and caught her as she fell, the last of her blood-spattered clothing gathered up in his arms as he hid her body from the silent onlookers.

The ship's master said thickly, 'I have a surgeon.'

Keen eyed him. 'I can well imagine.' It must have been the way he looked rather than what he said, because the master fell back as if he had seen his own danger in Keen's eyes.

'Take her to the gig, Hogg, and return to the ship. You go with the boat, Mr Stayt. I have work to do here.' He saw the barest hint of resentment in the lieutenant's dark eyes. He wanted to shoot, to kill the man with the whip. Anyone. Keen knew that look. *Perhaps I have it also*?

'Now, Captain Latimer.' Keen was surprised he had remembered the man's name, when moments earlier he had wanted to smash him to the deck. 'I intend that you shall put your best hands to work on a jury rudder. I will supply more men when required, but you will waste no more time, do you understand?'

'The girl?' The earlier anger showed itself. 'I'm responsible for every living soul aboard.'

Keen eyed him coldly. 'Then God help them. There are women in Captain Inch's ship, wives of the Gibraltar garrison officers. They can take care of the girl for the present, after my surgeon has examined her.'

The other man knew his authority was dwindling with each second.

'It must be said, Captain, that you've not heard the last o' this.'

Keen raised one hand and saw the man flinch. But he tapped his blue lapel and said, 'Nor you, I can promise that.'

Another boat ground alongside and he heard *Argonaute*'s carpenter and his selected crew climbing aboard.

Keen turned away, he was needed aboard the flagship for a dozen things but some last warning made him turn.

'If you are thinking, Captain Latimer, that it is a long, long way to New South Wales, let me assure you that you will not even see Gibraltar if you abuse your authority again.'

He climbed down into the cutter and waited to be pulled back to the ship.

He was breathing hard and thought his hands must be shaking. He saw the cutter's midshipman staring at him. He must have seen most of it.

Keen said, 'You are all eyes today, Mr Hext.'

Hext, who was just thirteen years old, nodded and swallowed hard.

'I – I'm sorry, sir. But, but – '

'Go on, Mr Hext.'

Hext flushed crimson, knowing that the oarsmen were watching as they pushed and pulled on their looms.

'When I saw it, sir, I – I wanted to stand with you – '

Keen smiled, moved by the boy's sincerity. It was probably hero-worship and nothing deeper, but it did more to steady Keen's mood than he could have believed possible.

He had heard it said that Hext wrote many letters to his parents although there was little time to post any of them.

He said, 'Never be afraid to help the helpless, Mr Hext. Think on it.'

The midshipman clung to the tiller bar and stared blindly at the towering masts and rigging of the flagship.

He would write about it in his next letter.

'Toss your oars!' he piped.

It was a moment he would never lose.

3

No Deadlier Enemy

Bolitho was leaning on the sill of the great stern windows when Keen entered his cabin, his hat beneath one arm.

Astern of *Argonaute* the other ships tilted over on the larboard tack, the courses and topsails braced round to hold the wind. Apart, and yet still with her escort, the *Orontes* was making better progress with her jury rudder, but the squadron's speed was still severely reduced.

The ship felt cold and damp. Bolitho thought of the Mediterranean and the warmth they would find there.

It was a full day since the trouble aboard *Orontes* and Bolitho could imagine the speculation on the lower deck, wardroom too, about the girl in the sickbay.

Keen looked at him and asked, 'You wished to see me, Sir Richard?'

It would not be lost on Keen that Ozzard and the others were absent. It was to be a private conversation.

'Yes. A letter has been sent to me by *Orontes*' master.'

Keen nodded. 'My cox'n collected it, sir.'

'In it he protests at your behaviour, *our* behaviour since you are under my command, and threatens to take the matter to higher authority.'

Keen said softly, 'I am sorry. I did not mean to involve you – '

Bolitho said, 'I would have expected no other action from you, Val. I am not troubled by that oaf's threat. If I were to press home a claim from his employers for salvage Captain Latimer would be on the beach before he knew it. His sort are scum, they work for blood money, like their counterparts in slavery.'

Keen waited, half surprised that Bolitho had not taken

him to task for interfering in the first place. He should have known.

Bolitho asked, 'Have you spoken to this girl?'

Keen shrugged. 'Well, no, sir. I thought it best to leave her with the surgeon until she recovers. You should have seen the whip, the size of the man who struck her – '

Bolitho was thinking aloud. 'She will have to be cared for by another woman. I did consider Inch's ship after your suggestion, but I'm not sure. Officers' wives and a girl sentenced to transportation, though for what crime we cannot yet know. I will *ask* Latimer for details of her warrant.'

Keen said, 'It is good of you to take the trouble, sir. If I had only known – '

Bolitho smiled gravely. 'You would still have acted as you did.'

Feet thudded overhead and blocks squealed as the officer-of-the-watch yelled for the braces to be manned.

In a crowded King's ship a solitary woman could be seen as many things, not least bad luck. Landsmen might scoff at such beliefs. If they went to sea they would soon know differently.

'See the girl yourself, Val. Then tell me what you think. At Gibraltar we can shift her to the *Philomela*. From what you say, Latimer would certainly take his revenge otherwise.'

Keen made to withdraw. He had meant to visit the girl and speak with the surgeon further about her. No matter what she had done in her young life, she did not deserve the agony and humiliation of a flogging.

Bolitho waited for the door to close and then sat down again beneath the stern windows.

Time and time again he kept thinking of Falmouth, of the sheer happiness of his homecoming, holding his new and only child Elizabeth in his arms, so awkwardly that Belinda had laughed at him.

Bolitho had always understood how difficult it must be for any woman to cross the threshold of the Bolitho home. Too many shadows and memories, so much expected of a newcomer. And in Belinda's case she had been replacing Cheney, or so it would seem to her.

It had hit Bolitho hardest when he had discovered that Cheney's portrait, the companion to the one she had had done of him, had been removed from the room where the two pictures had once hung together. She with the headland behind her, her eyes like the sea, and he in his white-lapelled coat, as the captain she had loved so much. His portrait now hung with the others, alongside that of his father, Captain James.

He had said nothing; he had not wanted to hurt her, but it still disturbed him. Like a betrayal.

He kept telling himself that Belinda only wanted to help him, to make others appreciate his worth to the country.

But Falmouth was his home, not London. He could almost hear the words so harsh in that quiet room.

He sighed and turned his thoughts to Allday. He had probably felt the new atmosphere at Falmouth. It was impossible to guess what he made of it. Or maybe Allday had been so concerned with the discovery of his son that he had had no time for speculation.

He pictured the two of them as they had stood here in the cabin. Allday, powerful, proud in his blue jacket with the prized gilt buttons, head cocked to listen and watch as Bolitho spoke with the young sailor, John Bankart.

Bolitho could remember when Allday had been brought aboard his frigate *Phalarope*, a victim of the press gang. It was twenty years ago although it did not seem possible. Ferguson, Bolitho's steward now at Falmouth, had been dragged aboard with him. No wonder they had remained so close.

Allday had been very like this young sailor. Clear-eyed, honest-looking, with a sort of defiance just below the surface. He had met with a recruiting party and signed on with little hesitation when he was around eighteen. He disliked farm life, and knew that as a volunteer he would get better treatment than pressed men in a King's ship.

His mother had never married. Allday had hinted uncomfortably that the farmer had often taken her to his bed, under the threat that otherwise he would get rid of her and her bastard son.

It had touched a nerve for Bolitho. The memory of Adam's arrival on board his ship after walking all the way from Penzance when his mother had died. It was too similar not to move him.

Bankart had already proved himself a good seaman and could reef, splice and steer, equal to many his senior in age and service. As second coxswain he would have little contact with his admiral. His duties would be confined to maintaining the readiness and appearance of the barge, going on errands to ships and the shore, and helping Allday in any way that he could. It seemed a satisfactory solution for the present.

He got up and walked into his sleeping compartment, then, after a slight hesitation, he opened a drawer and took out the beautiful oval miniature. The artist had caught her expression perfectly. Bolitho replaced it under his shirts.

What was the matter with him?

He was happy. He had a lovely wife ten years his junior, and now a daughter. And yet –

He turned away and re-entered the day cabin.

When they joined the fleet things would be different. Action, danger, and the rewards of victory.

He stared at his reflection in the salt-encrusted windows and smiled wryly.

Sir Richard, yet at the actual moment the King had seemingly forgotten his name.

Bolitho tried to gather his thoughts for the months ahead, how Lapish would react the first time the squadron's only frigate was called to arms, but it eluded him.

He thought instead of the portrait which had gone from the room which looked towards the sea, and wished suddenly he had brought it with him.

Far beneath Bolitho's spacious quarters and the view astern from its gilded gallery, *Argonaute*'s sickbay seemed airless. For the orlop deck, below the level of the waterline, was completely sealed, a place of leaping shadows from the swaying, spiralling lanterns where the massive deckhead beams were so low a man could not stand upright. From the day the ship had been built, the orlop had not, and would never, see the light of day.

Tiny hutchlike cabins lined part of the deck where the warrant officers clung to their privacy with barely room to move. Nearby was the midshipmen's berth where the 'young gentlemen' lived their disordered lives and were expected to study for promotion by the light of a glim, an oiled wick in a shell or an old tin.

The hanging magazine and powder stores, where a single spark could bring disaster, shared the deck with them, and below them the great holds carried everything to sustain the ship for many months if need be.

Right aft at the foot of a companion ladder the sickbay seemed bright by comparison with its white paint and racks of jars and bottles.

Keen strode towards it, his head automatically lowered to avoid the beams, his epaulettes glittering as he passed from one lantern to the next. Dark shapes and vague faces loomed and faded in the gloom, that other world away from sea and sky.

He saw James Tuson, the surgeon, speaking with his assistant, a tall, pallid Channel Islander named Carcaud. The latter was more Breton than English, but was intelligent and could both read and write. Keen knew that Tuson, who had been *Achates'* surgeon, took a great interest in his lanky assistant and had taught him as much as he could. They even played chess together.

Keen liked the silver-haired Tuson, although he knew him no more than in their previous ship. He was a fine surgeon, twenty times better than most of his profession who served the King's ships. But he kept to himself, not an easy thing in this teeming world between decks, and often went to the wardroom only for meals.

A marine, his crossbelts very white in the poor light, straightened his back and made Tuson turn towards the captain. It had been a wise precaution to place a sentry at the door, Keen thought. Many of the hands had been aboard one ship or another without a break for many months. Any woman might be at risk. One labelled a felon even more so.

Tuson murmured something and his assistant, bent almost double, melted into the shadows.

Keen said, 'How is she?'

Tuson unrolled his shirt sleeves and considered the question.

'She says nothing, to me anyway. She's young, under twenty I'd wager, and her skin is fine, and her hands have not worked in a field.' He turned away from the rigid sentry whose leather hat seemed to be wedged against the deckhead, and dropped his voice. 'There are several bruises. I fear she may have been raped or savagely molested.' He sighed. 'I'd not risk an examination under the circumstances.'

Keen nodded. The girl had suddenly become a person, someone real and not just a victim.

The surgeon was watching him thoughtfully; he rarely smiled.

'She can't stay here, sir.'

Keen avoided the issue. 'I'll speak with her.' He hesitated, 'Unless you advise to the contrary?'

The surgeon led the way towards the small, bright place. 'She knows where she is, but be patient, I beg you.'

Keen stepped into the sickbay and saw the girl lying face down on a pillow and covered with a sheet. She appeared to be sleeping, but Keen could tell by her quick breathing that she was pretending. The surgeon pulled down the sheet and Keen saw her back tense.

Tuson said in his soft, matter-of-fact tones, 'The scar is healing, but – ' He lifted a loose dressing and Keen saw the deep cut left by the whip. If he had not acted promptly, or had not gone over to the ship at all, she would be crippled or dead. In the lantern light the scar looked black.

Tuson pointed to hair which was long and dark brown; it was matted and tangled and as he touched it Keen saw her stiffen again.

He said, 'She needs a bath and some fresh clothing.'

Keen said, 'I'll send a lieutenant over to the *Orontes*

as soon as we anchor. She must have some possessions
surely.'

His words seemed to strike her like the whip and she
rolled over violently, covering her breasts with the sheet
and oblivious to the immediate droplets of blood which
broke from her scar.

'*No, not back there!* Please, not back to that, that place!'

Keen was taken aback by the outburst. The girl was
almost beautiful, something which bruises and disordered
hair could not conceal. She had small, well-shaped hands,
and eyes so wide they were almost starting from her face
as she pleaded with him.

He said, 'Easy, girl. Easy now.' He reached out to
steady her but saw Tuson give a quick shake of his head.

The surgeon said, 'This is the captain. He saved you
from the flogging.'

She looked at Keen's anxious face and said, '*You*, sir?'
It was little more than a whisper. 'It was you?'

She had a soft, West Country voice. It was impossible
to imagine her standing trial and being transported in that
filthy vessel with the other prisoners.

'Yes.' Around him the ship kept up her continuous
chorus of creaks and groans with the occasional boom of
water beyond the massive timbers as the keel crashed into
a trough. But Keen was conscious only of stillness, as if
all time had suddenly stopped.

He heard himself ask, 'What's your name?'

She glanced quickly at the surgeon, who nodded
encouragingly.

'Carwithen.' She clutched the sheet tighter as Tuson
readjusted the dressings on her back.

'Where are you from?'

'Dorset, sir, from Lyme.' Her small chin lifted briefly
and he saw it tremble. 'But I'm Cornish really.'

Tuson grunted, 'Thought so.' He straightened his back.
'Now lie still, and don't open the cut again. I'll have some
food brought down.' He turned to the door and beckoned
to his waiting assistant.

She looked at Keen once more and said in a hoarse
whisper, 'You really are the captain, sir?'

Keen knew that her guard was about to break. He had grown up with two younger sisters and knew the first signs. God alone knew, she had suffered enough.

He moved to the door, pausing as the hull dipped and then reluctantly lifted her eighteen hundred tons for the next challenge. The girl did not take her eyes from his face. 'What will you have done with me, sir?'

Her eyes were shining. He must not be here when the tears broke through.

Instead he asked bluntly, 'What's your first name?'

She seemed caught off balance. 'Zenoria.'

He backed away. 'Well, Zenoria, do as the surgeon directs. I will ensure that no harm comes to you.'

He passed the sentry without even seeing him.

What had he done? How could he promise her anything, and why should he? He did not even know her.

As he hurried up the first companion ladder he already knew the answers to both questions. It was madness. *I must be mad.*

It seemed to mock him and he was suddenly grateful to see the sky once again.

Lieutenant Hector Stayt leaned over the table and placed another copy of Bolitho's orders for his signature. They would be passed to all the other captains when they finally anchored at Gibraltar. That would be in two days' time if the wind remained in their favour. It had been a long, empty week since the incident aboard *Urontes*, but now, as the small squadron steered to the south-east with the Spanish coastline from Cadiz to Algeciras barely visible to the most keen-eyed lookout, the passage was almost over.

Bolitho glanced over Yovell's round handwriting before putting his own signature at the bottom. The same orders but each would be interpreted differently by the captains who read them. Once in the Mediterranean there would be neither time nor opportunity to get to know his officers nor they him.

He thought of Keen and his visits to their unexpected passenger. The French builders had allowed an extra chart space abaft the master's cabin, and this had been made as comfortable as possible for the girl Zenoria Carwithen. A cot, a mirror, some clean sheets from the wardroom had somehow transformed it. Ozzard had even managed to discover a spare officer's commode in the hold and had installed it for her use. They must not get too fond of the idea of having her aboard, he thought. Once at the Rock . . .

Stayt said, 'I did hear something about that girl, Sir Richard.'

It was not the first time the flag-lieutenant had seemed to read Bolitho's thoughts. It was unnerving and irritating.

'And?' Bolitho looked up from the table.

Stayt sounded almost indifferent now that he had his admiral's attention.

'Oh, she was mixed up in a riot of some kind, I understand. It was near to my father's property. Someone was murdered before the military arrived.' He gave a thin smile. 'Late as usual.'

Bolitho looked past him at the swords on their rack. One so bright and gleaming, the other almost shabby by comparison.

Stayt took his silence for interest. 'Her father was hanged.'

Bolitho dragged out his watch and opened the guard. 'Time to exercise the squadron's signals, Mr Stayt. I'll be up directly.'

Stayt left. He had a springy walk; it seemed to show his great self-confidence.

Bolitho frowned. Conceit anyway.

Yovell moved to the table and gathered up the papers. He glanced at Bolitho over his small gold spectacles and said, 'It wasn't quite like that, Sir Richard.'

Bolitho looked at him. 'Tell me. I'd like to hear it. From you.'

Yovell smiled sadly. 'Carwithen was a printer, sir. A fine one, I'm told. Some of the farmworkers asked him to print some handbills, a sort of protest it was, about two landowners who had been keeping them short of money and chattels. Carwithen was a bit of a firebrand by all accounts, believed in speaking his mind, especially when others were being wronged.' He flushed but Bolitho nodded.

'Speak as you will, man.'

It was strange that Yovell should know. He lived at the Bolitho house when he was ashore, but he was a Devonian, a 'foreigner' as far as local folk were concerned. Yet he always seemed to know about the people around him.

'Carwithen's wife had died previous to that, so they sent the girl out of the county.'

'To Dorset?'

'Aye sir, that were it.'

So something else must have happened since the 'riot', as Stayt had described it.

He heard the trill of calls from the quarterdeck as the signalling party were mustered under Stayt's eagle eye. Signals, especially in battle, should be few, short and precise.

Bolitho made up his mind and said, 'Fetch Allday.'

Allday glanced questioningly at the secretary as they entered, but Yovell merely shrugged his sloping shoulders.

'Sir?'

'Go with Yovell and fetch that girl aft.' He saw their surprise. 'Now, if you please.'

Keen would be busy on deck watching the other ships as they acknowledged and obeyed the signals from the flag.

Allday's jaw looked stubborn.

'If you thinks it's wise, sir – '

Bolitho eyed him firmly. 'I do.'

He saw Ozzard lifting his coat from a chair but shook his head. Any sort of liaison would be destroyed before it had begun if she found herself confronted by a vice-admiral.

From what Keen and Tuson had said she seemed to be an intelligent girl, and her father's influence had obviously gained her some education.

He was interfering, but he had seen Keen's face when-ever he had mentioned the girl. Bolitho had not forgotten what it was like; he must act before the girl was taken from the ship.

He was totally unprepared for what happened next.

Yovell opened the screen door and the girl walked hesitantly towards the stern cabin. Against Allday's powerful figure she looked small, but her head was up, and only her eyes moved as she paused below the skylight.

She was dressed in a white shirt and breeches of one of the midshipmen, and her long brown hair was pulled back to the nape of her neck with a ribbon, so that she almost looked as if she belonged in the gunroom. But her feet were bare, small like her hands, and Yovell explained hastily, 'Even the young gentlemen didn't have shoes small enough for her.'

Bolitho said, 'Sit down. I wish to talk with you.'

He saw the stiff way she held her shoulder. Tuson had said her back would be scarred for life. And that had been from just one stroke.

'I should like to know – ' He saw her eyes level on his; they were dark brown, misty. No wonder Keen was under some kind of magic. ' – what brought you to these circumstances.'

Yovell murmured, 'Tell, Sir Richard, lass, he'll not eat you.'

She started with alarm, her lips parting as she exclaimed, '*Sir* Richard!'

Bolitho wanted to glare at Yovell but said, 'Just tell me. Please.'

But she stared at him. 'But – but I've met the captain?'

Yovell said patiently, 'The admiral here commands all the ships, all the captains, Miss, and some two thousand eight hundred jack tars and marines.' He watched her gravely. 'A big job to do, so speak up an' don't you waste his time, eh?'

Bolitho smiled. 'He means well, er, Zenoria, isn't it?'

She looked at her hands in her lap. Then she said, 'They took my father, sir. He was a fine man, a clever man too. He believed in people's rights.' Her eyes took on a faraway look and Bolitho found he was holding his breath. Just to hear her speak. It was like hearing Cornwall again.

'I saw him hang, sir.'

'But why?'

'It was the squire, sir. He came to the house with some of his men and they tried to smash his press. My father soon showed them.' Her chin lifted with sudden pride so that she looked all the more vulnerable. 'He pulled the squire from his horse, and others came from the village to help him. Someone was killed. Then the dragoons came and took him away.'

'How old were you then?'

'Seventeen, sir. That was two years ago. They sent me to Dorset, to work in a big household and help teach the children there.'

It was difficult to speak as he wished with Yovell and Allday listening. But he had to be certain she was not lying, not a whore as stated by *Orontes'* master. It could be dangerous to be alone with her.

'Tell me about what happened in Lyme.'

Yovell said severely, 'Your warrant will come aboard, my lass, so no use lying about it!'

'For God's sake, man, hold your tongue!' Bolitho saw the girl cringe as if his anger was directed partly at her.

He said, 'Fetch her a glass, Allday.' He was trying to cover his own confusion. 'I must know.'

She dropped her eyes. 'Everyone knew about my father and what had happened. The master was always touching me, making remarks, telling me how lucky I was to have a roof over my head. Then one day he came to my room.' She was beginning to shake. 'He tried to – ' She took a glass from Allday but did not drink from it. 'He forced me to do things – ' She looked up, her eyes wild and pleading. 'I'd been making some repairs to the children's clothing.' She could barely get the words out. 'I took the scissors and I stabbed him.'

Bolitho stood up and walked slowly behind her chair. It was so clear in her voice. He could almost see it happening.

'And then?'

'He didn't die, sir, but I was sent to the Assizes. You know the rest, sir.'

Transportation for life.

'You may return to your cabin, Zenoria.' Bolitho looked

down at her upturned face. Nineteen years old, but in the midshipman's shirt with her hair tied back she looked like a child.

She stood up and handed her glass to Allday. It was still full.

'That Captain Latimer wanted me too, sir.' It was all she needed to say.

'Tomorrow my secretary will help you to write all this down. I cannot, *must* not pretend that I can help in this matter.' He touched her shoulder and this time she did not flinch. 'But I promise you, I shall try.'

He turned aft to the windows and waited to hear the door close.

When Allday came back he said simply, 'That were kindly done, an' that's no error, sir. She's sobbin' fit to bust now, but it'll do her good.'

'You think so?' Bolitho watched the flags soaring up *Helicon*'s yards, but saw only the girl's eyes, the pain that was so deeply lodged there. *I saw him hang.* He thought of the squire who had married his sister Nancy at Falmouth. A rich landowner who had always had his eye on the Bolitho house. Local people called him the King of Cornwall behind his back. But he was good to Nancy even if he was a braggart who lived too well in peace and war. He was also a magistrate, but even he would have recommended mercy rather than deportation. Or would he?

More calls trilled and he knew that the drills were ended for another day.

He watched the door and heard the sentry's heels bang together. Keen entered and exclaimed, 'May I speak, Sir Richard?'

Allday and Yovell left the cabin and Keen said, 'I have just heard, sir. I regret that you did not feel free to ask me when – '

Bolitho said quietly, 'Sit down, Val. We are not going to fight. I saw the girl because of you, not in spite of you.'

Keen stared at him. '*Me?*'

Bolitho gestured to a chair. 'She sat there. Now pray do likewise.'

Bolitho watched the emotions crossing Keen's features. He had rarely seen Keen angry, but this was different, protective.

He said, 'She will have to be put ashore once we anchor. It is only a temporary solution, but I think I can arrange it. From what she has told me and what was left unsaid, I believe there is some hope, if only – '

He broke off as Keen exclaimed, 'I can write to my cousin in the City of London. I am sure we can – ' He turned and looked at Bolitho, his eyes steady. 'It was good of you, sir. I should have understood.'

Bolitho poured two glasses of brandy and guessed that Ozzard was pressed against his pantry shutter.

'She has been cruelly used, Val.' He let his words drop like shot into a still pool. 'Raped, it would seem, and that's just the half of it.' He watched the pain in Keen's blue eyes. He had guessed correctly. Bolitho did not know whether it gave him satisfaction or grief.

Keen said quietly, 'I have a great affection for her, sir.' He looked up, his eyes defiant as if he expected Bolitho to explode.

'I know that, Val. I think I knew that day when you went down to visit her, maybe even earlier.' He nodded. 'That's settled then.'

Keen put down the empty glass although he had barely noticed what he was drinking.

'It's impossible! I am mad even to think of it!'

Bolitho said, 'How old are you, Val? Thirty-five or six?'

'A year older than that, sir. And she is just a girl.'

'A *woman*, Val, so remember it, eh? As you get older the gap between you will lessen, not widen.' He put his head on one side and smiled at Keen's expression.

Perhaps he had done wrong by both of them. The senior officer or the Governor at Gibraltar might refuse to allow the girl to remain there.

But at least the truth was out and Bolitho found that he was surprisingly lifted by it.

Keen said, 'I am deluding myself, sir.'

Bolitho touched his arm. 'We shall see – ' He glanced at the skylight as a lookout's cry floated down from aloft.

A minute later the midshipman-of-the-watch appeared breathless at the door.

'Beg pardon, sir.' He stared from Keen to his admiral. 'Mr Paget's respects, and we have just sighted a sail, sir.'

It was Midshipman Hext, his eyes now moving around the great cabin, doubtless remembering it for another letter.

Bolitho smiled gravely. 'And are we to be told where this sail might be, in due course?'

The boy blushed. 'I – I'm sorry, Sir Richard. It bears to the sou'east.'

Keen said, 'My compliments to the first lieutenant. I shall come up.' He still sounded different, as if only half his mind was working on the news.

Bolitho said, 'Signal *Rapid* to investigate.' His thoughts clung to that small moment of warmth they had shared and then he said, 'Might be news of the French.'

Keen's eyes cleared. 'Aye, sir.' Then he was gone.

But it was to be news of a graver sort.

As the other ship drew closer she was soon identified as the *Barracouta*. Bolitho took a telescope and joined Keen at the quarterdeck rail to watch as Lapish clawed his way to windward to draw closer to the squadron.

There were men at work on her yards and several of her sails were patched. Even as he watched Bolitho saw a great mass of cordage being hoisted aloft, the work not even faltering as the business of sailing the ship went on.

'She's been in a fight.' Keen nodded to his first lieutenant. 'Prepare to shorten sail, Mr Paget.'

Bolitho kept his face impassive as the men around the quarterdeck stared at him. So it was beginning already. The momentary calm was over.

'You are right, Val. Captain repair on board immediately.'

An hour later Captain Jeremy Lapish sat in Bolitho's cabin. He seemed to have aged since he had left the squadron to carry dispatches to Gibraltar.

He explained, 'I sighted a schooner inshore and closed to see what she was about.' He took a goblet gratefully from Ozzard. 'Before I knew where we were there were

two French frigates coming around the point with the
wind under their coat-tails.'

Bolitho saw the despair and misery on the young
captain's face. Just what he had feared had happened. The
schooner had been the bait and the two Frenchmen had
almost run Lapish's ship onto a lee shore.

'I shall read your report later.' Bolitho eyed him sternly.
'Did you lose any hands?'

Lapish nodded, his eyes dull. 'Two, sir.'

Quite rightly Lapish had run from his attackers.
Outsailed and outgunned, he had had little choice.

Would I have done the same? Bolitho looked at him.
'What of Gibraltar?'

Lapish shook himself from his thoughts. He had nearly
lost his ship so soon after taking command. Almost as
bad, he may have lost the confidence of his people.

He said, 'Gibraltar is closed, sir.' He laid a heavy
envelope on the table and they all looked at it as he added,
'Fever. It has struck down half the garrison.'

Bolitho walked across the cabin and back again. The
Rock was notorious for outbreaks of fever, but what a
time for this to happen.

'There is no deadlier enemy.' He looked at Keen. 'We
shall have to stand offshore until we know what is
happening.' To Lapish he said, 'Return to your ship.' He
wanted to share his pain, to commiserate with him. Instead
he closed his mind and said sharply, 'Think yourself fortunate to have a ship left to command.'

Keen left to see the crestfallen Lapish over the side.

Fever. Bolitho shivered. Just the word brought back the
nightmare, when he had nearly died of it. It might still
return.

He shook himself and tried to consider how the news
would affect them. With Gibraltar closed to them he
would have to decide for himself what to do.

He smiled grimly. He was no longer just an onlooker.

4

Bait

With the crash of a salute lingering in the air the small squadron came round into the wind and anchored in succession.

Bolitho stood by the nettings and saw the relief on Keen's face. The manoeuvre was executed well despite so many new hands throughout the ships.

He turned and looked up at the great towering mass of Gibraltar. In the past it had always been a refuge, a safe anchorage; now it seemed edged with menace.

There were few men-of-war present, and they were moored clear of the jetty near the other convict ship *Philo-mela* and some local craft. Several guardboats plied slowly back and forth. Bolitho saw that they carried redcoats and each mounted at least one swivel. It was as bad as that.

'We call the other captains aboard today.'

He saw Keen training his telescope on one of the boats which was pulling towards the flagship. 'Aye, sir. I think we have a visitor.'

The boat paused, the oars backing water below the main chains while the crew stared up at the two-decker as if she was part of another world.

A post-captain stood in the sternsheets and squinted up at the quarterdeck.

'I cannot come aboard, Sir Richard! I have to tell you that the Governor has taken charge here, the admiral is ill.' He kept his voice unhurried and level as if well aware of the countless ears and eyes which were gauging the danger.

Bolitho walked to the entry port and stood looking down at the boat. Each man in it would probably give all he owned to be allowed on board, even though he might bring the fever with him.

The sunburned captain in the boat called, 'I have sent a courier brig, *Firefly*, to Lord Nelson.'

It was strange that only Inch had ever met the little admiral and had rarely ceased to tell of it. Now Adam might meet him.

The captain added, 'I understand that officers' wives are taking passage in your squadron, Sir Richard. I have to tell you that if they land, they must do so now. It is their right to be with their husbands if they so wish. But they cannot leave until this fever is broken.'

Bolitho saw the *Orontes* swinging to her anchor, a guardboat idling nearby to deter anyone from trying to swim ashore.

It would require a lot of planning. Water, supplies, repairs. The squadron would need them all and more.

'I have dispatches from the Governor, Sir Richard.' A satchel was being lifted to the main chains on a boat hook. Bolitho saw Carcaud, the lanky surgeon's mate, leaning down to seize it in a flannel bag. Tuson was taking no chances even with that.

Bolitho could feel Keen watching him as he called, 'All the ladies are astern of me in *Helicon*. I have one woman aboard my ship.'

The captain shrugged apologetically. 'If she is not of the garrison, Sir Richard, I am ordered to inform you no other person can be landed.'

The boat began to move away, the oars stirring unwillingly. The captain raised his hat. 'I shall collect the ladies now, sir!' The contact was broken.

Keen lowered his voice. 'You did not tell him that the girl is a prisoner, sir?'

Bolitho watched the flannel bag being carried aft.

'I do not recall that he asked, Val.' He left a patch of shade and stared up at the Rock, its ancient Moorish castle shrouded in heat haze.

'The Governor might easily have shut her in a cell, Val. He has raised a state of seige here, one girl more or less would stand no chance.'

Keen stared after him, knowing that his lieutenants were waiting with their demands and lists.

Bolitho had to search through his dispatches and compare them with his instructions from the Admiralty. It was a great responsibility to his ships and his men. But he had still found time to think about the girl named Zenoria. It was unnerving.

He turned and looked at his officers. 'Well, Mr Paget, where shall we begin?' His face was quite calm; he was the flag-captain again. If one hint of this matter reached higher authority Bolitho's name would be smeared too. And yet he had not hesitated.

By the boat tier Allday peered up at the green-painted barge and frowned. It would not be lowered, here at Gib anyway. He climbed up to peer into the sleek hull, biting his lip as if he expected the hot pain to surge through his chest again. The boat was half filled with water. The seams would not open in the sunlight. He glanced down at Bankart and grinned.

'You've made a good start, lad.' He was pleased although still dazed by the change of events which had given him a son. That was the strange thing. They spoke a lot with each other, but apart from Bankart's dead mother they had nothing in common except the Navy. But he was a pleasant lad and did not abuse his small authority of second coxswain as some might.

Allday dropped to the deck and said, 'Time for a wet. We'll not be needed just now.' He glanced aft. 'The admiral's too busy for chatter.'

Bankart ducked beneath a gangway and asked, 'What is he like? I've heard tell you've been with him since – '

Allday eyed him fondly. 'Since around the day you was born, I reckon. A fine man. Brave, an' loyal to his mates.'

He thought of the girl in midshipman's clothing. All bloody hell would break if Keen wasn't careful. He had heard some of the seamen laying odds on whether the captain had had his way with her. 'All right for the officers, eh, lads? Poor Jack is the one to suffer!' Allday had silenced that one with his fist, but there would be plenty more who thought as much.

He said, 'I'll take you with me to the house when we gets home. It's a grand place, but they found room for me like one o' their own.'

The mention of Falmouth made him suddenly uneasy. He had seen Bolitho's dismay change to resentment over something Lady Belinda had said or done.

Allday would back Bolitho anywhere against all odds, but he felt sympathy for his lovely wife. It could not be a smooth passage to follow in Cheney's shadow. Bolitho would have to accept this. There was no going back.

He shook himself out of his mood as he caught the heady aroma of rum.

'A good wet, that's what we need.'

The surgeon was standing just inside the door of the make-shift cabin, wiping his strong fingers on a cloth, as Keen appeared. Keen glanced at the Royal Marine sentry and saw that his blank face was wet with sweat, for despite the hastily rigged wind-sails to every hatch the air felt hot and sluggish.

'How is she?'

Tuson eyed him for several seconds. 'I've removed the dressing, sir.'

Keen walked past him and saw the girl sitting on a stool, her hair released from its ribbon and covering her shoulders.

He asked, 'Does it still hurt very much?'

Her eyes lifted to his. 'It is bearable, sir.' She moved her shoulders warily beneath the shirt and winced. 'It feels stiff.' She seemed to realize that her borrowed shirt had fallen open and dragged it together quickly.

Then she said, 'I heard what happened today. About me.' She looked up and he saw the anxiety stark in her eyes. 'Will I be sent to that ship again, sir? I'll kill myself before – '

Keen said, 'No. Don't speak of it.'

Tuson watched from the door. The tall, elegant captain and the long-haired girl on the stool. Miles apart and yet there was something like a shaft of light between them.

He cleared his throat. 'I'll fetch some ointment for that scar, my girl.' He looked at Keen and added quietly, 'I shall be about ten minutes, sir.' Then he was gone.

She asked, 'Would you like to sit with me, sir?' She gestured to a heavy chest. Then she smiled. It was the first time Keen had seen her smile. She said, 'Not what you're used to, I'm sure.' Her sudden confidence left her and she added huskily, 'I am sorry.'

'Don't be.' Keen watched her hands in her lap and wanted to hold them. 'I wish I could make you more comfortable.'

She lifted her gaze and watched him steadily.

'What is it you want of me?' She sounded neither angry nor frightened. It was as if she had been expecting him to demand freely what she had already been brutally forced to give.

Keen said, 'I want to take care of you.' He looked at the deck. He thought she would call for the sentry or, worse, laugh at him and his clumsiness.

Without a word she moved from the stool and knelt down against his legs and rested her head on his knees.

Keen found that he was stroking her long hair, saying meaningless words, anything to prolong this impossible moment.

There were footsteps on a companion ladder and outside the door the sentry dragged the butt of his musket across the deck. Tuson was coming back.

Then she looked up at him and he saw that her eyes were streaming with tears, could feel them wet through his white breeches.

'You *mean* it, don't you?' The words were torn from her.

Keen stood up and raised her to her feet. Without shoes she barely reached his chest.

He touched her face, and then very carefully as if he was handling something precious and delicate he lifted her chin with his fingers. 'Believe it. I have never meant anything so much.'

Then as Tuson's shadow moved between them he stepped back through the door.

Tuson watched them and was surprised that he could still feel so emotional after what his trade had done to him. It was like sharing something. A secret. But it would not remain one for long.

Ozzard and his assistants had brought extra lanterns to the great cabin so that the windows overlooking the harbour seemed black by comparison.

It was the first time that all the captains of Bolitho's squadron had been gathered together like this. There was an air of good humour and perhaps some relief that they were staying away from the fever.

Keen waited until all the goblets had been filled and then said, 'Pay attention, gentlemen.'

Bolitho stood by the windows, his hands tucked behind him under his coat-tails.

A landsman would be impressed, he thought; his little band of captains made a fine sight beneath the slowly spiralling lanterns.

Francis Inch was the most senior, his long face empty of anxiety or concern about anything. Keen, the only other post-captain, looked tense as he glanced at his companions.

His mind was still turning over what had happened between him and their passenger. One good thing had occured, Bolitho decided. A Jamaican girl, one of the servants who had been travelling with the garrison wives, had pleaded not to be sent ashore. In view of the Governor's order this seemed a suitable solution for a companion for Zenoria Carwithen. It would not stop the speculation but might halve the gossip.

Philip Montresor of the *Dispatch* was a young, eager-faced man, who was not in the least daunted by the solitary epaulette on his right shoulder. Next to him, Tobias Houston of the *Icarus* looked old for his rank and had indeed gained it by a roundabout route through John Company and later the Revenue Service. He had a round, hard face like a weathered nut, and a mouth little more than a slit.

Commander Marcus Quarrell was leaning across to

whisper something to Lapish, who had commanded his
brig *Rapid* before him. Quarrell was a lively, friendly man
from the Isle of Man. But his humour was failing with
Lapish who still looked sunk in gloom.

Lieutenant Hallowes of the cutter *Supreme* was also
present and quite rightly, he was as much a captain as any
of them. For the present anyway.

They were a mixed bunch, Bolitho thought. The whole
fleet must be like this as their lordships tried to produce
ships and men for a war which even an idiot should have
expected.

He looked over their expectant faces, the gold and blue
of their uniforms, the confidence he had heard in their
voices.

He said, 'Gentlemen, I intend to sail with a minimum
of delay. In his dispatches the Governor has informed me
that an East Indiaman will be arriving any day now to take
passage around the Cape of Good Hope. With her trained
company and heavy artillery she will be able to offer a
suitable escort to the two convict vessels until they are
clear of French interference. I am sure the Governor will
be able to *persuade* the grocery captain.'

They all laughed. The HEIC was not known for losing
time on a fast passage no matter for what reason.

It hid Bolitho's relief. He had been afraid that the
Governor might demand one of his ships for the task;
there were too few already without that.

He continued, 'This is unlike the blockades of Brest and
the Bay. There, foul though it is for the ships involved,
they can be relieved and sent to England for restoring or
repairs in a couple of weeks. In the Mediterranean there
is no such relief. Toulon is our main cause of anxiety;
to watch the enemy and discover his intention will need
constant vigilance. But where can we go for our supplies
and, even more important, our fresh drinking water?
Gibraltar is eight hundred miles from Toulon, and Malta
about the same. A ship sent from Malta might be away
from her admiral for over two months.' He smiled wryly.
'Pleasant for her captain maybe,' he saw them grin, 'but
in the meantime the enemy could be away on the wind. I

have no doubt that Vice-Admiral Nelson has already found a possible solution. If not, I intend to act independently.'
He could see the captains of the seventy-fours considering what he had said. Each ship carried fresh water for only ninety days, and that was on a restricted ration. They had to find a source of water above all else.

'You must continue regular gun and sail drills at all times. Apart from improving both it will keep the people occupied.'

There was a smell of food and he guessed that Ozzard was waiting to serve dinner for the gathered captains.

He said, 'We will speak later, but do you have any questions?'

Montresor got to his feet. Like Keen he had fair hair and the fresh complexion of a schoolboy.

He asked, 'Are we to blockade the French at Toulon and the other ports, Sir Richard?'

Bolitho replied, 'Not entirely. Our main task is to catch them if they break out, and destroy them. They will be testing us, remember, feeling our strength as well as our ability.' He saw Keen's face. He alone knew what Bolitho had left until now.

'There is one French squadron, newly formed, but not yet reported in Toulon.'

Even as he said it he found it hard to believe, impossible to accept.

'Rear-Admiral Jobert commands it.' He saw their exchange of glances; for some it had not sunk in.

He looked round the great cabin. 'This was his ship, gentlemen. We took it from him some five months ago.' How had Jobert managed it? To obtain an exchange with some British prisoner of equal rank perhaps, but Bolitho had heard of no such arrangement.

'He will know our movements, also that my flag flies above the squadron. He is a brave and resourceful officer and will be out for revenge.'

Inch leaned forward and bobbed. 'We'll finish him this time!'

Bolitho looked at the three junior officers. 'Your importance is paramount. I have no doubt in my mind that Jobert was behind the trap laid for *Barracouta*.' It was little more than a guess, but fitted what he knew about Jobert. The look of gratitude on Lapish's face more than made up for it. He would not repeat his mistake.

Bolitho said, 'Jobert may intend to seek out any small, detached vessel and destroy her and so leave the flagship deaf and blind.'

With his ex-flagship and *Helicon*, another French prize, trailing their coats in his waters, Jobert would need little encouragement to level the score.

At the back of his mind Bolitho wondered if Admiral Sheaffe had known about this when he had last seen him. An encouragement for one was a goad for the other. *Perhaps I am the bait?*

Keen murmured bitterly, 'We should have done for him there and then!' It was unusual for him to sound so vehement.

Worrying about the girl and what would become of her now that they were moving deeper into the Mediterranean? What *should* be done with her? Perhaps, after all, his plan had gone wrong and might eventually do her some real harm.

He thrust it from his mind. The war would not wait. It was something greater than any of them had known.

He said quietly, 'So let us dine together, gentlemen.'

Inch beamed. 'And think of our loved ones, eh?'

Captain Houston gave a thin smile. 'Some can do more than *think* about them to all accounts.'

Keen looked pale but managed to remain silent.

Bolitho said, 'Captain Houston, I am not sure if that was meant to be offensive? If so, then I am offended.' His grey eyes were suddenly hard. 'I am waiting.'

The silence was oppressive like the humidity in the cabin.

Houston met Bolitho's gaze and said hesitantly, 'I meant no offence to you, Sir Richard.'

'I am glad to know it.' Bolitho turned aside. Houston was a fool. Worse, he might become the weak link in their slender chain.

He thought of Inch's words which brought Houston's

response. *I shall write to Belinda tomorrow*. But the thought remained motionless in his mind, like a cloud.

As the others made their way towards the long table with its gleaming candles, Keen said urgently, 'It is beginning, sir, I blame myself. I would not have had this happen – '

Bolitho faced him and, ignoring the others, gripped his arm with sudden force.

'Say no more on the matter. Tomorrow, next week maybe, we could join our lost friends, or be whimpering as our parts drop in Tuson's wings and limbs tubs.' He tightened his grip still more. 'It is something you could never have foreseen.' Then he smiled and released his hold. 'In truth, Val, I damned well envy you.' He turned away before Keen could speak.

Two days later, as a lordly East Indiaman dropped anchor in the bay, Bolitho's squadron weighed and put to sea in watery sunlight. Throughout the squadron every purser was worrying over fresh water and rations, and each captain considered the need to be sparing with cordage and canvas as they sailed farther and farther from the land.

A thousand miles ahead of the squadron the little brig *Firefly* lay hove-to under the flagship's lee.

Adam Bolitho stood on the broad quarterdeck and glanced across at the other ships and then up at the vice-admiral's flag at the fore. Like his uncle, and yet it was all so different. Several other visitors were aboard, and the flagship's own captain had barely paused to offer him a nod.

The solitary epaulette counted for very little here, he thought. But the challenge and the thrill of making his first rendezvous in his own command still held him. Even sighting the Rock in all its majesty had seemed exciting and personal. And now he was here in the old *Victory*, ignored perhaps, but here.

He shaded his eyes to look across at his small command. She was young and alive, the way he felt.

He owed it all to his uncle, although he would be the

first to deny it. Adam sighed. It was his uncle's birthday tomorrow, although without someone to remind him he would let it pass unnoticed. He would more likely be thinking of the day after, two years exactly since he had married Belinda at Falmouth. They had been a hard two years, much of them spent at sea, as was the way of the Bolitho men. Now there was little Elizabeth, but something was missing.

The flag-lieutenant joined him on the quarterdeck and eyed him curiously.

'The secretary is completing the dispatches you are to carry. It will not take long.'

'Thank you.'

'In the meantime Lord Nelson would be pleased to receive you. Please follow me.'

Adam walked aft, his mind awhirl. He was twenty-three years old and with *Firefly* had thought he had everything.

A voice announced, 'Commander Adam Bolitho, my lord.'

In fact it was just beginning.

5

Darkness at Noon

Bolitho paced slowly along *Argonaute*'s handsome stern gallery, his neckcloth untied, his shirt open to his waist. October it might be, but the air was hot, with little more than a light breeze to fill the sails.

He liked the stern gallery, a luxury he had never enjoyed in an English-built ship. Beyond the tall windows of his day cabin, or above on the poop, was the ship and all the responsibility she represented. Here on this narrow catwalk there was complete privacy, no eyes to watch him, to study his confidence or lack of it. Even the sounds were more muffled here, masked by the surge of water below the counter, the creak of the rudder-head as the helmsmen held the two-decker on course.

One sound did intrude, however. The regular staccato roll of a drum, the agonizing pause, and the crack of the lash on a man's naked back.

One more note in the punishment book, and little comment from the ship's company. Discipline was discipline, less harsh in many ways than that meted out by the lower deck if they found someone stealing from their own kind.

Crack.

Bolitho thought of the girl, and wondered why he had not told Adam about her when *Firefly* had joined the labouring squadron just long enough to pass some dispatches and collect letters for home. For *Firefly* was returning to England, Nelson's link with a far-off Admiralty.

Adam had said wistfully, 'I have only just come here,

Uncle.' He had brightened when Bolitho had given him a letter for Belinda. 'But I shall be back soon with any luck.'

Bolitho walked to the end of the gallery and rested his hand on the gilded shoulder of a life-sized mermaid, the twin of the one at the opposite side. He smiled. Well, almost. This one had been decapitated by a ball from *Achates* on that murderous day in May. Adam and Hallowes, who now commanded *Supreme,* had boarded this ship with a small handful of men, each knowing it was a last chance with the possibility of survival too unlikely to consider. Adam had told him about this mermaid and how he had clung to her before the last mad dash.

The old woodcarver at Plymouth who had fashioned a new head must have a sense of humour, he thought. He had given the mermaid a sardonic grin, as if she was enjoying a secret.

He had asked Adam of his impressions of Nelson and had seen him putting them together in his mind.

'He was not at all as I expected. He seemed restless, and in some pain from his arm. And although I am taller than his lordship, he seemed to fill the cabin. I cannot explain it. And his contempt for authority is astounding. The name of Admiral Sheaffe was mentioned and Nelson laughed. He said that Sheaffe's oceans were made of paper and fine intentions, that he had forgotten that it took men to win wars.'

'You liked him, despite his outspokenness to a subordinate?'

Adam had seemed uncertain. 'I am not sure, Uncle. Once I thought him vain, even shallow, and the next instant I was struck by his total grasp of the war out here.' He had grinned shyly. 'I know now that I would follow him to hell and back if he required it of me. But I cannot say why. It is just something I know.'

It was much as others had said. Hated by most of his superiors, but loved by the men he led, the majority of whom had never laid eyes on him. Bolitho wished he had been there.

Adam had said, 'He asked of you, Uncle, and wished you well.'

Now *Firefly* was gone, speeding to Gibraltar and then on to Spithead.

Without effort Bolitho could see Portsmouth as he had left it. Cold and wet, but so strong in his life.

He began pacing again. Nelson had left him in no doubt as to a suitable watering-place for his ships. Sardinia, and a small group of islands at the eastern end of the Straits of Bonifacio. The Madalena Islands as they were named lay less than two hundred miles from Toulon. Trust 'Our Nel' to know such things. No wonder he could thumb his nose at men like Sheaffe. Until his luck ran out.

Pipes trilled like distant birds. Without seeing it Bolitho knew the hands were being dismissed, the flogged man cut down, the gratings unrigged and swabbed clean. Justice had been done.

Bolitho thought of his instructions. It made him smile to himself. As a captain you received orders. A flag-officer had to discover his own solutions.

The squadron had been given a two-hundred-mile sector, west of Toulon and the main blockade to the Spanish frontier. It was of course possible that if the French did break out in force they might try again for Egypt and the Nile. It had been a very close thing the last time. If they succeeded in a new attempt, Bonaparte would look further to India. It would be like opening a vast sack of booty, to say nothing of a tactical advantage. Bolitho thought it just as likely that the French fleet would head for the Strait of Gibraltar and force their way to Biscay and double the size of their squadrons there.

If he had read Nelson's mind correctly, no matter what Adam thought, Nelson would want the lion's share of the fight for himself.

The sea seemed empty without half his ships. He had sent Inch with *Dispatch* in company with Lapish's frigate as scout and go-between. *Icarus*, her sails filling and then emptying in the weak breeze, followed astern, her gunports open as the sour-faced Captain Houston drilled his crews. The cutter was like a pale shark's fin far to windward, and *Rapid* was visible only from the masthead as she led her big consorts like beasts on a line.

Far to starboard the horizon looked deep purple. Corsica. He leaned on the rail and looked at the water as it bubbled from the rudder. In these light airs it would take longer than he had hoped to find anchorage and take on fresh water. The nearness of land would do wonders for the seamen and marines, he thought.

A door opened onto the gallery and Allday said apologetically, 'Cap'n Keen's respects, sir, an' *Rapid* has sighted a sail to the east'rd. Masthead reports it's just in sight.'

Bolitho nodded. 'I'll wait down here.' It was strange, he had heard nothing. Like his new chair, the gallery was private and personal.

He grinned at his reflection in the windows. Must be getting old.

Keen came down a few minutes later.

'A schooner, sir. Genoese according to Mr Paget – he went aloft with a glass.'

Bolitho walked into the cabin and crossed to his chart.

'So long as she's not Spanish. The Dons may not be in the war, not yet at least, but they are still an enemy and will tell the French everything they can about us.'

Keen suggested, 'She'll be a trader hereabouts, sir. I'd like to speak with her myself when we're up to her.'

Bolitho thought of *Rapid*'s commander, Quarrell. A good officer, but, like Lapish, he lacked experience.

'Yes, you go. The trader may know something.' He said with sudden anger, 'Like groping in the dark. I wonder what he's up to?'

Keen watched him. Jobert was rarely mentioned by name but he was always on Bolitho's mind.

Bolitho was saying, 'These islands, there are quite a few hiding places amongst them. It will be well to keep a sharp lookout until we know they are secure.' He tapped the chart with some dividers. 'On this hill for a beginning. A good man could see for miles from there.'

Keen waited, knowing there was more to come.

Bolitho rubbed his chin. 'I'd like to see for myself. Once you have investigated this schooner, signal *Supreme* to close on the flag. I intend to board her and go on ahead.' He saw Keen's uneasiness and added, 'Don't worry, Val,

I have no intention of becoming a prisoner-of-war a second time!'

Keen should have been used to Bolitho's unorthodox methods but he always seemed to have something new up his sleeve. It would certainly keep the cutter's little company jumping with their admiral dropped amongst them.

Bolitho pulled his shirt away from his damp skin.

'How are things, Val?'

Keen replied, 'She is well, sir. If only there was a way to reassure her.' He shrugged, the gesture one of helplessness. 'We do not even know ourselves – '

There was a rap at the door and after a small hesitation Midshipman Sheaffe looked into the cabin.

'Mr Paget's respects, sir. The schooner is hove-to.'

Bolitho said, 'We shall be up to her before dusk. We don't want to lose her.'

Keen smiled in spite of his thoughts. What Bolitho really meant was he needed to get started now that he had decided on something.

Bolitho saw Sheaffe's eyes watching, perhaps comparing them, and wondered what he would say if he knew what Nelson had said of his father. Sheaffe was very like his father in one way. Keen said that he had made no friends and in fact avoided any close contact. Not an easy thing in an overcrowded ship-of-the-line.

Bolitho said, 'Mr Sheaffe will come with me. Good experience.'

'Thank you, Sir Richard.' Either Sheaffe did not care what he was being told to do or he had been listening at the screen door.

Allday protested as soon as the others had gone, 'You can't go without me, sir!'

'Don't be such an old woman, Allday.' He smiled. 'I may go ashore, and I'll not have you undoing all the good the surgeon did by dragging you up a mountain.' He saw the stubborn light in Allday's eyes and added, 'Besides, I think my, er, *second* cox'n should be given the chance, eh?'

Allday nodded slowly but said mistrustfully, 'If you says so, sir.'

Bolitho had been right about timing. It was nearly dusk by the time they had the shabby schooner lying under their lee, and when Keen returned he had little to offer. 'The master says he sighted a frigate four days ago, sir, could have been a Frenchie. He did not loiter to find out. He is making for Lisbon.'

'In that?' Bolitho shook his head. Not only men-of-war had their problems.

But a solitary frigate must be assumed to be an enemy. Nelson had only two, otherwise there was just *Barracouta*. Spanish then? Unlikely to be sailing without company in these disputed waters. He marked the place on the chart which Keen had gleaned from the trader. Out of Toulon, or trying to get back into that port?

He made up his mind. 'I'll go over to *Supreme* before night closes in. See to it, will you, Val.'

Keen could manage very well without him, and Inch would be well able to take care of the rest of the squadron if anything happened.

He heard the calls shrilling and the clatter of tackles above the boat tier.

He felt sorry for Allday, but there was no point in overtaxing his strength. The savage wound had healed, but it had not gone away.

He waited while Ozzard fussed about with his seagoing coat and the hat with the tarnished lace.

In his heart Bolitho knew he needed to be alone, away from those he trusted, even loved.

'Barge alongside, Sir Richard.'

A last glance around the cabin. It seemed to be watching him. Waiting maybe for its old master to return.

Bolitho allowed Allday to clip the old sword to his belt.

Never in a thousand years, he thought. Then he loosened the blade in its scabbard and thought of those other times.

Aloud he said, 'I'll see him dead first.'

At the entry port where the side party had assembled Bolitho took Keen aside and said quietly, 'I shall see you

at our rendezvous.' He glanced at the sky. 'We are in for
a blow, so make sure that *Icarus* stays in close company.'

Keen opened his mouth to speak and changed his mind.
The breeze barely pushed the reefed topsails against the
shrouds as the ship lay hove-to, and apart from a few
arrowhead clouds the sky was as before.

Old Fallowfield, the sailing master, was nearby and
walked towards his helmsman. Even he was impressed.
He glared at a midshipman who was watching the vice-
admiral open-mouthed and growled, 'Wait till you can
fathom out the weather like that, Mr Penton, but I see no
chance o' you learnin' nothin'!'

Keen touched his hat. 'Aye, sir. I'll send *Rapid* after
you if need be.'

Bolitho glanced up to his flag. 'This would be a private
ship but for my presence, Val. Use my quarters while I
am away. They would have been yours.'

He tugged down his hat and clambered over the side as
the boatswain's mates trilled their salute.

It was good that Keen should also have some freedom
while there was an opportunity. What he did with it was
his affair.

As the early light filtered across the nearest island Bolitho
walked up the cutter's tilting deck, his shirt rippling from
his body in the wind. It was difficult to find somewhere
to stand, he thought, as *Supreme*'s deck seemed filled with
busy figures and snaking halliards. The topsail cutter was
only seventy feet in length but carried a company of sixty.
Bolitho had once served temporarily in one as a
midshipman. That vessel had been commanded by his
brother Hugh. Even so it was hard to believe that all these
busy seamen could eventually find enough space below
Supreme's flush deck to eat and sleep.

The squall Bolitho had predicted had swept down after
dark, and he felt sorry for the heavier ships he had left
astern. *Supreme* on the other hand flew with the wind;
her enormous boomed mainsail, jib and foresail bulging
under the pressure, she seemed to skip across the waves.

A cutter had proportionally more agility and sailpower than any other man-of-war and could manage to sail as much as five points into the wind.

He saw Hallowes shouting to his first lieutenant, a round red-faced man who looked old enough to be his father, which he probably was. Lieutenant Okes had been promoted from the lower deck and had last trod the planks as a master's mate. It was just as well Hallowes had more than proved his skill and courage as a fighting officer when they had seized *Argonaute*. But *Supreme* required a knowledge of seamanship which could only come from long experience.

The rising wind and sea had kept the hands fully occupied, too busy to worry about the presence of their admiral amongst them. But now, as the wind backed slightly and the sturdy hull thrust closer into sheltered waters, many of the men paused to stare. Bolitho, with his hair plastered down by spray, his shirt open from the throat and grubby from the cutter's lively motion, was not most people's idea of a flag-officer.

Bolitho watched as some seamen bustled past Midshipman Sheaffe, who was clinging desperately to a backstay. His face was pale green and he had been sick several times. Lieutenant Stayt was below, not sick, but out of sorts at being a passenger and always in somebody's way.

Hallowes crossed to Bolitho and said, 'With your permission, I shall round the next headland and feel inshore, sir!' He had to shout above the din of canvas and rigging. He looked very young and was obviously enjoying his freedom in spite of Bolitho. Two leadsmen were already up forward loosening their lines in readiness. The chart was a poor one, but hinted at shallows and some spurs of rock, although to the naked eye in the blue-grey light the sea looked deceptively welcoming.

Bolitho took a telescope and waited for the *Supreme* to complete the next leg of her tack before he steadied it on the land. Dark, lush green, with purple beyond. That must be the mountain, as it was described. More like a tall, bald hill, he thought as it swam into the dappled lens.

Bolitho stepped back as more seamen lurched past with a tangle of halliards and blocks, oblivious to everything but the boatswain's yell.

The long boom, which extended well beyond the counter, swung above the helmsmen at the tiller and filled out on the opposite tack. Spray dashed over the deck and Bolitho wiped his face with his sleeve. He felt alive again, the demands of land and flagship momentarily put aside.

He looked at *Supreme*'s armament, twelve tiny cannon and two swivels. But she could give a good account of herself in anything but a ship-to-ship action.

The headland fell back in a towering curtain of spray.

Hallowes saw Okes watching him and shouted, 'All hands! Shorten sail! Leadsmen in the chains, lively now!'

Hallowes waited until some of the way had gone from his command and said, 'Is it your intention to land here, Sir Richard?'

Bolitho hid a smile. Hallowes obviously still thought it incredible that he should wish to go ashore when others would do anything which was required.

'While your watering party is employed, I shall take a glass to that hilltop.' It was a long walk and a climb too. But now he had told Hallowes he felt better. He would have to do it to avoid a loss of face. It was as well Allday was in the flagship. He would not be strong enough for a long time, he thought sadly. If ever. He saw Bankart in his blue jacket below the great, single mast and wondered what he really felt about his father.

'Look, sir.' Hallowes leaned on the bulwark and pointed at the sea alongside.

As the bow wave receded Bolitho saw the seabed rising and falling beneath the keel, as if it were breathing. Scores, no, thousands of fish scurried this way and that, and every so often a line of solid rock showed menacingly through the pale sand.

'By th' mark five!' The leadsman's chant was somehow reassuring. The boats were already made ready for hoisting out over the sides, a gig and a jolly boat. Hallowes was sensibly going to replenish his own water supply before he rejoined the squadron.

He heard Sheaffe taking deep breaths. The worst was over.

'A pleasant landfall, Mr Sheaffe?'

The midshipman straightened his shoulderbelt and dirk and said, 'Indeed, sir. Am I to come ashore with you, sir?'

Bolitho grinned. 'It will do us both good.'

Stayt came on deck. Unlike Bolitho, he wore his uniform coat and hat and doubtless had his fine pistol close to hand.

'Stand by to come about! Hands wear ship!'

Feet pounded on the wet planking, and as the sails were checked and fisted into shape the anchor plummeted down into clear water.

Hallowes put his hands behind him and Bolitho saw that the fingers were tightly entwined. He was nervous, but that did no harm at all.

'Sway out the boats!'

Hallowes said, 'I'll send a good lookout up to that ridge, sir. With a glass he'll be able to see across the next headland, according to the chart.' He smiled self-consciously. 'And Mr Okes, of course.'

Stayt beckoned to Bankart. 'The gig!' His voice was sharp, and Bolitho knew that had Allday been here he would have reacted just as curtly. But Bankart had to learn.

Bolitho waited for the others to clamber down amongst the oarsmen. Lieutenant Okes was taking the jolly boat, his weatherbeaten face like some old figurehead, Bolitho thought. The Navy could do with a lot more Okeses just now.

Sheaffe and Stayt squeezed into the sternsheets with him and *Supreme*'s only midshipman, a spotty youth named Duncannon, piped, 'Give way, all!'

Bolitho clutched his sword between his knees and thought of Cornwall, of how he and his brother and sometimes his sisters had played amongst the coves and caves near Falmouth. He sighed. A thousand years ago.

What would Belinda think when she received his letter? He had tried not to dwell on it, to keep his mind free of personal encumbrances.

Sheaffe said, 'The jolly boat's ashore, sir.'

Bolitho saw Okes wading through the shallows, his white-stockinged legs like huge inverted flasks. There was a broad-shouldered seaman already leaving the others, naked but for some tattered trousers and wide-brimmed hat. One of Hallowes' best men, and as bronzed as any native. With a telescope carelessly jammed under one arm he was striding towards the trees and the hills beyond.

The gig grounded and Bolitho climbed outboard and then trod on firm sand as the seamen hauled the keel up the beach.

The trees looked almost tropical and their bushy tops moved in the sea breeze as if in a dance.

The gig's crew were already returning to the cutter to fetch some water casks.

Bolitho touched his forehead and then, as if to test his reaction, he felt beneath his dangling lock of hair and along the deep scar which had almost killed him. That had been a watering party too. It always made him feel uneasy.

It was a strange thing that the lock of hair was now tinged with white. The rest of his hair was as black as before. What was it? Vanity, or the anxiety about the difference in his and Belinda's ages which made him worry about it?

Two seamen armed with cutlasses and muskets strolled behind the little group as, with Bolitho in the lead, they started to make their way up the first slope. Once sheltered by the scrub and overhanging fronds it seemed moist and very warm. No birds sang or screamed out a warning. It was almost drowsy.

Stayt said, 'You could shelter two squadrons here-abouts, sir.' He was already breathing hard for one so young. 'Nelson was right.'

Did that innocent remark have a sharper edge? Was Stayt implying that if Nelson had not suggested Sardinia, nobody else would?

It was not long before they saw the glitter of a stream with a chattering waterfall at its head. Okes was already there, his booming voice calling for axes to cut a passage for his casks which would be hauled to the boats on crude sledges.

When they walked into bright sunlight again Bolitho shaded his eyes to look back at the anchored cutter. She looked like a graceful toy, her great sails folded like wings. Bolitho raised his glass and saw the bare-backed sailor settling himself on top of the adjoining hill, his long telescope propped on some loose stones. He should see the whole coastline from there.

Bolitho felt his shirt dragging at his skin. He was wet through but felt elated, and pictured himself swimming in that clear, inviting water.

He thought of Keen and whether he had been alone with the girl. Bolitho knew he trusted him, but it was more important that others should know it.

The climb to the top took longer than Bolitho had imagined but he was secretly pleased that he had managed it. The others looked weary and wet with sweat. Only Bankart seemed fresh. As Allday used to be. The thought stabbed Bolitho like a marline spike.

Bolitho looked down at the cutter again, her deck alive with tiny antlike figures, while the boats moved slowly between her and the beach like water beetles.

He moved his glass to the lookout and saw the sunlight flash from the man's glass. He had sensibly put some dried branches on his back to protect himself from the rising glare, and his hat was pulled across the telescope as an extra shield.

It felt good to be here. Bolitho wished he was completely alone. Stayt would soon protest if he even suggested it. He sat down on the hot ground and unfolded his small map. Where was Jobert now, he wondered? What was the overall intention of the French fleet?

He heard the others resting, the sound of a water flask being shaken. What would he not give for some of Ozzard's clear hock which he always managed to keep cool in the bilges?

Bolitho slipped one hand inside his shirt and touched his skin. It was only too easy to picture her in his arms. Her hands on him, whispering to him, arching with

pleasure when he entered her. He folded the map with
sudden despair. Of whom was he really thinking?

Stayt said, 'Look at the birds, there are enough of them
now!'

A vast flock of gulls swept round and down as if held
together by thread. There must be a thousand of them.
As they dived down and past the anchored *Supreme*
Bolitho saw swift darting movements in the water and
remembered the fish he had seen. The gulls had timed it
perfectly, and even at this distance Bolitho could hear
them mewing and shrieking as they plunged to the attack.

Work on the cutter's deck had stopped as the seamen
paused to watch as gull after gull rose flapping wildly, a
shining fish gripped in its beak.

Stayt said, 'We've a good lookout, sir. Never took his
eyes off the proper bearing even for that. I've never seen
birds act like – '

Bolitho said abruptly, 'The lookout?' He snatched his
glass and opened it quickly. As he swung it across the
bright water and darting seabirds his eyes stung with
sweat. For some reason the old wound was throbbing.
What was the matter with him?

Bolitho relaxed very slowly; the bronzed lookout was
still in position. He said, 'Put a ball into the rocks below
the crest. The bloody man's asleep.'

Stayt scowled and gestured angrily to one of the seamen.
'Did you hear that, man?'

The seaman grinned. 'Aye, sir. I'll wake our Jake up,
right 'nough.'

He dropped on one knee and raised the musket to his
shoulder. It might startle the boats' crews, but a sleeping
lookout was a real danger.

The crack of the musket sent the birds wheeling and
flapping away while here and there a fish dropped once
more into the sea.

Bolitho closed his telescope and stood up, his face
impassive even though he thought his heart was bursting.
The lookout had not moved although the telescope still
glinted as before.

'That man is not asleep.' He tried to keep his voice level.

'I fear we are in some peril.' He felt them stir, their eyes swivelling from the drifting musket smoke to his face.

Stayt exclaimed, '*Here,* sir?' He sounded stunned.

Bolitho snapped, 'Mr Sheaffe, you are the youngest, run back to the beach. Warn Lieutenant Hallowes.'

The midshipman was watching his mouth, his lips forming the words as if he could not believe what was happening.

'You, Bankart, go with him.' He forced a smile. 'As fast as you like.'

As the other two blundered downhill and into the trees Bolitho said, 'See to your weapons.' He cursed himself for not bringing a pistol. He stared around at the nodding fronds. But who would suspect danger in a place like this?

He walked deliberately down the slope, straining his ears in every direction, but only the rustle of the trees mocked him, as if a hidden army was on the move.

They reached the trees and Bolitho said, 'We'll circle around the hill.' He saw the doubt in Stayt's dark eyes, the way that the two armed seamen had suddenly hunched together.

Bolitho said, 'They must have seen us after the musket shot. But we're out of sight now. They'll think we're following the others.'

Stayt hissed, 'Who are *they,* sir?'

Bolitho drew his sword and gripped it firmly. How many times – He realized what Stayt had asked. 'Must be French.'

They seemed to outguess everything they did, where they went, what the ships were doing. It was unlikely that anyone knew he had moved to the cutter, but *Supreme* was one of his strength; even the wind on a lee shore was the same as that which had nearly done for *Barracouta.*

Stayt had drawn his hanger and together they moved slowly towards the hillside, avoiding patches of sunlight, anything which might betray them. He wondered if Sheaffe had reached the beach yet. Unlikely, even running at full tilt.

He gritted his teeth to prevent him from despairing aloud. *Why didn't I think? I should have realized it was*

just the kind of trap Jobert might think of. The secret was
out now, that musket shot would have made sure of that.

'Look!' Stayt dropped on his knees. There were two
men, taking their time, their weapons sheathed as they
strolled down through the trees. Sailors obviously, and as
they drew nearer Bolitho heard that they were speaking
French.

They must have left a larger party to go back to the hill
for the lookout's telescope. Bolitho could remember the
seaman exactly, the glass under one arm, a good reliable
hand. Now another carried it, and there was dried blood
on the case.

'*At them!*'

Bolitho bounded over the bushes and charged onto the
man with the telescope. He stared with utter astonishment
and then made to draw his cutlass. He was hampered by
the telescope. Bolitho slashed him across the face and as
he toppled sideways drove the blade beneath his armpit.
At no time did the man cry out. The other dropped to his
knees and reached out imploringly. The lookout must have
been popular for one of the seamen swung his musket and
smashed him in the skull. The musket rose again but Stayt
snapped curtly, 'Enough, you fool, he'll not move again.'

The man with the musket picked up the telescope and
followed Bolitho down the slope. But for their detour
they would have been ambushed and the alarm given
before they reached the beach.

He heard the dull bang of a cannon. *Supreme* had at last
realized what was happening and had fired a recall.

There was a sudden fusillade of shots and wild shouts,
then the brief clash of steel.

Bolitho broke into a run and burst through the last
bushes and onto the beach. In seconds he saw it all. The
grounded jolly boat, the gig caught halfway between the
beach and the anchored cutter. Lieutenant Okes stood by
the water's edge, a pistol in either hand. One he had just
fired, the other he trained on a zigzagging figure which
with several others was running towards his handful of
seamen. Bolitho found time to notice that Okes stood
quite still despite the yells and occasional musket balls,

more like a wildfowler than a sea officer. The pistol cracked and the running man tore into the sand like a plough and lay still.

That seemed to deter the others, especially as Bolitho and his three companions charged towards them. Stayt fired twice, his silver pistol must have two barrels, and each shot found its mark.

Okes mopped his face with his sleeve. 'Lor' bless you, sir, I thought the buggers 'ad done for you, beggin' yer pardon!'

Bolitho saw Bankart by the boat and Okes said as he reloaded a pistol. 'We'd 'ave bin caught in th' open but for that lad.'

Bolitho looked past him. 'Where's Mr Sheaffe?'

Okes dragged out his other pistol. 'I thought 'e was with you, sir?'

Bolitho beckoned to Bankart. 'Where's the midshipman?'

Bankart said, 'He fell, sir. Back there. There was a hole, he rolled down some sort of cliff.'

Bolitho stared at him. 'Cliff? There are none here!'

The others were clambering into the boats; there had been no casualties except for the lookout. Four corpses lay in attitudes of abandon, their blood already soaked into the sand.

Stayt tossed his hanger into the air and caught it by the blade before sliding it into its scabbard.

It was a neat trick for the blade had an edge like a razor. But Bolitho was in no mood for games.

'Can't leave him.'

Stayt said, 'I'll go.' He eyed Bankart coldly. 'Show me where it was, damn you.'

They reached the top of the beach and then saw Sheaffe stagger into the sunlight. His face was cut and bleeding but otherwise he seemed unharmed.

'Into the boats.' Bolitho put his hand on Sheaffe's shoulder. 'Are you all right?'

'I fell.' Sheaffe dabbed his lip. 'I hit two tree stumps.' He grimaced. 'Knocked the wind out of me, sir.' His eyes cleared as he saw Bankart. 'Where were you?'

Bankart faced him stubbornly. 'I brought the message, like I was ordered.'

Bolitho walked towards the gig. There was more to it than that, but he was grateful they had survived.

He climbed into the boat and stared across at *Supreme*. She was already shortening her cable, and her sails were flapping in disorder as Hallowes made ready to leave.

Bolitho rubbed his chin, unaware of the oarsmen's curious glances. The French must have landed a party to see what they were doing. But for the seabirds and the lookout apparently ignoring the spectacle, they might have been attacked when the French had had time to land more men. So where were they?

Another four-pounder banged out from the cutter and Stayt said harshly, 'They're aweigh!'

Hallowes, anchored where he was, had seen what the lookout would have reported had he been alive to cry out.

As if a piece of the headland itself was tearing adrift, Bolitho saw a ship coming around the point, her jib flapping as she tacked sharply to avoid the reefs.

She was a frigate.

Bolitho said, 'Pull, lads! With all your might!' They needed no urging.

If they had not realized the lookout was dead, this frigate would have sailed right across the bay and raked *Supreme* into a bloody shambles.

Then the gig ground alongside and men clambered wildly aboard to throw themselves into the business of setting more sail.

The two boats drifted away. Bolitho saw Hallowes, strained and anxious. It was a pity about the boats. They might need them. He clung to a stay and watched the frigate taking up her courses to hold on the present bearing.

Whatever Hallowes did, he could never beat clear of the land in time.

Bolitho said, 'Get your leadsmen to work! Mr Okes, do you know these waters well?'

Okes had somehow lost his hat. 'Aye, a fair bit, sir.'

He turned as the leadsman began his chant. 'The Frenchie won't dare come after us or he'll be in worse trouble.'

'I agree.' The frigate's captain would realize he had lost the bonus of surprise and would lie off and maybe attempt a cutting-out action with her boats at nightfall. That was half a day away.

Bolitho beckoned to Hallowes. 'I suggest you anchor.'

Hallowes nodded, suddenly unable to think clearly.

Okes remarked, 'The Frenchie's changed tack a piece, sir.'

The frigate was nearly a mile away with the next head-land already reaching out to hide her. It would take her captain most of the day to claw offshore, to beat back again and attack at leisure. But first he intended to try to cripple his small quarry.

Bolitho watched the forward division of guns shoot out their long orange tongues and saw the iron making ripples across the sea's face like streaks of light.

It was a poorly aimed attempt. The second one was not.

The sea boiled and shot skywards alongside and Bolitho heard the balls slamming into the lower hull, a terrible scream as someone was cut down by splinters.

Hallowes was staring at the chaos, torn rigging and punctured sails, with blood already trickling down the larboard scuppers.

'Anchor, damn you!' Bolitho shook his arm. 'You command here! So *do* it!'

Two balls hit the cutter together. One ploughed a black furrow across the deck and killed a man on the opposite side. The other smashed on to the mackerel-tail-shaped stern and blasted several buckets of sand and planking to fragments.

It was like being punched in the face. Bolitho fell on his side, dazed by the explosion and feeling the ache from his old wound probe through him from the fall. Men were crying out and he felt the deck shiver as something smashed down from aloft.

He clawed at his face and felt droplets of blood. An unknown voice shouted, ''Ere, sir! I'll give 'e a 'and!'

Bolitho gasped, 'Anchor, now!' His voice suddenly loud as the firing stopped.

He stumbled over an inert body and clung to some dangling ropes.

'Here, sir – ' The voice broke off as Bolitho dragged his hands from his face and stared round him.

Except that he could see nothing. It was noon when the frigate had fired, but he was standing in darkness, hands touching him, voices all round him in wild confusion.

'I'm here, sir.' It was Stayt.

Bolitho covered his eyes as the pain increased. 'I'm blind. Oh, dear God, I can't see!'

He groped out and found Stayt's arm. 'Get me below. Don't let them see me like this.' He gasped as the pain mounted. *I were better killed.*

6

Supreme

Captain Valentine Keen clung to the weather netting, his eyes raw from staring into sea and wind. Even his palms felt torn from gripping the tarred nettings to keep his balance.

All night long the gale had lashed the sea into a fury of leaping crests and great torrents of water which had boiled over the gangways and hurled men from their feet like flotsam. Now, as silver-grey streaked the sky, the motion was easier; dawn had come to mock their puny efforts.

There had been no point in trying to keep station on *Icarus*. Like the little brig *Rapid*, she had been out of sight throughout the onslaught. *Argonaute* had laid into the wind, hove-to under a reefed main topsail for most of the time. If the ships had attempted to remain under sail they would have been scattered miles apart before dawn.

The first lieutenant staggered towards him. 'I can get her under way again, sir.'

Keen glanced at the sailing master in his sodden tarpaulin coat. Old Fallowfield said nothing, but it looked like a shrug.

'Very well. Pipe all hands. Change the masthead lookouts too. We'll need good eyes today if we are to re-form the squadron.'

Paget had done well, he thought, and his voice had kept the men at it from nightfall until now.

'All hands! All hands aloft to make sail!'

The yells of the petty officers and here and there the slap of a rope's end drove the battered, weary men back to the braces and yards.

Keen tugged at his neckcloth. Like the rest of him, it

was sodden from spray and perhaps rain. The ship had responded better than he had expected. She was, as claimed, an excellent sailer.

He was vaguely pleased with his own efforts. He had controlled his ship throughout and the men and discipline which drove her. The deck trembled as the fore topsail and jib were set and, flapping wetly, brought the helm under control again. Tuson would be busy. Keen had seen several hands injured. Worse, one seaman had been swept overboard, a terrible death for anyone, to watch the wind driving your ship away, your friends unable to help while you drown alone.

'Steady she goes, sir! Nor'east by east!'

The sky was already clearing; it might even be a fine day after the night's fury. It was a strange sea, Keen thought.

'Take over the watch, Mr Paget.' Keen rubbed his sore eyes. 'As soon as the galley fire is alight, send the hands to breakfast by divisions. Tell the purser to break out a tot per man. They've earned it.'

Paget grinned. 'That'll rouse them, sir!' He turned away, obviously pleased to be left in charge with a big sea still running. Keen decided to mention him in his report; he needed a good first lieutenant, but the fleet needed those who could command.

Keen walked beneath the poop, his figure swaying in the darkness. He had not realized he was so tired and under so much strain. A scarlet coat loomed through the shadows and he saw Captain Bouteiller of the ship's Royal Marines waiting for him.

'Morning, Major.' Keen never really understood the marines although he admired them. Even the term 'major' for the officer-in-charge seemed odd.

Bouteiller said, 'I thought I should tell you myself, sir.' He had a clipped way of speaking, like a piece of equipment. 'The, er, passenger wishes to speak with you.'

Keen nodded. 'I see. When was this?'

The marine considered it. 'Two hours back, sir. You were very busy at the time.'

It was too dark to see his face, not that Bouteiller would give anything away. What was he thinking?

'Very well. Thank you.'

Keen groped his way to the small door and could almost hear the sentry holding his breath. For once guard duty would have been most welcome, he thought. Every other man and boy, even the afterguard, had been on deck fighting their natural enemy.

A lantern, shuttered low, swung from the deckhead and he saw the girl lying on the cot, one leg hanging over the side and swaying with the ship, as if it was the only part of her alive. Keen closed the door. Tuson would definitely not approve, he thought.

Very gently he took her ankle and raised her leg towards the cot. She was still wearing her shirt and breeches, and as a beam of light swung across her face Keen thought she looked incredibly young.

Then her eyes were wide open and she stared at him with terror, her fingers gripping the shirt to her throat.

Keen did not move and waited. The fear, like a storm-cloud, was slowly departing.

He said, 'I am sorry. I only just heard you were asking for me. You were asleep. I would have gone – '

She pulled herself into a sitting position and peered at him. Then she reached out and touched his coat and shirt.

She whispered, 'You are soaking, Captain.'

Even the simple formality tore at Keen's heart.

He replied, 'The storm has passed over.' He watched her fingers on his lapels and wanted to seize them, to press them to his lips. Instead he said, 'Were you frightened?'

'Not as much as the other thing.' Ozzard had told him how he had found her cowering, hands pressed to her ears, while a seaman had been flogged for insubordination.

She said, 'Such a big ship and yet there were times I thought she would break apart.' She played with a lapel, her lashes lowered. 'I thought you might be worried for me. I wanted to tell you I was safe.'

Keen said, 'Thank you.' Once during the storm he had imagined her beside him in the gale, her hair streaming, her teeth white while she had laughed, had ridden the storm with the ship.

'Yes, I was worried. You are not used to this life.'

Despite his guard he pictured the convict ship, what she would be like in a storm. He knew at once the girl had read the same thought.

She said, 'I still cannot believe I am safe.' She looked up, her eyes bright and dark in turns as the lantern pivoted round. '*Am* I safe?'

He saw his hands take hers and hold them. She did not protest or pull away, nor did she take her eyes from his face. 'Tell me, please.'

Keen said, 'I had hoped to put you ashore at Gibraltar as you know. Now it seems I must wait. I sent word with the courier brig, the one commanded by Sir Richard's nephew. Letters will be sent as soon as mine reaches the City. Maybe you will have to remain aboard until my ship is ordered to Malta. Part of our work here is to protect the convoys. In Malta I have friends too.' He found he was pressing her hands in time with his words. 'One thing I do know, Zenoria,' he let his voice linger over her name, 'you will not be put aboard any convict vessel. I shall see to that.'

She asked quietly, 'All this, you do it for me? You do not know me, sir, only what others have told you. You have seen me stripped and beaten like some whore.' Her chin lifted. 'But I am not.'

He said, 'I know that.'

She looked past him into the leaping shadows. 'Would you care if we were somewhere else? In London maybe, or where your wife might see us?'

Keen shook his head. 'I have never married. Once I – '

She responded by holding his fingers in hers. 'But you loved somebody?'

Keen nodded. 'Aye. She died. It was a long time ago.' He looked up. 'I cannot explain it, but it is real. Call it Fate, God's will, call it luck if you wish, but it is there, and it is not imagination. Some might say that everything is against me – ' He tightened his grip as she made to speak. 'No, it must be said. I am so much older than you,

I am a King's officer and my duty lies with my ship until this damned war is won.' He raised her hands to his mouth, just as he had seen himself in his thoughts of her. 'Do not laugh at me but hear me. I love you, Zenoria.' He expected her to pull away or to interrupt but she sat completely still, her eyes wide. He continued, 'It is like a great weight hoisted from my mind.' He said it again, slowly, 'I love you, Zenoria.'

He made to rise, but she threw her arms round his neck and whispered, 'Do not look at me.' Her voice was in his ear. 'I am dreaming. It cannot be happening. We are both bewitched.'

Very gently he prised her away and studied her face, the two bright lines of tears on her cheeks.

Then, still holding her, he kissed each cheek, tasting the salt, feeling his elation, the swift, impossible happiness.

He said, 'Do not speak. Try to sleep now.' He stood back, her hands still in his. 'It is not a dream, and I mean what I said.' His mind rushed on. 'You can come aft for breakfast later on. I shall send Ozzard.'

He was speaking quickly, and he knew it was to prevent her from stopping it here and now.

He reached the door but her arms were still outstretched as if she was holding on to him.

Outside the little cabin there were two sentries and a marine corporal who was relieving the guard, hissing out his orders in a fierce whisper.

Keen nodded to them and said, 'Good morning, Corporal Wenmouth, I think we have ridden out the storm, eh?'

He strode aft and did not see the astonishment on their faces.

Keen entered the stern cabin and stared around at the shadows and at the tossing water beyond the windows.

He was tingling, almost helpless with an excitement he had never known before. He threw his hat on to the bench seat and said aloud, 'I *love* you, Zenoria.'

With a start he realized that Ozzard was watching him from the other screen door, his paws folded over his apron.

Ozzard asked politely, 'Breakfast, sir?'

Keen smiled. 'Not yet. I am expecting, er, company for that in an hour or so.'

'I see, sir.' Ozzard made to leave. 'Oh, I *see*, sir!'

Others might be less pleased, but Keen did not care.

'Is everything satisfactory, Miss?' Ozzard hovered by the table, seizing a dish as it slid dangerously towards the edge.

She turned and looked up at him.

'It was lovely.'

From across the table Keen watched her profile as she spoke with Ozzard. She was beautiful, with her hair loose now across her shoulders; even the midshipman's shirt could not disguise it.

She turned and saw him watching her. 'What is it?'

He smiled. 'You. I could admire you all day and find something new every minute.'

She looked at her empty plate. 'That is nonsense, sir, and you know it!' But she looked flushed. Perhaps even pleased.

Then she said quickly, 'Tell me about your Sir Richard, Have you known him long?'

Keen listened to her voice. So alien here in a man's world. Yet so right.

'I have served under him several times. I was with him when he nearly died of fever.'

She studied his features as if to remember them. 'Was that when you lost your love?'

He stared at her. 'Yes. I did not say so – '

'It was written on your face.' She nodded to Ozzard as he removed the plate, then said, 'War, fighting, you have seen so much. Why must you do it?'

Keen glanced round the cabin. 'It's what I am. I have been at sea since I was a boy. It is what I am trained to do.'

'And do you never miss your home?' Her eyes were misty again but she seemed quite controlled.

'Sometimes. When I am on land I want to get back to my ship. At sea I think of fields and cattle. My brothers both farm in Hampshire. Sometimes I envy them.' He hesitated; he had never spoken like this to anyone.

She said, 'Now I can tell *you* not to be afraid. Your words are safe with me.'

Overhead, feet slapped across the wet planking, and near the skylight a man laughed, another snapped a reprimand.

She said, 'You love these men, don't you? Where you lead, they will follow.'

He reached across the table, the one where he had sat with the other captains. 'Give me your hand.'

She offered it; they could barely reach one another.

He said, 'One day we will walk ashore together. Somewhere, somehow, but we shall.'

She pushed some hair from her eyes and laughed, but her eyes were sad.

'Like this? I would be some companion for one of the King's officers.' She squeezed his hand and whispered. 'The King's finest officer.'

Keen said, 'I boarded a Genoese trader the other day.'

She looked surprised at his change of subject.

Keen added, 'I bought a gown for you. I will have my servant bring it to you.' He felt unsure and clumsy. 'You may not like it, or it might not fit, but – '

She said softly, 'You are a sweet man, Captain. Even to think of it when you have all this to do. And I *will* like it.'

Keen ended lamely, 'I have two sisters, you see – ' He broke off, confused as the sentry beyond the screen doors shouted.

'Surgeon, sir!'

Keen released her hand. It felt like being cast adrift. Guilty.

He called, 'Enter!' Then he said, 'I do not wish this to end – '

Tuson entered and eyed them impassively. His hands looked red, as if he had been scrubbing them.

'Some breakfast?' Keen waved him to a chair.

The surgeon gave a wry smile. 'No, sir. But I'd relish some strong coffee.'

He looked at the girl. 'How are you today?'

She dropped her eyes. 'I am well, sir.'

Tuson took a cup from Ozzard. 'More than can be said for your companion, young Millie.'

Millie was the Jamaican maidservant. She seemed to have no other name.

Tuson added, 'I think she'd risk fever on the Rock rather than go through another storm like last night.'

Keen looked up at the skylight as the masthead lookout shouted to the deck.

Tuson said, 'Sounds like another ship.' But he was watching the girl, her small hands gripped into fists, the quick movements of her breasts. Keen must have said something. She looked different.

She said to Keen, 'Is it friend or foe?'

Keen restrained himself from getting up and opening the skylight. They would come to him when he was needed. Another lesson Bolitho had taught him well.

He replied, 'Both of our ships were sighted an hour ago.' He watched her mouth. 'While you were asleep.'

She held his gaze. 'I did not go back to sleep.'

Tuson pricked up his ears, but masked his curiosity.

The sentry called, 'First lieutenant, sir!'

Paget entered, his coat black with spray. 'The masthead has sighted a sail to the sou'west.' His eyes stayed firmly away from the girl at the table. This made his interest all the more obvious.

Keen said, 'Southwest?' Without looking as the chart he could picture the other vessels. *Icarus* was almost three miles abeam, and *Rapid* far ahead, little more than a shadow against the murky horizon.

Paget added, 'I went aloft myself, sir. She's a Frenchie, I'll stake my life on it.'

Keen eyed him thoughtfully. He was learning more about Paget every day.

Paget waited and dropped his shot with great skill. 'She's rigged like us, sir. Sail-o'-the-line, no doubt about it.'

Keen was on his feet, unaware that the others were watching him, Paget with pride at what he had discovered without being ordered, Tuson with interest as he studied Keen as he had Bolitho on many occasions. Weight of

command, a captain's ability, determination, it was all
there. Only in the girl's eyes was there tenderness, anxiety
too for this other side to Keen's character.

'She will know what we are about.' Keen paused by
the stern windows and pictured the other vessel. 'She is
following us. Reporting our movements to another ship
maybe.'

Paget said stubbornly, 'She's made no signals, sir. I've
put Mr Chaytor aloft with a glass. He'll tell me if he sees
any hoists.'

Keen walked reluctantly to the chart and wished
suddenly Bolitho was here. The French were using one of
their heavy ships, even though frigates had been reported.
Argonaute could come about and give chase. It might be
hopeless, it would certainly take a long time with a southerly wind across the starboard quarter.

He said, 'Make a signal to *Icarus* to remain on station.'
In his mind he saw not the ship but the sour face of her
captain. 'Then signal *Rapid* to close on the flag.'

Paget hesitated by the door. 'Shall we chase her, sir?
We might catch her if the wind backs a mite further. I
reckon this ship'd outfly anything!'

Keen smiled grimly, warmed by Paget's enthusiasm.

'Make the signals, then call all hands and set the
t'gan's'ls, after that the royals too.'

Paget glanced quickly at the lively crests astern, blurred
and unreal through the salt-caked glass. It was blowing
hard to set more canvas just yet. But his captain seemed
to hold no doubts. The door closed and moments later the
shrill calls and the stampede of feet made the ship stir
herself yet again.

Tuson asked, 'She'll run, won't she, sir?'

Keen brought his mind back to the cabin. 'I've no
doubt.' He smiled. 'I'm a poor host. What did you come
to see me about?'

Tuson stood up and swayed to the slope of the deck.

'News of last night's injuries, sir. Ten in all. Broken
bones mostly. It could have been far worse.'

'Not for the wretch who went outboard. But thank you.

They are in good hands. I think you know how I appreciate your presence amongst us.'

Tuson walked to the door. In his plain dark coat with his white hair hanging neatly over his collar he looked more like a cleric than a ship's surgeon.

He never drank. Keen had seen his eyes on some of the others when they had been filling their glasses. Something terrible must happened in his past.

The door closed and he said quietly, 'A good man.'

They faced each other across the table.

She spoke first. 'I will leave.' She looked at her bare feet, small against the checkered canvas. 'I saw you just now. The man. The one who cried out aboard that ship after the whip had cut my back. The one who comforted me, and now who insists he loves me.' She walked round the table, her slim figure angled to the deck. 'What will become of us?'

He waited until she had walked up to him and said, 'I will make you love me.'

He shut his mind to a cry from the masthead. That must be Chaytor, the second lieutenant.

'She's making more sail, sir!' So the French ship was in pursuit, did not want to lose them.

She reached up and laid her palm on his cheek. When he made to hold her she said quickly, 'No. Not like this.' She held her hand to his face for several seconds, her eyes never leaving his. Then she said, 'I shall go now.' She sounded reassured, satisfied by what she had discovered. 'If Ozzard can take me?'

Keen nodded, his mouth quite dry.

'Do not forget.'

She turned by the door and looked at him. 'That would be impossible.'

Ozzard opened the door and she was gone.

Keen walked round the cabin, touching things, seeing none of them. Then he paused by the new, high-backed chair and smiled at it. What would he have done?

Then he went on deck and saw Paget and the officer-of-the-watch studying the braced yards and the set of every sail. The great mainyard was bending like some huge bow. Even the master glanced at him with some apprehension.

A midshipman called, '*Rapid*'s acknowledged, sir!' He saw Keen and fell into a confused silence.

Keen gripped his hands together beneath his coat-tails and felt suddenly chilled.

Lieutenant Chaytor yelled, 'She's set more sail, sir!'

Keen looked at Paget. 'Shorten sail, if you please. Take in the main course.' He saw something like relief on their faces.

Keen watched *Icarus* responding, her sails being fisted to the yards as she followed the flagship's example.

Minutes dragged past. Perhaps he was wrong. Suppose the French captain wanted to close and fight? Two to one, but it could happen. He let out his breath very slowly as the masthead called, 'She's shortening sail, sir.'

Keen walked to the foot of the mizzen and touched the boarding pikes which were racked around its fat trunk.

That Frenchman *wants me to turn and go after him. He's goading me. It is what he expects of me!* The realization was still a shock.

He said, 'As soon as *Rapid* is close enough, tell her to make all sail and find *Supreme*. Quarrell will have noted the first landfall on his chart.'

Paget watched him guardedly, aware of Keen's sharpness, his change of mood.

'Tell him that our admiral must know we are being followed but not pursued. There is no time to write him separate orders.' The same chill swept through him. The French captain expected him to begin a chase. It would divide their force even further. The realization made him feel pale. He added, 'Tell *Rapid* to make haste. As soon as Quarrell understands, *we* shall set all plain sail.' He glanced at the masts and added, 'Even if we tear the sticks from her.'

Later, in the stern cabin again, Keen heard Paget repeating his orders, his voice booming through a speaking trumpet.

Rapid would live up to her name. He felt suddenly

anxious and when he looked at Bolitho's chair it was with
the thought it might remain empty for ever.

Bolitho sat on the side of a low bunk in *Supreme*'s tiny
cabin. It was stiflingly hot between decks and he knew it
must be evening.

Someone squeezed through the door and said, 'Getting
dark, sir.' Bolitho reached out and seized his arm. It was
Hallowes; he sounded beaten and subdued, so much so
that he had not noticed what he had said, Bolitho thought
despairingly.

He touched the damp bandage across his eyes. *Perhaps
it will always be dark for me?* Why the sudden fear? He
should have expected something like it to happen. God
knew, he had seen enough good men struck down. But
like this?

He said, 'Tell me what you're doing!' There was a bite
in his tone, and he knew it was to crush his own self-pity.

During the afternoon Hallowes had tried to recover one
of the boats. A strong swimmer had volunteered to go out
for it. It was maddening for Hallowes to see both of his
boats drifting in the distance, out of reach and
unconcerned.

It was strange but men who could swim well were rare
in the Navy. This one had got only twenty yards when a
solitary musket shot from the shore had killed him. There
had been a great groan from the watching seamen as their
messmate threw up his arms and vanished, a pink cloud
rising above him.

The French sailors who had been landed earlier must be
still there, watching the cutter and waiting for their own
ship to recover them.

Hallowes said tightly, 'I've had all the guns loaded with
grape and canister, sir. We'll give a good account of
ourselves when those devils come at us.'

Bolitho released his hold and sank back against the
curved hull. The sobs and cries had all but finished. Seven
men had been killed in that brief mauling. One, the
diminutive midshipman named Duncannon, had died lying

across Bolitho's lap. He had felt the boy sobbing quietly,
his tears mixing with his blood.

Bolitho said, 'Help me on deck. Where's my flag-
lieutenant?'

'Here, sir.' Stayt had been with him and he had not
known. The realization made him suddenly angry. They
had all depended on him; now they were losing heart so
fast they would have no fight in them despite what
Hallowes thought.

He said, 'Put more swimmers over the side. If we can
get the boats we might kedge *Supreme* closer to the headland. There are rocks there. We'd be safer from that
damned frigate.'

'Aye, sir.' Hallowes sounded doubtful. 'I'll see to it
right away.'

He hurried away and Stayt murmured, 'Ready, sir?'

Bolitho stood up carefully to avoid the deckhead. Every
time he moved the pain in his eyes returned, stinging like
fire, pricking them into torment.

He held Stayt's arm and felt the man's pistol bump
against him.

The frigate had left them alone, prepared to wait until
nightfall. They were in no hurry. It would have been
different if they had known they had the English admiral
almost in their hands. Bolitho winced as his eyes stung
with emotion. A useless, helpless admiral.

On deck it felt clammy although a steady breeze slapped
wavelets along the hull like catspaws.

Stayt whispered, 'He's had them all keep down, sir.
Behind the bulwarks. They all seem to be armed.'

'Good.' Bolitho moved his head from side to side. He
could smell the land, could picture it in his mind. What a
place to die, he thought, like the young midshipman, the
hill lookout, all the others he had not even known.

He heard Okes' resonant voice and Sheaffe answering.

'Where's my cox'n?'

Bankart was right behind him. 'Present, sir.'

If only Allday were here. Bolitho held his bandaged eyes
in his palms. No, Allday had done and suffered enough.

Hallowes said in a hushed voice, 'The swimmers are here, sir.'

Sheaffe sounded very near. 'I'm going, Sir Richard. I learned when I was a child.'

Bolitho held out his hand, 'Here, take my hand.' He said, 'I was taught early too.' Somehow he had known it would be Sheaffe. 'Listen to me. When you reach the boat, either of them, no matter, I want you to stay there. Drop a stream anchor if you will, it's shallow enough. Who is with you?'

The seaman's name was Moore. He had a soft Kentish dialect. Like Thomas Herrick, Bolitho thought desperately.

'Keep together.'

Sheaffe asked, 'But why must we stay out there?'

Bolitho wanted to tear the bandages from his face. It was a nightmare, and he felt the urge to scream as the pain probed his eyes again.

'What can you see?' Bolitho moved towards the bulwark and grated his knee against a gun truck.

Stayt touched his left shoulder. 'The headland's that way, sir. Then as you turn slowly right there's the bluff on the other side of the bay, where the frigate first appeared.'

'Yes, yes.' Bolitho gripped a belaying-pin rack. He could see it, he remembered it. Just those last moments before he had been cut down.

'The French will come around the headland.' He moved his face. 'What say you, Mr Okes?'

Okes replied, 'Most like, sir. They'll be closer to their bloody – beg pardon, sir – to their friends ashore.'

'My thought exactly.' He touched the midshipman's bare back. The flesh felt icy, like a corpse.

'Off you go. Take care, both of you.' As they moved away Bolitho said, 'No heroics. When you see boats on the move, yell out.' He heard them splash down the side and he half expected a shot to follow.

'Is it very dark?' He felt so helpless. Like a child in the night.

'Aye, sir. No moon as yet.'

'When they reach the first boat,' he had almost said *if*,

'be ready. We shall see nothing, but if Sheaffe can see the French coming we shall open fire.'

Hallowes asked, 'Shoot blind, sir?' He stammered, 'I'm sorry, sir. That was stupid of me.'

Bolitho reached out again and touched his coat. 'No. But that is exactly what we shall do.'

Stayt said in a low voice, 'The Frogs will follow the coastline and expect to get between us and the beach. Once alongside they could overwhelm us.'

'It's what *I* would do.' Bolitho gripped his sword and let it fall into its scabbard again. Even that seemed to mock his helplessness. How could he tell Belinda? He could not face being a prisoner-of-war again. He would die first.

Hallowes asked, 'If they board us – '

Bolitho said quietly, 'Fire the ship.' He felt his words rip into the young lieutenant like canister. He added, 'There is no easy way, Lieutenant. The enemy must not take your *Supreme* as a prize.' He pulled him closer so that the others were excluded. 'Strike if you must to save the people. But sink the ship.' He let his words sink in.

When Hallowes spoke again his voice was changed. Firm, determined. 'I'll not let you down, sir.'

Bolitho turned away to hide his agony. 'I knew that when I recommended your appointment.'

Oh, Belinda, the foolish things I said and wrote. Now it is all too late.

He thought of Keen and knew he would command the squadron in his own way. He would fly an admiral's flag one day. Bolitho gasped. So God help him!

A man murmured, 'I 'eard somethin'!'

Another said, 'An oar in a boat.'

Hallowes said, 'They've got one of the boats, sir.'

Bolitho thought of Sheaffe's unsmiling features. His father would be proud of him. Or would he? Did he even envy his son as he did leaders like Nelson.

Bolitho rested his head in his hands. *He'll not have to envy me any more.*

The cry came across the water and seemed to hang above the gently swaying deck like an echo.

'Sheaffe's seen 'em!'

There was a single shot, and someone jeered, 'Couldn't hit a bloody barn door!'

Stayt said, 'By God, that fool with the musket has marked down their position well enough, sir.' He sounded excited, ready to kill, as Keen had described him aboard the convict ship.

'They're still coming.' Stayt must be crouching down, eyes level with the bulwark to seek out the dark shapes on the water.

'Three boats at least, sir.'

Voices murmured along the deck and Okes rumbled, 'Not a bloody squeak out of any mother's son, right?'

Bolitho heard the metallic clink of a swivel gun being depressed, and here and there a handspike squeak as a four-pounder was made snug against the side, each little muzzle pointing blindly into the darkness.

Bolitho said, 'Bankart, come here.' He felt the young seaman beside him. As Allday would have been.

'I shall use you as my eyes.' To Stayt he added, 'Go forrard and take charge of the foc's'l. Be ready to cut the cable if need be.' He heard Stayt move away and felt suddenly lost without him.

He thought of the girl Keen had brought to the flagship, the look in his eyes whenever he mentioned her name. If *Argonaute* was called on to fight, she might still be aboard.

The pain pricked his eyes again as, like an additional torment, another memory came to him.

Called on to fight. Cheney had been aboard his ship when the decks had thundered to the roar of broadsides. *Cheney.*

'Ready, lads!' Hallowes was drawing his sword, his face hidden in the darkness as was his despair.

'As you bear!'

Bolitho leaned forward; he had heard the splash of oars. *'Fire!'*

The night exploded.

7

Surrender or Die

The whiplash bangs of *Supreme*'s four-pounders were deafening. Hemmed in by the land, the explosions echoed from every side, as if two ships were engaged in battle.

Bolitho gripped Bankart's arm. 'Tell me!'

Bankart winced as the packed charges of grape and canister smashed into the leading boat like an iron flail. It was just possible to see the leaping feathers of white spray, the sudden glare of an exploding lantern before the darkness shut down again.

Hallowes yelled, 'Easy lads! Sponge out and reload!'

Bolitho cocked his head and heard someone screaming, others shouting and thrashing in the water. It had been a lucky broadside, and must have completely destroyed one of the boats.

A solitary voice was shouting commands, and Bankart whispered, 'Th' boats is splittin' up, sir.'

Okes growled, 'Pity they don't try to rescue their mates. We'd 'ave got them too in the next broadside!' He meant it.

'All loaded, sir!'

'*Fire!*' Gun by gun the shots crashed out and men retched and coughed as the smoke funnelled inboard.

Bolitho clutched his bandage. He had seen some flashes through it. Not much. Like lightning through a curtain. It was something.

A few musket shots whined overhead and one hit the hull. Half dazzled by the guns, the officers and lookouts were now finding it hard to locate the enemy's boats.

Bolitho said, 'What do you see?'

Bankart replied, 'One o' th' boats is 'ead on, sir. Comin' straight for us, starboard bow.'

Bolitho grasped his fingers around his sword until the pain steadied him. Around him he heard men whispering to one another, the hiss of steel as cutlasses were drawn, boarding pikes handed to the gun crews.

'Fire as you bear!'

Again and again the four-pounders blasted the night apart, the grape ripping across the water like lethal hail. But none found a mark.

Bankart said excitedly, 'I saw th' Frog's boat in the flashes, sir!'

Bolitho twisted his head. Where were the others?

'Repel boarders!'

Hallowes cheered like a madman, like the time when he and Adam had boarded the *Argonaute*.

'At 'em, Supremes!'

Bolitho heard the thud of grapnels, screams rising seemingly at his feet, the rasp of steel and several shots, from friends or enemies he could not tell.

A man cannoned into him and Bankart dragged at Bolitho's arm.

'Back, sir! That one's done for!'

A voice yelled, 'Port quarter, lads!'

Bolitho gritted his teeth as more shots clanged around him. As he had expected, he heard a boat crash into the stern, the yells and curses of boarders and defenders alike as they came to grips with blades, axes and pikes – there was not time to reload. He was pushed aside and two figures fought one another with Bolitho pressed against the bulwark. At any second he expected to feel the slashing agony of a blade or the thrust of one into his body. A man screamed almost in his face; he could feel his terror, his pain, before a sickening thud silenced him. How often had Allday protected him like that, had driven his cutlass into a man's head like an axe into a log.

He exclaimed, 'Thank you, Bankart!'

Stayt said between gasps, 'It's me, sir. Thought you looked surrounded, so to speak.' A pistol exploded at waist-height and Stayt said savagely, 'Take that, you bugger!'

'They're falling back!'

Someone raised a cracked cheer, and Bolitho heard men tumbling into a boat, others hurling themselves into the water to escape the maddened English seamen.

Okes bellowed, 'Stand aside, you booby! Let me at that swivel!'

Bolitho heard the thrash of oars; he knew that if he could see he would be looking down on one of the French boats right alongside.

Stayt pulled his arm. 'Here we go!'

The swivel gun gave a tremendous crack. For a split second beforehand Bolitho thought he heard someone scream, pleading perhaps as he realized what Okes intended.

Stayt said quietly, 'There can't be a man left alive there.'

Bolitho could barely hear him, his ears still cringing from the last explosion.

A whistle shrilled and he heard Hallowes shout, 'Cease firing!' Then, with a break in his voice, 'Well done, my Supremes!'

Stayt said, 'We've lost a few. Not too many though.'

'Silence on deck!'

The sudden quiet was almost worse. Bolitho heard some of the wounded gasping and sobbing. How would they manage without a surgeon?

Then he heard the distant splash of oars – so there had been another boat, maybe several. But for Sheaffe's warning they would have swamped the cutter's defences no matter what it cost them.

Unable to contain themselves the seamen cheered and cheered again. Bolitho felt the pain returning and wanted to lay his head in his hands. But somehow he knew Stayt was watching him.

'Get Lieutenant Hallowes for me.' He fought back the need to cry out and asked between gasps, 'Where's Bankart?'

Over his shoulder Stayt said casually, 'Gone somewhere, sir.' It was all he said.

Hallowes arrived and knelt beside Bolitho. 'I am here, sir.'

Bolitho felt for his shoulder. 'That was bravely done.'

Hallowes said huskily, 'But for my men –'

Bolitho shook him gently. 'Because they respect you. You led, they responded in the only way they know.'

Hallowes did not speak for several seconds and Bolitho could guess why. In victory and defeat he had known emotion more than many. Hallowes was just discovering the pride as well as the pain of command.

Hallowes said, 'They'll be back.'

'Not tonight. Too costly. Thanks to Sheaffe.'

Hallowes sounded as if he was grinning. 'Your idea, sir, with respect.'

Bolitho shook his shoulder. He seemed to need a physical contact. Without it he felt completely cut off, a burden.

'Call him alongside. We may need that boat.'

He heard the insane bellow of *Supreme*'s copper foghorn and wondered what Sheaffe and his companion had thought as the fight had exploded on board the cutter.

Stayt came back and helped Bolitho to seat himself with his back against a small companionway. Everyone was talking, friends seeking out friends, others sitting in silence, remembering a messmate who had been killed or badly wounded.

Bolitho knew they would not survive in daylight when the frigate came for them. After their bloody repulse, the French would be out for revenge and give no quarter.

He felt the other officers standing or squatting near him. Hallowes was in command. What would he do?

Hallowes asked, 'What would you advise, sir?'

Bolitho held his eyes again, hating the spectacle he must present to these men.

'We must try to break out.'

Hallowes sounded relieved. 'I was going to suggest that, sir.'

Strangely enough, in that brief angry fight during which he had not even been a spectator, Bolitho had lost all sense of direction. The headland, the bluff at the end of the bay, even the rocks seemed all jumbled together.

'Mr Okes?'

Okes belched and Bolitho smelled rum. He had been having a well-earned wet as Allday would call it.

The thought touched off Stayt's words. What *had* happened to Bankart? He was close by now; he had heard him several times. Was it fear? Everyone was afraid in a fight, but he thought of Allday and tried to shut it from his mind, like something foul and unclean.

Okes rambled on, unperturbed by his murderous attack with the swivel. 'With the Cap'n's permission, I'll send the boat for t'other one. We could warp *Supreme* clear. I think the wind 'as backed, not greatly, but this beauty don't need *that* much.'

Hallowes said, 'See to it, Mr Okes. And thank you.'

Okes strode off and Bolitho pictured his thick legs in their white stockings when he had shot down the running Frenchman.

He said, 'That man is worth a pot of gold.'

Stayt said, 'The others have gone, sir.'

Bolitho laid back and tried to ignore the pain, to think of something which might distract him. But it was hopeless. If anything it was getting worse and Stayt knew it.

The flag-lieutenant said quietly, 'We could parley with the French, sir. Their surgeon might be able to help.'

Bolitho shook his head vehemently until Stayt said, 'I felt I should speak out, sir. I'll not mention it again.'

He stood up and leaned over the bulwark to stare at the blacker mass of land.

It was spoiled now. The smell of blood and gunpowder was too strong.

He considered Bolitho's driving, almost fanatical determination. If only he could sleep and escape from his pain.

A voice called, 'The two boats are comin', sir!'

Bolitho stirred and exclaimed, 'Your hand, get me up!'

Stayt sighed. Perhaps the strength which was holding Bolitho together was what they all clung to.

They would soon know.

*

There was something unreal about the way *Supreme*'s weary company set to and prepared to weigh anchor.

Bolitho remained by the companionway and tried to picture the cutter's deck as, with barely a word of command, the seamen went to their stations. Below the long bowsprit the two boats were already in position with extra hands to throw their weight on the oars if the cutter looked about to go aground.

Leadsmen whispered together on the forecastle, and behind his back Bolitho heard Okes rumbling to the helmsmen at the tiller bar while Hallowes attended to the shaken-out sails. Bolitho heard someone cursing that a French ball had ripped a hole through the topsail big enough for two men.

He tried to remain calm as he felt figures brush past him as if he barely existed.

A petty officer called in a hushed voice, 'Anchor's hove short, sir!'

Bolitho shivered as a warm breeze rattled the loose rigging and made the deck tilt, as if *Supreme* was eager to get away.

Hallowes had told him that the nearest beach was about half a cable away. The French were bound to have left men there. They would soon know what Hallowes was trying to do.

Okes said, 'Stand by!'

Hallowes called, 'Ready! Two more men on the larboard braces!'

'Anchor's aweigh, sir.'

Bolitho craned forward and tried to put a picture to every new sound. The anchor being winched home and made fast to its cathead, loose or severed lines being flung aside to leave the deck clear, almost the whole company was now employed either in the boats or in the business of making sail when required.

If they had to fight, they would be lucky if they could loose off a single gun in time.

Okes hissed, 'Helm down, boy!' The tiller creaked, and Bolitho heard a sail slap impatiently as the wind plucked at it.

A man cried out with shrill urgency, but his voice was muffled, far away, and Bolitho knew he was one of the badly wounded who had been carried below to die. The cry rose to a higher pitch, and Bolitho heard a seaman hauling on a halliard nearby utter a terrible curse, urging this unknown sailor to die and get it over with. The cry stopped, as if the man had heard the curse. For him at least it was over.

'Let 'er pay off!' Okes raised his voice as the cutter gathered way, and the oars of the two boats ahead of her thrashed the sea like wings. The lines would be lifting from the water as the gig and jolly boat took the strain of the two. They had steerage way, not much, but Okes sounded breathless, confident, 'Good. Warmly done, lads!'

Hallowes said, 'We have to use whatever passage we can, sir.'

Bolitho had not heard him approach.

Hallowes continued, 'I've a party by the anchor to let go if we get into trouble.' He seemed to chuckle. '*More* trouble, that is.'

Stayt asked, 'How long?'

Hallowes said, 'As long as it takes!' Bolitho pictured him looking everywhere as his command edged painfully ahead at a walking pace. The pumps thudded and creaked and Bolitho guessed that *Supreme* had been badly damaged and was taking a lot of water.

The leadsman called, 'By th' mark five!'

Bolitho recalled when he had been about twelve and in his first ship. Like little Duncannon, he thought. Too young to die. But he remembered watching the leadsmen sounding their way through a sea mist off Land's End, while the upper yards and wet sails of the big eighty-gun *Manxman* had been out of sight from the deck. Skilled seamen, like those who were sounding now, their hard fingers feeling the marks on their lines or guessing the depths in between.

'Deep six!'

That was plenty of water for the cutter even with her bilges filling from several shot holes.

The French would know now, Bolitho thought, not that they could do much about it. The clank of pumps and the occasional cry from the leadsman would mark their slow and precarious passage better than anything.

Stayt waited for Hallowes to go aft and said, 'She may be small, sir, but in these waters she feels like a leviathan.'

There was a splash alongside and Bolitho knew it was the dead seaman being dropped overboard. No prayer, no ceremony to mark his brief passing. But if they lived through this he would be remembered, even by the ones who had cursed his reluctance to die.

Bolitho cupped his bandaged eyes in his fingers and shook as more pain tested his resistance. It came in waves, slashing down his defences like a bear's paw.

How could he go on like this? What would he do?

'By th' mark seven!' The other leadsman called, 'Sandy bottom!'

They had primed their leads with tallow which would pick up tiny fragments from the seabed. Anything helped when you were feeling your way.

Bolitho dragged his hands down to his sides. *Like a blind man.*

Hallowes was speaking with Okes again. 'I think we might recover the boats and make sail, eh, Mr Okes?'

Okes answered but Bolitho could not hear. But he sounded doubtful. Thank God Hallowes was not stupid enough to ignore Okes' skill.

He said, 'Very well.' The deck leaned slightly and he added brightly, 'The wind is backing, by God! Luck is with us for a change!'

After an hour, which felt like an eternity, the gig fell back and there was a quick change of crew. The returning hands were utterly exhausted and fell to the deck like dead men. Even Okes' promise of rum did not move them.

Next it was the jolly boat and Bolitho heard Sheaffe speaking to the *Supreme*'s only master's mate.

The midshipman came aft and said, 'I have reported back, sir.'

It sounded so formal, so empty of what the youngster

had done, that Bolitho forgot about his own pain and despair.

'That was a *fine* piece of work, Mr Sheaffe. But for you we would have been swamped by the enemy.' He heard Sheaffe dragging on his shirt, his teeth chattering. It was not the night air, it was the sudden realization, the shock of what he had carried out.

'Go and rest. You'll be needed again before long.'

Sheaffe hesitated and then sat on the deck near Bolitho. He said, 'If this does not disturb you, sir?'

Bolitho looked towards his voice. 'Your company is welcome, believe me.' He leaned against the companion-way and tried not to anticipate the next wave of pain.

Sheaffe had his knees drawn up to his chin and was instantly asleep.

Bankart crouched down and whispered, 'I've brought you some wine, sir.' He waited for Bolitho's fingers to grip the goblet. 'Mr Okes sent it.'

Bolitho sipped it. Strong, rich Madeira. He drank it slowly, let it run through him, restore him. He could not remember when he had last eaten; perhaps that was why the wine seemed so potent. He touched his face below the bandage. Several cuts and some dried blood. He needed a shave badly. He tried to smile. Allday would soon see to that. Big and powerful like an oak, yet he was as gentle as a child when need be. Both Bolitho and Keen had good reason to remember it.

'What is it like to discover your father, Bankart?'

The question seemed to shock him. 'Well, it's fine, sir, it really is, like. My mother'd never tell me, y'see, sir. I always knew 'e were in the Navy, sir.'

'That was why you volunteered?'

There was a long pause. 'I suppose it were, sir.'

Bankart poured him another goblet of wine, and when Sheaffe was roused to take charge of the jolly boat again and take up the tow Bolitho barely stirred.

Okes left his helmsmen and walked over to the companionway. He was satisfied with what he saw.

Hallowes asked, 'Is he asleep at last?'

Okes fumbled with a red handkerchief and blew his nose loudly.

'Aye, sir. So 'e should, arter what I put in 'is Madeira!'

Bolitho felt a hand on his arm and twisted round with sudden fear as his senses returned.

Stayt said, 'First light, sir.'

Bolitho touched his bandage and tried not to show his pain.

'How do I look?'

Stayt sounded as if he was smiling. 'I've seen you somewhat better, sir.' He took Bolitho's hand. 'I've got a bowl of warm water and a towel of sorts.'

Bolitho nodded, grateful and ashamed as he dabbed his mouth and face with the wet towel. Such a simple thing and it was unlikely that Stayt realized how it had moved him.

'Tell me what's happening?'

Stayt thought about it. 'I reckon we're about a mile from where we set out, sir.' He sounded neither bitter nor even surprised. 'We're in some shallows at the moment – ' He broke off as the leadsman called, 'By th' mark three!'

Bolitho forgot his pain and dragged himself to his feet. Three fathoms of water and a mile from their last anchorage. He felt the wind on his cheek and heard the splash of boats as his head rose above the bulwark. One of the coxswains was calling out the time for the stroke. The oarsmen must be worn out, he thought.

'Is it really light?'

Stayt said, 'I can see that bluff, sir, and just make out the horizon. Sky's a bit angry. Could be in for a blow, I'm thinking.'

Hallowes was calling, 'Rouse the hands! I'm going to make sail.'

Okes replied, 'No choice, sir. Them boats are useless now.'

The deck lifted on a swell and Bolitho felt a catch in his throat. The open sea was waiting for them.

The cranking pumps, the tattered sails, nothing would stop them once they found searoom. *Room to bustle in.*

Stayt was watching him and saw him give a small smile.

Hallowes said, 'Recall the boats. Be ready to shake out the mains'l! Get the topmen to report on damage now that they can see it!' He was speaking quickly, sharply.

Bolitho had known such moments many times. Covering doubts and uncertainties, to show confidence when there was little.

A call shrilled and someone gave a mocking cheer as the lines to the boats were slacked off and the oarsmen slumped over their looms.

'By th' mark five!'

Hallowes rubbed his hands. 'We'll show 'em!'

Who, Bolitho wondered?

Men charged past him hauling on tackles as first one boat and then the other was hoisted into position on the tier.

The cutter seemed to stir herself and Bolitho wished he could watch as men swarmed to their stations. Somewhere overhead a sail cracked out noisily in the damp air.

'*Shallows ahead!* Fine on the starboard bow!'

'Hell's teeth!' Hallowes yelled. 'Stand by to let go the anchor!'

Okes said in a harsh whisper, 'Belay that, sir! We'll swing round an' strike if we does!'

Hallowes sounded confused, 'If you believe – '

But Okes was already acting and thinking. 'Let 'er come up a point! Steady as she goes!' He must have cupped his hands, Bolitho thought as his voice boomed along the deck, 'Set the jib, Thomas!'

'Here we go again.' Stayt sounded dangerously cool. 'Shallows, the lookout said. I can see breakers, for Christ's sake.' He added, 'Forgive me, sir. I am not used to this.'

Bolitho lifted his chin as if to see some light beneath his bandage. There was only darkness.

'Nor I.'

Okes barked, 'Now, lee helm!'

Bolitho heard several shouts and a clatter of rigging as, with a fierce jerk, *Supreme* surged into a bar. Gear torn

loose in the one-sided fight rolled about the deck and a
four-pounder reared up on its trucks as if it had come to
life. The grinding, shaking motion continued for what
seemed like an age, with Okes coaxing his helmsmen or
throwing an occasional instruction to his petty officers.

The shaking stopped and after a while a voice called,
'Pumps are still holding it, sir!'

Stayt said between his teeth, 'A damned miracle. There
were rocks an arm's length abeam but we hit only sand!'

'Deep six!' The leadsman must have been nearly hurled
from his precarious perch, Bolitho thought. But they were
through.

'*Loose tops'l!*'

Once in open water nothing could catch the cutter even
with her damaged hull.

Men were calling to one another, the fear and the danger
forgotten or put aside for this moment in their lives.

Stayt said, 'Our surgeon will know what to do, sir. As
soon as we sight – '

He broke off and gasped, 'It can't be!'

The lookout called, 'Sail, sir! Fine on th' weather bow!'

Bolitho heard Stayt murmur. 'It's the frigate, sir.'

Bolitho was almost glad he could not see their stricken
faces. The French captain had not been so overconfident
that he had waited around the headland. While Hallowes'
men had toiled at their oars, the Frenchman had spent his
night clawing to windward and towards the bluff where
he had first appeared. Now he held the wind-gage and was
sweeping down on them, with only his braced topsails
visible against the dawn horizon.

Bolitho did not need Stayt to describe it. He could see
the hopelessness of it as if he were seeing it through
Hallowes' eyes.

Another mile and they could have lifted their coat-tails
and run from the frigate's guns. But they were still on a
lee shore despite the change of wind, and the two vessels
were converging on some invisible rendezvous. No escape
this time.

Hallowes shouted, 'Run up the Colours, Thomas! Have
the guns loaded and run out!'

As men ran to obey Bolitho was conscious of the other silence. No yells or threats, and certainly not a cheer. Men facing certain death could still work well, but their minds would be elsewhere, seeking refuge with a memory, which moments ago had been a hope.

'Bankart!'

'Present, sir!'

'Go below and fetch my coat and hat.'

Filthy and bloody, but he was still their admiral and would be damned if they should see him already beaten.

Crash – crash – crash. The frigate was already firing some of her forward guns. Balls hurled waterspouts into the air or ricocheted across the sea in short, fierce spurts.

Bolitho heard Okes murmur, 'Will you fight, sir?'

'Would you have me strike?' Hallowes sounded calm, or was he beyond that?

More shots made the air quiver and Bolitho heard a ball crash down close by, the water tumbling across the weather shrouds like lead shot.

'Bring her up a point, Mr Okes!' Hallowes was drawing his sword. Bolitho touched his own and wondered what would become of it. He would fling it into the sea if he was given time and life to do so.

Another series of bangs made Stayt swear under his breath and a ball slapped through a sail and parted a stay like a piece of cotton.

'*On the uproll!*'

Stayt said fiercely, 'He's no chance, sir! Most of his pop-guns won't even bear yet!'

Bolitho said, 'It is his way. There is nothing else now.'

'*Fire!*'

The air cringed as the four-pounders recoiled inboard on their tackles, their explosions almost blanketed as the frigate fired yet again.

The deck jumped and wood splinters flew over the cowering gun crews.

Then a second salvo tore overhead and a man fell kicking and screaming into the sea alongside. *Supreme* was moving so fast despite her torn canvas that the man was soon lost far astern.

'How is it now?'

Stayt said tonelessly, 'Lighter, sir.' He winced as more balls slammed close alongside and one hit the bows with a terrible jerk. Torn rigging drifted down from aloft and trailed from the spars like shabby banners.

The gun crews did not look up but sponged out, rammed home fresh charges and tamped down their shot, because it was what they were trained to do, if necessary until death itself.

More shots struck the hull, and Bolitho said, 'She can't take much more.'

'Sail to loo'rd, sir!'

Men gaped at each other, not understanding, unable to judge anything in the ear-shattering din of cannon fire.

Stayt shouted, 'It's *Rapid*, sir!' He almost shook Bolitho's arm. 'She's catching the sun right now, sir! She's hoisted a signal! By God, the squadron must be here!'

Another explosion rocked the deck and men screamed as splinters scythed them down. It must have been a full broadside for someone yelled with disbelief, 'The Frenchie's goin' about! The bastards are runnin' for it! You showed 'em, Cap'n!'

But Stayt said bitterly, 'Hallowes is down, sir.' He took Bolitho's arm. 'That last bloody broadside.'

'Take me to him.'

The seamen had been cheering at this impossible intervention but now fell silent as their blind admiral was led aft to where Hallowes was being held by Okes and the master's mate.

Bolitho murmured, 'How bad is it?'

Stayt swallowed hard. 'Both his legs, sir.'

Bolitho was guided to Hallowes' side.

Hallowes said in a strong voice, 'I didn't strike! Given the chance – ' He broke off and cried out, '*Help me!*' Then mercifully he died.

Bolitho had been holding his hand and felt it die. He lowered it to the deck and said, '*Given the chance*. That was the measure of this man's courage.' He was helped to his feet and turned to where he knew Okes was waiting.

'*Supreme* is yours, Mr Okes. You've more than earned

her, and I'll see that your appointment is confirmed if it
is the last order I give.'

'*Rapid* is heaving-to, sir.' That was Stayt.

But that was all part of something else. It did not seem
to belong. Here there was only this moment and the pain.

'Take good care of her.'

'I – I will, sir. It's just that I didn't want, didn't
expect – '

Bolitho tried to smile. 'It is your moment now, Mr
Okes. Seize it.' He felt the pain grinding into his eyes
again and knew they were all watching him. He said,
'Never fear, Mr Okes, *Supreme* has a fine new commander,
and she will fight again.'

Okes stared after him as Stayt and Sheaffe guided the
bandaged admiral to the bulwark.

Then he said brokenly, 'Aye, sir, an' please God, so
will you.'

8

The Fire Still Burns

As *Argonaute*'s anchor cable took the strain men were already hoisting out boats while others were mustered into a landing party. *Icarus* had dropped anchor too, and even without a telescope Keen could see the busy activity on her upper deck and gangway.

The island looked so peaceful, he thought. It would be sunset in an hour and he needed to get a landing force of Royal Marines ashore with another detachment from Houston's ship in case any French were still present.

He removed his hat and rubbed his forehead. Could so much have happened in a single day?

He looked across at the anchored brig *Rapid*, with the listing and scarred cutter lashed alongside.

Why had he sent *Rapid* to find Bolitho? Instinct, a sense of danger? It had almost been too late. Perhaps it was too late. He thought of her young commander as he had described the scene, the frigate turning away when one more broadside would have finished what she had begun. Quarrell had said simply in his Isle of Man dialect, 'I knew I couldn't fight the Frenchie, sir, so I hoisted *Enemy in sight* as Sir Richard once did, and the enemy took the trick as fact and made off. But for it, *Supreme* and my own command would have been on the bottom!' His voice hardened. 'I would not have hauled down my colours with the admiral out there watching us, no more than poor John Hallowes did.'

Keen recalled the shock when he had seen Bolitho being hoisted up the side on a boatswain's chair, something he would always refuse even in bad weather. The whole ship had held her breath, or so it seemed. Keen had wanted to

run across, to take hold of him, but some last warning
had told him that for Bolitho the moment of return had
almost broken him.

It fell to Allday who had stepped past the marines and
watching officers to take Bolitho's elbow and say in an
almost untroubled voice, 'Welcome aboard, sir. We was a
mite worried, but now you're back, so there's an end to
it.'

As they had walked past, Keen had seen Allday's face
and had known his demeanour was a lie.

All day they had continued to the watering place, with
the squadron's surgeons aboard *Supreme* doing what they
could.

Keen gripped the nettings and stared at the streaks of
coral-coloured cloud. Calm, storm, gale and bright
sunlight. It changed like the pages in a book.

Paget joined him and touched his hat. 'Shall we rig
awnings, sir?'

'No. We will begin to take on water tomorrow at first
light. I want, no, I need to be out of this place quickly. I
intend to join the squadron without delay. My bones tell
me that things are moving fast.'

Paget eyed him doubtfully but chose his words with
care. Nearly everyone knew how the captain felt about
Bolitho.

He said, 'It may be serious, sir. If he is blind – '

Keen swung on him angrily. 'Damn you, how would
you know?' He relented just as swiftly. 'That was unfor-
givable. I am tired but so is everyone else.' He nodded. 'I
know it must be faced. As soon as *Supreme* is ready I will
send her south to Malta. Her wounded can be cared for.
I shall make my report for the admiral there. He will be
concerned about his convoys, no doubt.' He glanced at
Paget's impassive face. *He is wondering if I am going to
put her aboard for Malta.*

But Paget said, 'It is a bitter blow.'

Keen turned away. 'Call me when the Royals are ready
to leave.' He hurried aft past the immobile sentry.

It was like a group painting. Stayt, still in his stained
coat, sitting on the stern bench with a goblet between his

fingers. Ozzard slowly polishing the table which did not need it, and Allday standing quite motionless as he stared at the old sword which he had returned to its rack. Yovell was slumped by Bolitho's charts.

Keen glanced at the sleeping compartment and thought of the girl in there with Tuson. The surgeon had asked for her to assist him; he did not explain why.

When Keen had gone to her she had exclaimed, 'Of course! I had no idea what had happened!' No tears, not a trace of hesitation. She had been in there for most of the day.

Keen asked, 'Anything?'

Stayt made to rise but Keen waved him down. The flag-lieutenant replied wearily, 'I think the bandage is replaced, sir. There were splinters as well as sand.' He sighed. 'I fear the worst.'

Keen took a glass from Ozzard and swallowed it quickly. It could have been brandy or beer, he was too concerned to notice. It would be up to him to decide what to do. The other captains would obey, but would they trust him? It might take an age before *Supreme* reached Malta or they joined with the other ships of the squadron. How could Bolitho remain here? Suffering and fretting, destroying himself with each agonizing day.

To send him to Malta would mean losing another ship. It was brutal, but a fact which Bolitho would have been the first to emphasize.

The sentry called, 'Officer-of-th'-watch, sir!' Even his voice was hushed.

The lieutenant hovered in the doorway. 'First Lieutenant's respects, sir, I am to inform you that the boats are ready. Signal from *Icarus*, sir, asking permission to proceed.'

At any other time Keen would have smiled. Captain Houston was always trying to be a jump ahead of the flagship.

But not this time. 'Signal *Icarus* to await orders!' He saw the lieutenant flinch and tried again. 'I am sorry, Mr Phipps. My compliments to the First Lieutenant and I shall come up in a moment.'

The youthful lieutenant had been a midshipman in Keen's *Achates*. Keen eyed him sadly. 'Yes, it is true about Lieutenant Hallowes. He died bravely, I'm assured. I know you were his friend.'

The ex-midshipman withdrew. He was still too young to shrug off grief and it showed.

'Boys, all boys.' Keen realized he had spoken aloud. He said, 'I shall return as soon as the boats are gone. Come for me if you hear anything.' He glanced at Allday's broad shoulders. 'Anything at all.'

Stayt stood up and walked to the door. 'The same for me.'

Allday turned slowly and looked at his companions.

'I should have been there with him, y'see.'

Yovell took off his glasses. 'There was nothing you could have done, man.'

Allday was not hearing him. 'By 'is side. Like always. I must speak with my lad about it.'

Ozzard said nothing but polished all the harder.

Allday said, 'He should have let me kill that bloody *mounseer* up there on deck when I had the chance.'

He spoke so quietly that it was all the more fearful to watch him.

Yovell suggested, 'Have a tot of rum.'

Allday shook his head. 'When it's over. When I know. Then I'll drink a bloody keg of it.'

Bolitho lay very still in the cot, his arms at his sides. He was not relaxed and every muscle in his body seemed to be stretched taut.

How long was it? Everything merged and overlapped in his mind. The cutter, the sounds from the wounded, then being half carried into a boat and a voice he thought he recognized saying, 'Attention in the boat there!'

What a sight he must have been. Then more hands, some gentle, others less so, as he was hoisted into a boat-swain's chair and hauled up the ship's side like a piece of cargo.

Tuson had spoken only to identify himself and had got

to work with his examination. They had cut away his clothes, and someone had dabbed and cleaned his face and throat before applying something to the scars which stung like nettles.

Tuson had left the dressing until last. Feet had moved round the cot, and Bolitho had felt the edge of his scissors clipping carefully at the bandage.

He had asked, 'What time is it?'

The surgeon had answered severely, 'Please desist from talking, sir.'

Then Tuson had said, 'Hold that mirror. That's right. I want you to reflect the sunlight from the open port when I say so.'

It was only then that Bolitho had realized that the girl was there helping Tuson.

He had made to protest but she had touched his face, her hand surprisingly cool.

'Easy, sir. You're not the first man I've seen.'

The bandage had come away and Bolitho had almost cried out as Tuson's strong fingers had probed around his eyes and rolled up the lids. It was agonizing and he heard the girl exclaim, 'You're hurting him!'

'He's already hurt! Now, girl, the mirror!'

Bolitho had felt the sweat running down his chest and thighs, like a fever as the pain scraped into his very sockets. It had been a blurred, jumbled nightmare, punctuated by sharp, raw probes from some instrument.

The girl had stood beside the cot with the mirror, and another held his head firmly like a vice as the torture continued. Bolitho had tried to blink, but could not feel his eyelids move. But there was light, red and pink, and shadows which he knew were people.

Tuson had said, 'Enough.' The light faded as the mirror was removed. Then a new bandage had been carefully tied; it had been soft and damp, and after the probing and the pain it was almost soothing.

That must have been several hours ago. Twice more the bandage had been removed and changed, with more agonizing manipulation and some oily liquid which had at first made his eyes sting worse than before. Then the pain had eased.

When he had asked Tuson about the liquid Tuson had said offhandedly, 'Something I picked up in the Indies, sir. Useful at times like these, really.'

Bolitho listened to the girl's voice. It made him think of Falmouth, and the thought made his eyes smart all the more.

She said, 'I don't know how you can work in this light, sir.'

Tuson replied, 'It's far better than I'm used to.' He rested his hand on Bolitho's arm. 'You must rest.' A sheet was pulled over his nakedness and Tuson added, 'I see that you have gained a few honourable scars for King and Country, sir.'

To the girl he said, 'You'd better go and get some food inside you.'

'I'll come if you need me, sir.'

Bolitho raised an arm over the cot and turned his head towards the door.

She came to him and took his hand in hers. 'Sir?'

Bolitho barely recognized his own voice. 'I just want to thank you – '

She squeezed his hand. 'After what you've done for *me*?'

She seemed to run from the cabin and Tuson said heavily, 'Fine girl.'

Bolitho lay back in the cot and pictured the deckhead as he had seen it each morning.

'Well?'

'I can't say, sir, and that's the truth. Both eyes are scarred, but there is little I can decide until the ruptures heal or – '

Bolitho persisted, 'Will I see?'

Tuson walked round the cot. He must be looking through an open gunport, Bolitho thought, for his voice was muffled.

Tuson said, 'The left eye is the worst. Sand and metal particles. Your cheek was cut by a sliver of metal – a bit higher and there'd be no eye for us to worry about.'

'I see.' Bolitho felt his body relax. It was easier somehow when you knew the worst, the inevitable truth. *He thinks I'm done for.*

Bolitho said, 'I must speak with my flag-captain at once.'

Tuson did not move. 'He is busy, sir. It can wait.'

'Don't you *dare* to tell me what can and cannot wait!'

Tuson rested his hand on his arm again. 'That is *my* duty, sir.'

Bolitho covered the surgeon's hand with his own. 'Yes. My apologies.'

'None needed. All men are different. I once took off a seaman's leg and he didn't even whimper. Then he thanked me for saving his life. Another damned me to hell for sewing up his head after a fall from aloft. I have seen and heard everything, from quarterdeck to the lowliest mess.' He yawned. 'Why do we do it? Why do *you* do it, Sir Richard? You have given so much for your country. You must realize the consequences of staying at sea year in and year out? There is an inevitability about it which cannot be ignored or silenced.'

'Death?'

Tuson replied, 'There can be worse things than death.' He added, 'I shall leave you now, it seems your captain is here anyway.'

Keen sat down beside the cot and asked, 'How is it, sir?'

Bolitho tried to push his despair into the darkness. It was important, maybe vital, how he replied.

'I saw some light, Val. The pain is less, and as soon as I have had a shave I shall be more of a man again.'

Keen said, 'Thank God.'

Bolitho found his arm. 'And thank *you,* Val, for saving us.' He clenched his other hand into a fist to contain his emotion. 'Tell me what you are doing.'

When Tuson returned he found them both in deep conversation. He said sternly, 'This must cease, gentlemen!'

Bolitho held up his hand. 'A moment more, you impatient sawbones!'

To Keen he said, 'Finish watering then, and we shall make haste to gather the squadron. Jobert had tried to scatter our strength, destroy our ability to follow his movements. Like you, I feel it is near the time for his next move. Send Yovell to me.' He heard Tuson tutting. 'And I'll have my own report sent with *Supreme*.'

Almost to himself he said, 'I was with Hallowes when he died. Both legs gone. He had promise, that one.'

Bolitho laid his head on the pillow and tried to move his eyelids beneath the bandage. He could hear Keen and the surgeon whispering outside the door and suddenly wanted to get out of the cot, to go on deck and make as if he was the same as before.

Keen was saying, 'But in truth, will he recover?'

'And in honesty I do not know. I would have said it was hopeless, but with him I am not so sure.' He shook his head. 'He's like a ship in a storm, suddenly bent on its own destruction. It seems as if nothing can stop him.'

Keen saw Allday carrying a bowl of hot water and a razor. He had heard what Tuson had said to Bolitho about terrible odds against survival. He touched his side and felt the wound beneath his shirt. First one, then the other. Now Hallowes was gone.

He hesitated by the little cabin with its scarlet-coated sentry. Then he tapped on the door and stepped inside as she called on him to enter.

She was sitting on the big chest, the gown he had bought from the Genoese trader spilled across her lap, filling the place with light. She looked at him and said quietly, 'It is lovely. So good of you. You are a kind man.'

She laid it carefully across the cot and stood up. She had been crying, for Bolitho, for them, he could not tell.

She said, 'You have done so much, and I have nothing to give you.'

She turned away abruptly and when she faced him again he saw that her shirt was unbuttoned to her waist. Very deliberately she took his hand, her eyes fixed on his with a kind of defiance, then she pulled it inside her shirt and pressed it to her breast.

Keen did not move and felt the rounded skin beneath his hand burning into him, consuming him.

Then she did lower her eyes and said in a small voice, 'That is my heart. Now I have something to give. It is yours for as long as you will it.'

Then with equal gravity she withdrew his hand and closed the shirt.

Someone was shouting on the poop, and feet clattered on a ladder. But for just a few more seconds they stood motionless together.

Then she said, 'Go now. They must not see us like this.'

He stooped and kissed her lightly on the forehead and then left the cabin.

For a long while afterwards the girl stood watching the closed door, her hand touching her breast as he had done.

Then she said softly, 'Indeed I do love thee too.'

In two days the ships had completed taking on fresh water and with a brisk southerly wind to speed their passage they soon left the islands astern.

Keen had watched as *Supreme*, her shot holes crudely patched, her pumps still cranking, had cleared the anchorage and headed for open water. At the head of that same beach several of her company had been buried, including Lieutenant Hallowes. It was a sad parting, Keen had thought.

On the fifth day, with *Rapid* in the lead, they entered the Golfe du Lion.

Keen was walking the quarterdeck, his chin sunk in his neckcloth and deep in thought when the masthead sighted a sail. It was soon identified as *Barracouta* – the squadron would be one again.

But today was also special for Bolitho, and down in the cabin he was seated in his high-backed chair, breathing deeply as Ozzard opened one of the stern windows and his assistant Twigg put a cup of coffee in his hand.

Bolitho listened to the sea and the creak of the rudder-head. The ship was alive around him. He heard Allday speaking with Yovell, Ozzard bustling about. They were all so bright. Did they think they could deceive him?

He heard Tuson enter the cabin, the soft, bare-footed step of the girl who was with him.

Tuson put down his case and said, 'Plenty of light today.'

Bolitho nodded. 'We have sighted a ship, I believe?'

Tuson grunted. '*Barracouta*, sir.'

Bolitho tried not to show his dismay. Keen had not come to tell him. Even he thought it was over. He gripped the arms of the chair and said, 'Then Captain Inch will not be far away.'

He listened to his voice, his empty words. But he would play their game too. Not give in to his true thoughts.

'Now then.' Tuson moved the bandage slightly and began to unwind it. 'Keep your eyes shut until they have been bathed.' He was breathing hard, concentrating so that it was almost physical. The bandage went and Bolitho was aware of the complete silence around him. A warm pad dabbed at his eyelids, and for an instant a jab of pain shot through him.

Tuson saw him recoil and said, 'In a moment I shall tell you – '

Bolitho held out his hand. 'Are you here? Zenoria?' He felt her grasp his hand between hers.

He said, 'I want you to be the first one I see, not these ugly characters!'

She laughed, but he recognized the anxiety.

Tuson said flatly, 'In your own time, sir.'

Bolitho touched his left eye then his right with his fingers. He could feel himself holding her hands so hard he must be hurting her. He gritted his teeth together. He tried again, but was suddenly afraid.

Tuson said, 'Now, sir, if you please.'

Bolitho gasped aloud as the eyelids opened. It was as if they had been stitched down and were tearing themselves apart. Vague, distorted lights beamed past him from the stern windows, shadows too, but *there was light*.

Tuson was ready, another soft pad forcing moisture into each eye. They stung once more but Bolitho saw the pale

oval of the girl's face, the checkered floor covering, something shining. He craned his head around, not caring how
he looked, straining with desperation as he tried to focus
on something familiar.

Then he turned back to the girl, who was kneeling by
his chair. Her eyes, which he remembered so well, were
shining up at him and her lips were parted in a smile,
encouraging him.

Tuson seemed to be behind the chair. He put one hand
over Bolitho's left eye.

Bolitho said, 'Not too clear yet.'

'There will be discomfort, but the liquid I am using will
clear it eventually. Now look at the girl, sir.'

Bolitho could sense the others watching, not daring to
move. He felt his lips cracking into a smile. 'That is a
pleasure indeed.' He saw her flinch under his one-eyed
stare but she said, 'Bless you, sir.'

Bolitho whispered, 'My captain is a lucky man.'

Tuson placed a hand over his right eye and said remorselessly, 'Now the left.'

Bolitho blinked rapidly and saw Allday's gilt buttons,
the two swords at his back.

He whispered, 'Allday, old friend, I – ' He wiped his
face as if there was a cobweb across it. Something like a
shadow was covering Allday.

Bolitho turned despairingly to the girl again. The eyes,
the mouth, and then the shadow moved over her so that
she seemed to draw away although he held her hands and
knew she had not moved.

Tuson snapped, 'Bandage.' He stooped over Bolitho and
peered at his eyes. 'Early days, sir.'

He had tested the right eye first to give him hope.
Tuson had known that the other one was the most badly
damaged.

The disappointment left Bolitho spent, unprotesting as
the bandage brought back the darkness.

A door opened and he heard Keen ask, 'Well?'

Tuson replied, 'Better than I dared to hope, sir.'

Bolitho said, 'Blind in one lamp, not too fine in the
other, Val.'

The girl said, 'I'd better go, sir.'

Bolitho held out his hand. 'No. Stay with me.'

Keen said, 'The squadron is in sight, sir.' He sounded defeated. 'I shall report to you on the hour.'

Bolitho held the girl's hand like a lifeline. He leaned back in the chair and said, 'If the weather allows, Val, I want all captains to repair on board tomorrow. But first signal *Barracouta* to convey Inch's report on board directly.'

He had expected Keen or certainly Tuson to protest; their silence brought home the reality more firmly than any words.

Doors opened and closed and then Bolitho asked, 'Are we alone?'

'Yes, sir.'

Bolitho reached out and touched her hair. He must speak with his captains. They needed leadership, not despair. Jobert would use every weakness like a weapon.

He felt her move and said softly, 'Don't cry, my girl, you have given too many tears already.' He continued to stroke her hair, soothing himself and unable to see the pity in her eyes.

Then he said, 'You must help me. Then when I meet my little band tomorrow they will find their vice-admiral, not some helpless cripple, eh?'

Later, when a boat brought Inch's report to the flagship and Keen carried it aft to the great cabin, he found Bolitho sitting as before, but with the girl asleep against his legs.

Keen said, 'I am glad she kept you company, sir.'

Bolitho touched her hair again but she did not stir. 'You understand, don't you, Val? I *needed* her presence, her voice. I have become too used to the ways of men, the demands of strategy.'

Keen let him talk and all the while Bolitho's hand stroked the girl's long hair as she lay curled up at his side.

Bolitho continued in the same empty voice, 'When your day comes to hoist your own flag, let nothing distract you. I was reluctant to let go of the personal contact when I became an admiral. I longed to be a part of whichever ship flew my flag, used to think of individual faces and

names, the *people,* d'you see? Because I could not stay
apart I now blame myself for those who died, with
Supreme all but lost.'

'You must not think like that, sir.'

Bolitho said, 'So when your tune is piped, Val, forget
the faces, the pain you may cause them!' He was shouting
and the girl opened her eyes and stared up at him, then
questioningly at Keen.

'But I *cannot!*' He lowered his head, the anger gone
from him. 'And it is tearing me apart.'

Bolitho took the girl's hand. 'Go now. But please visit
me again.'

He held her hand to his lips. 'Brave Zenoria.'

The door closed and Bolitho heard Allday escort her to
her cabin.

Keen waited, feeling useless because he could not help.

Bolitho said, 'Open the report, Val. There's work to be
done.' He touched the bandage and added briskly, 'So let's
be about it.'

The following morning, while the ships lay hove-to in
their various angles, the captains boarded *Argonaute* as
ordered.

In his cabin Bolitho sat facing a mirror and tried to
compose his thoughts, as he had throughout the night. He
could not accept what had happened, but he had told
himself a thousand times he would not submit to it.

He listened to the shrill of calls as the last captain was
piped aboard.

Bolitho smiled bitterly. It was more like being an actor
than a sea officer. Should he have done this? Bravado or
necessity? He felt different in some way, and it was not
solely because of a clean, new shirt and a careful wash
under Allday's supervision.

'Ready, sir?' Tuson always seemed to be there.

Bolitho pressed his hands onto his knees and answered,
'Aye.'

The bandage was removed from his right eye, the now
familiar pad with its sweet-smelling ointment did its work,

and Tuson said, 'With respect, Sir Richard, you are a better patient than you *were*.'

Bolitho opened his eyes and stared at his cloudy reflection in the mirror. The small scars on his face were less noticeable because of his sunburned skin, but the eye glared back at him, angry and red-rimmed. It did not look like the one he could feel in his head.

He looked beyond the mirror, at Ozzard carefully brushing his uniform coat with its gleaming epaulettes. His best coat. It had to be a perfect performance. Allday craned forward to make certain he had not missed a single stray hair with his razor, and Yovell was busy with some papers at the table. The scene was almost set. He raised his eyes and saw the girl looking down over his shoulder.

She smiled gently, like a conspirator, which she was. She moved a comb over Bolitho's hair, loosening it across his forehead so that it partly covered the other bandage on his left eye. She had already arranged his queue and tied a ribbon which even Allday admitted was better than anything he could do.

Bolitho heard faint voices and the stamp of feet. The captains' meeting would be in the wardroom beneath his cabin. He had to leave his quarters free; for escape if things went wrong.

He said, 'Thank you, Zenoria, you have done your best with poor material.'

Their glances met in the mirror. She did not reply, but he saw the pleasure on her face. With her hair tied back again she had a look of determination in her brown eyes.

Bolitho tried to think of Inch's report, rambling as usual, for he loved to write lengthy descriptions of everything no matter how trivial. But each report contained something useful. This one had an item which was more than that. A key perhaps, or was it one more sly trap?

Tuson insisted, 'Don't overtax the eye, sir, and most certainly keep the other one covered. If you get proper treatment soon – '

Bolitho looked at him. The eye felt as if there was something in it. Tuson told him that would pass, given time.

Bolitho said, '*Your* care has been excellent.'

Tuson would not be deterred. 'Unless you avoid the other demands of this squadron, I cannot answer for the consequences.'

The door opened and Keen stood watching him, his hat beneath his arm. Bolitho noticed that he too was wearing his best dress coat. The second principal player, he thought.

'They are assembled, sir.'

Bolitho glimpsed him in the mirror and saw the quick exchange of glances with the girl who dressed like a boy. He saw too how her hand moved to her breast, and the look of understanding on Keen's face.

Bolitho touched his bandage. He was glad for them, no matter what difficulties lay ahead. He was not jealous, only conscious of a sense of envy.

He stood up and adjusted to the roll of the deck. The ships lay-to in a hot southerly breeze from Africa. It would be good to get this done and be under way again.

He slipped his arms into the coat and held one up as Allday clipped on the old sword.

Allday muttered, 'You watch yourself, sir.'

Bolitho touched his thick arm and smiled, 'I have work to do. I believe I have the makings of a plan.' He added quietly, 'But thank you, old friend.' He glanced at their faces, trying not to blink as his eye pricked painfully. 'And all of you.'

Keen felt a chill at his spine. He knew that look, that voice. Something neither pain nor a bandage could disguise.

The fire still burns.

9

Attack

Bolitho sat restlessly by his table and watched Keen's fingers busy with his dividers as he completed some more calculations on the chart.

Several times Bolitho had leaned forward to examine his progress and had felt the same rising sense of despair. It was like being half blind; as for reading the chart, it was out of the question.

He thought of his little squadron, so recently met in the Golfe du Lion and now drawing farther apart with each turn of the glass. *Helicon* and *Dispatch* had spread all the canvas they could muster and headed for the islands to take on fresh water. Bolitho frowned and immediately felt a painful response in his left eye. When they returned they would stay together as long as possible and wait no longer for Jobert to choose the next move.

Inch's report had been excellent. He had ordered *Barracouta* to stop and search any coastal vessels he could find, and from one he had discovered that two large French men-of-war had been seen in Spanish waters, just beyond the frontier and less than two hundred miles southwest of Toulon. No wonder few French ships had been sighted by Nelson's blockading squadron around the great port. This small fragment of news had been like a glimmer of light.

At the captains' conference Bolitho had first sensed doubt if not disbelief, but although he had been unable to see their faces clearly he had felt his words gaining their attention.

Spain was still an ally of France whether she liked it or not. On the face of it you could almost feel sympathy for

her, for Bonaparte had offered her few alternatives. He
had demanded six million francs a month as a subsidy
plus other important assistance. To avoid the outrageous
ultimatum, Spain had the choice of declaring war on
England once again. France had made it clear that a final
option was that she would make war on Spain if neither
alternative was met.

It seemed unlikely, if Inch's report was true, that Jobert
would have used Spanish waters without instruction from
a much higher authority in Paris. A further move to
involve the Dons in the conflict.

Bolitho felt uneasy when he recalled the conference. It
had seemed like an eternity before the captains had
returned to their ships. How did they see him now? Unde-
terred by his injury? Or had they seen through his pathetic
attempt to convince them of his ability to lead?

Lieutenant Stayt stepped through the screen door.

'Captain Lapish is ready for his orders, sir.'

'Very well.' Keen glanced at Bolitho and laid down the
dividers. He knew how loath Bolitho was to release his
only frigate. But if a fight was coming each ship needed
to be self-sufficient for as long as possible. You could
ration gunpowder. You could not survive without water.

As the flag-lieutenant withdrew Keen said, 'Lapish
knows what to do. I spoke with him when he came
aboard.' He gave a wry smile. 'He is more than eager to
make amends, I feel.'

When Lapish entered Bolitho said, 'Return to this
station as soon as you can.' He saw him nod, but his eyes
were smarting from so much use and he could see little of
the young captain's expression.

'You know what to do?'

Lapish said, as if repeating a lesson, 'I am to transform
my ship into a two-decker before I resume blockade duty,
sir.' There was no doubt in his voice, but Bolitho guessed
he probably thought his admiral was not only half blind
but unhinged as well.

Bolitho smiled, 'Aye. Use all your spare canvas and
hammock cloths. It has been done before. Lashed to the
gangways and painted buff with black squares for

gunports, no one could tell the difference from a third rate at any distance.'

He added forcefully, 'If they come sniffing too close, either board or sink them.'

Bolitho knew that the lithe frigate would be able to catch up with the two seventy-fours, complete her watering and still return to the French coast ahead of them. Once on station she would be seen as one of his squadron. It would leave Bolitho with a full muster, and Lapish would be able to discard his crude disguise and run down on him should he sight any enemy movements. Lookouts, friends or enemies, usually saw what they expected to see. That would leave *Rapid* in a role of paramount importance, his only feeler.

After Lapish had been seen into his gig by Keen, *Argonaute* made sail and, with *Icarus* in company, altered course to the southwest. The two ships sailed in line abreast and thus extended the range of their masthead lookouts. *Rapid* was so far ahead that she was barely visible even from the fighting-tops.

Keen returned to his chart and explained, 'The Frenchmen were sighted around the Cabo Creus, sir. An ideal anchorage, and less than twenty miles from the frontier with France. If they are still there, shall we go for them?'

Bolitho toyed with the dividers. 'It might provoke Spain. On the other hand it would show the Dons we are prepared to discount their one-sided neutrality. For once it will put Jobert on the defensive.' The more he considered it the less could he think of an alternative. Jobert had made all the moves, and had nearly succeeded in crippling Bolitho's squadron. He must be provoked into coming out into the open. Winter would soon be upon them and, Mediterranean or not, the weather would favour the enemy, not the ships battling up and down on blockade duty.

A convoy to Malta would be expected within the next few weeks, and the enemy would know it. From the moment the supply ships anchored briefly at Gibraltar their spies would pass on the news of the vessels, and probably their cargoes as well.

There were not enough men-of-war available. Nelson was right about that too.

Bolitho massaged his eye. He would probably find the sheltered anchorage empty. Suppose they met with Spanish patrols? Fight or retreat?

He said grimly, 'Landfall tomorrow, Val.'

'Yes, sir.' If he was anxious about the girl being aboard with a prospect of battle he did not reveal it in his voice.

Bolitho said, 'It would be something to show for our setbacks, Val. Tit for tat. Jobert would be out for revenge. That is a bad incentive for any flag-officer.'

He turned away and walked to the stern windows. *It is what I am seeking.*

After Keen had gone Allday entered and asked, 'Is there anything you need, sir?'

Bolitho immediately sensed the emptiness in his voice. 'What's wrong?'

Allday looked at the deck. 'Nothin', sir.'

Bolitho slumped down in his new chair. 'Out with it, man.'

Allday said stubbornly, 'I'll keep it battened down, if you don't mind, sir.'

There was no point in pushing him further. Allday was like the oak and had deep roots. He might tell him in his own time.

Allday took down the beautiful presentation sword and tucked it under his arm. He seemed to need something to occupy his mind.

Tuson was the next visitor. Bolitho had learned to tolerate the surgeon's regular treatment and to disguise his pain when the dressings were changed.

How many days had it been? He opened his left eye and stared fixedly at the stern windows. Watery sunshine and a deep blue horizon. He tensed, feeling the hope surge through him. Then clenched his fists as the same shadow returned to curtain off his vision.

Tuson saw him tighten his fists and said, 'Don't despair, sir.'

Bolitho waited for the bandage to be retied. It was

almost better to see nothing from that eye than to lose hope.

He asked abruptly, 'What is the matter with my cox'n?'

Tuson looked at him. 'Bankart, sir. His son. Pity he's aboard, if you ask me.'

Bolitho touched his shirtsleeve. 'Come on, man, you can speak with me, you should know that.'

Tuson shut his black bag. 'How would *you* like it, sir, if your nephew proved to be a coward?'

Bolitho heard the door close, the tap of a musket as the sentry changed his stance beyond the screen.

A coward. All the bitter memories surged through him as the word hung in his mind like a stain.

That moment when Midshipman Sheaffe had been left behind, probably injured. The times on *Supreme*'s deck when Bankart had been missing. There was not much Tuson did not glean from the men who came to him for aid.

He remembered Stayt's voice aboard the cutter; he had known even then.

How could he waste time on such things when so much was expected of him? He thought of his instructions to Lapish. *Board them or sink them.* The intruding hardness in his voice. Had blindness done that to him? But he recalled how he had hacked down the French seaman who had been carrying the lookout's telescope. Without a thought, with no hesitation. No, it was something inside him. Perhaps Belinda had seen it and feared for him because he was being destroyed by war with the same ruthlessness as by a ball or a pike.

But he *did* care. About people. About Allday most of all. Tuson had laid his finger right on it. How would he have felt if Adam had been a coward?

That night, as *Argonaute* dipped and lifted in an untidy sea of tossing white horses, Bolitho lay in his cot and tried to sleep. When eventually he dozed off he thought of Belinda, or was it Cheney? Of Falmouth and of a sea battle which became a nightmare, for he saw himself dead.

The next day *Rapid* stopped a Portuguese fisherman but only after she had put a ball across her bows.

Eventually the news was passed to the flagship. The fisherman had passed Golfo de Rosas below the cape two days earlier. A large French man-of-war lay at anchor there.

Bolitho paced up and down his stern gallery, oblivious to the wind and the spray which soon soaked him to the skin.

The French ship would not sail towards Gibraltar. She might remain at anchor, or she could decide to head for Toulon.

Argonaute would stand between her and any such destination.

He sent for his flag-lieutenant.

'Signal to *Icarus*. *Remain on station*. *Rapid* will stay with her.'

Had he been able to he would have seen Stayt raise one eyebrow. Bolitho groped his way to the table and stared helplessly at the chart.

Then he faced Stayt and grinned. '*Argonaute* will sail under her old colours tomorrow.'

'Suppose it is Jobert, sir? He'll surely recognize the ship.'

'It won't be. He will be with his squadron. When we know where *that* is – ' He left the rest unsaid.

Minutes later the flags broke brightly from the yards and were acknowledged by *Icarus* and eventually by the little brig.

If the wind changed against them he would have to think again. But if not, and the master seemed confident it would remain southerly, they might stand a chance of closing with the enemy.

The very coastline which the enemy had seen as a refuge might soon become the jaws of a trap.

In his cabin Captain Valentine Keen took a few moments to ensure he had everything he needed for the next hours. Around and below him the ship seemed quiet except for the regular groan of timbers and the muffled sluice of water against the hull.

It is always like this, he thought. Uncertainty, doubt, but beneath it all a determination which was without fear. He saw his reflection in the mirror and grimaced. In a short while he would go on deck and give the word to clear for action. He felt the touch of ice at his spine. That too was normal. He checked himself as thoroughly as he would a subordinate. Clean shirt and breeches. Less chance of infection if the worst happened. He touched his side and felt the soreness of his wound. They said lightning never struck twice in the same place. He was still looking at his reflection and saw himself smile. He had put a letter to his mother in his strongbox. How many of those had he written, he wondered?

There was a light tap at the door. It was Stayt.

'Sir Richard has gone on deck, sir.' It sounded like a warning.

Keen nodded. 'Thank you.' Stayt vanished in the gloom. An odd bird, he thought.

It was almost time. He loosened his hanger in its scabbard, and made certain his watch was deep in his pocket in case he should fall.

He heard low voices outside the door and pulled it open before anyone could knock.

For a moment he could only see the pale oval of her face; she was covered from chin to toe in his boat cloak which he had sent to her earlier.

It looked black outside, but he sensed figures moving about and heard the creak of the helm from the quarterdeck.

He led her into the cabin. Soon, like the rest of the ship, it would be stripped bare, ready to fight.

Perhaps the French ship would not be there, but he discarded the thought. The wind was fresh, and no captain would wish to fight it and end up on a lee shore.

He took her hands. 'You will be safe, my dear. Stay with Ozzard in the hold. He will take care of you. Where is your companion?'

'Millie has already gone down.' She was staring up at him, her eyes very dark in the shaded lantern.

Keen adjusted the boat cloak and felt her shoulder tense

as he touched it. He said, 'It will be cold below. This will help.'

He was conscious of the need to go, the seconds and the minutes. He said, 'Don't be afraid.'

She shook her head. 'I only fear for you. In case – '

He touched her mouth. 'No. We shall be together soon.'

A man coughed in the darkness. That would be Hogg, his coxswain.

He held her against him very gently and imagined he could feel her heart beating and remembered holding her breast in his hand.

He murmured, 'In truth, I do love you, Zenoria.'

She backed away and turned once to look at him. To remember, to reassure, he did not know.

He snatched up his hat and strode out towards the quarterdeck. He found Bolitho by the weather nettings, his body angled to the deck as *Argonaute* blundered her way on an uncomfortable larboard tack, as close-hauled as her yards would bear.

The quartermaster called, 'Nor'west, sir! Full an' bye!'

Keen could see it in his mind. All night the ship had clawed and beaten her way into the wind, to pass the cape well abeam and then turn again towards the land and the small gulf where the Frenchman was said to be lying. All the backbreaking work of resetting sails and changing tack a dozen times would offer them an advantage once they made their final approach. They would hold the wind-gage; even if the enemy managed to elude them there was only one course of escape, and he would find *Icarus* and *Rapid* blocking his path.

Keen thought of the girl in his arms, the crude comment made by *Icarus'* captain. He had made an enemy there, he thought.

Bolitho turned and asked, 'How long?'

Keen watched the painful way he was holding his head and sensed his hurt like his own.

'I shall clear for action at dawn, sir.'

Bolitho clung to the nettings as the ship shuddered into a massive trough; it seemed to shake her from beakhead to taffrail.

'Will the people be fed?'

Keen smiled sadly. 'Yes, sir. The galley is ready.' He had nearly answered 'of course'. He had learned well under Bolitho.

Bolitho seemed to want to talk. 'Are the women below?'

Keen said, 'Yes, sir.' He thought of the Jamaican maid called Millie. He suspected she was having an unlawful liaison with Wenmouth, the ship's corporal, the very man chosen to protect her from harm.

He admitted, 'I hate the thought of her being down there when we fight.'

Bolitho touched his bandage. '*If* we fight. But she is better here for the present, Val, than abandoned in some unknown harbour.' He tried to rouse his enthusiasm. 'You are lucky to have her so near.'

The calls trilled between decks and petty officers bawled at all hands to lash up and stow their hammocks. In minutes the upper deck, which had been deserted but for the duty watch, was overflowing with men as they ran to the nettings to tamp down their pod-like hammocks where they would offer the best protection against splinters and musket balls.

There was a strong smell of frying pork from the galley funnel, and from one hatchway Bolitho heard the thin note of a fiddle. Time to eat, to change into fresh clothing, to share a tot and a song with a friend. For some it might be the last time.

Keen had gone forward to speak with the boatswain and Bolitho twisted round to seek the officer-of-the-watch.

'Mr Griffin!'

But the shadow was not the lieutenant but Midshipman Sheaffe.

Bolitho shrugged. 'No matter. You can tell me what is happening.'

Sheaffe stood near him. 'Mr Fallowfield says it will be first light in half an hour. It is cloudy, as you can see, sir – ' He broke off and said, 'I beg your pardon, Sir Richard.'

Bolitho replied, 'I am getting used to it. But I shall be glad when the day comes.'

Eventually it was time. Keen came aft again and touched his hat.

'The galley fire is doused, sir. It was a hasty breakfast, I'm afraid.'

Bolitho smiled. 'But a bracing one, I gather, from the smell of rum.'

Shadows moved about, merged and separated, and there was a new greyness in the light.

'Deck there! Land on the lee bow!'

Bolitho heard Fallowfield blow his nose. Probably out of relief.

Keen exclaimed, 'A timely landfall, sir. I can wear ship presently, but first – '

Bolitho turned towards him, his hair blowing in the wind.

'Remember what I told you, Val. Clear your mind of everything but fighting this ship.' The hardness left him and he added, 'Otherwise our brave Zenoria will be widowed before she is wed!'

Keen grinned. It was infectious.

He cupped his hands and then paused as a thin shaft of frail sunlight ran down the main topgallant mast like liquid gold. Then he shouted, 'Mr Paget! Beat to quarters and clear for action, if you please!'

Bolitho took a deep breath as the drums rolled and the calls trilled yet again to urge, guide and muster the ship's company into a single team.

Bolitho did not have to see it to know what was happening. The crashes and thuds below decks as screens were removed and personal belongings taken below. Powder from the magazine, sand scattered on the decks so that the gun crews would not slip, and to contain the blood if any was to be shed.

Bolitho felt Allday beside him and raised his arm for him to clip his sword into place.

Together. Another fight, victory or failure, how much would it count in the end?

He tried not to think of the ceremony when he had been knighted. All those complacent pink faces. Did they really care about men like these, what it cost in lives to keep landsmen in comfort?

Paget's voice. 'Cleared for action, sir!'

Keen said, 'Well done, Mr Paget, but next time I want two minutes knocked off the time!'

'Aye, *aye*, sir.' It was a game. Captain and first lieutenant. Like me and Thomas Herrick, Bolitho thought.

He saw the nearest gangway taking shape, the lines of packed hammocks like hooded figures. The breeches of the upper deck's eighteen-pounders stood out sharply against the holystoned planking; life was returning to the ship.

Keen shouted, 'Alter course, three points to starboard! Steer north by west!'

Paget raised his speaking trumpet. 'Man the braces there!'

Keen gripped the quarterdeck rail and watched as the great yards were hauled round while the rudder went over. It was not much, but it took the strain out of the sails and shifted the wind more across the quarter.

As the bows lifted he saw a hint of land for the first time, tilting to larboard as if to slide the ship to windward. He turned to inform Bolitho but said nothing as he saw the vice-admiral standing as before, with Allday close behind him. Bolitho had seen nothing, and Keen was both moved and troubled.

Allday gave him a brief glance, but it told Keen everything. It said, *I shall be here.*

Keen said, 'Aloft with you, Mr Griffin, and tell me what you can see.'

He saw Midshipman Sheaffe and his signals party by the halliards and a huge French Tricolour trailing across the deck.

Keen took a telescope and climbed into the shrouds. The land was touched with sunlight, but without much substance. They were steering almost parallel with it and about two miles distant. The whole gulf was only ten miles across, and at the end of it the craggy-nosed cape leaned out protectively to make a perfect shelter or anchorage.

Bolitho called, 'Any ships?'

'None yet, sir.'

Bolitho sighed. 'Bit different from our last commission together at San Felipe, eh?'

Then he seemed to lift from his mood. 'Run up the flag, and then get the t'gallants on her. We shall need all our agility today if we are to be lucky.'

Keen gestured to the first lieutenant but paused as the voice from the masthead made them all look aloft.

'Deck there! Ship, dead ahead!'

Keen stared up until his eyes watered, fretting with impatience until Lieutenant Griffin yelled, 'Sail-of-the-line, sir! At anchor!'

Keen saw the big Tricolour break out from the gaff, while men swarmed up the ratlines to set more canvas.

The anchored ship was not visible from the deck, but even allowing for Griffin's telescope they could be up to her within the hour.

'Steady as she goes, sir! Nor' by west!'

Keen heard Bolitho say quietly, 'And it seems we are to be lucky after all.'

By the time the sunlight had reached the upper deck Bolitho could feel the tension rising about him while the lookouts called down their reports. He was torn between asking Keen what he was doing phase by phase or leaving him unimpeded by his questions.

Keen joined him suddenly and shaded his eyes to look at the set of the sails. Beyond them the clouds had broken up slightly to allow the sun to colour the ship and the sea around it.

He said, 'The Frenchman is anchored by the bow only, not fore and aft.' He let his words sink in so that Bolitho could form his own picture. With the wind still from the south the other ship would be swinging towards them as if on a converging tack, only her larboard bow exposed.

Keen added, 'No sign of excitement. Yet. Mr Griffin says there are craft alongside, a water-lighter for one.'

Bolitho thought suddenly of *Supreme*, of Hallowes holding his hand in death.

'That is very apt.'

'I intend, with your assent, sir, to pass between her and the land. There is ample depth there. Then we can hold the advantage, and rake her as we cross her bows.' A corner of his mind recorded the hoarse shouts of the gun-captains, the harsher tones of the fearsome gunner's mate Crocker. He was with the first division starboard side. He would enjoy that.

'Ship, sir! Larboard bow!'

Keen snatched a glass from Midshipman Hext. Then he said, 'Spaniard. One of their corvettes.'

Stayt murmured, 'Having a job to close with us, sir. She's almost in irons.'

Keen said, 'Watch for her hoist, Mr Sheaffe. She'll challenge us soon.' He raised his voice. 'You, on deck! Keep your eyes on the Frenchman, not on this little pot of paint!' Someone laughed.

Bolitho said, 'My guess is that there'll be no signal. The Dons won't want to be too open about their collusion.'

The little corvette was changing tack, the choppy water seething along her gunports as if she had run aground.

Beyond her the land looked high and green, a few white specks here and there to mark isolated dwellings.

There might be a battery, but Bolitho doubted that. The nearest garrison of any size was said to be in Gerona, only twenty miles inland. Enough to deter any would-be invader.

The small Spanish man-of-war was within a cable's length now. Bolitho heard the clatter of tackle from *Argonaute*'s forecastle as an anchor was loosened at its cathead as if they were preparing to drop it. Many eyes must be watching *Argonaute* from the Frenchman. Her preparations, like her design, would be noted.

Bolitho fretted at his inability to see. He took a telescope from Stayt and trained it across the nettings. He saw the corvette, watched her heeling over, her red and yellow ensign streaming almost abeam as she came up into the wind. He could ignore the blindness, forget that without the glass he would be helpless again. Tuson would rebuke him severely for straining his good eye. But the surgeon was in his sickbay, waiting for the next harvest.

Bolitho thought of the girl, her lovely eyes as she had exchanged glances with Keen. Could they ever find happiness? Would they be allowed to?

Fallowfield growled, 'Be God, sir, the wind's a veerin'!'

Men ran to braces and halliards again and Keen said, 'From the sou'west by my reckoning, sir.'

Bolitho nodded, fixing the chart's picture in his mind. Veering. Lady Luck, as Herrick would have said, was with them.

Keen shouted, 'Be ready to brail up the forecourse, Mr Paget!'

A thin voice floated across the water from the corvette. Bolitho said, 'Wave your hat to them!'

Keen and Stayt waved to the Spaniard, who was being rapidly driven towards the larboard quarter.

A mile to go. Bolitho gripped the rail and peered through the crossed rigging and straining jib sails. He could see the enemy, angled towards the starboard bow just as Keen had described her.

Keen glanced meaningly at Paget. 'Load, if you please.'

The order was instantly piped to the decks below and Bolitho could imagine the gun crews toiling with charges and rammers in semi-darkness behind sealed ports, their naked backs already shining with sweat. He had seen and done it so often from the early age of twelve. The men at the guns, the red-painted sides to hide the blood, and here and there an isolated blue and white figure of authority, a lieutenant or a warrant officer.

It did not seem to take long before each deck had reported ready.

Bolitho heard Captain Bouteiller of the Royal Marines whispering instructions to Orde, his lieutenant. Like the rest of the marines, he was crouching out of sight of the enemy. One sign of a scarlet coat would be enough to rouse a hornet's nest.

'Take in the forecourse!' Paget sounded hoarse. It had to appear as if they were shortening sail and preparing to drop anchor.

Bolitho stood away from the rail, his hands clasped behind him. It could not last much longer. One thing was certain, Jobert was not here. He would have been ready to fight as soon as his old flagship was revealed in the dawn light.

'Five cables, sir!'

Bolitho felt a trickle of sweat run down to his waist. Half a mile.

'The Frenchie's hoisted a signal, sir!'

That was it. No coded acknowledgement meant instant discovery for what they were.

Keen yelled, 'Belay that order, Mr Paget! Get the t'gan's'ls on her!'

Calls shrilled, and high above the decks the topmen spread out on the yards like monkeys to release the extra sails.

Fallowfield said, 'Wind's steady, sir. Sou'west. No doubt about it.' He sounded too preoccupied to care about the enemy closing towards the starboard bow.

'Three cables, sir!'

Faintly above the din of wind and rigging they heard the urgent blare of a trumpet.

Voices called from every hand, the anchor was catted again and, as the marine marksmen swarmed up to the fighting tops with their muskets or manned the swivels there, the rest of the detachment spread themselves along the poop nettings, their weapons already resting on the tightly packed hammocks.

Keen watched unblinking, gauging the moment, knowing that Bolitho was sharing it, and that Paget was ready to act on each command.

'*Open the ports!*'

Along each deck the port lids lifted on their tackles, like drowsy eyes awakening.

'God, they're cutting their cable, sir!'

Keen bit his lip. Too late. '*Run out!*'

Squeaking and rumbling, the *Argonaute*'s powerful armament poked through the open ports like snouts. The muzzles of the big thirty-two-pounders on the lower

gundeck were already lifting or dipping as their captains
practised their aim.

Bolitho took Stayt's glass again and trained it on the
other ship. He saw her foretopsail breaking free from its
yard and men swarming aloft while others crowded the
forecastle above the cable. The water-lighter was still
lashed alongside, its hull lined with staring faces as *Argonaute* bore down on them.

The cable parted and the French two-decker began to
fall downwind, more canvas flapping in disarray as men
fought to bring her under command.

'Stand by, starboard battery!'

Keen's eyes narrowed in the strengthening sunlight as
he waited for the Tricolour to tumble across the deck, and
the Red Ensign to break out from the gaff in its place. At
the foremast truck Bolitho's flag flapped stiffly to the
wind, and Keen heard one of his midshipmen give a shrill
cheer.

Argonaute's tapering jib boom crossed the other ship's
bows barely a cable away.

Keen lifted his hanger. He heard the grate of a handspike
from forward and saw the starboard carronade being
inched round; her massive sixty-eight-pound ball would
be the first to fire. The rest would shoot as they found
the target, not in a full broadside, but deck by deck, pair
by pair.

'As you bear, lads!' The hanger's blade made a streak
of light.

'*Fire!*'

10

Retribution

Without changing tack or altering course one degree
Argonaute swept past the drifting French two-decker, her
hull jerking violently to each resounding bang. So
conscious were the gun-captains of this moment that each
pair of cannon sounded like a single explosion.

Bolitho swayed and almost slipped as the deck tilted
into another offshore roller. He felt his nostrils flare in
the acrid smoke, his ears quake to the thunder of gunfire.
The attack was begun by the carronade, but at a range of
almost a cable it was more of a gesture than any danger
to the enemy.

Keen wiped his face as the last division of guns recoiled
inboard on their tackles and men scampered to sponge out
and reload. The Frenchman had been badly mauled, and
smoking scars along her tumblehome marked the accuracy
of the carefully aimed attack. A few guns fired in return,
and one ball smashed into *Argonaute*'s lower hull like a
mailed fist.

Some of the crews were calling to each other, racing to
beat their time, to be the first to run out and be ready to
fire again.

Keen watched narrowly as the Frenchman set her forecourse and then her main topsail. She was under command,
but almost beam-on to sea and wind as she fought to bear
up to her attacker.

He shouted, '*Ready!* On the uproll, Mr Paget!' He
glanced at Bolitho, just a fraction of a second, but he saw
him as he always remembered. Straight-backed, facing the
enemy yet now unable to see them. 'Full broadside!' This
might be the only time. He caught a vague glimpse of the

Spanish corvette, now well astern, a helpless and astonished spectator.

More shots hammered alongside and somewhere a man
screamed out in agony.

Keen held out his hanger, his eyes watering again as the
sunlight warmed his face.

'*Now!*'

As the whistles shrilled and *Argonaute*'s topgallant masts
began to tilt once more, the whole broadside thundered
out with such violence it was like hitting a rock.

Smoke and charred wads drifted everywhere, but not
before Keen had seen the broadside tear across the less-
ening gap, the wavecrests breaking to the force and the
weight of iron.

He saw the enemy ship shiver, then sway over as the
full onslaught smashed into her. Wood and rigging flew
in all directions, and the labouring hull was masked by
falling fragments and leaping talons of spray.

'*Stop your vents! Sponge out! Load!*' Paget's voice
echoed above the wind and the squeal of tackles like a
clarion call.

Allday said in a sudden pause, 'We hit 'em, sir! Even
her canvas is shot through!' He sounded tense, slightly
wild, like men usually are when battle is joined.

Bolitho held the quarterdeck rail, afraid he might lose
his balance again. He thought he had heard the broadside
strike home even at this range.

He said tersely, 'Close the distance, Captain Keen!'

Lieutenant Stayt lowered his telescope and looked at
him. He had seen Keen's quick glance as his mind had
registered Bolitho's sharp formality.

'Alter course to starboard, Mr Fallowfield!' Keen broke
off as several balls crashed into the hull, and some
hammocks burst from the forward nettings in a wild
tangle, like exultant corpses.

Keen shouted, 'That was chainshot!' He looked at the
sailing-master. 'Close as you can!'

Men ran to the braces while along the upper deck's
eighteen-pounders others worked like demons with hand-

spikes and tackles, training, and holding the enemy firmly in their ports.

'*Fire!*'

The broadside thundered out again, and Bolitho heard someone cheering, like a demented soul in Hell, he thought.

Allday exclaimed, 'Her mizzen's gone! She's tryin' to come about, to save her stern from the Smasher!'

Bolitho seized a glass and pressed it to his right eye. All the jokes about Nelson at Copenhagen were not so funny now. He saw the hazy outline of the French ship, shortening as *Argonaute* turned towards her, the bowsprit pointing directly at her poop.

The other captain had not regained control completely when the second broadside struck and raked his ship from bow to stern. Instead of continuing to turn, she was falling downwind, her afterpart shrouded in fallen spars and canvas, while here and there along her battered side a few guns fired independently, and on her gangway tiny stabbing flashes showed that her marksmen were fighting back.

'Steady as you go!'

Keen crouched down to peer through the pall of smoke and straining rigging. The wind had risen; he had to hold the gage or lose all the advantage his attack had gained. He saw the water-lighter tilting over, spilling men and casks into the sea, the hull so pitted with holes it was a wonder it had taken so long. On the opposite, disengaged side, another harbour craft, a big yawl, had cast off, and was probably trying to beat away from her big consort before she shared the lighter's fate.

Keen made up his mind. 'Mr Fallowfield, lay her on the starboard tack!' The Frenchman was still beam-on to the wind, her progress further hampered by the trailing wreckage of spars and rigging alongside. The shattered lighter was sinking rapidly and he realized that she was still made fast by the bow to the two-decker. Either they had not had time to cast off, or the men so ordered had been scythed down by the last murderous broadside. But Keen had been in enough fights to know how quickly the

balance could alter. The French captain had kept his mind
above the disaster which had caught him unprepared, and
had found time to order his gun crews to load with chainshot. A well-aimed fusillade could bring down a vital spar
– victory and defeat were measured by such delicate
distinctions.

Orders were yelled and men hauled at the braces yet
again. Bolitho felt a shot fan past him, heard a crack and
something like a fierce intake of breath as the musket ball
hurled a marine from the nettings, the side of his skull
blasted away. His companions left their stations as the
afterguard was piped to the mizzen braces, while the ship
tilted steeply and began to plough over to the opposite
tack.

Keen joined Bolitho and shouted above the noise of
gunfire and bellowed orders, 'They see you, sir! Put on
my coat!'

Bolitho clung to a stay and shook his head. 'I *want*
them to see me!' More shots hissed past him and smacked
into hammocks on the opposite side or cracked against the
planking. Bolitho could feel the anger rising inside him,
driving away reason and caution had there been any. Keen
did not understand. Bolitho was afraid to release his grip
and move about as any sane man would. His bright epaulettes marked him down as a prime target; better that than
lose his balance again while his men fought for their very
lives around him.

Crash – crash – crash, the French ship returned fire yet
again.

Bolitho raised the telescope and jammed it to his eye.
It was heavy, difficult to hold steady with one hand. He
saw the French ship suddenly stark and huge, towering
over the *Argonaute*'s starboard bow. Keen's sharp change
of tack had pared away the distance. The French captain
had no chance now to break off the action, to turn and
fight or even to run.

He saw the enemy's helpless stern rising still higher,
isolated from the rest of the ship by the great gap in her
silhouette left by the fallen mizzen.

Keen said fiercely, 'We shall pass barely a boat's length away, sir!'

A masthead lookout waited for a pause in the firing and yelled hoarsely, 'Ships to larboard, sir!'

Keen shouted, 'Send an officer aloft!' He ducked and coughed as a ball slammed through the nettings and hurled blasted hammocks everywhere. But for the alteration of course there would have been a solid rank of marines there.

A ship's boy, a mere child, who was running almost doubled over with fresh shot to a quarterdeck nine-pounder, was caught even as he reached the gun. The horrified crew of the nine-pounder were drenched in blood as the ball cut the boy neatly in half so that the legs appeared to run on after the torso had fallen to the deck.

'Steady she goes, sir! Nor'east by east!'

'As you bear!'

Keen waved to the forecastle although he doubted if the carronade crew needed encouragement this time. Every gun had extra hands to work it, men taken from the disengaged weapons on the larboard side.

More shot whined overhead, and several sails danced as holes appeared and broken rigging clattered across the nets and gangways.

Captain Bouteiller yelled, 'Get those bloody sharpshooters, Orde!'

A swivel banged loudly and Bolitho recalled Okes firing into the French longboat. He felt the deck quiver by his feet and knew that a ball had almost taken him. He did not move. He wanted them to see him, to know who had done this.

A voice filtered through the noise. 'They're Spaniards, sir!'

Bolitho heard Keen shouting orders. Spaniards. Some local vessels coming to drive the attacker from their waters.

'*Fire!*'

The ship jerked violently as the carronade fired almost point-blank into the enemy's stern.

It was a direct hit, and the whole ornate stern appeared to fall inboard as the massive ball exploded within the poop, its packed charge of grape bursting amongst the crowded gun crews and turning the confined deck into a slaughterhouse.

As *Argonaute* continued to edge remorselessly around the enemy's broken stern, the murderous broadside swept across and into her. The lower gundeck had somehow found time to load with double shot, as if each officer knew it was their last chance before *Argonaute* was carried either past or into their enemy by the freshening wind.

Keen watched, chilled by what he saw, as the enemy's main topmast was carried away and one of the muzzles on the enemy's lower gundeck exploded in a sheet of fire. Some terrified seaman had forgotten to sponge out before a fresh charge was rammed home, or maybe the gun was old and had outworn those who crewed it.

Keen shouted, 'The Dons'll be up to us in an hour, sir, despite the wind! Shall we discontinue the action?'

More shots roared from *Argonaute*'s lower battery, the long thirty-two-pounders wreaking terrible havoc on the other vessel, which now appeared to be out of control with either her helm shot away or none left to take charge aft.

Bolitho did not speak and Keen swung round on him, fearful that a marksman had found him.

But Bolitho was staring towards the other ship, his head on one side as if to force a clearer view.

Keen persisted, 'She'll not fight again for a long, long while, sir!'

'Has she struck?'

Keen stared at him. He barely recognized Bolitho's voice. Curt, with all pity honed out of it.

'No, sir.'

Bolitho blinked as a ball from the enemy cut through the shrouds and a man screamed shrilly like a woman in agony.

'She must *never* fight. Continue the action.' He caught Keen's arm as he made to hurry away. 'If we leave her she'll anchor. I want her destroyed. Totally.'

Keen nodded, his mind reeling to the crash and roar of cannon fire, the excited chatter from the marines as they fired their long muskets, reloaded with almost parade-

ground precision, and then sought out fresh targets on the
enemy's decks.

He stared sickened as blood ran down the enemy's side;
he could imagine the horror between decks.

Paget stared up at him, his eyes very clear in his smoke-
grimed face.

Keen jerked his head and seconds later the broadside
thundered out, measured and deliberate, with barely a gun
firing back in reply. Keen watched through his telescope
and saw the Frenchman's foremast begin to dip through
the smoke.

He gestured to Stayt, who snatched up a speaking
trumpet and then climbed nimbly into the mizzen shrouds.

'*Abandonez!*' But only musket shots answered him.

Argonaute's sails filled and gathered the wind as
Fallowfield guided her clear of the drifting, dismasted
hulk.

Keen glanced quickly at Bolitho but there was no change
in his expression.

Keen raised his hanger, then thought of the girl who
was sheltering in the hold far below his feet and the corpses
that lolled by the guns. Someone had mercifully thrown
some torn canvas over the ship's boy who had been halved
by the enemy's iron.

It was no longer a battle. The enemy was like a helpless
beast, waiting for the fatal blow to fall.

He saw the nearest gun-captain watching him, his
trigger-line already taut.

'Prepare to fire!' He heard his order being piped to the
lower gundeck and braced himself for the broadside.

A voice shouted, 'White flag, sir!'

Keen looked at Bolitho, half expecting him to order the
broadside to be unleashed.

Bolitho felt his glance and turned towards him. He could
see only a misty outline, the blue and white of Keen's
clothing, the fairness of his hair. His eye stung with smoke
and strain, but he managed to keep his voice level as he
said, 'Order them to abandon ship. Then sink her.'

Paget called, 'There's a lot of smoke, sir. I think she
may have taken fire.'

Bolitho waited for the deck to settle then walked across to the quarterdeck rail. He heard faint shouts from the other vessel, smelt the breath of charred rigging which at any moment might turn the beaten ship into an inferno.

He said quietly, 'War is not a game, Val, nor is it a test of honour for friend or foe.' His tone hardened. 'Think of *Supreme*. There was no mercy for poor Hallowes, and I will offer none to the enemy.' He turned and walked to the opposite side, his foot slipping on blood where the marine had fallen when the ball had missed Bolitho by mere inches.

Paget yelled, 'No, it's the yawl which has taken afire, sir!'

Keen raised his glass and saw the smaller vessel drifting clear of the two-decker. To his astonishment he could see men leaping overboard, making no attempt to quench the flames. A stray ball from *Argonaute*'s last broadside perhaps, or maybe some burning canvas had dropped from the two-decker's broken spars like a torch to a fuse.

Bolitho must have heard the busy speculation on the quarterdeck and said sharply, 'Get the ship under way, if you please! That yawl must have been loading powder aboard the Frenchman!'

Calls twittered and men rushed yet again to their stations while others spread out on the yards above the pock-marked sails as their ship slowly turned towards the welcoming horizon.

The explosion was like a volcano erupting, catching men in their various attitudes of shock or dismay, and shaking the hull as if to carry vengeance even to *Argonaute*.

The two-decker's hidden side took the full blast of the explosion, and even as the water began to descend again like a ragged curtain she started to heel over. The explosion, which had completely obliterated the yawl without leaving even a floating spar to mark her passing, must have stove in the two-decker's bilge like a reef.

Keen watched, his mind refusing to contain the swiftness and the horror of the explosion. Much nearer and *Argonaute* might have shared the same fate.

Bolitho crossed the quarterdeck and paused to face the silent group of young officers there.

'That will save *us* the trouble, gentlemen.'

He turned to see Allday was marking his line of retreat. The smoke had played havoc with his eye and he could barely see their faces. But their shock was plain enough, as he had meant it to be.

As he made his way aft several of the smoke-blackened seamen raised a cheer: one, more daring than the rest, touched Bolitho's back as he passed.

Keen's men, *his* men. He wished those at home who took such people for granted could see them now. They did not care about the cause or the reason, and none had come to this place of his own free will. They fought like lions, for each other, for the ship around them. It was their world. It was enough.

He thought of the disbelief in Keen's voice when he had ordered him to continue the action. For those few moments he had felt something more than anger, more than the hurt which had been done to him by the shot which had all but blinded him. It had been hate. Something white hot and without mercy which had almost made him order another broadside. The enemy had already been defeated before some half-crazed soul had raised a white flag on a boathook. He considered it warily, almost fearfully. *Hate.* It was beyond his reckoning, as alien as cowardice, like another person.

The deck tilted and, with the wind filling her newly spread maincourse, *Argonaute* stood away from the dying ship and the great spread of flotsam and floundering survivors. They at least would be picked up by the Spaniards.

Keen had watched his face, had seen the effect of his callous remark on his youthful lieutenants and midshipmen.

Keen had seen Bolitho in almost every situation and if he loved any man he would look no further. But at moments like this he felt as if he knew him not at all.

*

Tuson wiped his fingers individually on a small towel and regarded Bolitho sternly.

'Much more of this, Sir Richard, and I cannot answer for your sight.'

He expected a sharp retort but was more shocked to see that Bolitho did not seem to notice. He had moved to the stern windows and sat staring at the glittering water astern, listless, the life drained out of him.

The ship echoed and quivered to the bang of hammers, the squeal of tackles as fresh cordage was run up to the yards to replace that lost or damaged in the swift battle.

There was almost a carefree atmosphere throughout the ship. It was their victory. Five men had been killed and two more had been badly wounded. Tuson had described the rest as mere knocks and scrapes. The fierceness of their attack had cut down their losses more than Bolitho had believed possible. He had heard what Tuson had said; there was no point in arguing or disputing it.

Through the thick glass he could see the misty outline of *Icarus*, her topsail almost white in the noon sun. *Rapid* was on station ahead and, apart from the repairs and the five burials, there was little to show for the destruction of a French third-rate. Keen had noted that her name was *Calliope* before the terrible Smasher had reduced her stern to boxwood.

Tuson was saying, 'If you want my advice, sir – '

Bolitho looked towards him. 'You are a good man. But what advice? When I try to walk I lose my footing like a drunken sailor, and I can scarcely tell one man from another. *What* advice?'

'You won a battle despite these things, sir.'

Bolitho gestured vaguely towards the screen. '*They* won it, man.'

'You could request another flag-officer – ' Tuson persisted stubbornly as Bolitho turned on him, 'so that you could obtain better treatment.'

'I do not command in the Mediterranean, and I'll not ask favours even of Nelson. The French will come out, I know it,' he touched his chest. 'Here, I feel it.'

'And the girl? What of her?'

Bolitho leaned back and felt the sun deceptively hot through the glass against his shirt.

'I shall make arrangements.'

Tuson gave the nearest thing to a smile. 'You do not wish to *involve* me, is that it, sir?'

There was a tap at the door and Keen stepped into the cabin. In the three days since the battle he had barely been off his feet, but, like his company, the swift victory had removed the strain, the earlier uncertainty.

Keen did not look at the surgeon in case he should discover bad news.

He asked, 'Are you well, sir?'

Bolitho gestured to a chair. 'No worse, anyway.'

Keen watched him, the way Bolitho tapped one foot on the canvas deck covering.

'*Rapid* has signalled a vessel to the sou'west, sir. Small one closing under all sail.'

'I see.'

Keen tried to conceal his concern. Bolitho sounded uninterested. All the fire and determination he had shown when they had dished up the Frenchman seemed to have vanished.

The marine sentry shouted, 'Midshipman-o-th'-watch, sir!'

Keen sighed and walked to the screen door. He looked at the small untidy figure and asked, 'Well, Mr Hickling, don't keep me in suspense.'

The boy screwed up his face as he tried to remember his message, word for word.

'Mr Paget's respects, sir.' His eyes moved past Keen to the other cabin, to Bolitho framed against the glittering seascape. Hickling was only just thirteen, but had been on the lower gundeck throughout the engagement and had seen one man cut down by splinters. And yet he seemed unchanged, Keen thought.

Hickling continued, 'The sail is reported as the brig *Firefly*, sir.'

Bolitho lurched to his feet and exclaimed, 'Are they sure?'

Hickling watched his admiral curiously and without awe. He was even too young for that.

'Mr Paget says that *Rapid* is quite certain of it, Sir Richard.'

Bolitho touched the midshipman's shoulders. '*Good* news.'

Hickling stared at his hand, not daring to move as Bolitho added, 'Your lieutenant spoke highly of your behaviour under fire. Well done.'

The midshipman hurried away and Keen said quietly, 'That was good of you, sir. Not many would care.'

He watched Bolitho return to the bench seat, noticed the way he took deliberate steps, as if feeling the ship's movement, looking for a trap.

Bolitho knew Keen was watching him, feeling for him. *How can I share it? How can I tell him that I am beside myself with worry? Hate, revenge, callousness, they should play no part in my life, and yet –*

He said, 'I care because I have not forgotten, Val. When I was his age, you too, remember it? Kicked and bullied, neither respected nor trusted, when one kind word could make all that difference?' He shook his head. 'I hope I never forget while I breathe.'

The surgeon walked past with his bag. 'Good day, gentlemen.' He looked at Keen. 'I trust, sir, now that young Mr Bolitho is drawing near, we may get an ally in this trying situation.'

Bolitho frowned. 'Bloody man!'

Keen closed the door. 'He makes good sense.'

The sudden shock made Bolitho start. Adam did not know. What would he think?

Keen said gently as if he had read his thoughts, 'Your nephew is already proud of you. So am I.'

Bolitho did not reply and was still staring astern when Keen left to go on deck.

Keen nodded to his officers and studied the clear sky. Bright but cool. He walked to the rail and glanced down at the maindeck, the marketplace as Bolitho called it. The sailmaker and his crew were busy with their needles and palms, repairing, preserving. The boatswain and the carp-

enter were conferring on their stocks of timber, and there
was a heady smell of tar in the air.

But Keen was thinking of the aftermath to the battle.
Holding her in his arms, the relief, the unbelievable happiness which each gave to the other, like something pure
and bright being lifted from a blacksmith's furnace.

She had buried her face in his chest while he had held
her so closely that he had felt the remains of the scar on
her back through the shirt.

The last terrible explosion had bellowed against the hold
like a thunderbolt, Ozzard had told him. The girl had held
his hand and that of Millie the maid. She had more courage
than any of them, Ozzard had insisted.

Keen saw Allday by the restacked boats on their tier.
He looked angry, his face inches from the second
coxswain's. It looked bad. Like the surgeon, Keen was
beginning to regret Bankart's presence in the ship.

'Deck there! Sail, fine on th' larboard bow!'

Keen glanced at Paget and nodded. *Firefly*'s arrival could
not have been better timed. Young Hickling had no idea
how welcome his news had been.

News from home, perhaps a letter for the admiral. There
would be no time yet for anything from London about
Zenoria. But at least things were being done, war or no
war. He thought of her in his arms, how right it had felt,
and how he longed for her.

Paget watched him and turned away satisfied.

The captain looked happy. To any first lieutenant that
was more than enough.

Bolitho stood up yet again as familiar sounds thudded
overhead and voices murmured near the skylight. The
hands had been piped to the braces and the flagship was
preparing to heave-to and receive the brig's commander.

How he wanted to be there at the entry port when
Adam came aboard. But that was Keen's privilege, one
captain greeting another.

Bolitho heard the side party being mustered, some
marines falling in to do Adam his rightful honours.

It was not just tradition which kept him away, and Bolitho knew it. He was afraid of what his nephew would say and think when he met him.

Allday moved from the sleeping cabin and held out his coat for him. Bolitho was so preoccupied that for once he did not sense Allday's grim mood.

There might be a letter from Belinda, and she –

He raised his head as Paget's voice echoed along the deck.

Argonaute's helm went over and, with her sails flapping noisily, she swung heavily into the wind, swaying steeply for a while until the remaining sails were reset.

For a brief moment he had seen the brig through the streaming windows, her ensign making a dab of colour, like metal in the wind.

He wondered if *Firefly*'s arrival had been noted by some unseen fishing boat, her purpose already known by a spy at Gibraltar or a traitor in London?

He heard a boat passing close by, the bark of an order as the coxswain steered her towards the chains. Command. Adam had earned it twice over.

Allday watched him dully. He could not bear to see him so helpless and unsure. He had tried to shield him when they had engaged the Frenchman, fearful for Bolitho's safety as he had stood there, unwilling or unable to move away.

Bolitho said, 'It's good to have him back if only for a moment, eh, Allday? Inch will rejoin us in a day or so, then we will go and seek out Jobert together!'

Allday took down the old sword. He hated Jobert, what he had made Bolitho become.

Pipes trilled and the marines slapped their muskets. Bolitho saw it clearly, as he had a thousand times, for others and for himself.

It seemed to take an age before Yovell opened the outer screen door and Bolitho walked to greet him, careful to stay where he could reach support from a table or chair, desperate not to show it.

But there were two visitors, not one.

He grasped Adam's hands and knew that he already had the news.

'How is it, Uncle?' He did not try to hide his anxiety.

'Well enough.' He shied away from it. 'You are failing in your duty, sir, who is our visitor?'

Adam said, 'Mr Pullen.' He sounded uncomfortable. 'From the Admiralty.'

The man had a bony handshake. 'On passage for Malta, Sir Richard.' He sounded as if he was smiling. 'Eventually.'

'Well, be seated. Allday, fetch Ozzard.' He knew Adam was staring at him, measuring his hurt as Keen had done.

'And what brings you here, Mr, er, Pullen?'

The man arranged himself in a chair. He was all in black. Like a carrion crow, Bolitho thought. He turned to keep the light behind him, knowing they would see the bandage and nothing more.

'I have certain affairs to manage in Malta, Sir Richard. Admiral Sir Hayward Sheaffe has given me instructions.'

Bolitho forced a smile. 'Secret, eh?'

'Certainly, Sir Richard.' As Ozzard hurried to him with a tray he said, 'Some watered wine will suffice, thank you.'

Adam said, 'I wish to speak with you, Uncle.'

Bolitho sensed something in his tone. 'Will it not keep?'

The man called Pullen took an envelope from his coat and laid it on the table. Bolitho stared at it, feeling trapped, stripped of his pretence. 'May I ask the same of you, Mr Pullen?'

The man shrugged. 'I would imagine that you have many things on your hands, Sir Richard. You have been in battle, although to glance around you you would scarce believe it.'

Bolitho controlled a sudden irritation. 'We destroyed a French seventy-four.' That was all he said.

'Excellent. Sir Hayward will be pleased.' He regarded the glass of watered wine. 'I'd not trouble you, Sir Richard, it is after all a nuisance but a necessity none the less. I am required to serve notice on your flag-captain to attend a court of inquiry in Malta with all dispatch.'

No wonder Adam had tried to warn him. Bolitho said calmly, 'To what purpose?'

Pullen seemed satisfied. 'Two bothersome reasons, I understand, Sir Richard. He behaved somewhat foolishly by ignoring a government warrant and then removing a woman,' his voice lingered on the word as if it were obscene, 'from custody. I feel he can explain his reasons no matter how misguided, but I must point out – '

'Who had made this accusation?'

Pullen sighed. 'It was a written report, Sir Richard. As I said, it should not concern or trouble you. A nuisance, nothing more.'

Bolitho said quietly, 'You are impertinent, sir. That woman was being abused, flogged! Captain Keen was doing his duty!'

'That is in the past, Sir Richard.'

Bolitho stared at him and replied, 'This is a battle-ground, *Mr* Pullen, not a safe and secure office. Here, *I* command. I could have you seized up and flogged to within an inch of your life and none would question my order.' He heard the man's quick intake of breath. 'It would be months before anyone acted on it, and I would like to know if you might call that a *nuisance!*'

Pullen swallowed hard. 'I meant no offence, Sir Richard.'

'Well, it was taken! Do you imagine that I'll stand by and permit a gallant officer to have his name smeared by this – this absurdity?'

Pullen leaned forward, his confidence returning. 'Then it is not true, any of it?'

'I do not have to answer that.'

Pullen stood up and placed his glass, still full, on the table. 'Not to me, sir. But you will see in your orders that you are also required to attend with your captain.'

Bolitho stared at him. 'Leave this station? Do you know what you are saying? Have you no conception of what the enemy intends to do?'

Pullen said, 'It is out of my hands, Sir Richard.' He gave a brief bow. 'If I may, I would like to withdraw while you decide.'

For a long moment Bolitho stood stock still beneath the skylight. It was like a bad dream. Like his failing sight. It must soon clear away.

Adam said bitterly, 'He explained nothing, Uncle. You did not tell me about this woman.' He hesitated. 'We must see that there is no gossip.'

Bolitho took his arm. 'She is aboard this ship, Adam.' He turned him slowly to face him. 'If that wretch made it sound coarse and indecent, he has done more harm than I imagined. She is a fine, brave girl, wrongly charged, falsely transported, and we shall prove it.'

The door opened and Keen walked slowly aft, his hat dangling from one hand.

Keen said, 'But in the meantime she will be sent in irons to another transport.' He looked at Adam. 'You see, I love her. I love her more than life itself.'

Adam glanced from one to the other, instantly aware of the strength of Keen's sincerity, of his uncle's compassion.

Adam said, 'Pullen plays cards.'

They both stared at him, at his dark features which had become so grim.

'I could accuse him of cheating and call him out – '

Bolitho crossed to his side and grasped his shoulders. 'Enough of that. We are in enough trouble. Keep your steel covered.' He squeezed his shoulders. 'Bless you.'

Adam said wretchedly, 'I have a letter from Lady Belinda.' He held it out. 'I think I know why you did not read Pullen's brief, Uncle.' He sounded shocked, stunned by the realization.

Bolitho asked, 'Do you have to leave immediately?'

'Aye.' Adam looked down and his unruly hair fell across his forehead. 'I heard about John Hallowes, Uncle. He was my friend.'

'I know.' They walked together to the screen. 'I shall have to quit the squadron when I am most needed, Adam, over this tragic affair. I will place Inch in command until we return.' He looked at Keen. 'Have no fear. I shall not desert that girl.'

Adam followed Keen to the quarterdeck and saw Pullen waiting by the entry port. Who was behind these accusations, he wondered? The fact that they were true seemed less important.

He touched his hat to the side party and then looked at Keen.

He said, 'You have my loyalty, sir.' He touched his sword. 'This too when and if you need it.' Then he followed Pullen into the boat.

Keen waited only until the gig was under oars and then crossed to his first lieutenant.

'We shall make sail as soon as a letter has been sent over to *Firefly* from the admiral.'

It was obvious that Pullen had wanted to remain on board as an observer until they reached Malta where he would change his role to that of jailer. Now he would be there waiting for them, his determination sharpened by Bolitho's hostility.

'I'm sorry about all this, sir.' Paget flinched under Keen's stare but stood his ground. 'We all are. It's not fair.'

Keen dropped his eyes. 'Thank you. I once believed it was enough to fight a war. Apparently there are those who think we are better used fighting each other.'

A boat carried a hastily penned letter across to the brig and by the time dusk had closed in *Firefly* had already dipped below the horizon.

Keen walked the quarterdeck and watched the red sunset. *Firefly* had brought only bad news after all.

11

A Time for Caring

It was early morning when Bolitho made his way to the quarterdeck. Two days since *Firefly* had found them and Adam had given him the news.

Argonaute was lying comfortably on the larboard tack under topsails and jib, her decks damp from the night air, her seamen moving about in the half-light, clearing up loose lines and holystoning the poop under the supervision of their petty officers. There was a sickly smell from the galley funnel, and all hands would soon be dismissed for their breakfast.

Bolitho saw the officer-of-the-watch glance at him startled, then move hastily to the lee side. The helmsmen too straightened their backs when moments before they had been clinging to the big double wheel, tired after their watch, thinking only of breakfast, poor though it might be.

One or two of the seamen looked up at him from the maindeck. They had seen very little of Bolitho since the injury, and later the smoke of battle had hidden him better than any disguise.

He shaded his eye and stared towards the land. Purple and deep blue above a steely horizon. There were clouds about, rimmed with pink and gold from the sunrise. The sea was calmer and the deck much steadier.

He walked a few paces inboard, his hands grasped firmly behind him. When he sought out individual figures he felt his heart quicken. He could recognize all but those in shadow between the guns.

He called to the lieutenant in charge of the watch.

'Good morning, Mr Machan.' The officer touched his hat and hurried towards him.

'A fine day, Sir Richard.' He sounded confused and pleased.

Bolitho studied him. Detail by detail. He could see him better than he had dared hope and recalled how he had once mistaken Sheaffe for another officer entirely.

He realized that Machan was visibly wilting under his stare.

Bolitho said, 'Is *Helicon* in sight from the masthead?'

They had seen Inch's ship and her consort just as night had closed in, but daylight would bring them all together again except for *Barracouta* in her odd disguise, and they would be reduced again as soon as the flagship left for Malta.

It was madness, but Bolitho knew that the orders left nothing to chance or conjecture. If Keen was required to face a court of inquiry he must go in his own ship. To be sent as a passenger in some courier brig would be as good as condemning him and holding the door wide to a court-martial.

He found he was pacing again, and that Machan had returned to his place at the lee nettings. The news would spread, first through the lower deck, then to every ship in the squadron. The admiral was up and about again.

Bolitho allowed his mind to grapple with Belinda's letter. He was still not sure what he had expected. Her letter was not brief, but lacked any personal contact. She had written of the estate, of Ferguson's plans for extending the market garden, of the old exciseman whose wife was having another baby.

It had been a strange experience, but he had not wanted Yovell or Ozzard to read it to him. Instead he had asked for the girl to be brought aft and to do it. Belinda's voice had become hers, but the letter had been light and evasive, no mention of London or the coolness of their parting.

Bolitho paused as a shaft of sunlight lanced through the shrouds, then took the letter from his pocket. He held it to the light, careful to hide what he was doing from the officer-of-the-watch and his midshipman.

He could just make out some of the words. Yesterday it would have been impossible.

It ended, 'From your loving wife, Belinda.'

He recalled the sound of her name on Zenoria's lips, how it had moved him and made him vaguely uneasy because of it.

The girl had handed him the letter and had said, 'She is a fine lady, sir.'

Bolitho sensed her despair and her envy. Keen had told her about Pullen.

Bolitho had said, 'Sit closer.' When she had joined him he had taken her hands, remembering how he had removed his coat with the proud epaulettes the first time he had met her.

He had said, 'I shall keep my word, have no doubt of that.' He had sensed her disbelief as she had replied, 'How can you help me now, sir? They will be waiting.' He had heard her frightened determination. 'They'll not take me alive. Never!'

He had pressed her hands between his. 'What I tell you must be our secret. If you tell my captain, he will be an accomplice and there must be no more blame.'

She had hesitated. 'I trust you, sir. Whatever you say.'

Bolitho put the letter back in his pocket. He was still not sure how to deal with the matter. But her spirits must be held high. Otherwise, she might throw herself overboard or do some other injury to herself rather than face arrest and custody again.

The masthead lookout yelled, 'Deck there, sail in sight to the sou'east!'

Bolitho could picture Inch's ship, her sails like pink shells in the frail sunshine as she headed towards *Argonaute*.

He thought of the girl again. She would soon hear of the other ship's arrival. Another turn of the screw, hastening her passage to Malta and heartless authority.

Keen came on deck, hatless and without a coat. He stared at Bolitho and made to explain.

Bolitho smiled. 'Easy, Val. I could not sleep. I needed to walk.'

Keen grinned with relief. 'Just to see you on deck again is like a tonic, sir!'

He became serious. 'I do not wish to burden you further, but – '

Bolitho interrupted. 'I have a plan.'

'But, sir, – '

Bolitho held up his hand. 'I know what you will say, that you will insist that the responsibility is yours. You are wrong. My flag flies over this squadron, and while it does I will pilot the affairs of my officers and in particular those of my own captain.' His voice sounded bitter as he added, 'Ever since my brother deserted to the American Navy there have been those who have been eager to bring discredit on my family. My father suffered because of it, and more than once I have been a ready target for their malice and plotting. Adam too, but then you know that. So I shall not have you brought down merely because it might hurt me.'

'You really think that someone intends you harm, sir?'

'I have no doubts at all. But nobody will expect me to release you from responsibility and take it on myself.' No wonder Pullen, the carrion crow, had seemed so confident. The realization chilled him, angered him with the same intensity as when he had almost ordered the last broadside on the French two-decker.

He heard himself say, 'Let me deal with it my own way, Val. Then we can go after the *real* enemy, if it is not already too late!'

Keen watched him and saw the emotions, like the lines on a chart. Perhaps Bolitho's injury had affected his reasoning more than he realized. Keen had heard about the attacks on Bolitho's family, the way it had been used in the past to prevent promotion or stem recognition which had been bravely earned.

But surely, in the middle of a campaign, nobody would be mad enough to exploit such deep-rooted malevolence?

Keen said, 'Just so long as Zenoria is safe, sir.'

'She is merely being used, Val. I'm certain of that.' He turned as the midshipman called, '*Rapid*'s signalling, sir!'

Bolitho watched the flags breaking from the yard and heard Keen say, 'You can *see* the signal, sir!'

Bolitho tried to conceal his excitement. 'Well enough.' He turned towards the poop. The other bandage would come off and to hell with Tuson's gloomy predictions. When Inch came aboard he would find his admiral again, not some faltering cripple. He strode beneath the poop and only once lost his balance as the ship dipped into a long trough.

The scarlet-coated sentry made to open the door for him but Bolitho said, 'No need, Collins. I can manage.'

The marine gaped after him, astonished that Bolitho had even remembered his name.

Yovell looked up startled from the desk, his spectacles awry as he saw Bolitho stride through the door.

'I want to prepare some instructions for Captain Inch of the *Helicon*, Mr Yovell. After that I will receive that gentleman on board before we part company again.' He watched Yovell opening drawers and searching for a new pen.

'And after that I shall want Midshipman Hickling to lay aft, if you please.'

Yovell nodded. 'I understand, Sir Richard.'

Bolitho eyed him keenly. *You don't, but never mind.*

Yovell said, 'The surgeon is waiting to see you, sir.'

Bolitho leaned both hands on his chair to study himself in the mirror. The small cuts had almost healed, and his eye looked almost normal. Even the occasional pricking sensation was less noticeable.

He said, 'Send him in.' He tugged the bandage. 'I have a job for him directly.'

Allday came through the other door and watched anxiously as Bolitho prepared to remove the bandage.

'If you're *sure*, sir?'

'I shall want you to perform as a barber later on.'

Allday glanced at Bolitho's black hair. It looked suitable, he thought. But he knew better than to say or do anything which might dampen Bolitho's new mood.

Tuson made no bones about it; he even raised his voice as he said hotly, 'If you won't listen to me, at least wait until you can be examined by someone more qualified, sir!'

The bandage had fallen to the deck and Bolitho had tried not to flinch or bunch his fists as Tuson had examined the eye for the hundredth time.

'It is no better,' he said at length. 'If you will but rest it, I – '

Bolitho shook his head. The vision was misty, clouded, but the pain held back as if surprised by his sudden action.

'I *feel* better, that is the important thing.' He turned to Tuson and added simply, 'Try to understand, my friend.'

Tuson closed his bag angrily. 'If you were a mere common seaman, Sir Richard, I'd say you were a damned fool.' He shrugged. 'But you are not, so I will say nothing.'

Bolitho waited until the door closed then massaged his eye until he realized what he was doing.

Then he stared at himself in the mirror for several seconds. He would find and destroy Jobert's squadron no matter what. And, like Inch, when his men looked to him at the cannon's mouth, they must find confidence and not lose heart.

To the cabin at large he said, 'So let us be about it!'

During the five and a half days it took for *Argonaute* to take passage to Malta Bolitho remained for much of the time in his quarters. It allowed Keen time and scope to complete his repairs, and to change his watch-bill whenever he discovered a weakness in his company. Gun and sail drill, he kept them at it on each monotonous day. They might curse their captain, but the results were clear to Bolitho as he heard the creak of gun trucks on deck or the yells of the petty officers as they drove some reluctant landmen aloft to the dizzy yards.

As he studied his orders and information he was conscious of their slow progress, sometimes only six knots, often less. He became very aware that it would take just as long to return to his patrol area if the enemy decided to move.

He trusted Inch as a skilful and experienced captain. He did not lack initiative, but often hesitated about using it. It troubled Bolitho, for over the years Inch with his eager horse-face had become like a brother.

Keen reported as soon as the masthead had sighted the island.

'It will be late afternoon, maybe in the dog watches, before I can anchor, sir, unless the wind freshens.'

Bolitho looked at him and saw Keen trying not to stare at his unbandaged eye. It was never mentioned now but it was always there, like a threat.

'Very well. I shall come on deck when we enter the Grand Harbour.'

Keen left him alone and Bolitho sat down in his new chair. What would the next move be? An order to remove him because of his injury? Replace him entirely? It was all too much of a coincidence to think, as Keen probably did, that he was imagining it.

There had been many letters sent home from the squadron in *Firefly*.

Bolitho frowned as he pictured his officers, his captains. Houston of the *Icarus* was the most likely. Anger and an obvious resentment made him first choice. He certainly had no love for either his admiral or his flag-captain.

He went on deck only briefly to train a telescope on the blue hump of islands as Malta appeared to drift sleepily towards them. He made up his mind. If things went badly wrong nothing he could say would save their accusations, or the girl either. But he had to be ready. He knew Keen had been to visit the girl in her cabin. It would have been a difficult farewell, each trusting Bolitho, neither knowing if or when they might ever meet again. They could not even speak freely with Tuson and a marine sentry close by.

Bolitho returned to his cabin. 'Ozzard, send for Allday. Now.' He walked to the windows and watched a small high-prowed fishing boat bobbing astern. Malta, fought over, won and lost, now accepting the Navy's protection more as a defence against the French than from any sense of loyalty.

Allday had obviously been very near. He entered the cabin and waited, his face expressionless as he gauged Bolitho's mood.

Bolitho said, 'Fetch her, please.'

Allday took a deep breath. 'I'm not at all certain about it, Sir Richard.'

'About what, old friend? You have heard *nothing*.'

Allday sighed. It was fine now, but there would be squalls later if it misfired.

He padded from the cabin, an unspoken argument left hanging in the air.

Bolitho swore silently as the deck tilted and he heard the clatter of blocks and helm as the ship altered course slightly. He had almost lost his balance again. It was unnerving, like the mist which hung over his eye like a piece of fine silk.

The door opened, then Allday closed it behind her.

'It is almost time.' Bolitho led her to a chair and watched her grip its arms, making a lie of her composure.

He walked behind her and touched her long hair. 'Are you sure, brave Zenoria?'

She nodded and held the chair even more tightly.

Allday muttered hoarsely, 'Lie back, Miss.'

She laid her head on the chairback and after a brief hesitation unbuttoned her shirt and bared her neck.

Bolitho took her hand. No wonder Keen adored her.

Allday said despairingly, 'I can't do it, sir. Not like this.'

She said quietly, 'Do it. Please. Now.'

Allday released a great sigh and then pulled her hair out behind her, his scissors poised like steel jaws.

Bolitho watched the hair falling to the deck and said, 'I will be on deck.' He squeezed her hand; it was like ice in spite of the cabin's humid air. 'Allday will care for you.' Then he bent down and kissed her gently on the cheek. 'Your courage will yet sustain all of us, Zenoria.'

Later, as he joined Keen on the quarterdeck and watched the white forts and harbour opening up to receive the slow-moving seventy-four, he had forcibly to restrain his anxiety.

The salutes began to boom across the placid water and a flag dipped above the nearest battery.

There were many ships at anchor and several large men-of-war. He raised a telescope and held it carefully to his good eye. A smart two-decker lay nearest to the jetty, a rear-admiral's flag flapping only occasionally from her mizzen.

He felt a catch in his throat. There was no mistaking the *Benbow*. Pictures flashed through his mind. He had been a rear-admiral, when was it? Three years back in the Baltic when his nephew had been the ship's third lieutenant and Herrick his flag-captain.

He tried to thrust her fat black and buff hull from his mind as, with something close to physical force, he continued to examine the busy anchorage.

Thank God. The lens settled on a sturdy brig which was anchored almost end on. No wonder he had not seen her. He waited impatiently for the gentle breeze to swing her again on her cable until the sunlight glinted on her gilded counter.

Bolitho read her name, *Lord Egmont,* although he already knew it well. She was one of the oldest in the fleet of Falmouth packets; he had known her since he had been a junior lieutenant.

He had felt certain she would be here; he had seen her name in his Admiralty instructions. But wind and sea, a change of events could have altered things, and even now –

He lowered the glass and the brig fell away into hazy distance again.

The last smoke from the salute still hung over the yards as men were piped to hoist out the two cutters in case the wind was insufficient to turn the ship at her anchorage. A swaying guardboat with a limp anchor flag in her bows waited, pinned down on the glittering water, probably the only interested group to watch their arrival. Warships were too common for comment; only the transports and the mail carriers from England excited real attention nowadays.

Keen cupped his hands. 'Be ready to let go, Mr Paget!'

He glanced quickly at Bolitho, his expression suddenly apprehensive, but not for himself.

Bolitho shaded his eyes and stared at the waterfront with its ancient fortifications and busy markets. A sailor's port, a warren of activity. He bit his lip. A place for spies too.

The admiral would be watching; Pullen too.

Keen said, '*Firefly*'s already gone, sir.'

'Aye.' Adam at least would be well out of it, no matter how he wanted to help. Is it something about us, the Cornish, he wondered? A senior officer had once told him to his face, 'Cornishmen? Pirates and rebels the whole bunch of you!'

It seemed to take an age before *Argonaute* finally took up her anchorage, her sails furled neatly to her yards. Awnings were spread and the ship settled down to await events.

Bolitho watched the boats coming to the chains, the officer-of-the-guard, a chandler from the dockyard, an embarrassed-looking ensign from the garrison who had come to collect Millie the maid. She seemed unwilling to leave and, despite the grins of the watching sailors, clung to the ship's corporal as if her life depended on it.

Keen watched from the poop, his thoughts elsewhere as visitors and some of his own officers waited to make their claims upon his time.

He saw Lieutenant Stayt speaking with the boatswain and then a party of seamen loosening the lashings on the barge in readiness for hoisting her outboard.

Bolitho was going ashore. Earlier than he had expected, and it made him uneasy.

The officer-of-the-guard touched his hat and handed Keen an official-looking envelope. He looked ill at ease, like someone performing his duty against his nature, but at the same time afraid of being tainted by too close a contact.

It was a summons from the admiral's headquarters to appear before a court of inquiry two days hence. The flag-officer-in-charge must have sent it as soon as *Argonaute*'s sails had been sighted.

Stayt waited for the guardboat to leave the chains and then came aft.

'I have to take Sir Richard's dispatches to the flag-officer here, sir.'

Keen nodded. So Stayt was taking the barge. That explained it. He noticed that Bankart, the second coxswain, was in charge of the bargemen. That was unusual, he thought. Allday usually handled her when they were in harbour or under the eyes of the fleet.

He heard Midshipman Hickling request permission to take the jolly boat to a nearby merchantman, and Paget's approval when he learned that there was a message to be carried across from the admiral.

Keen glanced up at the flag. When it was hauled down again it might mean the end for both of them.

Midshipman Sheaffe hurried up to the poop ladder and said, 'The admiral's compliments, sir, and would you see him at eight bells.'

Keen tightened his jaw. If Bolitho had any good news for him he would not wait for another hour.

Almost savagely he called to Paget, 'I want all boats lowered. Send a lieutenant in each one to examine the hull.'

It was unlikely that they had overlooked any damage from the brief battle, and Keen knew he was being unfair to give them extra work.

Eventually Keen heard the bell chime from the fore-castle. It was time.

He thought suddenly of his home in Hampshire. It would be cold there, probably wet too as the villagers prepared for winter and, if need be, an attempted invasion by the French. What would his brothers and sisters say when they heard the news of his court-martial, and he could see no alternative to one. His father would be distressed, especially as he had been against his youngest son entering the Navy in the first place.

He passed the sentry and stepped into the glowing lights of the stern cabin.

Keen was surprised to find Bolitho dressed in his long

boat cloak, and for an instant imagined that Stayt had misunderstood his orders.

But Bolitho said calmly, 'I am going ashore, Val. I will take your gig, if I may.' He gave a quick smile as if he was on edge. 'Less formal, I thought.'

Keen said, 'The ship is secured, sir, and both watches have been stood down.'

Bolitho watched him gravely. 'Except for certain lieutenants, I gather?' He nodded. 'Good. Never trust to luck where hull damage is concerned.'

Allday padded across the cabin and took down the old sword.

Keen watched. So Bolitho was not going to visit the admiral who commanded in Malta? It was getting a bit late for formalities anyway, he decided.

Bolitho settled his sword against his hip and said, 'Take charge of the gig, Allday.' He glanced towards the stern windows. The thick glass was twinkling with countless lights from the shore. Like the dawn, the night came swiftly.

There was a quick exchange of glances, but Bolitho faced Allday steadily and said, 'We don't have much time.'

Allday looked at Keen but said nothing.

They were alone. Bolitho said, 'I shall be aboard the *Lord Egmont* before I step ashore.'

Keen nodded. He had seen the packet preparing to up-anchor, men swarming on her deck to secure some extra cargo, probably her master's own booty.

Bolitho said, 'This were better done quickly, Val.' He raised his voice. 'Are you ready?'

Keen stared as the midshipman entered from the opposite screen door.

'I did not realize you were – '

He stared as the girl met his gaze and looked at him. She was dressed in a complete midshipman's uniform, and even wore a finely gilded dirk at her side.

Keen stepped towards her, his hands outstretched as she removed her hat, and he saw what Allday had done to her hair. It was short, the ends tied neatly with a black ribbon

as befitted a 'young gentleman' about to take charge of his
admiral's boat.

Bolitho watched them, suddenly glad of what he was
doing. With a court of inquiry about to begin and the
enemy stirred into the mood for revenge, there was little
room for mere people.

He said, 'I'll be on deck. No side party, eh?'

As the door closed Keen took her in his arms. He could
feel her heart pounding against him despite the padding
she wore beneath her shirt to disguise her figure.

'You did not tell me?' Even as he said it he guessed what
Bolitho had done, his sudden agitation as they had entered
harbour. The *Lord Egmont* would be sailing to Falmouth.
She was as familiar there as Pendennis Castle.

'He asked me to remain silent.' She looked up at him,
her lashes shining in the soft lights. 'I have a letter and
some money, in case – '

He hugged her against him still tighter. He had prayed
for her safety, even if it meant losing her. But now that
the moment had come he could scarcely bear it.

She said softly, 'Now I must tell you, my dearest one.
You must be brave. For both of us.'

A boat clattered alongside and Keen heard Allday's voice
taking command.

'When I reach England – '

She put her hands to his face and held it. 'I will be
waiting.' She watched him steadily. 'No matter what
happens, I shall be there. For you.' She kissed him slowly
and then stood away. 'I love thee, my dear captain.'

He watched her replace her hat and tilt it over her eyes.
She was very contained, like brittle steel.

'Ready, *sir?*'

He nodded, wanting to hold her again, but knowing it
would finish both of them.

'Carry on, if you please, *Mr* Carwithen.'

It was almost dark on deck and Keen saw that the
lantern by the entry port had been doused.

The boat was waiting below the stairs, and there were
few figures on deck to notice that someone was leaving
the ship.

Keen saw that Tuson was there, Paget too, but nobody spoke; even the master-mate of the watch stood back as Bolitho passed, as if he did not exist.

Keen brushed her arm, the small contact tearing him apart.

'It is their way. They will miss you too.'

She looked into the gloom and then touched her hat before she clambered down the side.

Bolitho glanced at Keen. 'The *Lord Egmont*'s master is an old friend, Val. I made certain he was still in command before I entrusted our passenger to his care.' He flung his cloak over one shoulder. 'There is not a moment to delay.'

Keen said, 'We were just in time, sir.'

Bolitho looked down into the boat where Allday would be worrying about his descent.

'A time to care, Val. There must always be room for that.'

Then without another glance he lowered himself down to the boat. As the oars slashed at the water Keen could just see Allday in the sternsheets, one hand covering hers on the tiller, but hidden from the oarsmen by Bolitho's shoulders.

Ozzard bounded across the deck and exclaimed in a desperate whisper, 'The gown, sir! She's forgot it!'

Keen watched until the gig had merged with the anchored shadows and then replied, 'No matter. I shall hand it to her myself, in England.'

Divided Loyalties

The residence of the flag-officer-in-charge of all His Majesty's ships, stores and dockyards in the island of Malta was a fine, imposing building.

After the dusty sunlight of the streets Bolitho found the room to which he had been ushered both welcome and cool. One long window looked out across the harbour, the crowded ships at the anchors, the criss-crossing wakes of cutters and gigs as the Navy got down to work for another day.

Waiting. In the Navy you always seemed to be doing it. As a midshipman or lieutenant, and even as a captain. When did it cease, he wondered?

He thought of the brig *Lord Egmont* and pictured her under full sail and heading for the Rock. She would not pause there for fear of fever, but would head out to the Atlantic and drop anchor only when she was in Carrick Roads, within sight of the Bolitho home.

He thought too of the brig's small cabin, and her master, Isaac Tregidgo, facing him across the table.

The master had a face like a block of weathered wood, lined and scarred by years at sea, fast passages and quick rewards. Tregidgo's name was legendary even amongst other masters in the Falmouth Packet Service. Storms, fever, piracy and war, the old man had faced them all. He must be over seventy, Bolitho thought, and he had known him all his life. Even his greeting had been typical.

'Sit ye down, Dick.' He had grinned hugely as Bolitho had dropped his boat cloak. 'An' I hears yewm been honoured by King George, no less,' he had wheezed in the thick air of pipe smoke and brandy. 'But yewm still Dick to me!'

Bolitho had heard the girl moving about in the adjoining cabin. It was little more than a hutch, but it was safe.

The master had eyed him curiously. 'Might 'ave guessed yewd be up to summat, admiral's flag or not.' He had raised a fist like a smoked ham. 'Not to worry, Dick. She's safe with me. I knows me crew are a bunch o' roughknots, but I often carry me grandchildren on short passages. The men knows better'n to cuss an' blaspheme in front o' them!' He had shaken the fist grimly. 'I'll give any man, even me own kin, a striped shirt at the gangway if I catches 'im at it!'

The brig had stirred at her cable and old Tregidgo had squinted at the deckhead. 'Wind's favourin' me, Dick.' He had added slowly, 'I'll see 'er right, just like you said in yer letter.' He had watched him from beneath his sprouting white brows.

'Yewm not seeing too well, are yew, Dick?' He had turned aside to hide his compassion. 'God will watch 'e.'

The girl had entered the cabin self-consciously, the midshipman's coat and dirk in her hands.

'Keep the shoes.' Bolitho held her hands. 'Mr Hickling will not miss them. You will have to remain a youth until you reach Falmouth.'

She had watched him with that same misty stare he had first seen. It was like an unspoken question. He was still not sure how to answer it.

He had said, 'I am sending you to my sister Nancy. She will know what to do.' He had gripped her hands tightly, knowing she would pull away as he added, 'Her husband is the squire and the senior magistrate.'

'But, sir, he'll have me – '

He had said, 'No. I am not overkeen on the man, but he will not fail over this.'

He wrapped his cloak around him and reached for the companion.

She had said, 'I shall never forget you, Sir Richard.'

He had turned to see the tears in her eyes, the sad beauty

which even her shorn hair and crumpled shirt could not conceal.

'Nor I you, brave Zenoria.'

On deck he had found the bewildered Hickling waiting for him. A midshipman had left with him. One would return. He had handed him his coat and dirk. Hickling would be safe, no matter what happened. No one could blame a mere midshipman for obeying his vice-admiral.

By the bulwark the old man said, 'I 'ear you've one o' th' Stayt boys as yer aide, Dick? From up north?'

Bolitho smiled. To a Cornishman 'up north' meant merely the opposite strip of coastline.

'Yes.' There were no secrets for long in Cornwall. Except from the revenue officers.

Tregidgo had gestured in the darkness towards the skylight.

'She's best along of me then.'

'Why d'you say that?'

'Well, 'er father was mixed up in the trouble near Zennor when a man got killed, an' the dragoons was called. Stayt was a magistrate, like the one who's wed to yer sister,' he had wheezed. 'The one they calls th' King o' Cornwall.'

The master had leaned closer and had murmured, 'It was 'im wot 'anged 'er father. I'm fair surprised young Stayt didn't mention that?'

So am I. Bolitho had lowered himself into the boat and had told Allday to head for the jetty. He had to think and he knew that Keen would want to see him as soon as he returned.

Sentries had barred his way to the repair docks until he had thrown off his cloak and they had stared with astonishment at his epaulettes. Allday had followed him anxiously, watching each step in case he lost his balance and fell into a dock.

There were some lanterns by the dock where *Supreme* lay. In the gloom she looked as before, her wounds and state of repair hidden in shadow.

Allday had whispered, 'Goin' aboard, sir?'

'No.' Unwilling or unable, he still did not know. But he had walked along the rough stones until he had drawn

level with the taffrail where the ball had struck and flung
him down.

Now, standing in the sunlight by the window, *Supreme*
seemed like part of a strange dream. A cruel reminder.

He thought again of Tregidgo's words about Stayt. On
his way here to present himself to the flag-officer-in-
charge, Bolitho had been tempted more than once to ask
Stayt directly about it. His flag-lieutenant had said
nothing, even though he must have been aware that the
girl was no longer on board.

Bolitho had sent Stayt ashore in the barge to protect his
reputation and any suggestion of involvement. Or had he?
Was the mistrust already there?

Two servants threw open the high doors and Bolitho
turned to face the man who seemed to fill the entrance.

Sir Marcus Laforey, Admiral of the Blue, was gross to
a point which even his immaculate uniform could not hide.
He had heavy-lidded eyes and a wide mouth, and when
he walked with some difficulty to a chair Bolitho saw that
one of his legs was bandaged. Gout, the curse of several
admirals he knew.

Admiral Laforey sank carefully into the chair and
winced as a servant eased a cushion beneath his foot.

When seated he looked like an irritable toad, Bolitho
thought.

The admiral waved his handkerchief. 'Sit down,
Bolitho.' The lids lifted slightly in a quick appraisal.
'Bothersome about all this, what?'

Bolitho sat down and got the impression that his chair
had already been carefully positioned so as not to be too
close.

Laforey had been on one land appointment after
another, and had not been in command at sea since before
the war. He looked dried out, obscene, and Malta would
very likely be his last appointment. The next would be in
Heaven.

'Read the report, Bolitho. Good news about the French
seventy-four. Make 'em think, what?'

Bolitho tightened his hold on his sword. With the chair
half turned towards the window his vision was blurred.

He stared at a point beyond the admiral's fat shoulder and said, 'I believe the French will be out soon, sir. Jobert may be hoping to make a diversion so that the main fleet can slip out of Toulon. Egypt or the Strait of Gibraltar – '

Laforey grunted. 'Don't speak to me about Gibraltar! That bloody fever, not safe to let anything or anyone land here if they've been there en route. This place is like a ship aground, there's always some sort of sickness amongst the people an' the military.' He touched his brow with the handkerchief. 'Good wine is gettin' scarce. Spanish muck an' little else, dammit!'

He had not listened to a word, Bolitho thought.

Laforey stirred himself, 'Now about this court of inquiry, what?'

'My captain is accused – '

Laforey wagged a spatulate finger. 'No, no, dear fellow, not *accused!* Others may have to do that. It is all a mere formality. I have not read the details but my flag-captain and this Mr, er, Pullen from their lordships assure me that it will be a matter of hours rather than days.'

Bolitho said evenly, 'Captain Keen is possibly the best officer I have ever had under me, Sir Marcus. He has shown his courage and excellence on many occasions, from midshipman to command. In my opinion he should rate flag rank.'

Laforey's lids lifted again and beneath them the small eyes were cold and without pity.

'Bit young, I'd have thought. Too many inexperienced popinjays about these days, what?' He glared at his bandaged foot. 'If I could hoist my flag above the Channel Fleet instead of this, this – ' he stared round resentfully, 'I'd soon make the mothers' boys shed a few tears!'

He tried to lean forward but his belly prevented him.

'Now, see here, Bolitho, what really happened, eh?' He searched Bolitho's face as if for an answer. 'Needed a woman, did he?'

Bolitho stood up, 'I will not discuss my officers in this fashion, Sir Marcus.'

Surprisingly Laforey seemed pleased. 'Suit yerself. The court will sit tomorrow. If Captain Keen is sensible I am sure that you will be able to put to sea without further delay. There is a convoy due, and I cannot stand incompetence, anything which might make life here even more unbearable.' He watched as Bolitho stood up. 'I hear you were wounded too, Sir Richard?' He did not expand on it. 'It is part of our service.'

'Indeed, sir.' Bolitho could barely conceal the irony in his voice. 'There will be many more if the French succeed in joining their fleets together.'

Laforey shrugged. 'I am afraid I cannot entertain you longer, Sir Richard. My day is full. I sometimes wonder if their lordships and Whitehall realize the extent of my responsibility here.'

The interview was over.

Bolitho walked down a passageway and saw a servant with a tray carrying two decanters and a single goblet towards the room he had just left. The admiral was about to extend his responsibility, he thought bitterly.

Stayt was waiting for him in the marble lobby.

He watched curiously as Bolitho shaded his eyes to stare at the harbour. Then he said, 'You asked about the *Benbow,* sir. She has recently completed an overhaul here.'

'And whose flag has she hoisted?'

'I thought you would know, sir. She is Rear-Admiral Herrick's flagship.'

Bolitho turned towards the shadows in the lobby to contain his feelings. The last part of the pattern, as he had known there would be. It was not imagination, now he knew it, even before Stayt said, 'Rear-Admiral Herrick is to take the chair at the court of inquiry, sir.'

'I shall see him.'

'It might be unwise, sir.' Stayt's deepset eyes watched him calmly. 'It could be misconstrued, by some, that is.'

Thomas Herrick, his best friend, who had nearly died for him more than once.

In his mind he could see Herrick's eyes, clear blue, stubborn at times, too easily hurt, above all honest. Now the word 'honest' seemed to stand out to mock him.

Stayt said, 'There will be a letter awaiting you aboard

Argonaute, I understand, sir. You will not need to attend the court. A written statement will suffice.'

Bolitho turned towards him, his voice hard. 'Will you write one also?'

Stayt met his gaze without flinching. 'I am ordered to attend the court to give evidence, sir.'

It was like being snared in an invisible net which was being squeezed tighter every hour.

'I shall be there, be certain of that!'

Stayt followed him into the dusty sunshine and waited on the steps which faced the harbour.

Bolitho said, 'Did you imagine I would stand by and say nothing? Well, *did* you?'

'If there is anything I can do, sir – '

Bolitho felt his eye sting and knew it was anger rather than injury.

'Not for the present. You are dismissed. Return to the ship.'

He strode down towards the jetty where Allday stood by the barge. There were other *Argonaute* boats nearby and Stayt would have to use one of them.

The boat coxswains stood up and touched their hats as they saw him. Their routine did not allow for emotions like his. Stores had to be arranged, and the purser would have been ashore since first light to carry out his bargaining with chandlers and traders alike.

Bolitho said, 'To the *Benbow,* if you please.'

Allday watched him enter the barge without any show of surprise. Herrick was here. It was only proper they should meet, no matter what some might think. Mates were mates, high or low.

'Give way all!'

The green-painted barge slid through the busy thoroughfare, other boats raising their oars or backing water to allow a flag-officer to have free passage.

Bolitho sat stiffly in the sternsheets, only his eyes moving as he focused them on familiar things, masts and rigging, seabirds and small clouds above the fortress.

Damn Laforey and his drink-sodden indifference, and anyone else who had a part in this. He glanced at the

stroke oarsman and quickly along the bronzed faces of the
barge crew. They all knew. Probably the whole fleet did
too. Well, let them.

Vague thoughts flashed through his mind, of Belinda's
letter, of Stayt's cool demeanour as he had mentioned his
summons to the inquiry, and of Inch and the squadron
who expected him to be above mere human reactions – or
did they?

It would certainly not be the first time he had acted
against the dictates of authority. He gave a small, bitter
smile. It must run in the family. His father, who to his
sons had always appeared as the stern, model example of
a sea officer, had once fallen out with his army equivalent
during a siege in the East Indies. Captain James Bolitho
had solved the problem by arresting the soldier for negli-
gence and then going on to win the battle. Had he lost it,
Bolitho had no doubt that the family's naval connection
would have ended there.

Allday murmured, 'She looks proud, Sir Richard.'

It sounded unusually formal. Allday never forgot
himself when others were present. Well, hardly.

The seventy-four-gun *Benbow* did indeed make a fine
sight. Newly painted, and her rigging like black glass,
yards crossed with each sail furled to match its companion.
The ports were all open, and Bolitho had no difficulty in
hearing their fearful thunder at Copenhagen and later
against the French 'flying squadron'. It never failed to tear
at his memory, of the time he had been a prisoner of
France and his subsequent escape. Allday had been with
him then. Had carried the dying John Neale after his ship
had foundered. Yes, many memories lay stored within her
deep hull.

The barge swept round in a wide arc and he saw the
side party rushing to their station, the Royal Marines
dressing into lines. His unexpected arrival would get them
on the move. Bolitho smiled again. Wrong, Herrick would
have expected it.

Benbow must be almost ready for sea, he thought. Only
a few local boats lay alongside and just one tackle was
swaying up cargo nets to the men on the gangway.

Bolitho murmured, 'Stand off, Allday, I'll not be long.'

He saw Allday's face in the sunlight, caught it for just a moment as he carefully steered the sleek barge towards the main chains. Bolitho was shocked to see the strain on his strong features, ashamed that he had not thought about his worries over his son.

'Oars – *up!*' The pale oars rose dripping in twin lines, their blades perfectly matched. Allday had done well.

Up the tumblehome to the piercing twitter of calls and then the drums and fifes of the marines. Pipeclay floated like white dust above the guard as they presented arms for his benefit. And here was Thomas Herrick, hastening to meet him, his round face beaming, and letting the formality blow away like the pipeclay.

Herrick exclaimed, 'Come aft, *Sir* Richard.' He gave a shy smile. 'I'm not yet accustomed to it.'

Nor I, Bolitho thought as they strode beneath the familiar poop. Here, and here, men had locked weapons and died. Up there shot had raked away seamen and marines alike, and where two small midshipmen were listening intently to the sailing master he had been struck down.

In the great cabin it was warm although the windows and skylights were all wide open.

Herrick bustled round. 'The stench of paint and tar makes this place like Chatham Dockyard!'

A cabin servant was placing goblets on a tray, and Bolitho sat down beneath a skylight, his shirt already clinging to his skin. He watched Herrick affectionately. His hair was tufted with grey and his body was stockier, probably from married life and Dulcie's cooking.

But when he turned he seemed just as before. The same clear blue eyes, the searching curiosity as he looked at his friend, originally his captain in another war when mutiny had been a greater threat than the enemy.

'I saw young Adam when he was here, er, Richard.'

Bolitho took a goblet and placed it beside him. Claret. Herrick's taste had risen with his rank.

Herrick added, 'A fine brig. It'll be a frigate next, what he's always dreamed of, the rascal. If he stays out of trouble – ' He paused, his eyes suddenly worried. 'Well, anyway, here's to you, dear friend, and may Lady Luck stay with you.'

Bolitho reached for his goblet but missed it and caught it with his cuff. The wine spilled over the table like blood, and as Herrick and the servant hurried to help Bolitho said, 'No. I can manage!' It came out more sharply than he had intended and he said, 'I'm sorry, Thomas.'

Herrick nodded slowly and poured another goblet himself.

'I heard, of course, Richard. It was a shock.' He leaned over and stared at Bolitho for the first time. 'Yet I see nothing, no damage, except perhaps – '

Bolitho dropped his gaze. 'Aye, Thomas, *except, perhaps*, they sum it up very well.'

He drank the goblet without knowing what he had done.

'About the inquiry, Thomas.'

Herrick leaned back in his chair and regarded him gravely.

'It will be here, in this cabin, tomorrow.'

'It is rubbish, Thomas.' Bolitho needed to get up and move about as he had done so often in this place. 'God, you know Valentine Keen. He's a fine man, and is now an excellent captain.'

'Of course I remember everything about him. We've sailed together often enough.' He became serious. 'I cannot talk about the inquiry, Richard, but you know that, you have had this filthy job yourself.'

'Yes. My flag-lieutenant warned me that I should not come.'

Herrick watched him worriedly. 'He was right. Any sort of discussion would, might be seen as collusion. We are all friends.'

Bolitho stared hotly at the windows. 'I was beginning to wonder.' He did not see the hurt in Herrick's eyes. 'When I flew my flag here, and you commanded *Benbow*, young Val was captain of *Nicator*, remember?' He did not wait for a reply but hurried on, 'Then, when I went to the West Indies and we fought over that damned island

San Felipe, Val gave up a larger vessel to come to *Achates*, a little sixty-four, because I asked him to be my flag-captain.'

Herrick gripped the table. 'I know. I *know*, Richard, but the fact is that we are all here to conduct an inquiry. I have my orders, otherwise I would say nothing more about it.'

Bolitho tried to relax. Anything and everything seemed to seize him like claws since his injury. He picked up the goblet and knew Herrick was trying not to watch in case he knocked it over again.

He said, 'I shall come myself. I had no intention of sending a written statement, as if it were just a secondary matter. My captain's future is in danger, and I'll not stand by and see him slandered by enemies I can only guess at!'

Herrick stood up and gestured to the servant, who immediately withdrew. Another Ozzard.

Herrick said steadily, 'Keen behaved wrongly when he removed a prisoner from a ship under a government warrant. The fact that she is a woman could only add meat to the pot.'

Bolitho pictured the filthy convict transport and young Zenoria as he had last seen her. The girl who would carry a scar on her body for the rest of her life. She would have died but for Keen. Nobody could have foreseen what would transpire from that one savage incident. It was a miracle that her mind had not been equally scarred.

Herrick said, 'Had she been an ordinary, male prisoner – '

'Well, she was not, Thomas. She was wrongly charged and wrongly transported. God, man, they wanted her out of the way because of her father!'

Herrick shifted under Bolitho's angry stare. 'But others will say – '

Bolitho stood up. 'My warm wishes to Dulcie when next you write.'

Herrick was on his feet too. 'Don't leave like this, Richard!'

Bolitho breathed slowly to compose himself before he faced the side party and marine guard.

'Who else will be present? You can at least tell me that, surely?'

He did not hide his bitterness.

Herrick replied, 'Admiral Sir Marcus Laforey will be taking part, and the inquiry will be conducted by his flag-captain.' He said abruptly, 'The woman, is she still aboard *Argonaute*?'

Bolitho picked up his hat.

'And I cannot answer *that*, Thomas.' He walked through the door. 'It might be seen as collusion.'

It was unwarranted and unfair, Bolitho knew it. But there was more at stake now than strong words.

It would not require a bad verdict in the court of inquiry to damage Keen's future. Rumour would soon spread. It had to be stopped, overwhelmed like a forest fire under a cloudburst.

The two flag-officers walked to the entry port together, but Bolitho had never felt so isolated from his friend. He had known him longer even than Allday, who had been pressed aboard that same ship.

He hesitated as the first rank of scarlet coats moved into his vision. The colour-sergeant on the end, his eyes fixed on the nearest buildings along the shore, was strangely stiff, even anxious.

Bolitho hesitated and then the face came back. Helping him on that terrible day, just an ordinary marine then.

He said quietly, 'McCall, I remember you well.'

The sergeant remained rigid, his captain watching beyond Bolitho's shoulder. But his eyes moved and he said, 'Thank you, sir.' He hesitated as if afraid he was going too far. 'It were a fierce battle, that 'un, sir, an' no mistake.'

Bolitho smiled. 'Aye, I'm glad you are doing well in the Corps.' His words seemed to have another meaning as he added, 'Take good care that others do not spoil your efforts.'

The contact was broken as the calls trilled once more.

Bolitho paused in the entry port and removed his hat to the quarterdeck. After tomorrow this ship might never seem the same again.

He knew Herrick was watching him, his eyes filled with concern. In case he stumbled because of his distorted vision, or because he knew that not for the first time his own honesty had come between them.

Captain Francis Inch leaned across his chart and tugged repeatedly at his left ear as he often did when he was contemplating his next move. Around him the cabin heaved and shuddered as *Helicon* rolled uncomfortably in a rising wind.

It was almost noon, but because of a thickening mist which even the wind was refusing to disperse visibility was reduced to a few miles.

He could see the ships in his mind, *Dispatch* directly astern, and *Icarus* a blurred outline at the tailend of the line. Inch hated the uncertainty of the weather. The wind had veered greatly in the two days since Bolitho had left the squadron. It now blew almost directly from the west, from France.

He studied his chart more closely, very aware of the other two captains who remained silent as they sipped their wine.

Two hundred miles southwest of Toulon and already floundering in the rising wind. If it did not back soon or drop in force they might be driven far off their station or, worse, scatter so that they would lose contact altogether.

He pictured the little brig *Rapid*, far ahead of her companions. Inch was working her hard, but he envied her commander Quarrell more than he cared to admit. At least he had freedom of movement, while they blustered along, keeping station, ponderous and slow. He looked up and saw the broken white horses through the stern windows.

Captain Houston said, 'I must leave soon, or I'll never find my ship in this.'

Montresor of the *Dispatch* said, 'Can't do anything unless the wind quietens down.'

Inch looked at them impatiently. Negative. Neither willing to search beyond the obvious. Montresor was proving to be a good captain but always seemed to take a lead from the sour-faced Houston.

The latter remarked, 'I still think it's madness to keep our one and only frigate on some wild deception when she could be with us.' Encouraged by Inch's silence he continued in his harsh voice, 'We can't possibly seek out local craft with only *Rapid* to do it.'

Inch glanced round his cabin. It looked French still in spite of the paintings he had hung around it. Pictures of country scenes, brooks and meadows, churches and farms. Like his own Dorset home. He thought momentarily of Hannah, his wife. She had already given him a little son, and another child was on the way. How could she imagine what he was doing, he wondered?

He said, 'Vice-Admiral Bolitho has explained about *Barracouta*. I accept his judgement.'

Houston said, 'Naturally.' He smiled wryly at Montresor, 'But then we have not known him as long as you.'

Inch showed his teeth in a dangerous grin. 'He made me acting-commodore until his return. That should be enough for *you*, I think.'

Houston's smile vanished at Inch's change of tone. 'I wasn't doubting the thinking behind this. It's just that – '

'Quite.' Inch listened to the groan of timbers, the distant crack of canvas as the ship leaned uncomfortably from the wind. It felt wrong and incomplete without Bolitho. He always seemed able to foretell what the enemy might do, and Inch had never known him to scoff at or underestimate what the French had up their sleeves.

Houston said, 'Maybe we should pass word to the squadron off Toulon. Nelson might have views on what we're about. I still think the French will head for Egypt again as they attempt to break out. We beat 'em once at the Nile, but they might favour a second attempt.' He stood up and swayed to the deck's slant. 'I must leave, with your permission.'

Inch nodded regretfully. There were many things he needed to discuss, but Houston was right: much worse and he would never fight his way back to his own ship.

He heard a voice on the wind, far away, lost.

Montresor said, 'They've sighted something.' He shuddered. 'Not a good day for it.'

There was a tap at the door, Inch's first-lieutenant had come in person.

'Signal from *Rapid*, sir. Sail in sight to the nor'west.' He glanced at the others. 'Wind's getting up, sir. Shall I order another reef?'

Inch tugged his ear. 'No. Prepare to see these gentlemen into their boats. After that I want to signal *Rapid* before we lose contact.'

He turned to the others as the lieutenant hurried away.

'*Rapid* is unlikely to report or even sight a fishing boat in this weather.' He watched his words going home. 'I must close on her immediately. So keep station on *Helicon* and be prepared to fight.'

Montresor stared at him. He had not been a captain long enough to learn how to hide his feelings.

'The French? You really think so?'

Inch thought of Bolitho, how he would have presented it.

'Yes, I do. The wind is right for them; equally it is unfavourable to us.' He shrugged his bony shoulders. 'However, we must do what we came to do. At least we are ready for them.'

The two captains left the ship with unseemly haste, *Helicon* heaving-to for the minimum of time before butting into the heavy rollers once again.

Inch stared up at the masthead, the pendant standing out and seemingly almost at right-angles to the ship.

He glanced at the compass; northeast by east. Spray swept over the weather nettings and made the watchkeepers duck and swear.

Savill, his first lieutenant, shouted above the wind, 'Masthead reports that *Rapid* has her signal still hoisted, sir.' He looked excited, glad perhaps that they were doing something other than beating up and down.

Inch considered it. That probably meant that Quarrell had sighted or anticipated more than one strange sail.

'Signal from *Dispatch*, sir. Her captain is safely on board.'

Inch grunted, fretting as he thought of Houston's boat smashing its way further astern to his own command.

The masthead lookout yelled, 'Signal from *Rapid*, sir! Two sail in sight to the nor'west!'

Inch looked at his second-in-command. *Two sails.* It would not be any of Nelson's fleet so far south in the Golfe du Lion, and certainly no trader would attempt to break the blockade in this weather, especially in company with another.

He pondered Houston's words. He was right about one thing, *Barracouta* would make all the difference if she were here.

'I think the French mean business this time, Mr Savill. Make more sail, if you please. I intend to close on *Rapid* now.' He took a telescope and climbed to the poop to look for *Icarus*. He saw the wet mist far astern; even *Dispatch* was shrouded in it. God, what a time for it to happen. He snapped to the midshipman-of-the-watch who had followed him like a terrier, 'General signal. *Make more sail.*'

He saw the flags break out to the wind, very bright against the low cloud.

It was his chance. For once he was not looking to the flagship for instructions. He was in command today. Hannah would look at him with those adoring, violet eyes when he told her. Nobody could have guessed or anticipated that Bolitho would be struck down by a stray ball, and not even in the midst of battle. Keen was in Malta, although to Inch it had seemed absurd that he should be taken away for some stupid inquiry. But, no matter the whys and the wherefores, Francis Inch was in temporary charge of the squadron.

It was like having a weight suddenly lifted. He knew he had no doubts and could deal with this without anxiety.

He glanced around the deck, proud of his ship and her company. He watched the hands moving out along the yards, their white trousers flapping wildly as they fought into the wind. Canvas thundered out and bulged to the pressure so that the deck heeled over even further. Another look astern. There was *Icarus* visible just briefly astern of

Dispatch. A ghost ship. He grinned into the spray. Houston was a miserable man, he thought.

'Deck there!' That was one of the lieutenants. Savill had done right to put an experienced officer up there. '*Rapid* has signalled. Three sail-of-the-line to the nor'west!'

Inch felt a tingle run through his body. *Three*. There was no doubt now. They might try to avoid a confrontation, but Inch had no doubts about what he would do. Must do.

'General signal, Mr Savill. *Prepare for battle*.' He made himself smile. 'After that, you may clear for action.'

He thought of Bolitho, and felt sudden pride that he had entrusted this day to him.

The drums began to roll, and as *Helicon* hurled spray over her beakhead the violence of sea and wind seemed like a foretaste of their destiny.

13

West Wind

Inch stared up at the topsails as spindrift floated through the drumming shrouds like ragged banners. There was much movement and the hull was staggering over each successive crest, every stay and ringbolt protesting to the violent motion.

But he knew that all the noise and discomfort hid the fact that their progress was slow, painfully so. Unless the wind backed in their favour – he pushed the conjecture from his mind.

'Bring her up a point, Mr Savill. Steer nor'east.'

He heard the muted cries of the topmen, the hiss of halliards and blocks as his men fought to obey him. He dare not let her pay off just to gain more advantage from the wind. He must leave that until the last moment, when manoeuvrability would count the most. The second lieutenant was up there on the crosstrees watching the oncoming vessels, although even his vision must have been impaired by spray and the persistent layers of wet mist. The land was only five miles abeam and yet it was invisible. The sea had changed completely in a single hour, from shark-blue to pewter, and then to angered crests which broke in the wind as it moaned through shrouds and running rigging like an onslaught of demented souls.

Savill lurched up the canting deck, his face and chest running with water.

'Cleared for action, sir!'

Inch bit his lip. They could not attempt to open the lower gunports on the lee side. They would flood the whole deck in minutes. He comforted himself with the thought that the three French ships would not be finding it easy either. How could he be sure they were French? Spanish maybe? He discounted it instantly as he pictured *Rapid*'s young commander. Quarrell would have signalled the fact by now.

He considered his feelings. *They were the enemy.* Another time, a different place. The same flag.

Savill said, 'No sign of *Icarus*, sir.' He grinned. 'A change indeed.' It was well known in the squadron that Houston always liked to be the first and the best. This time he was sadly lagging behind the others.

Three to three. Good odds. Maybe the enemy would try to avoid them. There was little chance, Inch decided. If they headed for open sea, *Helicon* would lead the others round to take better advantage of the wind. No, it was far more likely that the French commander would continue on a converging tack with that same wind offering him all the advantage.

Inch looked at his ship. Cleared of unnecessary gear, the nets rigged above the gangways, the arms chests opened below the mainmast. The gun crews were stripped to the waist, their bodies already wet from spray as they crouched around their weapons or listened to their captains. Inboard of the black breeches the lieutenants moved restlessly about, their bodies angled to the tilt and shuddering vibration each time that *Helicon* ploughed into a trough or roller.

'Run up the Colours, Mr Savill.' He looked round for the Royal Marines officer. 'Ah, Major, I suggest you tell your fifers to strike up a jig, eh?' He gave his wide horsy grin. 'It will be a while yet before we match points with the Frogs.'

And so *Helicon*, followed as closely as her people could manage by *Dispatch*, headed towards the distant sails; the small marine fifers marched up and down the deck playing jig after jig, sometimes barely able to keep on their feet.

Inch saw his gun crews watching and grinning at the miniature parade. It took their minds off the inevitable. Only here and there a man stared across the nettings or above a gangway to seek out the enemy. New men probably, he thought. Or those who had done it before too often.

He glanced at his first lieutenant. A good and reliable officer. He seemed popular with the hands and that was a real bounty. It was a difficult thing for a first lieutenant to be.

'Deck there!'

Savill remarked, 'God, he has much to say today!'

Several of the men near him laughed.

But all smiles faded as the lieutenant in the crosstrees continued, 'The leading sail is a three-decker, sir.'

Inch felt them all looking at him. A first or second rate – bad odds, but he had known worse.

'Signal *Dispatch*, repeated *Icarus*, *close line of battle*.'

The three-decker's captain would be quick to exploit any weakness in his adversary, Inch thought.

Eventually the signals midshipman lowered his glass.

'Acknowledged, sir.'

Inch paced back and forth, deep in thought. It was taking much too long.

He looked up as the air quaked to sporadic cannon fire.

'What th' devil?'

The masthead yelled, 'Firin' on *Rapid*, sir!'

Inch swore. 'Signal *Rapid* to stand away! What does that young fool think he's playing at? If he tries to harass one of those ladies he'll soon get a bloody nose!'

Savill had climbed on to the shrouds with his telescope and shouted, 'One of the ships is closing with *Rapid*, sir! Trying to cut her off from us!'

Inch stared at him. Facing a battle, and yet the French commander seemed prepared to waste time and strength on a small brig.

Houston's words seemed to mock him, as if he had just spoken them aloud. *Rapid* was their only link now that *Supreme* was in dock. But for Bolitho, she would have been on the bottom. Now, with *Barracouta* to the north, the brig's importance was paramount.

'No acknowledgement, sir.'

'God damn!' Inch looked round. 'Chase your younkers aloft and get the t'gan's'ls on her, Mr Savill. Then the

maincourse. Lively with it!' He watched the hands rushing
to obey the pipe, the wild freedom of the topgallant sails
as they were released from their yards. He felt the ship
shivering to the extra power, and when the mainsail thundered out he saw its yard bend and knew he was risking
everything to cut down the range before one of the French
guns scored a fatal hit on *Rapid*.

He said urgently, 'General signal. *Make more sail.*'

Savill glanced at the sailing master and saw him grimace.
'Aye, aye, sir.'

The cannon fire continued with just an occasional gun
being used. It would only require one of those massive
balls to bring down the brig's masts or hit something vital
below deck.

'Signal from *Dispatch*, sir!' The midshipman was almost
yelling. 'In difficulty!'

Inch snatched a glass and ran up a poop ladder where his
marines leaned on the muskets and waited for something to
do. He rested the telescope on the hammocks and felt his
heart go cold as he saw the other two-decker's outline
changing as she paid off to the wind. He did not notice
the anguish in his voice as he exclaimed, 'Steering's gone!'
He saw the sails being taken in, tiny figures risking death
on the madly pitching yards as they struggled to prevent
the ship from being laid over or dismasted. It was common
enough in a gale. The rudder or a parted yokeline, it was
just another hazard and could always be repaired. But
the gap was already widening, and *Icarus* was completely
invisible in the lurking mist.

He hurried down the ladder and saw Savill's anxious
expression; others were staring at him with dismay, when
moments earlier they had been ready and willing to fight.

'It will take *Dispatch* a hundred years, Mr Savill. She
will be as helpless as *Rapid* if we cry in our aprons and
do nought.'

Savill seemed to relax. 'You can rely on me, sir.'

Inch looked at him. 'I never doubted it. Now, have the
guns loaded, but do not run out until I order it.' He
turned away as the gun crews leaped from their various
stances to seize their rammers and handspikes.

Dispatch was continuing to drift. The enemy must be wondering what was happening. Some ruse or trap to make the French commander think again. Inch frowned. Not for long.

'We will engage to larboard, Mr Savill.' He narrowed his eyes as he stared across the packed hammocks. He could see the other ships now without a glass. The three of them were advancing in echelon, their masts and sails overlapping to create one monster leviathan.

The rearmost ship was the one which was firing on the brig. *Rapid* was trying to haul off, but the last waterspout from a falling ball showed how close it had been.

Inch's coxswain hurried towards him, his captain's hanger in his hands.

Inch looked at the curved fighting sword. 'No, the other one.' He thought of Bolitho in his best uniform while the ship had rocked to the thunder of broadsides. Bolitho had known that he stood out as the captain, a sure target at any time. But he had also known it was necessary that his own people should see him until the end. When was that? It seemed a lifetime ago.

He allowed his coxswain to buckle on his best sword, the one he had bought before getting married to his dear Hannah.

Just thinking her name was like a cry from the heart. He forced the door closed on her and shouted, 'We'll take 'em down with us, eh, lads!'

They cheered, as he had known they would.

Here they come. He watched the oncoming sails, writhing and altering their outline as each captain reduced his canvas and prepared to fight. The leading ship made a splendid, terrible sight as she suddenly opened her ports and the black snouts showed themselves deck by deck.

Inch watched in silence. It was as if his heart had already stopped. He was unable to move or drag his eyes from the enemy. She was a ninety-gun ship at least. She had a bright figurehead beneath her beakhead and when Inch raised his telescope he saw that it was fashioned in the likeness of a springing beast, a leopard, with both its front paws reaching out in anger. It was Jobert. It had to be.

'Open the ports, Mr Savill. Then run out to larboard.'

There was still time. Time to run. Inch hardened his heart. 'Have the boats cast adrift, Mr Savill.'

It was always a bad moment when the boats were cut free to drift on a sea anchor until recovered by the victors. Being left aboard on their tier doubled the risk of flying splinters when the enemy's iron pounded across the decks. But to any sailor boats represented safety, a chance to survive. Inch began to pace between the quarterdeck guns, his chin in his neckcloth, the bright sword slapping against his thigh. Except, for his men, there would be no survival.

Bolitho felt the sun across his shoulders, magnified by the thick glass, as *Argonaute* swung heavily to her cable. He could hear the watch on deck shouting as they hoisted one of the boats inboard. He put down his pen and looked moodily through the windows towards the shore and at the cluster of shipping which lay between it and the flagship.

It would soon be time to leave for Herrick's ship. Bolitho thought of yesterday's meeting, more so of the parting. It had grieved him, and he felt trapped, with few courses left to attempt.

He watched the craft. Huddled together, as if the great harbour was no longer a haven and they wanted to put to sea. The expected convoy had been sighted at first light. Bolitho had heard the warning gun while he had toyed restlessly with his breakfast. The harbour would be crammed with ships.

He could not finish the letter to Belinda before he had to leave. Boots tramped across the damp planking and he guessed the marines were preparing to see him over the side. Keen's gig had already left. Bolitho had spoken with him only briefly. They had shaken hands. It had reminded Bolitho of a highwayman he had seen doing just that with his executioner before the trap had dropped beneath his kicking legs.

Why had he told Belinda? Because she deserved to know? Or was it merely that he had to confide in her because he needed her? Was that it?

He sighed and stood up, the pen left beside the letter.

The ship was swaying quite steeply, and he wondered if the wind would be gone before he sailed. *If* he sailed.

He stared at himself in the mirror, much as Herrick had looked at him. His right eye felt almost normal, or perhaps he had become used to it. The left, he sighed again, it was no worse, but the least strain and he felt it, his balance still unsure. Even now, in harbour, he had to consider every move.

He heard Ozzard in the next cabin brushing his best coat, and thought of Keen in his as he had left the ship. He was youthful and mature all in one. No wonder they loved each other. He thought of the girl with the brown, misty eyes. How far had the packet reached, he wondered?

There was a light tap on the door, and as the sentry said nothing Bolitho knew it was Allday.

He too was in his best blue jacket with the gilt buttons which he prized. His nankeen trousers looked newly cleaned and his buckled shoes would do credit to a post-captain.

Allday watched him grimly. 'Barge is alongside, sir.'

'I'm coming. I want to be on time, not early.'

Allday nodded and tried to smile. 'Keep 'em guessin', eh, sir?'

'Something like that.' He saw Allday glance at the unfinished letter. 'For the next courier.'

Allday sounded distant. 'I heard that the convoy will unload today an' tomorrow. Then it'll sail for England again, or some of it will.'

Bolitho looked at him. 'What else have you heard?' Allday was a better source of information than any signal and usually far more accurate.

Allday said, 'Two of 'em are carryin' gold, from the Sultan o' Turkey, whoever he might be when 'e's at 'ome.'

For whatever reason or purpose, the Sultan's wealth would be more than welcome in England. It sounded like Nelson's hand behind it. He had received several favours from the Sultan after their victory at the Nile.

Ozzard entered and held out the coat for him.

Bolitho looked at the mirror. A changed man again. To

any outsider he would seem to be and to have everything. Rank, authority, a beautiful wife. Everything.

He touched the gold Nile medal which hung about his neck. *Is this what a hero looks like?* Hardly as he felt, he decided.

'Let us go.' Bolitho touched Allday's sleeve then drew him aside. 'I have not forgotten about your son.'

Allday met his gaze, his eyes steady but sad. 'I 'ave, sir. He wants to quit the service, an' good riddance, I say.'

Ozzard had gone on ahead and Bolitho heard Captain Bouteiller calling his marines to attention. But he said, 'You don't mean that, Allday.'

Allday stuck out his jaw. 'Don't you fret about 'im, sir. It's you I'm fair bothered for. After all you done for King an' country, an' now you're goin' across to *Benbow* to smash all of it!'

Bolitho said, 'Don't be ridiculous, man. You don't know what the hell you're saying!'

Allday took a slow breath; his chest wound bothered him sometimes when he became excited or angry.

'Yes, I do, sir, an' you knows it.'

As they walked towards the screen door Allday added fiercely, 'I've said me piece. One more thing, sir. I'll be right there with you.'

Bolitho swung round, shocked by the distress in his voice. 'I know that, old friend. Your loyalty means more to me than – ' He did not finish. If anything, Allday's simple acceptance had decided him. As Allday had known all the time.

Bolitho barely noticed the swift pull to *Benbow*. Through the entry port, more salutes, formal greetings and then aft to the great cabin.

Herrick's furniture had been removed and there were many chairs, even benches, all of which appeared to be filled with naval uniforms, some civilians, and one or two of the *Argonaute*'s own company. He saw Stayt, who still managed to stay apart from all the others, Keen with Paget sitting beside him. The latter was not required to attend, but Bolitho was glad he had made the choice.

Athwartships was a long table, its chairs backing on the

stern windows, so that the few officers already seated there were silhouettes against the sunny panorama beyond.

All heads turned as Bolitho entered, and as he walked down to an empty chair at the front he saw their searching glances. Awe, pity, curiosity. There would be some who would be glad to see a flaw in his record if only because Keen was under his command. Keen looked at him and gave a brief nod. Their glances held and spanned the years, midshipman and captain, now together once more. Fear, love, tragedy, they had both shared it, just as the girl Zenoria had seen and understood. She would, more than most.

From a vast distance Bolitho heard four bells chime. Ten o' clock exactly, to coincide with Herrick's arrival aft.

Bolitho stood with the others as the court found their seats. Herrick in the centre, grave-faced but very calm. Sir Marcus Laforey took some time to settle down at one end of the table while his servant adjusted a wooden gout-stool beneath his bandaged foot. Bolitho saw a young lieutenant nudge his companion. If Laforey caught them at it they would think the world had toppled on them. Mr Pullen from the Admiralty, still dressed in black, his face severe, two other captains whom Bolitho did not recognize, and lastly Captain the Hon. Sir Hedworth Jerram. Laforey's flag-captain was tall and thin with a long nose to match his haughty demeanour. As he rose now, he looked along his nose like a man who had discovered something unsavoury.

Herrick said shortly, 'This court of inquiry at the direction of their lordships is open. Those advised of the content of the inquiry will be required to answer questions. Some written statements may be used, but the court is gathered mainly to discuss the behaviour of Captain Valentine Keen of His Britannic Majesty's ship *Argonaute*, at the times and dates as specified.'

He looked at Keen for the first time. 'Please be seated. You are not on trial here.'

Bolitho looked at Captain Jerram. His expression clearly said, *Not yet*.

The captain stood facing the cabin, some papers grasped

loosely in his bony fingers. In a penetrating tone he described the squadron's departure from Spithead, and its eventual meeting with the convict transport ship *Orontes*.

'At some time during this operation we are to understand that several attempts were made to take this vessel in tow, she having lost steerage way. For some reason the squadron's flagship decided to take control of the damaged vessel, although prior to that the *Helicon*,' he glanced sharply at his papers, 'under Captain Inch, had already achieved some success.'

Keen said, 'The reason for that – '

Herrick tapped the table. 'Later, Captain Keen.'

Bolitho looked at Herrick's eyes. He was unhappy about this, but there had been no recognition in his voice.

'Shortly afterwards Captain Keen went in person to the *Orontes*.' His eyes fixed on Keen as if he expected an argument. He continued, 'And this is where the captain's behaviour becomes a matter for the court and perhaps a more serious one at a later stage.'

In the cabin you could have heard a pin drop. Even the ship was unusually silent. Just the creak of wood and the lap of water below the counter.

The Hon. Sir Hedworth Jerram said in his precise voice, 'A woman being transported to New South Wales was removed from that ship by the – by Captain Keen.'

Bolitho clenched his fist. Jerram had all but called him 'the accused'.

'*Argonaute*'s surgeon is present. Please stand.'

Tuson rose above the other heads and shoulders, his hair very white against his plain blue coat.

Jerram said, 'The woman in question had been punished?'

Tuson eyed him bleakly. 'Beaten, sir, yes. Whipped, sir, yes.'

Jerram snapped, '*Punished.* How bad was the injury?'

Tuson described the cut on the girl's back in his usual controlled voice. If they had been expecting the average ship's surgeon the court was soon made to realize they were mistaken.

Jerram persisted, 'But she was in no danger of dying?'

Tuson stared at him. 'If she had been returned to that ship – '

'Answer the question, if you please.'

'Well, no, sir, but – '

'Stand down.'

Jerram dabbed his mouth with a handkerchief. Bolitho watched Keen's profile. He looked pale beneath his bronzed skin. Bitter too.

Stayt was called next. As it was only an inquiry the court could ask what it liked through Jerram. No sort of cross-examination was permitted.

Bolitho gripped his sword until his fingers felt numb. A gathering of facts, it said in the book. An exclusion of others.

'You boarded the *Orontes*, Lieutenant Stayt. What happened?'

Stayt began, 'The ship's crew were in disarray and had been drinking.'

'Who said so?'

'I assumed that for myself.'

'I shall overlook your impertinence.' Jerram added, 'A punishment was being executed, I believe?' Before Stayt could reply he said sharply, 'And you were ordered to shoot the man carrying out the punishment. I understand, shoot him dead if he continued? *Am I* correct?'

Stayt said hotly, 'It was an ugly situation, Sir Hedworth. We were without support.'

'Or many reliable witnesses, it would seem?' He nodded. 'Sit.'

Jerram looked at his papers momentarily, although Bolitho had the feeling he knew every detail by heart.

Bolitho accepted that the procedure was right, but, without any mention of what had happened before and since – the loss of *Supreme*, of the squadron's vice-admiral too – and without Keen's appraisal of what had happened, the evidence was meaningless.

Jerram continued, 'No attempt was made to return the woman to the transport. *Orontes*' captain was treated shamefully in front of his company.' He walked to the opposite side, his feet tapping on the canvased deck. 'At

Gibraltar, when other women were landed, the prisoner was retained on board in Captain Keen's *care.*'

Someone at the rear of the crowd tittered.

'In fact a native girl was taken on board to look after this *prisoner.*'

His gold-laced sleeve shot out. 'Please stand, Captain Keen! Do you deny any of this? That you removed a female prisoner from *Orontes* for your own purposes, which we can only guess at?'

Keen said bitterly, 'Yes, I took her off that ship. She was being treated like an animal!'

'And that *upset* you, a King's officer!'

Bolitho stood up; he was on his feet before even Jerram had noticed him.

Herrick looked at him, seemingly for the first time.

'Yes, Sir Richard?'

'How dare this officer sneer at my flag-captain! I will not sit here and tolerate one more insult, do you hear?'

Keen was looking at him, imploring him to stop. But Bolitho did not, nor did he want to. All the frustration and disappointment had moulded together and he no longer cared what they might do, not even Herrick.

Jerram said, 'This is most unorthodox.' He was looking at Laforey.

Laforey grunted. 'Well, let's get on with it, what? Say your piece, Sir Richard, if you must. You are known as something of a firebrand, I believe.'

It was quite unintentional but his remark seemed to take the edge out of the confrontation.

Bolitho said in a calmer voice, 'Captain Keen is a fine and brave officer.' He turned and saw their eyes shift to the gold medal on his chest, the same one that Nelson wore with pride. 'I chose him as my flag-captain because of his record, and because I *know* him.' He sensed Jerram's restored confidence, as he had known it would return. Jerram would be quick to point out that his choice of a flag-captain, even his record, was irrelevant. *If he got the chance.* Bolitho was a good swordsman, his father had seen to that. He had never done well with any other weapon.

It felt like that right now: letting the opponent test your arm, lead him on, and then take him off balance.

Laforey said, 'All we must do is return the prisoner under escort surely? Then Captain Keen will have to answer for his actions at a later date. We are at *war*, gentlemen.'

Bolitho felt the touch of ice at his spine, but it was the same as the thrill of battle, heedless of the outcome.

'Why not ask me, Sir Hedworth?'

Jerram glared at him for several seconds. 'Very well, Sir Richard, since it seems we are forced to dally here. Where is the prisoner?'

'Thank you, sir.' Bolitho felt his left eye sting and prayed it would not fail him now. 'She has returned to England under my protection. I paid for her passage and will produce the bill for same if you intend to court-martial *me*. Not before. I ordered Captain Keen to bring her to the flagship. Do you imagine that any captain can act without his flag-officer giving consent or encouragement?' He glanced at Keen's face. 'I did both.' He continued, 'That girl was unlawfully transported, something I intend to prove, Sir Hedworth, in a far more convincing court than your charade here today! How could you possibly know what the *Orontes*' master said or did not say? My God, man, he's almost halfway to New South Wales!' His voice sharpened. 'And you will know about it when the proof is published, gentlemen, believe me, you *shall know about it*, and what greedy, dishonest men will do for revenge!'

Pullen stood up. 'You take all the responsibility, Sir Richard?'

Bolitho faced him, calm again. 'Yes. Captain Keen is under my command and will remain so until I am ordered otherwise.' He looked as steadily as he could manage at the black-garbed figure.

'When you explain to your superiors of admiralty, Mr Pullen, and you tell them what I intend, you may be surprised at the outcome, and when that happens I trust you will show the same zeal as you did when you tried to arrest a young girl who has already suffered brutality beyond measure.' He looked again at Keen. 'That too is being taken care of.'

Laforey asked irritably, 'Why did we not know about this?'

Bolitho tried not to blink his damaged eye. 'Some were too eager for the kill, Sir Marcus. To hurt or to damage me through another's reputation.'

Jerram dabbed his face. 'I can proceed no further, sir.' He looked at Herrick. 'At this stage.'

Herrick opened his mouth and then looked towards the screen doors as a lieutenant entered and after some nervous hesitation made his way aft.

He handed a piece of paper to Laforey, who thrust it across to Herrick.

Bolitho remained standing. He may have ruined his career, but Keen and his Zenoria were safe.

Herrick looked up, 'I think you should see this, Sir Richard.'

Bolitho took the paper and read it carefully, aware that every face was watching him. He could feel the rising tension, mounting to match his despair and anger.

He looked around the great cabin, the same one where he had planned each battle, had survived, when so many had not.

He said quietly, 'His Majesty's armed schooner *Columbine* has entered harbour.' His voice was so low that many craned forward to hear him better. 'My squadron was attacked last week and the *Helicon*,' he glanced at Jerram without expression, 'under that same Captain Inch, was severely damaged with many killed and wounded.' He saw Keen watching him, his handsome features quite stricken. Bolitho continued in spite of the catch in his voice which he could not control. *Dear God, not Inch too.* 'What we anticipated has happened. Jobert is out, and my squadron engaged them. When they needed me, I was here.' He picked up his hat. 'As Sir Marcus said, we are at war. It is a pity that some still do not realize the fact.'

Herrick said, 'You may leave with your flag-captain.'

Bolitho looked along the table and said in the same level tone, 'I have one more thing to say.' He glanced from face to face. 'God damn all of you!' Then he strode from the cabin, and after a brief moment Keen followed.

Herrick sat quite still for several moments.

Then he said, 'This court is dismissed.' He was stunned by Bolitho's anger, and yet not surprised. He had done and given too much to care any more.

Pullen said breathlessly, 'He'll never get away with this!'

Herrick said flatly, 'You didn't understand, did you? The French are *out*, man, and Nelson will be watching Toulon like a hawk, and be too hard-pressed to release ships to search for Jobert! Nothing stands between Jobert and his intentions but that man we all wronged just now!'

Laforey watched the people leaving the cabin. Silent now, as if they had pictured the battle through Bolitho's quiet voice.

Herrick helped Laforey out of his chair. 'I know Bolitho better than any man.' He thought suddenly of Allday. 'Except one possibly. To him loyalty stretches in both directions. If people try to scar him through others he will fight back like a lion.' He tried not to think of the blazing anger in Bolitho's eyes. 'But there are some battles he can't win.'

He waited for his captain to see the visitors into their boats and then returned to the cabin of which he had been so proud. *If I were still his captain he would have acted the same way for me. When he needed me, what did I do? My duty?* It was an empty word now.

If Bolitho had been with his squadron the result might have been exactly the same. But Bolitho would feel it deeply, nurse it like another wound until he conquered it. Or it killed him.

His servant peered in at him.

'Can I bring some hands to return the furniture, sir?'

Herrick eyed him sadly. 'Aye, do that. And clean it too. It smells rotten in here.'

While Herrick stared through the stern windows *Argonaute*'s green barge moved slowly amongst the other ships.

Bolitho noticed that the stroke was slower and guessed Allday was taking his time to give him a moment to recover himself.

Keen sat beside him, his face grave as he watched the harbour. He said suddenly, 'You should not have done what you did, sir.'

Bolitho looked at him and smiled. 'You had no control over events where that girl was concerned, Val. I took the responsibility because I wanted to. She has come to mean a lot to me, just as her happiness counts a great deal.' His face softened. 'With you it was a matter of humanity to begin with, then your heart took the tiller.'

Keen said in a low voice so that the oarsmen could not hear him, 'May I ask how you know who is behind this attack, sir?'

'No. Not yet.' Bolitho tried to find comfort in the fact that a simple bluff had worked, but it evaded him. All he could see was Inch facing the enemy. The schooner's message had little news of value, except that the enemy flagship was named *Léopard*.

Almost to himself Bolitho said, 'The French went for *Rapid*. Inch tried to support her and took the whole weight of the attack. Why did they want the brig, I wonder?' Keen watched his profile and wondered how much more there was about Bolitho he did not understand.

Bolitho shrugged, 'Remember *Achates*, Val?'

Keen nodded and smiled, 'Old Katie, yes, I remember her.'

'When Jobert attacked us we were outnumbered three to one. To draw him into close quarters we concentrated our fire on his smallest ship, the *Diane*, and so we took *Argonaute*.'

Understanding flooded Keen's face. 'And now he's done the same to us!'

Argonaute's shadow covered them as the barge glided alongside in the choppy water.

Bolitho gripped his sword. The wind was still strong. The same one which had blown from the west and had brought the French with it. He looked up at the faces of the waiting side party. Was this ship cursed after all? Still French, no matter what they could do to her?

As his head lifted through the entry port and the salutes died away, Lieutenant Paget, who had preceded them in the gig, raised his hat and yelled, 'A cheer for the Admiral, lads!'

Keen had seen the look in Bolitho's eyes; he said, 'It's *men*, not ships, sir.'

Bolitho raised his hat and held it above his head. He wanted them to stop cheering just as he needed it to continue to drive back his thoughts like beasts into the shadows.

When they reached the stern cabin it felt like sanctuary.

Bolitho sat down in his chair and tried not to rub his eyes. They both ached and the vision in his good eye was blurred from strain and, he knew, emotion.

'I would like to see the schooner *Columbine*'s commander immediately.' He saw Ozzard pouring some brandy. The little man looked both pleased and sad. He would remember Inch too. 'I must discover everything I can before we rejoin the others. There must be *something*.'

'Captain Inch may be safe, sir.' Keen watched him fondly. 'We can only hope.'

'A good friend, Val.' He thought of Herrick's face at the table. 'Losing one is bad enough.'

He got up and walked vaguely round the cabin.

'God, I'll be glad to leave here, Val. The land has no warmth for me.' He glanced at the unfinished letter. 'Inform the admiral that I intend to weigh before dusk.'

Keen hesitated by the door. 'I'll go to the schooner myself.' He added quietly, 'I can never thank you enough, sir.'

Bolitho looked away, unable to hold his depression at bay. 'She is worth it, Val. So are you. Now fetch that officer for me.'

The door closed and Bolitho picked up the letter. Then he screwed it up and with sudden determination began to write another.

My dearest Belinda – and suddenly he was no longer alone.

14

Speak with Pride

Bolitho stood quite still beside *Helicon*'s wheel which had somehow remained intact. He had forcibly to examine the ship's upper deck, masts and gangways if only to convince himself that the fight had been two weeks ago. It looked as if it had been yesterday.

The wind which had brought the French down like thunder on this shattered vessel had died away completely; in fact the last few miles before *Argonaute* had made contact with the squadron had been an additional torment.

There was a deep, oily swell, above which a hard sun, more silver than gold, laid bare the scattered ships, their disorder seeming to symbolize their combined shock and defeat.

Figures bustled about the decks, sailors from other ships, for there were not so many from Inch's company who were fit to work. The clank of pumps was a reminder of the damage, if anyone needed reminding, and as a crude jury-rig began to emerge from the tangle of cordage and tackles Bolitho wondered how the ship had managed to survive.

Ripped deck planking, great patterns of dried blood, black in the harsh glare, upended guns and charred canvas; only the dead were missing, and the wounded were below, fighting their own private battles while the ships' surgeons did what they could for the ones who still refused to die.

Bolitho could feel Allday watching with him, sharing it, remembering all those other times.

It had not been a battle. More like a slaughter. But for the arrival of *Barracouta*, tearing down on the scene under

full sail, *Helicon* would be on the bottom. If the wind rose
again she might still make that final journey, he thought.

Barracouta had tossed caution aside, had even shredded
her studding sails to the wind as she had endeavoured to
turn aside the enemy's calculated assault.

Allday said, 'Why not go back to the ship, sir. Good
bath an' a shave, might do wonders.'

Bolitho looked at him. 'Not yet.' He felt sick, stunned
by the savagery of the destruction all around him. 'If I
ever forget this day, remind me.' He added fiercely, 'No
matter what!'

He saw Tuson below the poop. Even that deck was
mauled and knocked out of shape. As if a giant had crushed
it and left great black scars, like burning clawmarks. So
many had died here, and many more were paying for that
day.

He asked, 'How is he now?'

Tuson regarded him impassively. 'The ship's surgeon
took off his arm too low, sir. I am not satisfied with it. I
would suggest – '

Bolitho seized his sleeve. 'God damn you, man, that is
my friend you are speaking of, not some bloody carcass!'
He turned aside and said quietly, 'Forgive me.'

Tuson watched him and said, 'I understand. But I would
like to deal with it myself.'

He did not say what Bolitho already knew, that *Helicon*'s own surgeon had made a bad wound worse by his
treatment. In fairness, he had been overwhelmed by the
ferocity of the battle, the tide of broken, frightened men
who had been dragged down to the orlop to face his knife
and saw, while the ship had quaked to the roar of guns,
the terrifying fire from the enemy.

'I must see him.' Bolitho watched some seamen flinging
broken timber and other fragments over the side. They had
not been in this ship and yet they moved like survivors, the
heart gone out of them.

Tuson said, 'I cannot promise anything.' He glanced at
Bolitho's profile. 'I am sorry.'

Beneath the poop there was still the stench of burning
and pain, death and anger. A few guns lay on their sides

or at the full extent of their tackles where they had recoiled
on a last broadside before their crews were scattered or
cut down. The sunlight shone through distorted gunports,
gouged into strange shapes by the intensity of the attack.

From the maindeck the sounds of hammers and
squeaking blocks became muted as Bolitho groped his way
down the companion to all that was left of the wardroom.
Inch's own quarters had been swept away completely,
charred beyond recognition, and had taken those of the
gun crews and afterguard who had stayed to the last.
Bolitho saw men glancing at him, parting to let him
through before returning to their work in saving the ship
and preparing her for a passage to safety. The regular clank
of pumps seemed to sneer at their efforts, and the cries
from the wounded as they waited for relief or death added
to a backcloth of hopelessness.

Helicon's wardroom seemed almost cold after the upper
deck, and even though the stern windows had been blasted
away it could not free the place of its stench.

Bolitho stood beside the cot and looked down at Inch's
pale features. He did not seem to be conscious and Bolitho
felt his heart chill as he saw the bloody bandage where
Inch's arm had been. The thing he had always feared most
for himself had happened to his friend.

Tuson drew down a blanket and said, 'He took a metal
splinter here, sir.' He replaced the blanket and added
heavily. 'Their surgeon says he removed it.' He sounded
doubtful.

It was then Bolitho realized that Inch had opened his
eyes and was staring at him. His eyes did not move, as if
he was concentrating all his strength to recognize and
discover what was happening.

Bolitho leaned over him and took his hand. 'I'm here,
old friend.'

Inch licked his lips. 'I knew you'd come. Knew it.' He
shut his eyes and Bolitho felt his grip tighten as the agony
tore through him. But the grip was feeble nonetheless.

Inch said, 'Three ships-of-the-line. But for *Barracouta*,
I'm afraid – '

Tuson whispered, '*Please,* sir, he's terribly weak. He'll need all his will to survive what I must do.'

Bolitho turned to him, their faces almost touching. 'Must you?'

Tuson shrugged. 'Gangrene, sir.' It needed no more words.

Bolitho leaned over the cot again. 'Don't give in. You've a lot to live for.' He wanted to ask Inch about the French ships, but how could he?

He saw Carcaud, the surgeon's mate, and two assistants waiting by an upended gun. Like ghouls. Bolitho felt his eyes smart. They would do it here and now, hold him down while Tuson did his bloody work.

Bolitho lowered his head, unable to look at him. Francis Inch, a man with all the courage and so much luck. Who would care? His pretty young wife and a few old comrades, but who would really spare a thought for the cost of unpreparedness, of ignorance?

Inch looked past him and saw Allday. A shadow of a smile creased his long face and he whispered, 'You've still got that rascal, I see!'

Then he fainted and Tuson snapped, '*Now!*' He glanced only briefly at Bolitho. 'I suggest you go elsewhere, sir.'

Bolitho barely recognized this Tuson. Steady-eyed, coldly professional. To him it was not a wrecked wardroom but a place of work.

Bolitho walked up to the quarterdeck again and saw that a young lieutenant, one of *Helicon*'s, was supervising the hoisting and rigging of two staysails. It would give them steerage way, but little else until they could replace some of the yards. Bolitho looked at the forecastle and decking again. Point-blank range, mostly grape by the look of it.

The lieutenant saw him and touched his hat. He said, 'Addenbrook, sir, fifth lieutenant.'

'Where were you?' Bolitho watched the strain and emotion on the lieutenant's grimy features. At a guess about eighteen and newly promoted like most of Keen's. Probably the first time in battle in his junior rank.

Addenbrook said, 'Lower gundeck, sir. The French laid off and concentrated their fire on us. Heavy artillery,

everything.' He was reliving it, the roaring, sealed world
of the lower gundeck. 'We heard the masts shot away, but
we kept firing, just like we'd been trained, what he
expected of us.'

'Yes. Captain Inch is a fine man.'

The lieutenant barely heard him. 'They kept coming for
us, sir, until half our crews were laid low. They still closed
the range and started to use grape.' He pressed one hand
to his forehead. 'I kept thinking, in God's name, why
don't they stop? My senior was killed, and some of my
men were half mad. They were beyond reason, screaming
and cheering, loading and firing, not like the men I knew
at all.'

Grape at close range. That explained the utter devas-
tation. There could have been hardly a gun to return the
fire by that time.

The lieutenant looked down at his stained uniform, scarcely able to believe it had happened, that he had survived
without a scratch.

'We were alone, 'til *Barracouta* joined in, sir.' He looked
up, his face suddenly bitter. 'We had no chance.' For just
a moment some pride cut through the hurt in his eyes.
'But we didn't strike to the buggers, sir!'

There was a splash alongside and Bolitho saw Carcaud
walk away from the gangway, wiping his hands on his
apron. He did not have to guess what he had pitched into
the sea. Was that all it took? He beckoned to the gangling
surgeon's mate.

'How is he?'

Carcaud pursed his lips. 'I don't think he knew what
had been done, sir, but later on – '

Bolitho nodded and walked slowly towards the entry
port, or what was left of it.

Helicon's first lieutenant appeared on deck, his head in
a bandage. He saw Bolitho and hurried towards him.

Bolitho said, 'You have done well, Mr Savill. If you
need any more men, signal the flag to that effect.' He saw
the man sway. 'Are you fit to be here?'

The lieutenant tried to grin. 'I'll manage, sir.' He had a
round Dorset accent – no wonder Inch liked him. 'I shall

lighten the ship as soon as I can rig some tackles.' His eyes sharpened. 'Not the guns though. We'll fight this old lady again once we can get her into dock.'

Bolitho smiled sadly. A sailor's faith in his ship. And he was probably right.

'You saw the French flagship, the *Léopard*, I understand?'

'Aye, sir.' His eyes were far away. 'I took a bang on the skull an' was pressed against a nine-pounder. I reckon that saved me in the next broadside.' He glanced aft. 'They were all cut down, smashed like a bowl of eggs. But, oh yes, sir, I saw her right enough.' He gave a rueful smile. 'Pity I've not got that Frenchie's extra boom. I could use it to hoist up some of the shot an' stores!' A man called out and he touched his forehead. 'If you'll pardon me, sir.' He hesitated and turned. 'Cap'n Inch just stood there an' damned th' lot of 'em, sir. He was a good cap'n, a real gentleman to the people.'

Bolitho looked away. *Was.* 'I know.'

In the barge he twisted round in the sternsheets to look for his other ships, his mind trying to grapple with the mauled squadron as *Helicon*'s lieutenants were fighting to restore life to their ship.

If *Barracouta* had not arrived the French would have gone for the other ships. He had already heard that *Barracouta* had been hurrying with the news that the enemy was moving out of Spanish waters when she had been chased by two French frigates. But for her speed, and the fact that the two enemy vessels had believed her to be a small two-decker, she would never have been able to help.

Once or twice he turned to look astern at *Helicon*. Scarred and burned, with only stumps for masts, she made a grim spectacle. How many had died? One more list of names to be considered. Jobert would not have wasted so much time if he had known the frigate was that near. But he had wanted to destroy *Helicon*, utterly. To pay him back for destroying his *Calliope* or because she was a prize ship? Or was it a savage warning of the fate he intended for *Argonaute* if he could not retake her?

He pictured each of his remaining ships in turn. Without

Inch, he was left with Houston and Montresor, who had yet to prove their ability in battle. Then there was *Rapid*, and with luck the cutter *Supreme* would rejoin them if the Maltese dockyard kept its promise. And one frigate. It was strange that Lapish, who had got off to such a bad start, had shown both skill and initiative. Bolitho wished in his heart that he was still captain of a frigate.

He sighed. 'We must fetch Captain Inch aboard the flagship as soon as he may be moved, Allday.'

Allday glanced down at Bolitho's squared shoulders, the stains on his arms and legs from his examination of the other ship.

'If you think he can.' He flinched as Bolitho looked up at him. Those grey eyes were still the same. It was hard to accept that one was half blind.

He tried again. 'You know how it is, sir.'

'Yes.' Bolitho stared at the *Dispatch*, hove-to above her own reflection. But for her steering failing. He turned the thought aside. It would merely have delayed the inevitable.

Jobert must have imagined that *Barracouta* was one of Nelson's ships, the vanguard of his blockading squadron off Toulon.

He said, 'But he'll not survive a passage to Malta.'

Allday persisted, 'He'll never leave 'is ship, sir!'

Bolitho shook his head. 'I think otherwise. This time.'

Keen was waiting for him, his face full of questions.

How different were *Argonaute*'s decks, Bolitho thought. Order, purpose. But despair was infectious; it would soon spread, with *Helicon*'s hull a constant reminder to them.

He said, 'Captain's conference, Val, this afternoon if possible. If the wind gets up, it might be days before I can speak with them together.'

Keen looked across at *Helicon* and said quietly, 'There's the heart of a ship, sir.'

Bolitho shaded his eyes and saw a thin fragment of sail being hoisted between the fore and mainmast stumps.

He said, 'Inch's heart.'

He pictured Jobert's squadron in his mind. It was not formed for a diversion or merely to seek revenge. If the

latter offered itself, then so much the better, but there was
far more to it. Was it to draw Nelson's blockade from
Toulon so that Admiral Villeneuve's main fleet could break
out in force? With Gibraltar under siege from another
fever, it was unlikely that any English ships would stay
there to act as a deterrent. Jobert might well try for the
Strait. Bolitho dismissed the idea at once. Jobert could
have done that already, could be in Brest by now if he
had managed to slip past the blockade there.

Bolitho made his way aft as Keen called out to the
signals midshipman to pipe his assistants on deck. Allday
watched him and noticed that he was so wrapped up in
his thoughts that he did not even falter or hesitate when
the deck tilted in the swell.

Bolitho walked through the screens and made his way
right aft to stare through the stern windows. He should
have been exhausted, worn down by shock and a sense
that he had failed. Instead his mind seemed to have taken
on a new edge, sharpened still further whenever he thought
of Inch, lying over there in his stricken ship.

Keen entered and said, 'The signal is bent on, sir.' He
sounded strained.

Knowing Keen, he was probably blaming himself for
what had happened. If he had not been recalled to Malta

Bolitho faced him. 'Dismiss any doubts from your
mind, Val. At least by going to Malta I discovered something I might never have known otherwise.'

'Sir?' Keen was astounded by Bolitho's demeanour.

'Hoist the signal, and call our gallant captains.' He
waited until Keen was almost at the door. 'And, Val, when
you next hold her in your arms you will *know* that Fate
left you no choice.'

Bolitho walked to the windows and out onto the gallery
with its two smiling mermaids.

He heard a shout and guessed that the signal had broken
aloft. He would speak with his captains. Repair the
damage. Restore their confidence. He saw *Helicon* drift
slowly into view.

But not you, dear old friend, you have done your share.

*

During the day the wind rose only slightly, but there were more clouds and perhaps a hint of rain.

Bolitho stood aft by the windows again and watched his captains as they sat in their various attitudes in the great cabin. Not the wardroom this time. He wanted no retreat. There was none. He had gone through the details of Jobert's squadron, its strength, and its possible purpose.

'There is nothing to gain from remaining in the gulf, gentlemen. I intend to sweep to the southeast'rd. If Jobert has headed west to pass through the Strait then we have already lost him. If not – ' he looked at their intent faces, 'then we must find him and call him to action.'

There were muffled shouts from the maindeck and the cabin quivered as two of *Helicon*'s thirty-two-pounders were lowered on board.

Bolitho said, 'Those guns will be conveyed to *Rapid* tomorrow.' He saw her young commander start up in his chair as if he had been only half listening.

Quarrell stammered, 'Too heavy, sir, I mean – '

Bolitho eyed him bleakly. 'You have shipwrights and a carpenter, I believe? I want you to mount two guns forrard as bow-chasers. By shifting ballast and stores and shoring up the deck you should manage it easily enough. I once commanded a sloop-of-war – she was not much bigger and had a very heavy bow armament. So *do it*.'

Captain Montresor said, 'My steering is repaired, sir. I had no way of knowing.' He looked bitterly at Houston. 'I *wanted* to fight. I didn't expect *Helicon* to stand alone.'

Captain Houston sat with his arms folded, unrepentant.

He said, 'My ship had fallen too far astern because of the wind and that damned mist. I saw *Dispatch* was in trouble.' His thin mouth opened and shut, each word rationed. 'I would have been a target and nothing more had I gone to assist *Helicon*. Anyway, I knew the Frogs would do for the lot of us piecemeal, so I decided to take Montresor in tow.'

Bolitho nodded. So typical of the man, he thought. Hard, uncompromising, but in this case right. His choice had been straightforward, in his view at least. Save a ship or lose the squadron.

He said, 'Jobert has a purpose for everything he does. So far he has been one step ahead of us.' He saw Keen watching him grimly. He knew that by quitting their station he was taking a huge responsibility, a greater risk to himself. It was odd, but it no longer mattered. After the court of inquiry at Malta he was a marked man anyway. He felt lightheaded. It was beyond personal risk and reputation now.

Houston said in his harsh voice, 'We shall have to consider where and when we will replenish water supplies, sir.'

Bolitho looked at him, suddenly aware of the shadow across his left eye. It taunted him but for once he was able to ignore it.

'There will be no watering, Captain Houston.' He glanced at the others. 'For any of us. Cut the ration, halve it if need be, but we stay together until this is finished.' He did not add *one way or the other* but the thought was obvious on their faces.

'I need all the information we can gather. Coastal craft must be stopped and searched thoroughly. If they are neutral, do it just the same. If not, sink them.' He felt the hardness creep into his tone, like that other time. It made him think of Herrick, the pain in his blue eyes when he had left *Benbow*. In his heart Bolitho knew Herrick had acted only as he saw fit. Bolitho hated any sort of favour-itism and despised those who used it for advancement or personal gain in the Navy. Yet he had done exactly that for Keen, and because Herrick was his friend. What would he have done had he been in Herrick's position and another had asked a favour of him? But the thought of what it had cost in lives made him shy away from an answer. Inch was a broken man. If he lived it was unlikely he would ever tread his own deck again. He saw some of them glance at him as he unwittingly touched his left eye. That thought was always there. *Suppose I lost the sight of my right eye?* Blind, as he had been in *Supreme*, but forever.

Captain Lapish asked, 'Will Jobert have any more ships at his command, sir?' He even sounded more confident than before.

Bolitho gave a grave smile. 'Are there not enough already?'

Houston muttered, 'Two frigates, y'say? And we've but one.'

Commander Quarrell exclaimed, 'My brig is worthy enough!'

Bolitho said, 'Save your steel for the enemy, all of you. Drill your people until they can point and fire in their sleep. Make each one aware that the enemy is human, not a god. We can and will beat him, for I believe we are the only bulwark 'twixt Jobert and his objective.'

The deck tilted heavily and a book slithered from the table.

Bolitho said, 'Return to your ships. If there is rain, gather it as part of the rations. Whenever you need to search or seek out small craft, use your boats to full advantage. I want our people to be ready to fight and to expect trouble in advance.'

Houston commented, '*Léopard* is a second-rate, I believe, sir?'

Bolitho saw the blunt reminder move round the others like a chill wind through corn.

He glanced at Keen. 'My flag-captain took on this ship and two frigates at once, Captain Houston. Battered we may be, but you will see that we are both still here!'

Quarrell laughed outright and grinned at his friend Lapish. They had both learned a lot in a short while. And they were still too young to nurse fear for long.

After the captains had been seen over the side Keen returned to the cabin and asked, 'Do you already know what Jobert is about, sir?'

'When I am certain I shall tell you, Val. Until then we must make sure that our ships do not grow slack or careless. A lack of vigilance now can mean only defeat.'

The sentry called, 'Surgeon, sir!'

Tuson entered and eyed them curiously. 'You sent for me, sir?'

Bolitho said, 'Make arrangements to ferry Captain Inch aboard. I fear the weather may change.'

Tuson nodded. 'He was speaking with me when I was

aboard *Helicon* earlier, sir. He is in great pain, but I would prefer him here in my care.'

Bolitho said, 'I know that.' He watched the surgeon leave and said, 'If *Helicon* gets into difficulties en route for Malta, it were better that Inch be with us. He'd be on deck, taking charge, otherwise.'

Keen smiled, 'Like you, sir.' He moved to the chart. 'A needle in a haystack. Damn Jobert! He might be anywhere.'

Bolitho walked to the table and caught his foot in a ringbolt and almost lost his balance. He felt the touch of fear once more. He thought of Inch returning home. What would his pretty Hannah think? What might Belinda think, for that matter? Even if Adam had not told her of the full extent of his injury, his handwriting in that last letter would make her realize something was wrong. The letter. He thought of the way his words had poured out; it had been as if he had been listening to his own voice. It was so unlike him; he was almost sorry he had written to her of his innermost hopes and fears, of the love which had burned with such passion and which he had imagined was gone forever.

Keen said suddenly, 'It breaks a confidence, sir, but, like you, I cannot bear to see Allday in the doldrums.'

'You know something, Val?'

Keen sat on a chair. Half of him needed to be on deck, but Paget could deal with most things now. The other half wanted to be here, with this one man who had risked so much for his happiness and had shown no regrets for it.

'My cox'n told me, sir. Old Hogg is a solid fellow and cares for little in this world but himself and, I believe, for me. Also Allday confides in him occasionally.' Water laced the stern windows and Bolitho tried not to think of Inch being swayed down into a lively boat for the crossing. A sudden shock could kill a man in his condition.

Keen said, 'It seems that young Bankart believed Allday would soon quit the sea after being wounded so badly at San Felipe. He had learned of his life in Falmouth with you, sir, of his security there. He wanted to share it. He had had enough of farm work, and a life at sea didn't appear to satisfy him even though he is a volunteer.' He watched Bolitho's profile and asked, 'Can we be certain that Bankart *is* his son, sir?'

Bolitho smiled. 'If you had known Allday when he first came aboard my ship, *Phalarope*, that was twenty years ago, remember, you'd not need to ask. He is exactly like him, in looks anyway.'

Keen stood up as the bell chimed out from the forecastle. 'As his captain I shall deal with it, sir. It might be better if he is discharged when we reach England.'

They stared at each other, startled by the word. England.

Bolitho looked away. It seemed likely they might never see green fields again.

'I shall speak to Allday myself, Val. A troubled man is often the first to fall in battle.'

Keen raised his head to listen to the sounds on deck.

He said, 'You brought the squadron together today, sir. I watched the others and saw the pride coming back to them.'

Bolitho shrugged. 'I should have been with them, with Inch. But recriminations will not give him back an arm.'

He heard a sudden wave of cheering and said, 'We'll go on deck. This will be an ordeal for Inch.'

Keen hurried beside him. 'I'll tell Mr Paget to stop the hands from doing it!'

Bolitho shook his head. 'No. Let them.'

On the quarterdeck Bolitho saw Big Harry Rooke, the boatswain, supervising the tackle on a chair to sway Inch's cot over the side. Across the water the listing *Helicon* was pitching heavily in the swell, her gangway lined with tiny faces as they watched the slow-moving boat which approached the flagship with such care. Bolitho adjusted his swordbelt and tugged his hat down over his forehead.

Another familiar face, broken with pain. Another of the Happy Few, who even if he defied death would never be the same again.

Paget looked at his superiors. 'Ready, sir.'

Bolitho stepped forward, 'Man the side, if you please.' He walked to the entry port and leaned out to watch the

approaching boat. He did not hold on, and knew the risk
he took for such a small gesture.

He heard the Royal Marines guard picking up their
dressing from Sergeant Blackburn, the hiss of steel as
Captain Bouteiller drew his spadroon.

He saw the boatswain's mates moistening their silver
calls on their tongues while the tackle took the strain and
all cheering stopped dead.

Keen looked at Bolitho, framed against the heavy swell.
He knew what this moment was costing him. But Keen's
voice was steady as he called, 'Stand by on deck!' He saw
Bolitho turn to look at him, their eyes understanding as
they had in the cabin. 'Prepare to receive *Helicon*'s
captain!'

After the din of calls and commands, as the cot was
manhandled towards the poop, Bolitho took Inch's hand
and said quietly, 'Welcome aboard, Captain Inch.'

Inch tried to grin but looked very pale and suddenly
older. He said in a hoarse whisper, 'Please let me see my
ship.'

They carried him to the gangway and Tuson himself
cradled Inch's shoulders so that he could look at the distant
seventy-four with her pathetic scraps of sail.

Inch said slowly, 'I'll not see that old lady again.'

Tuson wanted to look away, surprised that he could
still be moved by such men and such moments.

Bolitho watched as the little procession was swallowed
up in the poop and then said, 'And we'll not see his like
again, either.'

He swung away and added bitterly, 'Get the ship under
way. Signal the squadron to take station on the flag as
ordered.'

If anything, Keen thought, Inch's presence aboard
would be a reminder and a warning to them all.

On the larboard side of *Argonaute*'s orlop deck, in the
tiny berth which he shared with Mannoch, the sailmaker,
Allday moved a flickering lantern closer to his handiwork.
Allday was big and powerfully built, and his fists made a

cutlass look like a midshipman's dirk, but the model which
he had half completed was as delicate as it was perfect.
Wood, bone, even human hairs had been used to fashion
it, but Allday was ever critical of his work. He had made
models of every ship in which he had served with Bolitho,
and on occasions he had produced more than one.

He cradled the little ship in one palm and turned it
slowly before the lantern. It was a seventy-four, and he
grunted with grudging approval as the ship it represented
quivered and murmured around him.

Down on the orlop, which never saw the light of day,
the air was always thick. In the small berth it was still
heavy from the sailmaker's rum. He was a marvel at his
work and could run up a sail or a suit of clothes with
equal skill. But he loved his tot and was known by his
crew as Old Grog Mannoch.

Allday shifted his buttocks on his hard sea-chest and
thought of Bolitho, two decks above his head. It had been
painful to watch him when the bandages had first come
off; now it was hard to tell the extent of his injury and he
rarely mentioned it any more. He heard Tuson laugh, and
his assistant Carcaud say something in return. The sickbay
was just a few yards away on the opposite side. A place
to avoid at all costs. They were playing chess by the sound
of it. Inch had been given an empty cabin elsewhere. The
air down on the orlop could kill a man in his state, Allday
decided.

He recalled the girl as he had last seen her with her
shorn hair and borrowed clothes. There had been a nasty
moment when they had headed for the Falmouth packet
at Malta: one of the guardboats had passed almost directly
alongside. He had threatened his boat's crew with a
quilting if one of them had said a word about it. Some of
them had not even noticed. One midshipman was much
like another in the dark.

It had made Allday think seriously about getting married
himself. He grinned silently. *Who would want an old
bugger like me?*

There was a tap on the narrow door and he looked up,
surprised to see Bankart looking at him.

'Yes?'

'I'd like to talk a spell, if it's all right?'

Allday shifted along the chest to make room. 'What about?'

He looked at the youngster's features and remembered his mother. A clean, fresh girl. He had even thought of wedding her at the time. There had been so many of them, different faces, in many ports. The landlord's daughter of the inn near Bolitho's home was the only one who still held a firm place in his thoughts. He had thought her too young, but after what had happened to Captain Keen, well, you never know.

Bankart blurted out, 'I don't want bad blood between us.' He would not look at him. Like Allday, he was stubborn, and surprised that he had come to this place at all.

'Spit it out then.' Allday watched him sternly. 'An' no lies.'

Bankart doubled his fists. 'You may be me father, but – '

Allday nodded. 'I know. I'm not used to it. Sorry, son.'

The youth stared at him. 'Son,' he repeated quietly.

Then he said, 'You was right about me. I wanted to get ashore, to come to where you was.' He looked at him, his eyes bright. 'I wanted a 'ome, a real one.' He shook his head despairingly. 'No, don't stop me or I'll never get it out. I wanted it 'cause I was sick of bein' chased an' cheated. I'd always sort of looked up to you, 'cause of what me Mum said an' told me 'bout you. I joined up as a volunteer 'cause it seemed the proper thing to do, like you, y'see?'

Allday nodded, the model ship forgotten.

'Then Mum died. Best thing for 'er, it was. They wore 'er out, the bastards. I wanted somethin' of me own, so I got a mate to write to you. We was told you were leavin' the sea.' He looked at the deck. 'It was a 'ome I wanted more'n a father.' When he looked up again he exclaimed, 'I can't 'elp bein' afraid. I'm not like the others! I never seen men killed like that afore!'

Allday gripped his wrist. 'Easy, son. The sawbones'll

be comin' to see what's up.' He groped behind the chest and brought up a stone bottle and two mugs. ''Ave a wet.'

Bankart took a quick swallow and almost choked.

Allday said, 'That's the real stuff, not the muck that the pusser hands out! Most o' the others are scared too.' Allday let the rum float across his tongue and smiled as he recalled when Bolitho had drunk some in his despair and his relief. 'You must learn not to show it.' He shook his wrist gently. 'That takes *real* courage, believe me, matey.'

'It's different for you, I 'spect.' Bankart took a wary swallow.

'Maybe it is. Our Dick has taken good care o' me. He's a fine man. A friend. Not many can say that, an' I'd lay down me life for him, make no mistake on it!'

Bankart made to get up, his hair brushing a massive deckhead beam. 'I just wanted to tell you, I – '

Allday pulled him down again. ''Old still! I knew anyway, or most of it. I was the one who was wrong, I knows that now.' He took another full measure of rum. 'You don't belong in a King's ship. It took courage to volunteer, I can tell you that! They 'ad to *press* me!' He shook with silent laughter until the pain of his wound stopped him. 'No, a job ashore, with a good 'ome, an' I'll make proper certain you gets one. Until then, do what I tells you and keep out of trouble, see?' There were more voices and he guessed the sailmaker and one of his cronies were coming aft. 'We'll talk again, an' soon, right?'

Bankart looked at him, his eyes shining. 'Thanks, er – '

Allday grinned. 'Call me John if it's easier. But call me Cox'n when there's others about, or I'll tan your hide for you, an' that's no error, son!'

Bankart hesitated, unwilling to break the contact. He said quietly, 'I – I think I might be killed. I wouldn't want to let you down. I've seen the man you are, 'eard what they all say about you. I never bin proud of anyone afore.'

Allday did not even hear the door close. He sat staring at the unfinished model, at a complete loss.

The sailmaker banged into the berth with his friend and asked, 'All right, 'Swain? Good-lookin' lad that one.'

Allday looked down. 'Aye. He's my son.'

15

Fate

Bolitho walked up the sloping quarterdeck and allowed the wet wind to drive all tiredness aside. It was early morning, and around and above him the ship's company prepared for another weary day.

There had been some overnight rain, but Bolitho walked back and forth too far from any handhold if he should slip on the wet planking. It was a struggle but he was slowly regaining his confidence and blamed his earlier despair on self-pity and worse.

He heard Keen speaking with the first lieutenant and knew from the tone in his voice that they were discussing the punishment to be awarded to three seamen during the forenoon.

It was the same throughout the squadron. After *Helicon*'s departure there had been several outbreaks of disorder. Threats or actual violence used against petty officers or each other, with the usual aftermath of floggings. The flagship was no exception; even Keen's humanity had failed to prevent the latest flare-up of tempers, and the harsh justice which would follow.

Bolitho pictured his ships, each living her own life, controlled and led by her individual captain.

An admiral, even a junior one, was not supposed to concern himself with such abstract matters, Bolitho thought. He also knew that a ship was only as strong as her people.

When full daylight found them again his ships would be sailing in line abeam, *Argonaute* in the centre position. *Barracouta*, still in her rough disguise, was somewhere astern, ready to rush down from windward to wherever a signal dictated. *Rapid,* completely alone, was far ahead, tacking back and forth in the hope of finding a fishing boat or some trader who might have some valuable information for them.

They had sighted several such craft but had managed to catch only three. One of the ones which had eluded *Rapid*'s chase until she had been recalled to her station had been a fast schooner. It was customary for any merchantman to fly from a man-of-war, the flag did not matter. But out here any stranger might be an enemy, worse, a spy who would carry news of their strength and movements to Jobert.

It could not last. Bolitho knew it; so probably did his officers. He would have to admit failure and send the brig to seek out Nelson and tell him what had happened. It seemed likely that Nelson would scatter Bolitho's ships amongst his own fleet and wait for the French to fight their way out of Toulon. Jobert would not be considered. Bolitho guessed that the admiral in Malta, maybe even Herrick, imagined that Jobert had become like a crude joke or a figment of Bolitho's imagination.

It was the fourth day since they had parted company with Inch's ship. At any other time it would have been good sailing weather, with a favourable wind and fair visibility for the masthead lookouts along Bolitho's line of ships.

Keen crossed the deck and touched his hat. 'Any special orders today, Sir Richard?' His formality was for the benefit of the helmsmen and master's mate nearby. He sounded strained, or was he critical of his superior's actions and their results?

Bolitho shook his head. 'We will continue the search. The French may have left us alone, but I doubt it.'

Together they watched the ship taking shape around them, the sails and rigging picking up the sun's colour. Abeam, *Dispatch* rolled her bilge into a deep swell, so that her shining hull and lower gunports shone like fragments of glass.

Bolitho looked up at the mainmast, at the lookout's tiny figure.

He said, 'Change the lookouts every hour, Val. I want no tired eyes today.'

Keen glanced at him curiously. '*Today*, sir?'

Bolitho shrugged. He had not realized what he had said. Had he meant that he would need to break off the search and admit failure? Or was that same, chilling instinct offering him a warning?

'I feel uneasy, Val.' He thought of breakfast, and the fact he had been pacing the deck for most of the night. To regain his confidence, or was it because he had already lost it completely? 'Tell me if you sight anything.' He strode aft to his quarters where Ozzard and Yovell were waiting for him as usual.

Bolitho sat at the table and watched while Ozzard prepared his breakfast and poured some coffee. He felt in need of a wash from head to toe, and his shirt was crumpled and stale. But, as he had explained to Keen, as the water ration was cut, and if need be would be cut again, it had to be for everyone. Except for Inch, that was. It was painful to see him, sometimes delirious and on other occasions dulled into a state of collapse.

The amputation was still holding well, according to Tuson. But Inch needed to be ashore, in a hospital with those who could give him proper care. Bolitho knew from bitter experience that each shout from the upper deck, every change of wind and rudder, would stir even a dying sailor with old anxieties. Especially a captain.

Ozzard said, 'Just as you like it, sir.' He laid a pewter plate on the table. 'Last of the Maltese bread, I'm afraid, sir.'

Bolitho looked at the thinly sliced pork, fried pale brown in biscuit crumbs. The bread would be like iron, but Ozzard had managed to stop it going mouldy; anyway the black treacle which Bolitho enjoyed would deaden the taste.

He thought of the breakfasts at Falmouth, of Belinda sitting and watching his pleasure. *Like a schoolboy*, she had said. What would she make of this, he wondered? And down in the messes it was a hundred times worse.

He looked at the open skylight as voices drifted aft from

the quarterdeck. Then feet pounded along the passageway and he saw Keen coming into the cabin.

'I beg your pardon for disturbing you, sir.'

Bolitho put down his knife. It was not like Keen to leave the deck in a crisis.

'*Rapid* is in sight. She has news, sir.'

Bolitho thrust the plate aside and then spread the uninspiring bread with a thick coating of treacle.

'Tell me.'

'She sighted a ship and boarded it. More I cannot say, but *Rapid* is certainly making all efforts to close with us.'

Bolitho stood up, his mind busy. 'Make more sail and tell our ships to do the same.' With a physical effort he sat down again and bit into the treacled bread. 'I want to speak with Quarrell as soon as we are hove-to.'

Keen hurried away, and soon the deck quivered to the thud of bare feet and then the clatter of blocks and rigging.

But it was halfway through the forenoon watch before *Rapid* was able to beat up to the rest of the squadron. The first air of excitement gave way to silent resignation as the gratings were rigged and the hands piped aft to witness punishment. Two dozen lashes a man while the drums rolled and the spray pattered across the prisoners and onlookers alike.

Paget touched his hat. 'Punishment carried out, sir.'

Keen nodded and watched the hands dismissed, the gratings removed for scrubbing, while the flogged men were taken below to the sickbay. He handed the Articles of War to Paget and said, 'God damn this waiting!'

When eventually Quarrell climbed aboard from his gig he could barely control his excitement and pleasure.

At dawn *Rapid* had ordered the vessel to heave-to and await a boarding party. The lieutenant who had gone across in the boat had been thorough. The brigantine was a Greek trader, and her master had been able to speak English and had been more than willing to cooperate. The vessel had been loaded with olive oil and figs, but Quarrell described her as being so filthy that it was a marvel she obtained any cargoes at all.

Quarrell took a deep breath. 'The master was carrying

several bottles of wine and brandy, sir. My first lieutenant
saw them at once.' He turned and beamed at Keen. 'All
French, sir.'

They glanced at Bolitho. He said nothing so Keen
remarked, 'Your lieutenant had his wits about him, eh?'

Bolitho unrolled a chart across the table, his mouth
suddenly dry. 'Continue.' It was Quarrell's moment – to
prod him into haste would only fluster him.

The young commander said, 'When questioned about
the bottles, sir, the fellow admitted they had been given
to him in exchange for oil three days ago.' He watched
Bolitho's grave features. 'It was Rear-Admiral Jobert's
squadron, sir, no doubt about it. The Greek was able to
describe them, even the leopard figurehead on the
flagship.'

'Show me.' Bolitho held down the chart with a ruler
and dividers. He could feel Quarrell's eagerness, sense the
pride his discovery had given him.

Quarrell peered at the chart, at the marks and lines
which showed the squadron's position and progress.

'They were steering due east, sir.' He placed one finger
on it. 'That would put them about there.'

Keen leaned over the table beside him. 'Corsica.' He
gave a sigh. 'I should have guessed.'

Quarrell glanced from him to Bolitho. 'The Greek
master said that a French officer came aboard. He told
him they were going to take on fresh water.'

Keen frowned, 'Another long passage maybe?'

Bolitho stood up, his mind working busily. Fresh water.
Why did the mention of it always provoke such painful
memories?

'What have you done about the brigantine?'

Quarrell looked blank. There was no warmth in
Bolitho's voice.

'I – I knew how much you needed information, sir, so
I considered it my duty to – '

'You let him go? You put no guard aboard?'

'Well, no, sir.' Quarrell looked helplessly at Keen for
support.

Keen said, 'It could be the truth, sir.'

Bolitho walked aft to the windows and pushed his hand through his hair. He felt the deep scar on his temple, a ready reminder of that other time when collecting water had seemed such a simple mission.

Quarrell said, 'I could chase after him, sir.' He sounded lost.

'Too late.' Bolitho watched some fish jump from *Argonaute*'s shadow. 'He would give you the slip after nightfall. Heading for Corsica, you think? To take on water for three sail-of-the-line, and the two fifth-rates, what do you estimate?' He turned and looked at Keen, his eye throbbing painfully. 'Three, four days?'

Keen nodded slowly. 'We could still run him to earth, sir!'

Bolitho sat on the bench seat and clasped his hands together. He did not need a chart; he could see it clearly in his mind. Jobert's ships – if the wind stayed fair, they could be pinned on a lee shore or trapped until they came out to fight.

Keen said, 'So it was neither Egypt nor Gibraltar after all, sir.'

'Fetch my flag-lieutenant, Ozzard.' It was strange how he had managed to converse with Stayt without touching on the court of inquiry. Stayt was wary, withdrawn to such a point that they barely spoke except on matters of orders and signals.

When Stayt arrived his eyes moved swiftly across the group by the table. He asked, 'May I get something, Sir Richard?'

'The reports from the flag-officer in Malta. Bring them.'

Quarrell said, 'My first lieutenant was satisfied that the Greek told him the truth, sir.'

Bolitho said, 'Or maybe what the French wanted him to believe.'

Stayt laid down a folder on the table and Bolitho strained his eyes to look through it. Convoy arrival, escorts and departure times, passengers and equipment to be disembarked or carried elsewhere.

Bolitho pulled one paper towards him, the name *Benbow* standing out from the unknown clerk's writing.

Ignoring the others he snatched up the brass dividers and moved them quickly across his chart. It was all he could do to stop himself from cursing aloud as his good eye watered with the strain he was putting on it.

Three days, four at the most. It had to be. *Had to be.*

He looked up. '*Benbow* sailed from Malta in company with two homebound ships. There is one frigate as additional escort.'

Keen exclaimed, 'All that for just two ships? And we are expected to manage with – '

Bolitho held up his hand. 'I should have seen it, Val. Something that Inch's first lieutenant said after the battle.' In his mind he could picture the weary lieutenant with the bandaged head. *Pity I've not got that Frenchie's extra boom.* He could almost hear Savill's voice. The man who had seen it, yet had not realized what he had discovered.

Bolitho said, 'The ships are carrying a cargo of gold and precious stones. A king's, or should I say a sultan's, ransom.' He wanted to shout at them, to bang the table and make them realize the enormity of the discovery, and of Jobert's confidence. 'Jobert intends to attack that convoy and lift off the gold at sea. Corsica, Val? I think not. I believe this is what was intended from the start. Jobert and I got in the way. But now that way is clear.'

Bolitho looked at Quarrell. 'Return to your command and await orders.'

Quarrell backed away. 'I – I am sorry, Sir Richard.'

Bolitho eyed him calmly. 'Your lieutenant was convinced, so why not the rest of us?'

As the door closed Keen said, 'We have nothing definite, sir!'

Stayt added, 'If the French are really in Corsican waters, and we fail to seek them out or inform Lord Nelson – '

Bolitho looked past him. 'I *know*, gentlemen. I shall be held responsible.' He smiled shortly. 'And this time I shall have no defence.'

Once more he crossed to the chart. Keen was trying to warn and protect him. If they carried on as they were nobody would be able to blame him. He lowered his head to study the neat calculations. But if he went against everything but instinct, and a new, strange sense of destiny, he might still be wrong.

'In my estimation, we have two days. No more.' He touched the chart with the points of the dividers. 'Allowing for the weather, we should make a rendezvous with the convoy about there.' He turned away so that they should not see his expression. While they hunted fruitlessly along the rugged Corsican coast, the gold would be seized and Herrick overwhelmed. He would die fighting alongside his men. But he would certainly die.

Bolitho raised his voice, 'Mr Yovell! Come out, you quill-pusher, and I shall dictate my fighting instructions!'

Yovell padded across the cabin, smiling happily as if he had just been awarded a title.

Bolitho looked at Stayt. 'Warn the signals midshipman to be ready.' He thought of Sheaffe and wondered how he got along with his father.

Alone with Keen he said, 'It's a chance I *must* take.' He added with a wry smile, 'It was the wine and the brandy which alerted me. I could never imagine Jobert giving anything to a poor Greek trader unless he wanted *us* to know about it. Perhaps this time he has been too clever and overconfident.'

Keen doubted if Quarrell's information was enough to be certain of anything. Jobert may have laid some more bait, but he was wily enough to know how Bolitho might react.

Bolitho's change of mood, this new confidence which left him free to joke with his secretary, was unnerving.

Keen said simply, 'Then it will be a fight.'

Bolitho took his arm, the tone of Keen's voice making the vague strategy into stark, brutal reality.

'We shall face it together, Val,' he said quietly.

Keen smiled. 'Yes. Together.' But all he saw was her face, and for the first time he was afraid.

Commander Adam Bolitho pushed the unruly hair from his eyes as he stared up at the men working on the foretopsail yard. The sturdy brig *Firefly* was heeling hard over on the larboard tack, the sea creaming up to the sealed gunports and cascading along the lee scuppers.

He wore only his shirt and breeches and his clothes were plastered to his body like a wet skin. He would never tire of it. He wanted to laugh or sing as the brig, *his* command, dipped her bows steeply and threw up a sunburst cloud of spray.

He waited for the bows to rise again and then moved to the compass box. It gave him a marvellous feeling of pride. The vessel was heading due east, with the Balearic Islands somewhere below the larboard horizon.

Down again, and another great curtain of spray flew above the forecastle where other men worked busily to trim the yards.

Adam's first lieutenant, a youngster of his own age, lurched from the rail and shouted, 'Take in another reef, sir?'

Adam showed his teeth and laughed. 'No! It's not time yet!'

The lieutenant grimaced then smiled. It never was time with his young commander.

Adam moved restlessly about the poop while his *Firefly* lifted and thundered over the tossing water. Just days ago he had been under the Rock's shadow, ready to leave the Mediterranean and make his way back to an English winter. Instead he had received orders to return instantly to Malta.

The fever on the Rock was over, and the dispatch which Adam had locked in his strongbox was to tell the admiral at Malta to prevent a convoy from leaving for England. If it had already sailed Adam was to place himself under the orders of the convoy's senior officer. That too made him grin. Rear-Admiral Herrick. To Adam he was more like a fond uncle than a flag-officer.

It was exciting. His own command, and the sea to himself. The French were out, one squadron under Rear-Admiral Jobert had been reported on the move. If it had somehow managed to slip past his uncle's squadron, his ships were needed now at Gibraltar to close gates and cut off any attempt by Jobert to enter the Atlantic. A gigantic game of cat-and-mouse.

Adam wiped the spray from his lips. A game for admirals and great ships-of-the-line. While here –

He walked to the taffrail and stared at the frothing wake beneath the counter. Down there was his own cabin. A luxury beyond imagination. A place of his own.

He thought suddenly of the court of inquiry in Malta. He would learn the result when he reached there. Captain Keen might share the Bolitho curse of being hounded out of envy or revenge. They had passed the homebound packet *Lord Egmont,* and Adam had wondered about her. It would be just like his uncle to –

The lookout called, 'Sail! Weather bow!'

Morrison, his first lieutenant, hurried to the ratlines but Adam said, 'No, I'll go.' As a midshipman he had always enjoyed skylarking with his companions during the dogwatches. Up and down the masts, out and around the futtock shrouds. Few captains interfered. They probably thought it would keep their 'young gentlemen' out of mischief. He climbed rapidly up the ratlines, the wind ripping at his shirt. Once he hung out from the shrouds and looked down at the forward part of the vessel as the sea boiled over the catheads and tightly lashed anchors before frothing along the decks and leapfrogging over the black four-pounders.

He had always wanted a frigate. Be like his uncle had once been, one of the best frigate captains in the fleet. But when he looked at his lively *Firefly* he could scarcely bear to think of ever leaving her.

He found the lookout perched comfortably on the cross-trees, his battered face creased with curiosity as he watched his young lord and master swarming up to join him.

Adam pulled a telescope from his belt and tried several times without success to steady it towards the larboard bow.

The lookout, one of the oldest seamen in the ship, said hoarsely, 'I think there be two on 'em, sir.' He barely raised his voice but it carried easily above the roar of wind

and bucking canvas. Many years in all kinds of ships had
taught him that.

Adam wrapped his leg around a stay and tried again.
The mast was shaking so violently it was like a giant whip,
he thought.

He gasped, 'There she is! It's fine eyesight you have,
Marley!'

The seaman grinned. He didn't need a telescope. But he
liked the new commander. A bit of a devil with the girls,
or soon would be, he decided.

An extra lively wave thundered beneath the stem and
lifted the hull towards the sky like a surfacing whale. And
there she was, standing before the wind under close-reefed
topsails, her hull still hidden by leaping crests as if she was
driving herself under. Adam wiped the lens with his hand
and almost lost his hold as his ship dived once more.

He waited, counting the seconds until the jib boom
began to lift again, the sails flapping from it like wet
banners.

Adam closed the glass with a snap. 'You were right.
There are two of them.' He patted the man's thick
shoulder. 'I'll send you a relief.'

The seaman would have spat had he been able but
contented himself with, 'Nah, sir, I'll stay. They'll be
some o' Lord Nelson's ships.'

Adam slithered down a backstay, all dignity forgotten
as Morrison hurried to meet him.

'Two sail-of-the-line.' Adam dropped his voice, 'Same
tack as ourselves.'

Morrison grinned. 'We'd better not draw too close, sir,
or we might be given some more orders!'

Adam pushed his fingers through his black hair. It felt
sticky with salt. He knew he should be nervous, perhaps
even fearful. But the same excitement would not leave him
and he said, 'You may take in that reef now. And do
not worry yourself about more orders from on high, *Mr*
Morrison, for those two liners are French!'

The men scampered to shorten sail then Morrison took
a deep breath. 'What do you intend, sir?'

Adam gestured to the nearest four-pounder. 'Even we

are no match for them.' He became serious for a moment. 'We shall follow them and see what they are about.'

Morrison had been first lieutenant under the previous captain, who had managed to make daily life aboard *Firefly* little better than drudgery. Commander Bolitho was like a breath of clean air; he was very capable and nobody's fool.

He hinted cautiously, 'But your orders, sir?'

'Are to find the convoy or Malta, whichever comes first.' His mouth crinkled in a grin again. 'I think these two gentlemen will lead us to one or t'other, eh?'

Morrison hurried away to assist the second lieutenant. The old captain had never been like this.

He glanced aft again and saw Adam Bolitho beside the helm speaking with the master's mate. He acted more like a midshipman than a captain.

Aloud he said, 'He'll do me, that's for certain!' But only the wind heard him.

Two hundred miles east-northeast of his nephew's *Firefly* and ignorant of the fact Adam had been sent back from Gibraltar, Bolitho gripped the poop rail and watched his ships reeling and buffeted in the same gale.

The wind, which had veered to a strong northwesterly, showed no signs of easing, and when he steadied his telescope Bolitho saw the little brig *Rapid* standing out to windward, her hull and lower spars deluged with spray and spindrift.

It was to be hoped that Quarrell had made quite certain that the big thirty-two-pounders from *Helicon* were properly mounted and lashed firmly to their tackles. A gun breaking loose in a gale could kill and maim like a mad beast. It could also wreck the upper deck whilst doing it.

The sky was clear of all but a few streaky clouds, hard blue and with little warmth. He saw a party of seamen with a boatswain's mate hauling a ragged line through a block and preparing to reeve a new one to replace it. They were soaked in spray, and the salt would do little to help their thirst.

Too much rum or brandy would do more harm than good. Bolitho bit his lip and wondered at his earlier confidence. After pounding their way farther south with Sardinia's blurred coastline rarely lost from view, the hope of making a rendezvous with Herrick's convoy seemed like a bad dream. Even supposing Jobert was making for the same objective. He stamped on his doubts and turned from the rail to see Midshipman Sheaffe and his signal party watching him. They immediately dropped their eyes or became engrossed elsewhere.

Bolitho allowed his aching mind to explore his calculations yet again. The convoy would be very slow and precise in its progress. He had done all he could, with his small squadron spread out as far as possible without losing contact completely. Thank God for *Barracouta* and *Rapid,* he thought despairingly. But for them –

He heard Paget shout at a helmsman, and a muttered answer. Paget would stand no nonsense, and he at least showed no signs of doubt. He was a good man, Bolitho thought, and as a young lieutenant had fought under Duncan at Camperdown. There were not too many officers in the squadron who had seen a battle like that one.

Keen climbed up from the quarterdeck to join him. He had been down on the orlop to visit one of the midshipmen who had broken a leg after being flung bodily from a gangway in the gale.

Keen stared at the forecastle, his eyes red with strain, and Bolitho knew he had barely left the deck since the wind had risen.

Bolitho smiled, 'A strange sight, Val. Bright and bitter, like a dockside whore.'

Keen laughed despite his apprehension. He wanted to tell Bolitho to break off the hunt. It was finished before it had begun. Even if he had been right about Jobert, and it seemed less likely with each aching mile, they would not find him now.

Keen was sick and tired of it, and hated to think what it would do to Bolitho when the truth came out. Everyone said that Nelson had survived only on his luck. He had been fortunate. It was rare.

Bolitho knew Keen was watching him and could guess what he was thinking. As flag-captain he wanted to advise him. As a friend he knew he could not.

Bolitho looked at the cold sky and thought again of Falmouth. Maybe Belinda would have received his letter, or have heard the news from someone else. He thought too of the girl with the dark misty eyes. He smiled. Brave Zenoria, he had called her. She was the one good thing in all this endurance and failure.

Keen saw the smile and wondered. How did he go on like this? It was fanatical, unswerving, but it would not save him at a court-martial.

'How was the boy? Midshipman Estridge, wasn't it?'

'A clean break, sir. The surgeon was more troubled by some of his other injured hands. He's had more cuts and gashes than a small war!'

There was a seaman working beside one of the nine-pounders and Bolitho had seen him earlier. He was stripped to the waist, not out of bravado, but to try and keep his clothing dry. When he had turned, Bolitho had seen his back, scarred from shoulders to waist, like the marks of a giant claw. It made him think of Zenoria and what Keen had saved her from.

But when Keen laughed at his earlier remark the seaman had turned and looked up at him. Bolitho had rarely seen such hatred in a man's glance.

Keen saw it too and said tightly, 'I read the Articles of War before a flogging. I did not compose the bloody rules!'

Bolitho could sense his anger, something he had rarely shown even after the court of inquiry.

He saw extra marines at hatchways, their scarlet coats dark with flung spray. Keen was taking no chances. Better to prevent trouble than enforce the misery of suppressing it.

Bolitho said, 'I am going below.' He looked at him squarely. 'If I am wrong – ' He shrugged as if it were of little concern. Then he added, 'Some will be pleased. I hope that then they will let my family rest in peace.'

Keen watched him stride towards the poop ladder and felt a stab of pity as Bolitho caught his arm against the mizzen bitts.

Paget moved quietly beside him. 'May I ask what you think of our chances, sir?'

Keen glanced at him. The first lieutenant, the link between captain and ship's company, quarterdeck and forecastle.

He replied, 'Ask me again when we have run Jobert ashore.'

They both turned and Paget exclaimed, 'Not thunder too!'

Keen looked past him. Bolitho was climbing to the poop again, and wearing the old sword, with Allday a few paces behind him.

The lookout yelled with disbelief, 'Gunfire, sir! To th' south'rd!'

Bolitho looked at them. 'No. Not thunder this time.'

Keen stared. How did he do it? Moments earlier he must have been accepting failure. Now he looked strangely calm. Even his voice was untroubled as he said, 'General signal, Mr Sheaffe. *Make more sail.*'

He watched the flags hurriedly bent onto the halliards and sent soaring up to the yards for all his ships to see.

Bolitho wanted to grip his hands together for surely they must be shaking.

'Acknowledged, sir!' That was Stayt, appearing silently like a cat.

The distant murmur of cannon fire rolled across the water. It was a long way off. Bolitho said, 'We'll not fight before dawn tomorrow.' That was a fact which had to be faced. When darkness closed in the ships might be scattered by the blustery wind. By dawn it could be too late. *Benbow* was more than a match for any eager privateers or corsairs from the North African shore, but against a whole squadron she would stand no chance. He cocked his head to listen as the gunfire came again. Not many ships. Perhaps two. What could that mean?

He said, 'General signal. *Prepare for battle*. The people will sleep at their guns tonight.'

He touched the hilt of the old sword and felt a shiver run through his body.

He could recall as if it were yesterday the moment when he had been walking with Adam to the sally port on Portsmouth Point. Then he had looked back to search for something. So perhaps he had known it would be the last time.

16

Men of War

Rear-Admiral Thomas Herrick stood by the weather nettings, his chin sunk in his neckcloth while he watched *Benbow*'s seamen hauling on the braces to trim the yards and reset the reefed topsails.

Everything took an eternity; it had taken a whole day to make any progress and drained all their skill. Now at last they were past the southernmost tip of Sardinia, which lay some fifty miles to starboard. On the other beam was Africa at about the same distance.

Wallowing downwind of *Benbow* were two heavy merchantmen, *Governor* and *Prince Henry*. Herrick could only guess at the value of their cargoes.

He thought yet again of Bolitho's face in the stern cabin of this ship, the one which had once proudly flown his flag when Herrick had been his captain. He could not forget the bitterness in Bolitho's voice, the reckless contempt when he had damned the admiral's court of inquiry.

It was a strange coincidence which had decided Admiral Sir Marcus Laforey to take passage in *Benbow*. He had left his flag-captain in temporary charge, although the way Sir Marcus ate and drank it seemed unlikely he would ever return to Malta.

He heard Captain Dewar discussing something with the sailing master. Herrick sighed. He would have to make it up with his flag-captain, for Dewar was an excellent officer and very conscientious. Herrick blamed himself for Dewar's wariness. He had been foul company since the inquiry.

He felt the spray on his face and peered beyond the

starboard bow where, reeling like a ship in distress, his only frigate was tacking yet again to try to stand up to windward. She was the *Philomel* of twenty-six guns and, but for the grave news of the French squadron, she would have been completing a much needed refit in the dockyard where *Benbow* had been overhauled.

Herrick gripped his hands behind him and looked along the tilting maindeck. He thought too of Inch, another friend, one of their close-knit community. Was he dead, he wondered? It was unlikely he would have struck to the French.

He glanced at the sky, so clear yet so hostile. Perhaps by tomorrow the wind would have died down – any reduction would be a blessing.

Captain Dewar crossed the deck and said, 'Shall we lie-to tonight, sir?'

Herrick shook his head. He felt the ship lift under him and his sturdy legs bracing to take it. Unlike Bolitho, he had never got into the habit of pacing the deck. He liked to stand and feel his ship. He could think better that way, he had long decided.

'No. We need more sea-room. Before dark, pass the word for lights to be hoisted on the merchantmen. We can hold station that way. *Philomel* will have to manage on her own.'

Dewar gauged the moment as a wildfowler tests the wind before firing a shot.

'D'you think Vice-Admiral Bolitho has met with this, this Jobert?'

'If not, I'm sure he'll stand between us and the enemy.' He thought suddenly of the eight hundred miles which still lay ahead before they could moor beneath the guns of the Rock. Fever or not, it would offer a breathing space, and perhaps he might obtain another escort. But he said, 'If anyone can do it, our Dick will.'

Dewar eyed him curiously but remained silent. They were on good terms again. He would try again later.

Herrick toyed with the idea of going aft, but the thought of Laforey, with his gout and his steady drinking, turned him against it.

The masthead lookout yelled, 'Gunfire! To the west'rd!'

The sound must have carried more swiftly to his dizzy perch for even as Herrick made to speak he heard the distant bang of cannon fire and some intermittent shots from smaller weapons. Herrick's worried mind cleared as if he had ducked his head in ice water.

'Clear for action, Captain Dewar.' That was another thing which Herrick did not understand. He could never bring himself to use his captain's first name. Yet in other ways he had learned and used so much from Bolitho's example. 'Signal the convoy to close up.' He swore as the calls shrilled and *Benbow*'s six hundred seamen and marines dropped what they were doing and rushed to obey the awakened drums.

Damn the light and the wind. Everything was against them. How many were there? He forced himself to show a confidence which had eluded him after the lookout's cry. Who were they firing at? More crashes and bangs rolled across the tossing white horses, but the lookout stayed silent. They were still a long way off and the sullen explosions were using the stiff wind to carry their message.

'Signal *Philomel* to investigate.' Herrick opened and closed his hands behind him. The little frigate could always turn and fly with the wind if she got into danger. It would have helped so much if he knew her captain. His name was Saunders, that was all he had discovered.

Herrick strode to the opposite side and saw the nearest merchantman setting her topgallants to bear up on her companion. God, they looked like fat beasts for the slaughter, Herrick thought glumly. He heard the first lieutenant's voice urging the hands to extra efforts as they cleared the ship for action, each man fully aware that they now had two admirals on board.

Herrick considered his choices. Turn back for Malta? Even with the wind in their favour it was still another four hundred miles. In daylight the French would soon find them. So hold the present course? There was always a chance that the enemy was being engaged by an unexpected friendly force or that they might manage to lose them during the night.

He said, 'We will stand-to throughout the night, Captain Dewar.'

He seemed to see dear Dulcie in his thoughts. She was always so proud of him. He turned towards the western horizon which was already painted in the deeper hues of sunset.

A nervous-looking lieutenant, one of Laforey's staff, hovered at his elbow and said timidly, 'My admiral has nowhere to go, sir, now that the ship is cleared for action.'

Herrick bit back a rude retort. There were too many ears around him.

He replied calmly, 'I am most sorry, but as you see, all our people are having the same *inconvenience*.' Under his breath he muttered, 'Bloody fool!'

A shrill voice pealed down from the mainmast cross-trees. Dewar had sent his signals midshipman aloft with a telescope.

'Deck there! Two sail-of-the-line to west'rd, sir! They wear French colours!'

Herrick glanced quickly along the deck before him. Every gun manned, other half-naked figures waiting to trim or set more sails. Marines in their scarlet coats and crossbelts, ready to fight. *Benbow* could and would give good account of herself, as she had proved several times. Even her company was lucky to have so many trained and seasoned seamen. She had been too long out of England to have to rely on the press and the sweepings of the assizes. Two to one were acceptable odds. If Lady Luck had been less kind, the enemy might have been amongst them soon after dusk, and it would have been impossible to fight and protect the merchantmen at the same time.

He saw *Philomel*'s masts strain hard over as she fought across the eye of the wind and then filled her sails on the opposite tack. Herrick smiled grimly. Bolitho had always loved frigates; he on the other hand preferred something steadier and more powerful under his feet. Maybe his early experience of a tyrannical captain and a mutinous company had soured him against them in his later years.

The midshipman called down again, 'Small vessel is

engaged with them, sir!' His shrill voice cracked in disbelief, 'A *brig*, sir!'

Herrick stared up at the topmast. Whoever commanded that brig was trying to warn him. How could he know? He rubbed his eyes and saw the second signals midshipman peering up at his friend. More like a lover than a would-be officer, Herrick thought.

He snapped, 'Alter course. Steer sou'west by south.' He waited for the signal to be run up. 'What the devil is Captain Saunders about?' A few isolated bangs echoed across the water as *Philomel* gathered the wind and increased speed towards the enemy.

'Recall that madman! I shall require him right here very soon!'

Eventually the midshipman lowered his glass and called, '*Philomel* does not acknowledge, sir.'

'God damn it, is everyone blind?' He thought of Bolitho as he said it and was ashamed. He added, 'Alter course anyway, Captain Dewar.'

The slight change of direction laid the two big merchantmen almost in line abeam under *Benbow*'s lee. It might at least make them feel more confident when the enemy's full strength became apparent.

The nervous lieutenant returned and Herrick glared at him.

'Well?'

The lieutenant stared round at the gun crews, the sanded decks, the marines' bayoneted muskets.

'Sir Marcus sends his compliments, sir, and – '

Herrick had an idea. 'Tell my servant to give the admiral a bottle of my best port.' As the lieutenant hurried towards the poop he shouted, 'And another after that!' He looked at Dewar. 'That should keep him quiet, damn him!'

The darkness moved across from the opposite horizon like an endless cloak; even the wavecrests seemed to diminish as men became shadows, and the sea lost its menace.

But the gunfire continued on and off, the quick, snapping bang of the brig's cannon, followed by the angry bellow of heavier artillery.

Captain Dewar took a glass of brandy from his coxswain and watched as his admiral did likewise.

'Whoever is doing that is a brave man, sir.'

Herrick felt the brandy sear his salt-cracked lips. There were a few other brigs reported in this area, but in his heart he knew which one had tossed caution aside to warn him.

He said slowly, 'At first light I intend to engage.'

Dewar nodded and wondered why Herrick had said it. He knew his admiral by now. He had never doubted that he would attack.

Bolitho lowered his head and stood between two deckhead beams. The orlop deck, a place of spiralling lanterns and prancing shadows. After the long, open gundecks overhead it seemed all but deserted. The surgeon's mate and his loblolly boys in their long aprons stood around the makeshift tables where Tuson would perform his grisly work. Freshly scrubbed tubs for the wings and limbs of his amputations were a grim reminder of the work which went on here once a battle was joined.

Carcaud was checking over a line of instruments which seemed to blink like lamps as the lanterns swung above them. He, like most of the men Bolitho had seen while he had walked tirelessly through his flagship, avoided his glance. It was as if they felt unsure of him in their presence instead of standing aloof on the quarterdeck amongst his officers.

At the door of the sickbay Bolitho paused and waited for Tuson to look up from his preparations. There was a smell of dressings and enforced cleanliness. The only other occupant peered at Bolitho from a cot. Midshipman Estridge was not entirely saved by his broken leg; Tuson had had him rolling bandages although he was lying on his back.

Bolitho nodded to him and then said to the surgeon, 'It will be daylight in an hour.'

Tuson regarded him bleakly. 'How is the eye, sir?'

Bolitho shrugged. 'It has been worse.' He could not

account for his strange disregard for danger, even death. He had been on every deck, had made sure that everyone had seen him. He had imagined that down here at least, a place he had always dreaded, he would have felt anxiety. If anything he felt only relief. It was a level of recklessness he did not remember in the past. Resigned perhaps, so where was the worth in worrying any more?

Tuson looked at the low deckhead. It almost brushed his white hair. 'The ship is full of sounds.'

Bolitho knew what he meant. Normally you could recognize the general movement of men, of seamanship and the daily routine of eating and working.

But now, with the ship cleared for battle, the noises were all overhead, concentrated around the guns as they lay behind sealed ports, their crews huddled against them, trying or pretending to sleep. Soon those same guns would be like furnace bars, and no man would dare to touch them with bare hands.

The sounds of sea and wind were muted here. The sluice of water against the bilge, the occasional clatter of a pump as men, unfit to fight, carried out their regular soundings of the well. It was uncanny, eerie, he thought. They must be so close to the enemy, and yet, with the coming of darkness, the distant gunfire had ceased. As if they were alone.

Tuson watched him. He had already noted that Bolitho had changed into a crisp new shirt and neckcloth, and his uniform coat bore the glittering epaulettes with the twin silver stars. He pondered on it. Did Bolitho not care? Did he have a death wish? Or was it that he cared too much, so that his own safety had become secondary? He was hatless, and his black hair shone in the moving beams, and only the loose lock of hair which, Tuson knew better than most, hid a terrible scar showed any signs of greyness. An odd mixture. He would be handed his hat and sword when he returned to the deck.

Tuson had never seen it, but the silent ceremony was almost legendary in the squadron, perhaps throughout the whole fleet. Allday with the sword was as well known as a bishop with his mitre.

Tuson said, 'I have had Captain Inch taken forrard, sir. The place is less comfortable,' he glanced briefly through the door at the empty table and the waiting instruments, his crew standing or sitting like scavengers, 'but I feel that he will be better placed there.'

A midshipman's white breeches appeared on the companion ladder and after a slight hesitation he said, 'Captain Keen's respects, Sir Richard, and – '

Bolitho nodded. It was little Hickling, who, although quite unsuspecting, had helped him to smuggle the girl aboard the packet brig at Malta.

'I am ready, thank you.' He looked at Tuson, a lingering glance in which the surgeon later realized he could see no flaw or injury.

'Take care of the people.'

Tuson watched him leave. 'And you take care of *you*,' he murmured.

Bolitho, with Hickling panting behind him, made his way, ladder by ladder, to the quarterdeck.

It was still very dark, with just occasional whitecaps beyond the sides to distinguish sea from sky. But the stars were fainter, and there was an air of morning, stale and damp.

Keen waited by the rail. 'The wind's eased, sir. Still fresh enough to keep 'em guessing.' He sounded relieved that Hickling had found him. Keen had never known Bolitho tour a ship alone before. Not even with Allday, as if he needed to feel the mood of each man under his flag.

Allday clipped on his sword and Ozzard handed him his hat before scuttling away to the hold where he would remain until the day was won or lost.

Bolitho could distinguish the litter of flags on the deck, the occasional movements of the signals midshipman and his assistants. Stayt was here too, and Bolitho guessed that he had taken time to clean and load his beautiful pistol.

'Just a matter of waiting, Val.' He wondered if the other ships were following astern, if *Rapid* and *Barracouta* were on station. It must have been a long night for most of them, Bolitho thought. He remembered the Battle of the

Saintes when he had commanded his first frigate. It had taken an eternity for the two fleets to draw near enough to each other to fight. All day, or so it had seemed, they had watched the tremendous display of the French masts as they had lifted above the horizon. Like knights on the field of battle. It had been awesome and terrible. But they had won the day, if too late to win a war.

Keen stood beside him, silently preparing himself and searching his thoughts for any weakness. The sporadic gunfire had been a clear message that the convoy lay somewhere ahead and was under attack. Once he glanced at Bolitho to see if there was any surprise or satisfaction that he had been proved right, that he had found the enemy, when any honest man would have admitted that he had doubted his wisdom in acting on *Rapid*'s information. But even in the gloom he recognized Bolitho's quiet determination, rather than any hint of relief.

And they were going to fight. It did not sound as if many vessels were involved. Keen saw the girl again in his mind and wanted to speak her name aloud if only to reassure himself. It only took a second for a man to die. The cause and the victory did not matter to the one who heard the cannon's roar for the last time.

He pictured Inch down on the orlop, hearing the din of war, unable to help or be with his friends. Keen had visited him after he had left the quarterdeck to speak with his lieutenants on the gundecks. Inch was very weak and in great pain from the two amputations to his arm.

Keen felt the sweat cold on his spine. He had been wounded, and still felt the raw wound on occasions. But to lie on a table, with his men all around watching and suffering, waiting their turn, how could anyone stand it? The flensing knife and then the agony of the saw, choking on the leather strap to stifle the screams. He recalled what he had told Zenoria. *It is what I am trained to do.* The words seemed to mock him now.

Luke Fallowfield, the sailing master, banged his red hands together and the sound made several of the men nearby start with alarm. We are all on edge, Keen thought. The odds no longer matter. It is like a reckoning.

Bolitho looked abeam and saw the first hint of dawn, a faint glow on the horizon's edge. Many eyes would be watching it. Measuring their chances, the margin of life and death.

Keen strode to the compass and peered at the flickering light.

'Bring her closer to the wind, Mr Fallowfield. Alter course two points to starboard.'

Men moved like eager shadows in the darkness, and Bolitho thanked God he had Keen as his captain. If they wandered too far east they would never be able to beat back in time to close with the convoy. He bunched his fists and pressed them against his thighs. They needed light, and yet many were dreading what they might see.

Bolitho touched his left eyelid and wanted to rub it. He thought of all Tuson's arguments and warnings. They would count for nothing today.

The helmsman called, 'Sou'sou'west, zur. Full an' bye!'

Bolitho heard the main topsail flap as if with irritation as *Argonaute* nudged still further into the wind, her yards braced hard round to hold her on the same tack.

Soon, soon. He thought momentarily that he had spoken aloud. He heard Keen telling Paget to put more lookouts aloft, one to take a telescope. When he looked up he thought he could see the white crossbelts of the marines in the maintop, a man stretching out in a yawn. Not tiredness this time, he thought. It was often the first sign of fear.

It was strange, he thought, that he might fall today and Falmouth would not hear of it until next year. A Christmas in the big grey house below Pendennis Castle, singers from the town to wish them well, and to amuse little Elizabeth.

He stopped his drifting thoughts and said, 'Union Flag at the fore, if you please.'

He heard the squeal of halliards as his red command flag was hauled down and replaced seconds later by the biggest Jack in the ship. It was still hidden in darkness, but when the sun came up Jobert would see it. He felt strangely elated, with no sense of anxiety at all.

Paget's shadow turned from the quarterdeck rail. 'Colours aloft, Sir Richard!'

Bolitho nodded. Paget sounded much as he felt. Committed, a chance to end the waiting.

'Deck there! Sail on the lee bow!'

Bolitho said, 'Well done, Val. We are in a perfect position!'

A gun echoed across the water, just the one, and Bolitho thought he saw the flash for just a split-second.

Another lookout yelled, 'Convoy ahead!'

'Make a general signal.' Bolitho moved restlessly across the deck, his fingers to his chin.

The lookout's cry made him look up again. 'Two sail-of-the-line, weather bow!'

Bolitho said, 'So there we have it, Val. Two of the devils.' He glanced at Stayt, 'Make to the squadron, *Enemy in sight.*'

When he looked across the lee side again he saw the horizon, salmon-pink, like an unending bridge.

Above the braced yards of the foremast the flag flicked out, huge and bright, and completely isolated from the ship, which remained in shadow for a few more moments.

'General chase, sir?' That was Stayt.

Bolitho opened his mouth and then shut it again. Two ships-of-the-line. It was not the numbers, but the bearing. It did not fit the pattern. Again he felt the touch of warning. 'No. Signal the squadron to maintain station.' He did not turn as more gunfire cracked over the array of white horses.

Some of the Royal Marines in the foretop were staring up at the flag above them and cheering, their voices wild above the press of wind and canvas.

Bolitho loosened his sword in its scabbard without even noticing what he had done. *Into battle.* All the resentment and suffering would be forgotten. It was their way.

Another gun banged out but from the squadron astern. Keen exclaimed, 'Hell's teeth, who is doing that?'

Stayt called, '*Icarus*, sir.'

Stayt clambered into the shrouds as the first light

touched the masts and yards of the two ships which followed in their wake.

'From *Icarus*, sir. Enemy in sight to the nor'east.'

Keen stared. 'I don't believe it!'

Bolitho walked to the rail and grasped it firmly. It felt cold and damp. Not for long.

'Inform *Barracouta* and *Rapid*.' He watched the breathless signals party hoisting more signals and then walked to the shrouds where Stayt hung with one arm bent over a ratline while he levelled his telescope.

'*Three sail-of-the-line, sir.*' His lips moved as he read the flags. '*And two other vessels.*'

Bolitho found that he could accept it, even though he could see his squadron caught in the prongs of the converging ships, like the neck of a poacher's bag.

The two ships originally sighted must have arrived by sheer coincidence or had been sent from hiding by another commander. But Jobert was here, and the balance had tilted completely. Five to three, and one of them would be Jobert's powerful three-decker. The two lesser vessels, as yet unidentified, must be the two frigates. The odds were formidable and his choice nonexistent. He watched the sun's rim as it lifted above the sea and painted the sails of friends and enemies alike in pale gold.

Bolitho took a glass and rested it on the hammock nettings, waiting for *Argonaute* to dip her flank into a trough. He saw the overlapping cluster of the convoy, and felt his heart tighten as he recognized *Benbow*'s familiar hull and raked masts, her ports already open, her guns still in black shadow.

A ripple of flashes spat from the two Frenchmen, and he watched thin waterspouts leap amongst the waves and then be shredded by the keen wind.

Jobert's squadron must have sailed down the other coastline of Sardinia, making all speed while he had dealt with *Helicon* and her wounded. Now like tracks on a chart they were all met. Jobert's ships on the larboard quarter and not yet visible from the quarterdeck. The other two converging to starboard, firing towards *Benbow* as they advanced. Chainshot and langridge to dismast or at least

cripple her. Jobert would finish it. More gunfire crashed
out, and Bolitho shifted the glass to stare at a small frigate
which had appeared around the two seventy-fours. She
must be Herrick's other escort, perhaps the one which had
challenged the enemy and so foiled their surprise attack.
She was out of control, and almost totally dismasted. She
must have attempted to harry the enemy's rear, like a
terrier going for a bear, but had drawn too near to their
stern-chasers.

A marine was shouting, 'There be another, lads!'

Bolitho saw a second set of sails filling and shortening
as a brig appeared close to the crippled frigate.

It was impossible. The one thing which unnerved him.
She was Adam's brig, *Firefly,* her tiny four-pounders spit-
ting defiantly at the enemy but unable to draw off their
advance.

Benbow was changing tack, the sunlight laying bare her
ranks of black muzzles as she turned towards the enemy.
Bolitho saw the double line of guns shoot out their vivid
orange tongues, the smoke billowing inboard as if
Herrick's ship had taken fire.

Bolitho said harshly, 'Prepare to engage Jobert's
squadron.'

Herrick would have to defend himself; the treasure ships
could wait.

Keen cupped his hands. 'Stand by, Mr Paget! Wear
ship, and lay her on the larboard tack!' He hurried to the
compass as his men flung themselves on the braces and
halliards.

'We will steer nor'east, Mr Fallowfield!' He was round
again even as the first signal broke from the yards.
'General, *Form line of battle!*'

The deck tilted to the thrust of rudder and braced yards,
and Bolitho watched as first one, then the other of Jobert's
ships appeared to glide into view.

'Steady she goes, sir! Nor'east!'

We have the wind-gage, Bolitho thought, but not for
long. It would be every ship for herself.

More crashes came from the convoy but Bolitho ignored
them. He caught a glimpse of *Dispatch* as she floundered

round to follow her flagship, resetting her topgallants and even her maincourse to keep on station. *Icarus* was hidden astern of her, but every captain knew the odds, and there were the two frigates waiting to pounce if one of the bigger ships became disabled.

He said, 'Signal *Barracouta* to engage the enemy.'

Keen looked at him, a muscle in his throat jerking as a full broadside vibrated against the hull like a peal of distant thunder.

Bolitho met his glance. 'Lapish must do his best.'

It might baffle the enemy when they saw a two-decker suddenly clap on more sail and dash into the fray. If Lapish used that surprise he might bring down some spars unless. . . . Bolitho closed his mind to the appalling risks he was telling Lapish to take.

He heard Allday whispering fiercely to Bankart, and saw the youth shake his head, his stubborn determination somehow pathetic as the distant guns roared out once again. Bankart stood his ground. Whatever it was costing him, he was more terrified of showing fear.

Bolitho raised his telescope and trained it through the black rigging and for a few moments saw familiar faces leap into view before he found the enemy. There she was, her leaping leopard savage and realistic in the strengthening sunshine, the rear-admiral's flag streaming out from her mizzen.

Keen crossed to join him, his fingers drumming a silent beat on his sword hilt.

Bolitho said, 'We must stop her, Val.' He felt him watching him. 'Jobert will sacrifice every ship and man he has just to snatch the gold with us helpless to stop him.'

Keen nodded, his mind still reeling from the change of events. To begin with he had been able to ignore the danger in the face of their timely arrival. Now there seemed no chance even of survival. He watched Bolitho's expression, the way he covered his left eye while he rested the glass on a seaman's bare shoulder to get a clearer view.

It seemed to steady him. He was able to accept what must happen. But first –

Bolitho lowered the glass. 'Load and run out. Then – '

He looked at Stayt. 'Hoist the signal for close action.' He handed the glass to Sheaffe's small assistant. 'I'll not need this again, I think.' He walked away from the others and stared at the blue water and the endless desert of small crests.

Throughout his small squadron it would be the same, he thought. Brave men afraid to die, cowards fearful of living. They would follow his flag wherever it led. He saw their faces, Montresor, Houston, Lapish and young Quarrell nursing his two big guns. And Adam. Back there in his first command, in his twenty-third year. Or perhaps, like Inch, he had already paid for his impudent courage.

He looked up as the signal for close action broke out, and recalled that other time when men and boys like some of these had died to keep it flying. He shifted his gaze to the bright flag at the fore, and as guns cracked out from the convoy he was surprised to discover that all hate and bitterness were gone.

They were the luxuries of the living.

17

Beneath the Flag

The two converging lines of ships appeared to be closing rapidly, although Jobert's squadron still stood at about three miles' range.

Keen watched fixedly and then said, 'He's not reduced sail yet, sir.'

Bolitho wanted to climb to the poop and see what was happening in the convoy. There the firing had become general, and the last time he had looked Bolitho had seen *Benbow* wreathed in smoke as she engaged the two French seventy-fours on either beam at once. It was never a comfortable plan; it meant dividing the gun crews and left few hands to carry out repairs and remove the wounded.

The sharper crack of small weapons told him that Adam's *Firefly* had thrown any caution to the wind as she tacked as close as she dared to the two big Frenchmen. Adam knew *Benbow* wore Herrick's flag. Not that he would need any encouragement to fight. Bolitho thought of Keen's comment. Jobert had hoisted no signals either and had obviously drilled his ships for this very moment.

Keen asked without lowering his glass, 'Shall I shorten sail, sir?'

'Yes. Take in the courses. Otherwise Jobert will over-reach our line before we can cripple some of his ships.'

Paget shouted, '*Barracouta* has gone for the frigates!' He sounded excited. 'God, she's crossing the stern of one of 'em!'

Lapish had used his disguise well. While the two French frigates had held their station, one astern of the other, he had swept suddenly towards them with all the wind in his favour. His starboard battery was blasting into the enemy while he cut so dangerously close across the leader's stern that it looked as if they had collided. Smoke and flame belched from the Frenchman, and somebody gave a wild cheer as the main topmast plummeted over her side, the attendant tangle of rigging and snapped spars dragging her over and giving Lapish's gun crews the rare chance of a second broadside, before *Barracouta*'s helm went down and she changed tack towards the French line.

Even some of Keen's seamen paused as they fisted and kicked the main and forecourses against their yards, to stare as their one frigate curtsied round before the second enemy vessel had time to follow. Her two broadsides had rendered the other ship momentarily helpless and the list of killed and wounded must have struck them hard.

Bolitho made himself watch Jobert's flagship. Like her consorts, she was painted in black and white stripes, her gunports rising up her tumblehome in a checkered pattern.

Keen said, 'He intends to overreach us, sir.'

Bolitho said nothing. *Léopard*'s jib boom appeared to be pointing directly at their own.

Then Keen said, 'They're shortening now, sir.' He sounded tight with concentration. Relief too, for if Jobert's ships crossed their line of battle, they could smash into the convoy while Keen lost vital time trying to head round and engage. The reduction of sails might settle their final embrace.

The range was less than two miles now, and seemed to make Jobert's flagship loom even higher above the choppy wave crests.

'Stand by, starboard batteries!' Keen drew his sword, his eyes slitted in concentration.

Bolitho heard the order being piped to the lower gundeck and imagined the faces he had come to know.

He said, 'We must try to break the line. Pass astern of Jobert, and let Montresor and Houston tackle the others. Ship to ship, broadside to broadside.'

He saw the stabbing lines of flashes as Jobert's three-decker fired a slow broadside. The sea boiled violently as the heavy balls screeched above him and tore rigging to shreds and punched a dozen holes in the sails. Men swarmed aloft with the boatswain's bellowing voice guiding them to the worst damage.

Less than a mile now. More shots crashed overhead, and two balls hit the lower hull like battering rams. Bolitho wiped his eyes as smoke swirled over the quarterdeck in a freak downdraught before being sucked away downwind.

'Signal *Rapid* to assist *Benbow*.' Bolitho tried not to consider Quarrell's chances, but it would lend heart to Herrick – he bit his lip – and Adam. Please God he was still safe.

Paget yelled, 'He's resetting his tops'ls, the bugger!'

Bolitho watched as *Léopard*'s topmen struggled out on their yards while the helm went over and Jobert's ship changed tack as if to avoid a final encounter. As she presented her full broadside she fired. It was like one gigantic explosion and Bolitho had to seize the rail as many of the balls struck *Argonaute*'s side or crashed across the forecastle. Wood fragments whirled in the air and most of the starboard carronade's crew were cut to bloody fragments.

Keen's sword flashed down. '*Fire!*'

The gun-captains jerked their lanyards and *Argonaute* swayed over to the thrust of her combined broadside. The lower battery, their main armament, reacted badly; some of the crews there must have been stunned or unnerved by the weight of the enemy's iron.

Some of *Léopard*'s sails lifted and writhed, and her fore-topsail was torn apart by the force of the wind through the ragged holes. It was not enough to make her even falter.

Dispatch was closing with the second Frenchman, and Bolitho could hear *Icarus* firing from extreme range at the rearmost two-decker. He hurried to the nettings, the crews of the unemployed nine-pounders staring at him, their eyes wild, their naked bodies heaving with exertion as if they had been running.

Bolitho watched his two ships closing with the enemy, *Icarus* almost hidden in a rolling fog of gunsmoke.

He shouted, 'Follow Jobert!' He winced as more balls

slammed into the hull and a man screamed briefly as he was cut down.

Keen shouted, 'Put up your helm! Close with her, man!'

Fallowfield glared at him and then gestured to his helmsmen, who clustered around the big wheel as if it was a last refuge.

Small flashes lit up *Léopard*'s fighting-tops and several musket balls, almost spent, slammed harmlessly into the hammocks. The Royal Marines crouched against their frail protection and waited for the command to fire; some even glanced at Captain Bouteiller willing him to give the order.

Keen called, 'Set the forecourse!'

The hands had been waiting and Bolitho saw the great sail billow from its yard, cutting away the vision of the enemy like a huge curtain.

More shots whimpered across the quarterdeck and poop and Allday muttered, 'Stay close to me, lad. They're out of range, but – '

Stayt pulled out his pistol and stared at it as if he were seeing it for the first time.

The air was filled with noise, gun-captains yelling and gesturing to their crews who wielded their handspikes to heave the smoking barrels round towards the enemy. Overhead, seamen called to one another while severed standing and running rigging flapped out in the wind and defied their grasping fingers. Occasionally the spread nets would jerk as something broke free and plummeted down from aloft, and Bolitho knew it was a miracle that more damage had not been done.

He heard two bangs, loud and resonant, and knew *Rapid* was using her borrowed thirty-two-pounders. They would give the French ships something to worry about. They might even draw one of them away from Herrick who was being raked from two sides at once.

He saw a frigate falling downwind, her foremast trailing over the side, antlike figures swarming amongst the wreckage to hack it away. A cheer from some of the gun crews stopped abruptly, as if to a word of command.

Bolitho gripped his sword and saw *Barracouta* reel over

as another burst of crossfire tore into her and brought down more spars and flailing rigging.

Keen murmured, 'Bad luck. But he's knocked one of them out of the fight!' He ran to the side as Jobert's ship fired again, some of the balls ripping overhead with just a few feet to spare.

Stayt said abruptly, 'We can't mark him down!' The words were wrung from his lips as if he were feeling every shot. '*Must get closer!*'

Bolitho shouted, 'Captain Keen! Head for the convoy!' It was suddenly more than clear that Jobert intended to take the merchantmen as he had planned, and abandon his captains to stop or delay Bolitho's ships from interfering.

A great shower of sparks burst from *Dispatch*'s maindeck and timber splashed down alongside. For an instant Bolitho imagined that a magazine had exploded, but it must have been a powder charge which had burst before it could be rammed home. As the French ship drifted away from her Bolitho saw that she too was badly mauled, and *Dispatch* was already nudging round, her lower battery firing again and again, although many of her upper gun crews had been cut down by the explosion. *Icarus* too was obeying the signal, and appeared to be overlapping her enemy, her sails filled with holes and some of her guns unmanned or smashed.

With her helm over, *Argonaute*'s bowsprit followed Jobert's ship as if to impale her. The arrowhead of sea between them was torn again and again by leaping fins of spray, many followed by the terrible thud of iron striking deep into the hull.

Stayt remarked, 'We're alone!'

Bolitho looked at him. Stayt sounded so calm, almost matter of fact. A man without nerves, or one resigned to the inevitable.

'Larboard battery!' Keen's sword caught the sunlight. '*Fire!*'

There were some wild cheers as the Frenchman's sails bucked and split, and telltale puffs of smoke along her tall hull told of their success. Keen's regular drills were paying off even now.

Stayt ducked as musket balls scythed over the hammock nettings, and two seamen were hurled to the deck, one screaming as he clawed at his stomach. The dead man was thrown over the side, the other dragged to the nearest hatch and eventually down to Tuson.

Bolitho shuddered. It was happening there now. The knife and saw, the dreadful agony while some poor wretch was held on the table.

Stayt coughed.

Bolitho looked at him and saw him falling very slowly to his knees, a look of intent concentration on his dark features.

Midshipman Sheaffe ran to his aid and put an arm round his shoulders.

Bolitho said, 'Get him below!'

Stayt looked up at him, but seemed to have difficulty in focusing his eyes. He had one hand to his waist, and already his fingers were wet with blood.

Stayt tried to shake his head but the pain made him cry out.

'*No!*' He stared at Bolitho, his eyes desperate. '*Hear me!*'

Bolitho knelt beside him, his ears cringing to the crash and roar of cannon fire. *Léopard*'s masts were no longer at a distance; they were rising up alongside, huge and formidable, as the two ships continued to drive together.

'What is it?' He knew Stayt was dying. Men were falling everywhere; one of the helmsmen was dragging himself into the gloom of the poop, his efforts mocked by the great pattern of blood he left behind him.

'It was my father . . . I wanted to tell . . .' He coughed violently and blood ran from his mouth. 'I wrote to him about the girl, never thought what he might . . .' He rolled up his eyes and gasped, 'Oh dear God, help me!'

Sheaffe said, 'I'll carry him, sir!'

Sheaffe's voice seemed to give Stayt some impossible strength. His eyes turned towards the midshipman and he started to grin. It made him look terrible. 'Admiral Sheaffe, it was. A friend of my father, y'see.'

He turned back to Bolitho and shut his eyes tightly as

shots scored across the deck, killing a seaman who was thrusting his rammer into a gun and taking off the arm of his companion like a dead twig.

'Always hated you. Thought you knew, sir. All fathers together.' He tried to speak clearly but there was too much blood. He was drowning in it. 'Yours, mine and this young mid – ' He coughed again and this time the blood did not stop.

Sheaffe lowered him to the deck, and when he looked up his face was like stone. Then he picked up the silver-mounted pistol and thrust it into his belt.

Keen hurried across the deck and shouted, 'We're all but into her!' The deck bucked and splinters flew like hornets, hurling men aside or leaving them too badly injured to help themselves. He saw Stayt's body and said, '*Damn them!*'

Bolitho walked to the nettings again and, using a marine's shoulder for support, climbed up to look at the other vessel. On every hand the battle raged, flotsam and broken spars drifted abeam, while here and there a lonely corpse floated beneath the thunder of cannon fire, like an uncaring swimmer.

He saw Jobert's command flag above the smoke, the sparkle of musket fire as the sharpshooters sought out targets. The shot which had killed Stayt had probably been aimed at him.

He turned his back on the black and white ship and glanced down at the bronzed marine. It was sheer madness, and he expected to feel the crushing agony between his shoulderblades at any second. His epaulettes would make a fine marker.

But he could feel the same recklessness, the need to make these men trust him, even though he had led them to disaster.

He said, 'Aim well, my lad! But save the admiral for me, eh?' He clapped the marine on his rigid shoulder and saw his wildness change to astonishment, his face split into a huge grin.

The marine exclaimed, 'God's teeth, sir, I got two o' the buggers already!'

He was levelling and firing again as Bolitho jumped down to the deck.

The hull shook violently as more shots hammered into it, and an eighteen-pounder was lifted by an invisible hand and toppled onto some of its crew. The barrel must have been as hot as a furnace, but the men soon died, their screams lost in the bombardment. The foretopsail blew in ribbons, and without warning the main topgallant mast staggered and then plunged to the deck like a forest giant.

Bolitho stared through the smoke, his eyes stinging and streaming. They had to get alongside. A sudden gap in the smoke made him realize how close they were to the convoy. He saw *Benbow,* her flags still flying, but her mizzen gone, firing without a pause into the ship nearest to her. The other one was almost dismasted, and he saw the two little brigs firing at her before the smoke swirled down again.

His foot touched Stayt's outflung arm and he looked down at him. In those few minutes he had learned more about the man than ever before. How petty and empty all the jealousy and hate seemed now.

He looked at Keen. 'We have the wind. Use it.' His voice hardened, 'Ram her!' Then he drew his sword and heard Allday pull out his cutlass.

'Now! *Hard over!*'

Keen swung away. It was pointless to try to protest or explain. Jobert's company would overwhelm them. They would have no chance. But they never had from the beginning.

He shouted, 'Man the braces! Put up your helm, Mr Fallowfield!'

But the master's mate had taken charge. Fallowfield lay near the wheel where he had died, his ear to the deck as if he were listening for something.

'Mr Paget! Prepare to ram!'

Paget stared up at him and then ran towards the fore-castle, his hanger already drawn as, with ponderous intent, *Argonaute* turned towards her enemy, her jib boom like a lance, her sails so torn and holed that even the jubilant wind, a cruel spectator to the fight, could barely offer steerage way.

Dispatch was alongside another ship, her guns still firing even though her muzzles were grinding against those of her enemy.

Jobert had now realized Bolitho's intention but could do little about it. By changing tack directly towards the convoy he had the wind abeam. He could neither turn towards *Argonaute,* nor could he allow the wind to carry him away without exposing his stern to a murderous broadside.

Oblivious to the din, Bolitho watched the shrieking balls as Jobert's guns tried to traverse onto the slow-moving ship with the huge Jack at her foremast.

French sailors were already running along the gangway, firing towards *Argonaute,* some falling or pitching overboard as they came under fire from Bouteiller's marksmen. A swivel blasted out from somewhere, and Bolitho saw one of the scarlet coats fall. It was Lieutenant Orde, his sword still in his hand as he stared up at the sky.

Keen gripped the rail, watching transfixed as the big three-decker, once so aloof and distant, loomed above them. Men were firing down, and he felt the planks jerk by his feet. A heavy ball hit Stayt's body so that it convulsed as if he were only shamming death. The Frenchmen were running to the point of impact, and the chorus of their cries and curses was like one tremendous voice which even the battle could not quench.

Keen turned as Bolitho touched his sleeve. 'Are the guns ready?'

Keen nodded. 'At *this* range, sir?' The jib boom thrust slowly through *Léopard*'s foremast shrouds. It looked such a gentle motion but Keen knew the whole weight of his command was behind it. He waved his sword to the lieutenant at the larboard battery. The seconds seemed like hours and Keen had time to consider several things at once. The great chorus of voices and then, in that fragment of time before the trigger-lines were jerked taut, he heard Bolitho say, 'Fine words do not a broadside make, Val.'

Then the space between the hulls vanished in a frothing

torment of flame and smoke. Burning wads floated towards the torn sails, and the crash of metal against the enemy's hull was like a thunderclap.

The mass of French seamen and marines were gone, and *Léopard*'s side below the gangway was running bright red, so that the ship herself seemed to be bleeding to death.

Then like a last convulsion the two vessels ground together, the shrouds and spars entangled, guns, men and wind all suddenly silent. As if their world had ended.

Bolitho was almost knocked over by the marines from the poop as they charged towards the forecastle, some hatless and wild-eyed, their bayonets glittering in the smoky sunshine. The ships rolled more heavily together and, through the dangling creepers of rigging and strips of blackened canvas, Bolitho saw the stab of musket fire and the gleam of steel as the two sides came together.

From above the smoke the marksmen kept up their fire, and Bolitho saw Phipps, the fifth lieutenant, clutch his face as a ball smashed into his forehead. He had been one of *Achates'* midshipmen. In the twinkling of an eye he had become nothing.

The ships were being carried slowly and heavily downwind and away from the convoy. It would give Herrick a chance, but no more than that unless. Bolitho saw several seamen cut down by a blast of swivel, the canister shot raking them into bloody ribbons while they screamed and kicked out their lives.

Bolitho shouted, 'Take the ship, Val! *Hold her!*' He saw the shocked understanding on Keen's face and repeated, 'No matter what!' Then with his sword in his hand he ran along the starboard gangway with Allday and Bankart behind him. He found time to wonder what was keeping Bankart from hiding below, how long it would be before it all ended, as it had for too many already.

Allday rasped, 'God, they're aboard us!'

Bolitho saw Paget by the foremast and shouted, 'Clear the lower battery! Every man on deck!'

Then he found himself by the starboard cathead, and already the place was littered with corpses. Seamen and marines, friends and enemies, clawed for handholds on the

beakhead, and slid down stays and torn sails to get at each
other. Bayonets thrust; others hacked at the boarders with
anything they could find, cutlasses and axes; one man was
even using a rammer like a club until a ball brought him
down and he tumbled outboard between the grinding
hulls.

From the quarterdeck Keen watched despairingly as
more enemy uniforms appeared through the smoke, some
already on the larboard gangway. They would swamp his
company. He stared round and saw Hogg, his coxswain,
fall to the deck, one hand reaching out for help even as
the light died in his eyes.

They were all dying, and for two ships full of bloody
gold.

He yelled, 'Open fire with the nine-pounders, Mr
Valancey! Mark down their poop!'

It was almost impossible to speak or breathe as the
smoke billowed over the decks and men slipped and
hacked at each other, stamping on the corpses of their
companions.

There was a cracked cheer and Keen saw more men
swarming up from the lower gundeck, Chaytor, the
second lieutenant, waving them forward with his hanger.

The nine-pounders lurched inboard on their tackles and
blasted grape into the smoke, some of which might find a
target on the enemy's stern and amongst her officers.

Keen saw a seaman running towards him and his startled
mind made him realize it was one of the enemy, a single
seaman suddenly cut off from the rest of the boarders.

He lunged forward, seeing the stranger through a mist
of combined pain and fury. Hogg was dead, Bolitho would
soon be killed or captured as he led his own counter-
attack.

The French seaman aimed a pistol but a mocking click
from the hammer made him stare wildly before flinging
the useless weapon away. He raised his heavy cutlass and
kept his eyes on Keen's face.

He was young and nimble-footed, but the madness of
battle blinded him to Keen's skill.

Keen parried the heavy blade, the weight and power of

the man's thrust carrying his attacker almost past him. Then Keen slashed him across the neck and, as he fell, shrieking, hacked him once again across the face.

He turned away, the anger giving him an unnatural strength; he did not even look round as more shots whimpered past him or slammed into the deck.

Then he stared towards the forecastle. It was the most terrible scene of all.

Captain Inch, naked but for his breeches, was hurrying to the larboard ladder, his raw stump jerking violently as he waved his sword and yelled, 'Stand fast, Helicons!' The words were torn from him, the agony of his wound making it pitiful. He shouted again, his voice rising above the clash of steel and the screams of the dying, 'To me, Helicons! Repel boarders, my lads!'

Keen wiped his eyes with his sleeve.

'In God's name, he thinks he's in his own ship again!'

It could not last. The packed, stamping figures were being forced back, and there were some French boarders already fighting amongst the fallen cordage and bodies on the maindeck.

A midshipman, unarmed, driven beyond reason, ran for a hatchway, his ears covered with his hands as he tried to escape.

Keen saw it was Hext, one of the youngest aboard. As he reached the hatch coaming he slipped on some blood and fell sprawling. A tall Frenchman bounded towards him, his cutlass already swinging. The boy rolled over and stared at him. He did not cover his face or plead, he just lay and watched death.

But Inch was there, and drove his blade under the seaman's ribs, swinging him round, the man's weight tearing the sword from his grasp. The sailor dropped beside Midshipman Hext, his bare feet drumming in agony on the deck.

Keen saw a boarding pike come from the smoke. It took Inch in the back. As he fell to his knees the pike was torn free and then driven into him once more.

Bolitho watched Inch fall, and then, along the length of the deck, above the swaying, exhausted figures he saw

Keen looking at him. For a moment longer the battle seemed elsewhere. They shared the moment. All their memories, and the brave Zenoria. The brightness of hope and love, the illusion of a precious discovery.

The voices roared through it and Bolitho swung round to face a French lieutenant.

Savagely he slashed the young officer's blade aside and then seized his lapel and drove the knuckle bow into his jaw. The lieutenant lurched aside and gasped in terror as Allday's great cutlass swept across the sunlight like a shadow.

Allday wrenched the blade free and gasped thickly, 'We can't 'old 'em!'

Bolitho saw his men falling back; they were trapped here; both gangways had as many Frenchmen on them as Keen's people.

Bolitho shouted, 'Hold fast, lads!' A seaman dropped on his knees and tried to fend off another bright blade. He screamed as his severed hand fell beside him. Bolitho lunged over the wounded man's shoulder and felt the Frenchman against the sword, then reel over as the point grated off his crossbelt and slid into his chest.

He turned to rally some seamen and marines on the other side and then saw something rising above the great pall of smoke.

Allday croaked, 'Bastards are alongside! 'Nother of 'em!'

One of the French seventy-fours must have fought free of Bolitho's ships and was coming to assist his admiral.

There was a crazed cheer and Bolitho saw that the newcomer had lost her mizzen. Guns bellowed from her side, and Bolitho felt the jerk of iron transmit itself even to *Argonaute*'s own deck.

It was an impossible dream, the stern-faced figurehead in breastplate and with outthrust sword. Admiral Benbow.

Cheering and whooping, Herrick's marines and seamen swarmed across in a tide of smoke-blackened, battered men, who had already fought and won their battle to protect the convoy.

Suddenly Bolitho was being carried forward on *Argo-*

naute's new strength and almost fell into the swirling water
as two seamen hauled him roughly over the forecastle rail
and onto the bowsprit. Caught between *Benbow*'s men
and Keen's own company, the French were already
fighting their way onto one gangway, a bridge of escape
to their own ship, and still held the advantage over those
below them.

Bolitho heard Bouteiller yell, 'Royal Marines, *still!*'

He could not see them but pictured the scarlet coats,
no longer smartly pressed and clean, as they responded to
their captain's command. Dazed, wild, even the fury
within them was not enough to withstand their familiar
discipline.

They stood or knelt along the opposite gangway, their
muskets rising as one. A marine fell dead from the rank,
but nobody flinched. Revenge would come later.

Bouteiller yelled, '*Fire!*'

The musket balls crashed into the packed mass of boarders and, even as the living struggled free from the dead,
the marines were already charging towards them, shouting
and screaming like demons as they went in with their
bayonets.

Bolitho slipped, but held on to the massive bowsprit,
his feet kicking at the spritsail yard and shrouds while
he stared with stunned disbelief at the deck below him,
Léopard's forecastle. But for the lanyard around his wrist
he would have lost his sword for ever.

There was more firing from that other existence beyond
the smoke. Ships locked together or surging towards the
French rear-admiral's flag, Bolitho could not tell. A
command flag was supposed to lead and direct. Now it
had become a beacon, a guide for carnage. Men fought
and struggled all around him; it was impossible to grasp
direction or time. Bodies were sometimes pressing against
him, with brief flashes of recognition as a wild face found
his. Someone even managed to shout, ''Tis the admiral,
lads!' Another yelled, 'You keep with us, Dick!'

It was wild, terrifying, and yet the madness was like
rich wine. Bolitho locked hilts with another lieutenant and
was astonished that he found it so easy to disarm him with

one twist of the wrist which tore the weapon from his hand. He would have left it at that as the yelling, panting seamen carried him along, but a marine paused and glared at the cowering officer. All he said was, 'This is for Cap'n Inch!' The thrust carried the lieutenant to the rail, the point of the bayonet glinting red through the back of his coat.

Bolitho dashed his wrist across his face. It felt like a furnace and he was almost blinded by sweat.

He saw the gouged planks across the broad sweep of quarterdeck where Keen's grape had fired so blindly. Bodies lay scattered near the abandoned wheel, others ran to meet the rush of boarders, probably unable to accept what had happened.

A sailor darted under a bayonet and headed for Allday. He stared at the Frenchman and then lifted his cutlass. He almost laughed through his despair. It was so easy.

As he raised the blade and tightened his hold on the cutlass he suddenly cried out, the pain in his old wound burning through his chest, rendering him helpless, unable to move.

Bolitho was separated from him by an abandoned gun, but hurled himself towards him, his sword hitting out.

But Bankart leaped between them armed only with a belaying pin.

He screamed, 'Get back! Don't you touch him!' He threw himself protectively against his father, sobbing with anger and fear as the Frenchman darted forward for the kill.

Bolitho felt the ball fan past his face, although his dazed mind did not record the sound of a shot.

He saw the Frenchman slide back and drop to the deck, his cutlass clattering beneath the feet of the crowd.

Bolitho saw Midshipman Sheaffe, his face white with strain, with Stayt's pistol still smoking in one hand, his puny dirk in the other.

Then he forgot him; even the fact that, with Allday about to be cut down, his son had found himself and the courage which he believed would never be his.

Bolitho saw Jobert by the poop ladder, saw him

shouting to his officers, although the din, the mingled roar of victory and defeat, made it impossible to understand.

Lieutenant Paget, his coat sliced from shoulder to waist and cut about the face by wood splinters, waved his bloodied hanger to his men.

Bolitho stared through the smoke, now almost blind from it, or was it something worse? He could not even find the will to care any more.

Paget yelled, '*Get him!* Cut the bastard down!'

Bolitho found himself lurching through the jubilant seamen, some of whom were strangers from Herrick's ship.

It had to stop. The past could not repair anything; nor must it destroy.

He knocked a marine's musket aside with the flat of his sword. He heard Allday gasping behind him. He would die rather than leave him now.

Bolitho shouted, '*Strike, damn you!*'

Jobert stared at him, his eyes shocked. He peered past Bolitho and must have sensed that only he was keeping him alive. There was a great wave of cheering and someone yelled, 'There goes their flag, mates! We beat the buggers!'

The voices and faces swirled round, while the cornered Frenchmen in various parts of their ship began to throw down their weapons. But not Jobert. Almost disdainfully he drew his sword and tossed his hat to the deck.

Paget gasped, 'Let me take him, Sir Richard!'

Bolitho gave him a quick glance. Paget, the man who had faced the odds of Camperdown, was no longer the calmly efficient first lieutenant. He wanted to kill Jobert.

Bolitho snapped, 'Stand back.' He raised his sword and felt the raw tension in his wrist and forearm.

So it was a personal duel after all.

There was silence now, and only the groans and cries of the wounded seemed to intrude. Even the wind had dropped without anyone noticing it. Jobert's command flag flapped only slightly and in time with the bright Union Flag on the ship whose jib boom still impaled the shrouds.

The blades circled one another like wary serpents.

Bolitho watched Jobert's face, as dark as Stayt's. It was

all there. He had been a prisoner before, and his flagship had been taken from him only to rise again and repeat the disgrace. The impossible had happened. Jobert was a professional officer, and did not have to look farther than the man who now faced him for the reason. A last chance to even the score, to give him the seeds of a victory even if he never lived to see it for more than minutes after Bolitho had fallen.

Jobert moved around the deck and even the English sailors fell back to give him room.

Paget pleaded desperately, 'Can I take him?' He saw Bolitho's foot catch on some broken rigging, the way he staggered. Paget whispered, 'Fetch Captain Keen, for God's sake!' The messenger scuttled away, but Paget knew he would be too late.

Then Jobert struck, lunged forward again and again, his foot stamping hard down as he advanced. He turned still farther and made Bolitho twist his head as the sunlight lanced down through the ragged sails and blinded him.

Was it imagination or did he see a quick flash of triumph in the French admiral's eyes? Did he know his weakness? The blades glanced together and the steel hissed as each fought to retain balance and the strength to hold the other at arm's length.

Clash – clash – clash, the blades struck, parried and parted.

Midshipman Sheaffe stared wildly at Allday. 'Stop him, can't you, man?'

Allday clutched his shirt against his burning wound and replied, 'Get a marksman, lively now!'

Bolitho stepped carefully over some more rope. His arm throbbed with pain and he could barely see Jobert's intent face. *Why prove anything? He is beaten, finished. It is enough.*

Jobert's blade moved like lightning, and when Bolitho swung his own to beat it aside he felt it pass through his coat below his armpit, the searing pain as the edge cut across his skin. Bolitho smashed his hilt down on Jobert's wrist so that they lurched together, chest to chest.

Bolitho could feel the strength going from his arm, the

biting pain of the cut on his side like a branding iron. He could feel the man's breath on his face, see the strange darkness in his eyes. Everything else was lost in mist, and even when he heard Herrick's voice coming through the packed figures around him, it was like an intrusion.

He raised his arm and thrust at Jobert's chest with all of his remaining strength. Jobert staggered back against a quarterdeck cannon and then stared with horrified disbelief as the old sword flashed forward and struck him in the heart.

Bolitho almost fell as the sailors surged around him, cheering and sobbing like madmen.

He handed his sword to Allday and tried to smile at him, to reassure him, like those other times.

Herrick pushed his men aside and seized his arm.

'My God, Richard, he might have killed you!' He studied him anxiously. 'If I'd been here I'd have shot him down!'

Bolitho touched the hole in his coat and felt the blood wet on his fingers.

The cheering dazed him, but they had every right to give vent to their feelings. What did they know or understand of strategy, or the need to defend two unknown merchantmen? Why should they obey, when the harvest was so savage, so cruel?

He looked down at Jobert and saw a seaman prise the sword from his outflung hand. Jobert's dark eyes were half open, as if he were still alive, listening, and watching his enemies.

'He wanted to die, Thomas. Don't you see that?' He turned and peered across to his own ship and saw Keen shading his eyes to look at him. Bolitho raised his arm in a tired salute. He was safe. It would have been the final blow had he fallen.

He felt Herrick's hand holding his arm as someone brought a dressing to staunch the blood.

'He lost the fight. He would not surrender his pride too.'

Bolitho made his way through his blackened and

bleeding men. It did not seem real or possible. He looked up at the sky above the masts and lifeless sails.

He turned and looked at his friend and added quietly, 'In his way, Jobert was a victor after all.'

Allday heard him and then put his arm around his son's shoulders. He had not the words, not now anyway.

Bankart glanced at his father's face and smiled.

Pride of friend or enemy did not need any words.

Epilogue

It was six months before Richard Bolitho returned to England. The stark memories of that last desperate battle were still clear in his mind, although at home they had been overtaken if not completely forgotten amidst other events.

For Bolitho and his little squadron it had been a costly victory in life and in other suffering. His ships too had taken great punishment and had been forced into the dockyards at Malta and Gibraltar.

The results of their triumph over Jobert's squadron had been as astonishing as they had been destructive. So badly crippled were most of the ships involved in the line of battle that two of the French seventy-fours had been able to steal away and avoid capture. None of Bolitho's vessels had been heavy enough or in such good repair that they could capture them. An undamaged frigate had also escaped. Jobert's big flagship, although seized, would be spared the shame of fighting again under her enemy's colours. A fire had broken out between decks which had killed many of her wounded, and it had taken every able hand, English and French to save her from complete destruction. She would probably end her days as a hulk or stores vessel.

They had succeeded in capturing all the rest although at one time Bolitho had feared that two at least would founder on passage to shelter.

He often thought of the familiar faces he would never see again. Most of all, Captain Inch, dying on his feet, inspired by some last thought that he had had to be with his friends. Captain Montresor who had fallen at the last moment even as the French flagship's colours had dipped into the gunsmoke. So many more. Needless to say, Houston of the *Icarus* had survived unscathed and complaining although his ship had been in the thick of the fighting from the first broadside. The two smallest vessels, *Rapid* and *Firefly*, had come through the onslaught with few casualties, although any one of those great French broadsides could have sunk them.

With the two brigs as her only companions, *Argonaute*, repaired if not recovered from the battle, sailed for England and arrived at Plymouth in June 1804.

Again, vivid pictures stood out in Bolitho's thoughts as he relived the moments which followed their arrival. The wild excitement, the flags and the gun salutes as *Argonaute* finally dropped anchor. There had been little wind and their progress up-Channel had been slow. Enough it seemed for the entire population to know of their return.

He remembered it so well. The exhilaration of the cheering people on the waterfront, much of which was soon to dissolve into empty sadness when they discovered that their loved ones would never return.

Admiral Sheaffe had been there in person. Bolitho had imagined he would have challenged the man, that he in turn might have revealed the jealousy which had made him use Keen as an instrument to hurt him. Instead the admiral had made a great display of greeting his son. That was a moment Bolitho knew he would never forget.

The admiral, watched by his aides and some personal friends, had put his hands on the midshipman's shoulders.

Bolitho had seen the youth's face. Perhaps he had recalled Stayt's last words, or the time when he had been almost left behind when *Supreme* had been in danger, and Bolitho had waited for him.

He had said in a steady voice, 'I beg your pardon, sir. I do not know you!' Then, his eyes blind, he had hurried away.

Again, once ashore, when Keen had seen the girl running the last few yards along the cobbles, her long hair streaming behind her, Bolitho had felt both happiness and envy.

Oblivious to the onlookers and grinning sailors, Keen had held her against him, his face in her hair, barely able to speak.

Then she had looked at Bolitho, her eyes misty, and had said very softly, '*Thank* you.'

Bolitho was not sure what he had expected. For Belinda to be in Plymouth, waiting like Zenoria to learn the truth, to enjoy the reality of their survival.

The rest of the time it took to complete his affairs in Plymouth was blurred. He had taken passage in *Firefly* to Falmouth. One more brig arriving in Carrick Roads would excite little attention. Bolitho dreaded another hero's welcome, the noise, the curiosity of those who had not seen the true face of war.

So on this bright June morning he stood by the bulwark with Adam while the brig swung carelessly to her anchor. Home.

On either hand the green hillsides and moored vessels, the fields of various hues and colours which stretched inland in their own patterns. Houses and fishermen's cottages, and the grim grey bulk of Pendennis Castle which commanded the harbour entrance. Nothing had changed, and yet Bolitho had the feeling it would never be the same again.

Time to part again. Adam was under orders for Ireland with fresh dispatches and no doubt more to collect. If nothing else it would make him an excellent navigator.

'Well, Uncle?' Adam watched him gravely, his eyes troubled.

Bolitho saw Allday by the rail, peering down at the gig alongside. Allday must have guessed or felt Bolitho's mood of uncertainty. He had sent Bankart with Ozzard by coach with their chests and bags.

Until the next time. Allday sensed that he needed to be alone on this particular day.

Bolitho said, 'It will always be like this, Adam. Brief farewells, even shorter greetings.' He glanced around the neat deck. It was hard to believe that this vessel had been within a stone's throw of a powerful seventy-four and had survived. *Rapid* too, although Quarrell had pleaded for the borrowed guns to be removed. Their recoil had done more damage than the enemy.

Adam said, 'I wish I could step ashore with you, Uncle.'

Bolitho put his arm round his shoulders. 'It will keep. I am glad for you.' He looked up at the impatient masthead pendant. 'Your father would have been pleased, I know that.'

Then he strode to the side where the first lieutenant, his arm in a sling, stood with the boatswain's mates for a last farewell.

In the gig Allday watched Bolitho without speaking, saw him look astern once and wave back and forth to his nephew.

The brig was already shortening her cable and, once the gig had been hoisted, would be on her way. Allday found that he could watch her like a mere onlooker.

He thought of his son, on his way overland to the Bolitho house. Would he ever return to the sea? Surprisingly that decision no longer counted. *My son*, even thinking the words made him feel happy and grateful. He had saved his life, would have died for him but for the middy's pistol.

He glanced at Bolitho's impassive features and knew he was worried about his eyes. Lady Belinda would be up there at the house, fretting and waiting for him. That might make all the difference.

Tonight Allday would slip away to the inn. To see if the landlord's daughter was still as smart as paint.

They climbed onto the hot stones and Bolitho thanked the boat's coxswain and put two guineas in his hard hand.

The man gaped at him. 'Us'll drink to 'e, zur!'

They pulled away, one of them whistling cheerfully until they reached hearing distance of their ship.

Bolitho walked towards the town where he would take the narrow road to the house. He looked up and tried not to blink, to lose his balance as he had that day when he had faced Jobert for the last time.

He heard Allday's heavy tread behind him; it was a strange feeling. There were few people about. They were either in the fields or away fishing. Falmouth existed on earth and sea alike. He saw a weary woman carrying a huge basket of vegetables as she made her way towards a narrow lane.

She stopped and straightened her back and saw him. She smiled and attempted an awkward curtsy.

Bolitho called, 'A fine morning, Mrs Noonan.'

She watched them until they turned the corner.

Poor woman, Bolitho thought. He recalled seeing her husband die violently aboard his *Lysander,* it seemed a thousand years back, and yet like yesterday.

A long shadow crossed the square and Bolitho looked up at the tower of the Church of King Charles the Martyr, where twice he had been married. He wanted to walk past, but felt unable to move. It was as if he was being held, then guided towards those familiar old doors. Allday followed him with something like relief. In his heart he had known this was why Bolitho had not taken the coach from Plymouth.

Bolitho walked uncertainly into the cool shadows of the church. It was empty, and yet so full of memories, and of hopes. He paused and looked at the fine windows beyond the altar and remembered that first time, the sunlight streaming through the door.

He felt his heart pound until he thought he would hear it.

He must go, discover his feelings, explain to Belinda, learn to put right his mistakes.

Instead he walked to the wall where the Bolitho tablets stood out from all the others.

He reached up and touched the one which was slightly apart from the men. *Cheney Bolitho.*

He knew Allday was in the main aisle, watching him, wanting to help when there was none to give.

Bolitho moved back very slowly to the altar and stood looking at it for several minutes.

This was the day of their marriage, when they had joined hands here. He spoke her name aloud, very quietly. Then he turned on his heel and walked down to where Allday waited for him.

Allday asked, 'Home now, Sir Richard?'

Bolitho hesitated and then looked back at the small tablet.

'Aye, old friend. *It will always be that.*'

Bestselling War Fiction and Non-Fiction

☐ Passage to Mutiny	Alexander Kent	£2.50
☐ The Flag Captain	Alexander Kent	£2.50
☐ Badge of Glory	Douglas Reeman	£2.50
☐ Winged Escort	Douglas Reeman	£2.50
☐ Army of Shadows	John Harris	£2.50
☐ Up for Grabs	John Harris	£2.50
☐ Decoy	Dudley Pope	£1.95
☐ Curse of the Death's Head	Rupert Butler	£2.25
☐ Gestapo	Rupert Butler	£2.75
☐ Auschwitz and the Allies	Martin Gilbert	£4.95
☐ Tumult in the Clouds	James A. Goodson	£2.95
☐ Sigh for a Merlin	Alex Henshaw	£2.50
☐ Morning Glory	Stephen Howarth	£4.95
☐ The Doodlebugs	Norman Longmate	£4.95
☐ Colditz – The Full Story	Major P. Reid	£2.95

NAME ....

ADDRESS ....

....

....

U.K. CUSTOMERS: Please allow 22p per book to a maximum of £3.00.

B.F.P.O. & EIRE: Please allow 22p per book to a maximum of £3.00.

OVERSEAS CUSTOMERS: Please allow 22p per book.

Whilst every effort is made to keep prices low it is sometimes necessary to increase cover prices at short notice. Arrow Books reserve the right to show new retail prices on covers which may differ from those previously advertised in the text or elsewhere.

A Selection of Arrow Bestsellers

☐ A Long Way From Heaven	Sheelagh Kelly	£2.95
☐ 1985	Anthony Burgess	£1.95
☐ To Glory We Steer	Alexander Kent	£2.50
☐ The Last Raider	Douglas Reeman	£2.50
☐ Strike from the Sea	Douglas Reeman	£2.50
☐ Albatross	Evelyn Anthony	£2.50
☐ Return of the Howling	Gary Brandner	£1.95
☐ 2001: A Space Odyssey	Arthur C. Clarke	£1.95
☐ The Sea Shall Not Have Them	John Harris	£2.50
☐ A Rumour of War	Philip Caputo	£2.50
☐ Spitfire	Jeffrey Quill	£3.50
☐ Shake Hands Forever	Ruth Rendell	£1.95
☐ Hollywood Babylon	Kenneth Anger	£7.95
☐ The Rich	William Davis	£1.95
☐ Men in Love	Nancy Friday	£2.75
☐ George Thomas, Mr Speaker: The Memoirs of Viscount Tonypandy	George Thomas	£2.95
☐ The Jason Voyage	Tim Severin	£3.50

NAME ....

ADDRESS ....

....

....

U.K. CUSTOMERS: Please allow 22p per book to a maximum of £3.00.

B.F.P.O. & EIRE: Please allow 22p per book to a maximum of £3.00.

OVERSEAS CUSTOMERS: Please allow 22p per book.

Whilst every effort is made to keep prices low it is sometimes necessary to increase cover prices at short notice. Arrow Books reserve the right to show new retail prices on covers which may differ from those previously advertised in the text or elsewhere.